THE MYTH OF EXILE

DESMOND TRAYNOR was born in Du
College, Dublin and Trinity College, Dub ...u anu worked, in
various guises, in Holland, America, Italy, England and Spain. Now based
back in Dublin, he writes about books, film, theatre, music and travel for
many Irish and international newspapers and magazines, including *The
Sunday Tribune*, *The Irish Times*, *The Irish Independent*, *Film Ireland*, *Film
West* and *Graph*.

His short stories have been widely anthologised, and he was nominated
for Hennessy Literary Awards for 'Best Emerging Fiction' in 1998 and 2000,
winning a Special Merit Hennessy Award in 2000.

His critical articles have appeared in the *Irish Literary Supplement*, *Alumnus*,
New Voices in Irish Criticism 3, and the *Irish Studies Review*, and he teaches
creative writing at Rathmines Senior College.

This is his first novel.

Desmond Traynor is one of those brave writers who not only looks at the
edge, but in the end attempts to define the edge. His prose is crisp and clean
and provocative. He questions the nature of stories and story-telling, while at
the same time celebrating their value. In an era of so many mindless, fearful, housebroken novels, it's a breath of fresh air to have someone acknowledge the pulse of our wounds.

COLUM MCCANN, author of *This Side of Brightness* and *Dancer*

This is an excellent novel, very well-written, clever, and highly entertaining.
The writing is wonderful, the central character is interesting, and the oblique
look at modern Irish society is just what everyone wants. It is also a refreshing-
ly honest insight into the psyche of a young Irish male – apparently there are
some serious men in the country, and it's nice to find out what's going on in
their heads. From that point of view this is a fairly unusual novel in the Irish
context. The style reminded me of nothing so much as a younger W.G. Sebald.

ÉILÍS NÍ DHUIBHNE, author of *The Inland Ice* and *The Dancers Dancing*

Not just a rich and vibrant novel of our time, but a profound critical medi-
tation on home and homeland. Desmond Traynor has read and assimilated
the great Irish writings on exile, but he adds to that tradition with a book of
deep feeling and lyrical, humorous insight.

PROFESSOR DECLAN KIBERD, author of *Inventing Ireland* and *Irish Classics*

For Jane

The Myth of
Exile and Return

DESMOND TRAYNOR

For John,
Enjoy! (If that's the word.)

Best wishes,
Desmond Traynor

— SILENZIO PRESS —

First published 2004 by
SILENZIO PRESS
P.O. BOX NO. 9591, DUBLIN I
IRELAND

A CIP record for this title is available from
The British Library.

1 3 5 7 9 10 8 6 4 2

ISBN 0 9547008 0 5

Set by Susan Waine in 11pt on 13pt Adobe Garamond
Printed by ColourBooks Limited, Dublin

ACKNOWLEDGEMENTS

Many thanks to: Éilís Ní Dhuibhne, Colum McCann, Declan Kiberd, Jonathan Williams, Christopher Banahan, Brendan Kennelly, Gerald Dawe, David Marcus, Ciaran Carty, Andrew Ryan, Patrick Chapman, Helen Casey, Michael Farrelly, Dublin Corporation for a Bursary in Literature, The Arts Council of Ireland for an ArtFlight and a Travel Bursary, Temple Bar Properties for a Writer's Studio, and the Tyrone Guthrie Centre at Annaghmakerrig for a residency. Most of all, thanks to Jane Humphries, for love, encouragement, support and organisation.

no'vel 1 *n.* fictitious prose narrative of book length portraying characters and actions credibly representative of real life in continuous plot; **the ~ ,** this type of literature; hence ~E`SE *n.*, style characteristic of inferior novels, ~E'SQUE *a.*

no'vel 2 *a.* of new kind or nature, strange, hitherto unknown.

Oxford English Dictionary

CONTENTS

Every word I write is autobiography. Every word is fiction.

WILLIAM S. BURROUGHS

IRLANDA

If Socrates leave his house today he will find the sage seated on his
doorstep. If Judas go forth tonight it is to Judas his steps will tend.

JAMES JOYCE, *Ulysses*

1

OKAY, HERE WE GO AGAIN.... Stop me if you think you've heard this one before. But don't stop me yet. Don't stop me now. Because it never stops.

The myth of exile and return is an old one, perhaps as old as time itself, or our memory of time; or as creation, or the myth of creation. Or the creation of the myth of creation. Did time precede creation chronologically, or did creation begin contemporaneously with time? But that's another myth, for another time. The story of going out, whether voluntarily or under duress, and coming home, or longing to and failing, is certainly as old as Western, and indeed Eastern, civilisation.

Why did we create this myth, make up this story and tell it to ourselves, and continue telling it right down to the present day? We invent when we have to, to explain something better and understand it more fully. Or maybe we make things up only when we want to think of something in a more beautiful way than before, by contemplating a more beautiful expression of it, or what we consider a more beautiful representation of it, at that time, in that place. Imposing a form and structure will order the chaos, contain the loss, tranquillise the madness, we think...we suppose. Poor fools; if only we knew.

But let us not lose heart yet, on this, the very first page of our fable. We must still pursue perfection, even in the sure and certain knowledge that it does not exist in this world. And what other world is there, save the one each of us carries around inside ourselves?

Let us begin this odyssey, this hejira. Or should I say, immrama?

I have been imagining Edward for a long time: what characteristics to give him, how to realise his personality in prose on paper. Most importantly, I have been considering my relationship to him, and his to me, if I may be permitted to use that overused word.

We were together from the very beginning; our story started *ab ovo* with us as embryos, lying in unison in the warm dark past, two halves of the same whole, struggling to be born into the light of the here and now. After vagitus, we were separated at birth, and taken from our mother too. Shortly after that, we were parted forever. I have never met him, or her, since then.

Was this his initial defining experience of the nominal theme of this tome, nostalgia: homesickness as a disease, the regretful, wistful memory of an earlier time, the sentimental yearning for some period of the past, the pain of returning, or of not returning, home? Who knows? And was it mine?

No, I myself do not have such feelings.

So we were, and presumably still are, twins. How many tales, ancient and modern, concern a set like us, parted and reunited, lost and found, with manufactured mis-meetings and mistaken identities, all happily resolved eventually in a credulity-stretching recognition scene? Will this story, our own, be crowned in the end by some similarly implausible paradoxical denouement? We'll see.

Our germination was a gemination, and though born under the sign of Saturn, we were Gemini. Sometimes I think there is something in all this astrology; at other times I think the whole thing is just a big bunch of bullshit, an admirable evasion by whoremaster man, to lay his goatish disposition on conjunctions in the sky. We were born at a certain time in a particular place, so it follows that I am rough and lecherous, and he meek and mild. Fut! We would have been what we are, had we been born under any other star. For, whatever way you care to look at it, the central premise for the casting of horoscopes is invalidated for me, because my brother and I were born in the same place, as far as I know, at more or less the same time, give or take a few minutes, yet we're as different as it's possible for two men to be. Or are we? That's something else we'll have to see about.

Consider the Greek Dioscuri, or even the Indian Aswins. Edward is the immortal one, while I am merely mortal. But he is immortal because of what I do with my mortality. Are these preordained roles interchangeable, or even reversible? We'll see about that too.

At conception there was a sundering and a pairing, and after gestation, post-parturition, another sundering which made another pairing possible. The twins were cut in twain, and will the twain ever meet? Will that conceivable second pairing ever take place? Once again, we'll see.

Would it have been better if we had been from our mother's womb untimely ripped, and I don't mean like Caesar when we were nearly full term, but if the protective pocket of amniotic fluid we floated in had been prematurely and peremptorily pierced, if we had never drunk the waters of Lethe, never eaten the honey of generation? On finishing the following, you can decide.

Which one of us came first, I have never discovered. All I know is that he is the double who follows me and haunts me and won't let me be, the shadow I cast and look at and want to be, and that we were safe together briefly in that uterine cave, that home we shared, the first one that can be shared, the first that anyone and everyone has, the womb, that little room, as sheltering but assailable as a tomb, when we roll away the stone.

Who was this woman, our mother? And who, for that matter, was our father? Who is it that can tell us who we are? Was there good sport at our making? I doubt it, at least not from the feminine side. We all want to solve the riddle of our birth, but few of us are any happier when we find out the truth, if it is the truth we find. We grow only more disillusioned, and become resigned.

She was probably young, and in a vulnerable situation, which was exploited by someone in a position of authority over her. I see her now, recently orphaned, taken in and looked after by a kindly and well-respected uncle, who was gradually revealed to her as a cheap, pervy, suburban, low-rent de Sade. Or maybe she was a priests' housekeeper, doting on the caring and sensitive soul of the young curate, who was struggling to live up to the high ideals of his vocation, reconciling the contemplative life with the demands of his harassed, harassing, poor parishioners. Or the maid in a decaying old Big House in the country, maintained by asset-rich, cash-poor, *nouveau pauvre*, faded gentry, used roughly by the arrogant raffish young master, or his played-out old sot of a father, or both. Our date of birth was officially recorded as January 1st 1960, so such handy stereotypes were still in full swing, a long way from being laughingly left behind.

Or perhaps she was the possessor of a climactic clitoris, the purveyor of a vagarious vagina; a 'bad girl', an 'easy lay', as they used to say. Or some dubious mixture of these offered explanations is responsible for our coming into existence. 'It takes two to tango' as they still sometimes say, and also 'There's a pair of them in it'. Or neither proposition will suffice. Who knows? Speculation of this kind is futile and fruitless. I try not to concern myself overmuch with such thoughts.

The fact remains that from the start, born as we were 'the wrong side of the sheets' (to press into service another quaintly outmoded expression), we were prime targets for swallowing all that old baloney about Original Sin, that our origins were sinful, that the sins of the fathers were visited on the sons, that there was an innate depravity common to all human beings in consequence of The Fall, that we fell into being in this fallen world from some great good place that we must struggle to make our way back to, that the carnal deed of our begetting was wrong and we would have to atone for it through the suffering of penance to have any hope at all of being counted among the ranks of the righteous, and dwelling in the abode of the blessed.

But there is no such thing as an original sin. We have no homes to go to. The righteous are not necessarily right. It ain't necessarily so. Let copulation thrive, as they say still, or would if they knew how; and do say, in a different way: fuck around.

We were put up for adoption. Why the authorities didn't try to keep us together, I have never found out. Maybe it was a rule of thumb that no prospective foster parents would take two bawling baby boys. The sight of one screaming male infant in swaddling clothes was usually enough to deter even the most intrepid, but two specimens of same definitely proved too much, and made them realise with a shock to the system exactly what they were letting themselves in for.

Yet how many myths begin with the rescue of an abandoned child? There is Moses, sent bobbing downstream in his bullrush basket, to be found by the Pharaoh's Daughter. There is Oedipus exposed on the hill with the metal pins in his feet, to be reared by shepherds. Others of whose trade came to worship Christ, along with the Three Wise Men. The Jew and the Greek. The child of Jerusalem and the child of Athens. Edward and I were nobody's children. We are all the children of Jerusalem and Athens. We are all nobody's children.

Who were these people, our adoptive parents, and how did they come to choose us? The ones who took me are unimportant for the purposes of this story, or so I tell myself, but the ones who got Edward deserve some detailed description, which will be theirs in due course, and an intricate introduction, which they will get now.

I can still remember them clearly, or think I can, sauntering slowly into the nursery on an otherwise ordinary afternoon, giving all the possible candidates for the bounty of their munificence a desultory perusal. Which poor soul would be their sole beneficiary? They looked comfortable, even prosperous, she in a fur coat, he in a camel hair. Maybe this was their Sunday best, glad rags donned for special occasions, and they weren't always so particular about keeping their sunniest side out and looking the part. But this evident affluence was enough to induce the silence that betokened good behaviour in all the more savvy of us aspirants. Only one source of squalling remained among us babes who weren't in arms: my brother in arms.

She strolled over to him and smiled down, her face nervous but kindly, with sad, beaming eyes, and her body was tense but poised as she hunkered down towards him. His screeches subsided as she swam into his ken, and he extended his little right arm with its forefinger pointing in her direction. She took the offered digit between her finger and thumb and, glancing back up at her hovering husband, inclined her head slightly in silent assent.

His ruse had worked, as it would continue to throughout his life. He got attention in the most obvious way, and achieved his aim by second-guessing us all. You might think his success wasn't as a result of craft and cunning, but that he merely bundled through luckily in a gauche, guileless fashion. Maybe simple chance had something to do with it, but to conclude that happy accident was entirely responsible for his good fortune is to fall further into the tender trap of his wily ways. Believe me, I know the slyness of my brother, despite, or perhaps because of, my own shyness. Worldliness can be recognised, even by the most unworldly. To the pure, all things aren't pure. I know him, what he is, or imagine I do. I know myself, what I am, or so I imagine, too. My jealousy, the seed of which was planted that day and has been growing ever since, is legitimate, since he can be a bastard. Literally, he is. But then again, so am I. But the stain, as it used to be called, bothers him more than it does me, at least as far as I can see. It prevents him from having the ideal image of himself, whereas it sits comfortably with any picture of me. Although, to be sure, he's not the one sitting thinking about it now. Fine word, 'legitimate'. Now, gods, stand up for bastards.

What motivated this middle-aged, middle-class couple to take in one of our kind? Their own childlessness, and a willingness to share? A longing that their name would not die with them, that their worldly goods could be left to a creature of their nurture, if not their nature? That they could rear another human being, guiding it through the perilous waters of its early years, and watch it progress steadily towards maturity? Who knows? But it has always bothered me that, even if the truth was deliberately kept from them by the powers that be, they did not even notice on that day long ago the awful and obvious similarity of countenance between their choice and me.

One more tale from the orphanage, before we leave it. Lying in my cot late that night, the first after the departure of the last vestige of my own flesh and blood, my very kith and kin, I became acutely aware of a distant delicate music playing in my ears, and my eyes had a new vision before them, not of their immediate surroundings. In my nostrils was the fragrant aroma of what I took to be fresh flowers, which did not emanate from the environment I was in, and on my lips and in my mouth was what I only later discovered to be the sweet taste of milk and honey, which I had not then been fed. There is a happy land. I also felt much warmer than I usually did in that badly heated, under-resourced, revolting shithole of a glorified workhouse.

I began to notice that the curtains which fluttered gently in the mild breeze above my head were not the heavy institutional linen ones I was used to, but a soft, cotton fabric with a bright, light blue, floral design. A half-moon shone through the slight parting, and the comforting rays of a night-light fell on the floor from outside the bedroom door, soothing an anxious infant, in contrast with the strict policy of no namby-pambying, all-pervading darkness maintained by the regime in my regular quarters.

Then it came to me, as clear and unclouded as dawn on a fine spring morn: I was inside his mind and heart and body, experiencing the same experiences he was experiencing, thinking, feeling and sensing the same thoughts, feelings and sensations as him. I was being stimulated by his stimuli. I wondered if he could reverse the process, if he could come inside me and inhabit my consciousness, surrounded by my circumstances. Was he reacting to what was all around me, expanding towards what gave me pleasure, contracting from what caused me pain? I intuited that this was indeed the case. And if you ask me to tell you how I knew, I cannot tell you because I do not know. Only I felt it, and feel it still, and am deliciously but excruciatingly bifurcated, a poor, bare forked animal, torn in two.

From that night on, when we were still only howling infants, mere mites recumbent in our cribs, this strange form of telepathy has existed between us. I can access him when I want to, as he can me. Neither of us can block the other one out, or cut him off. It can be startling and surprising by times, inconvenient and uncomfortable too. But it has been a great source of consolation and diversion to me over the years. And to him too, I imagine, although I should not presume to speak with any authority for him, even if that is precisely what I will be doing for most of this book. For although we can send signals to each other, and transmit what encompasses us and how it encroaches on us, convey what impacts on us and how it impinges on us, we cannot communicate directly with each other, in any concretely constructed spoken or written language. We must be content with and contend with impressions and nuances, empathy and fellow-feeling. By this method we have managed to keep in touch.

I made it out of that place too of course, eventually. Farmed out to an oldish couple who had already bred a brood of their own, long past childbearing age themselves, but in need of some feckless, unfortunate young fool to lend them a hand and help them out for their remaining declining years, their own flock having fled as far as they could away from that nest of vipers, as quickly as ever they could. It fell to me to play the role of the runt of their litter. Here I will succumb to the temptation to indulge once again my abhorrent love of cliché, by employing phrases like: 'Better the devil you know than the devil you don't', and: 'Out of the frying pan, into the fire'. You get the picture, without me having to elaborate. Suffice it to say that I would rather have remained parentless than have been parented by them, if you don't mind me verbalising that noun. I will add nothing more, at least for the time being.

For I find I cannot bring myself to tell you much about them. My foster parents, I mean. I loathe my childhood and all that remains of it (yet I am all that remains of it, so do I hate myself?), but this is not text as therapy, at least I fervently hope not, nor was it meant to be. This is not the caterwauling of catharsis, even if it does contain some characteristic catch-phrases and catachreses. I am purged of purgation. No intentions where none intended. No good intentions where no good intended. No nothing where no anything. No anything where no nothing. But something still remains. My remains. The remains are all that remain. The remains will be removed. The remains will be remaindered.

So some snippets of information about the strange strangers I grew up with may still slip through the vigilance of my net from time to time. But I will endeavour to be guarded when it comes to my guardians. Who will guard the guardians? Who will guard the guards of my guardians? Who will guard me? And who will guide us?

What is that knocking at the front door?

Faces and names. If only they could be one and the same. You wouldn't have to put a name to a face, or a face to a name. There would be no nameless faces, no faceless names. Face the music, name that tune.

Since we are identical twins, it must follow as the night the day, that our faces are identical, although it may now be somewhat easier to differentiate us, one from the other, than it was back then, by how much or how little our respective visages have or have not, relative to each other, been belaboured and altered by the desiccation and destruction wrought by the fearsome forces of the passage of time.

When I look in the mirror, this is what I see: the eyes, which are the mirrors of and the windows to the soul, are a pale translucent blue, and sometimes wear a piercingly ocular and oracular stare, unswerving and unnerving. They are doing it now, as they look at me looking at myself, as I look at myself looking for him. Seek and ye shall find. Finders keepers, losers weepers. Jeepers creepers, where'd ya get those peepers? See the eyes; the eyes have it. Are you looking at me?

The ears, tapering like those of a less pointed more humanoid Mr Spock, project from either side of my head above and beyond the call of duty. The lobes are more pendulous than most. They may be big, but all the better to hear you with. A word in my ear. A word to the wise. A word to the wise guy. These aural appendages can thankfully be covered and hidden by hair.

The hair, swept back off the high forehead (sign of intelligence in medieval physiognomy), is still dark brown verging on black, even if a few streaks of grey are beginning to intrude and make themselves visible, and still luxuriant, even if receding ever so slightly around the temples. Soon the colour of widow's weeds will have the shape of a widow's peak. The growth, despite what seem like half-hearted attempts to impose order, is still quite unruly and unkempt around the back and sides, which are not short, but not too long either.

The skin, stretching taut and tight over the skull beneath it, though strikingly pale just now owing to the prolonged absence of exposure to sunlight, has been known to be rubicund and ruddy. The cuticle is cute, but is there anything subcutaneously? The epidermis is epideictic, but is there a dermis below? Like an onion, you can peel back layers. Like a snake, this coat can be shed. So the covering of camouflage is both thick and thin, depending on how deep you want to dig. Deep down, I'm superficial. On the surface, I'm deep. Is this why the brow is slightly furrowed, and the eyes have crow's feet? It could also be because occasionally I smile, and even laugh. But I have, and maybe even am, a good skin. Is he? But will I save it? And with it, my soul? Will he? His own, I mean.

The nose, jutting out like an overhanging crag from the side of a cliff, would in olden days have been called Fractured Coriolanian, but in modern times I prefer to call it Grounded Concorde. These are hard times. It is without doubt the most distinguishing and maybe even distinguished feature of my face, and therefore his as well. That's as plain as the noses on our faces.

The mouth, which can pout preposterously when its plump lips protrude, at present gives the impression of equanimity with them pursed. Like the equatorial line of latitude, it is long and even. Through it the oracle has spoken, is speaking and will speak. This lengthy observation makes me bite my lip.

The teeth, though still all my own and healthily pearly white, shiny with encrusted enamel, are slightly crooked and have a few gaps (sign of lechery in medieval physiognomy). This snaggle-toothedness some have found attractive on occasions, but more often than not it is not considered aesthetically pleasing. He didn't let this slightly unsightly idiosyncrasy bother him. I did. But then his Mama and Papa footed the exorbitant orthodontic bills, and he had them straightened. Mine didn't, and so my dentition remains as nature intended. But it's no skin off my nose that he came in for such luxurious pampering by the skin of his teeth. Or I tell myself it isn't. In the teeth of such depravation, I got the bit between mine. Brace yourself.

The chin, though weakly intellectual and somewhat small for all that composes itself above it, is not without its saving residual graces of strength. Even when streaked with stubble, you can tell that I can take it on the chin. I am not, nor is he, a chinless wonder.

So that's my face, and presumably his also, more or less. You might suggest that I should make him go to the nearest looking-glass, and by studying his reflection in it through his eyes, I could compare and contrast the aspect of our respective miens more accurately. But I can't make him do things he doesn't want to do. I can't even ask him to do things he does. You'll just have to take it on trust that he pretty much resembles me, or the description I've given you of myself. I'll be his mirror, as he'll be mine. We'll both be yours. Will we ever meet, face to face? Who knows? That's something else we'll have to wait and see about. I may be a lame duck, but I don't fancy Duck Soup. For now, we're still at the mirror stage. But faces are faeces, and so are fasces. He has that in his countenance which I would fain call Master. He has the emblems of authority parading before him. All a load of codswallop. Faces are shit.

Then there are the faces of his foster parents, almost as familiar to me as those of my own. I will write only of the former. Then there are their names. Mine went by the appellations of Mr and Mrs Tough, while his were known as the Tenders. I will write only of the latter.

They gazed down on him from the start through eyes brimming over with love. His mother beheld him as though he was the only baby in the world, happy, one supposes, to have a child to care for at last, after all the years of trying and failing, watching hope slowly giving way to disappointment, even if the infant was not the actual fruit of her own womb. His father looked bemused, but determined to bring up junior as best he could, imparting wise words of sound advice, introducing this little person to the wonder of the good things in life, even if not a jot of the seed of the tiny tot had actually sprung from his own loins.

His mother's brow would furrow occasionally in concern, troubled lines etched briefly across an otherwise calm face at his smallest sigh, but she smiled radiantly at each moment of recognition she received from him. His father could seem stern, his bulbous nose faintly frightening, but the distant aloofness occasionally evident in his eyes was merely a mask which one felt belied his essential benevolence. There's no art to find the mind's construction in the face.

Of course, they did not contribute in the slightest whit to the genetic make-up of my brother, no more than mine did to me, so we cannot look for any hereditary characteristics, inherited from them, in his nature, no more than we can from mine, in mine. But maybe one of the things this story is, or is trying to be, is a not very well controlled laboratory experiment designed to throw some additional light on the 'nature' versus 'nurture' controversy. Will he be more well-adjusted because of the childhood he is going to have than I am because of the one endured by me? And does the fact that I know the answer invalidate the results of my research? This is no place for placebos. We are bound not to be bound by the double-bind. Look at how different the children of the same parents brought up by those same parents can be from each other and you'll see the futility of imposing general theories on particular practicalities, regardless of position in the family. Still, it may keep us amused.

They gave him a name, which I've already told you. Mine put a name on me, which I haven't yet revealed. They called him Edward. So we'll call him Edward. They should have called him Edgar, in my opinion. But I cannot influence what his parents did, so I am not responsible for the appropriateness or otherwise of his name. You thought, especially given our family names, if not our given ones, that I was making all this up? Think again. We had different proper names, with the same meaning. Different sounds, with the same sense. His parents had looked up what his name means in a book designed to help people name their baby, as he had later overheard them say. I can safely say that mine hadn't. They knew they were calling him 'Guardian of Prosperity'. It goes without saying that mine didn't. He was going to have some prosperity to guard, while poverty was to be my only portion. Given this initial inequality, how could we both be good guardians? In naming him, his were claiming him. In naming me, mine were shaming me. They

23

called me Edmund. So we'll call me Edmund. We're the two Eddies. So welcome to the show. But even if his had called him Edgar, we'd still be the two Eddies. So welcome back once again, my friends, to the show that never ends.

2

WE PROVED ADEPT at adapting to the perils of adoption, each in our own peculiar way. Granted, we only officially found out much later that our foster parents weren't our real parents, or better say our birth parents, since the set had by each one of us had seemed real enough to the one who had them. But I knew something was amiss from the start, and I suspect that he did too. I had those scenes from the orphanage implanted in my mind, and I assure you they were not just another case of false memory syndrome. At least, I don't remember them as such. But it is strange to be told at a certain age that things you thought were true up until then, or it was thought you thought were true, were not in fact the case. You realise that everything you've seen could be seen in another way, that what you've taken for granted could be taken in a different way. You look at your life all over again in the light of the new information. Perspective is altered and so alters; significance is shifted and so shifts. So although we both knew that our parents weren't our parents, that we were at best warmly welcomed or at worst tacitly tolerated house guests, and were conscious of the artificiality of the arrangements which obtained, we weren't supposed to know this, and so were supposed to act differently when we did know, or when they knew we knew. Or maybe we weren't supposed to act any differently at all. How do I know? Still, there's lots of room for lots of double spin there, as if there wasn't enough room for enough of it already.

While I was frequently left alone, and never brought out into company, he was never left by himself, and was regularly surrounded by people. Although we were both, to all intents and purposes, only children (that is, children with no siblings, as opposed to mere children), since my elder brothers and sisters did not pay any attention to either their parents or to me, our early years were strikingly dissimilar. When any of his large extended family and their wide circle of friends were around, they foostered and fussed over him, and so he learned to perform for them in public. My lot, on the other hand, did not entertain visitors, family ties or not, and so I learned to reflect to myself in private. I remember lying many's the time in my cot with the teat of a bottle of milk long gone cold in my mouth, the rubber nipple like ersatz flesh, with only my thoughts to keep me warm. I was killing time, even then. He was having a good time, as now.

I didn't cry.

When it came to our negotiating the much-vaunted oral, anal and phallic stages (let's save the later latency and genital bits for later), he managed to muddle through, successively and successfully, as most people do, it seems to me (despite what the adherents of the originator of this particular system of apprehension might like to have you believe). I, on the contrary, could not navigate any of them. 'Old Age Pensioners Like Greens', I ask you. It's always easier to swallow the rubbish of bad medicine while spoon-fed with the aid of a handy, sugar-coated mnemonic. His progress was monitored conscientiously at every step with well-informed watchfulness, while mine went for the most part unnoticed and unremarked. Does that make me oral receptive – very trusting, dependent on others? Or oral aggressive – aggressive and dominating? Or anal receptive – very generous and giving? Or anal retentive – mean, stubborn, obsessively tidy? Or phallic – self-assured, vain, impulsive? Or genital – well-adjusted, mature, able to love and be loved? Judge for yourself. In my humble opinion, there are no personality types, not even through getting fixated on, or regressing to, one of these sacred stages. I am not a textbook case, as this text should show. I am not a type either, be it yours or mine. I'm a million different people, from one day to the next. Is that enough to make me a novelist? I hope someone with enough verve leaves no stone unrolled in suing me for plagiarism. And what about him? Let's wait and see.

I don't mean to try to set up here some silly opposition between his experience and mine, and have it run through this tale manifesting itself repeatedly as a series of fortuitously fortunate anecdotes about him and all that concerns him and hard luck stories about me and all that goes with me, which would doubtless appeal to all classes and kinds of bleeding hearts and mavrone merchants everywhere. I can categorically state here in simple black and white that I care not for these simple black and white categories. But if our piss and our shit are the first faltering gifts we offer to our parents, indeed to the world at large, then no dutiful child, indeed no child of the universe, likes to see his all, however modest, ignored or even scorned, especially when their only sibling has his little presents received with grateful thanks and much rejoicing, albeit by a different set of parents. The odour of his offering ascended into heaven, while the smell of my sacrifice fell by the wayside back down to earth. It was then that I knew what it felt like to bear the mark of Cain, even if I had not exactly killed my brother Abel, even if my sense of disgruntlement was only over the relative reception of our respective excreta, and even if it was he and not I who was to become the fugitive and the wanderer over the earth, while I and not he remained confined at home, an internal rather than external exile. Why did Cain kill Abel? Because he was able. Because he *was* Abel.

But facile foils aside, I will never forget the time when, inside him once again as he wanted me to be, he was picked up by his adoptive mother and held fast against her breast, and gripped so tightly with her arms fastened around him, that even I knew this gesture must mean all beauty, all truth, all love.

I do not recall mine ever doing the same to me.

When it comes to mothers, nothing, and no one, is innocent. There are no empty signs, however small, no exchanges without value, however trivial. Everything, however little, is made to mean too much. We all have mothers. We do. We all love our mothers. We do, except for the very odd outsider you might meet. And they have us. They do. And they love us. They do, except for the very odd Madame you might meet.

If his mother was pure love, mine was not so much unadulterated hatred, as undiluted indifference. That is the best way to differentiate them. What did he see when he was inside me, when I was looking at her? And what did he hear, smell, taste and touch? I know I wrote in the last instalment that I wouldn't write much about my foster parents, but insofar as they contributed to forming me, I feel I must do my bit, however little, to misforming them. Or rather, to informing on them. Even if I may seem misinformed. For this is writing as revenge. And this is the best way to present my mother, through him, since I was and perhaps still am too close to her to even approximate any semblance of objectivity. I know I'm only surmising what he saw, that though you're getting her through him, ultimately you're still only getting her through him through me. But it gives me the illusion of the distance necessary to pluck out these painful memories from my mind and pin them down on the page in prose. So here goes.

She intimidated him with her girth, as she retrieved the bottle I'd thrown out of my cot and stuffed it back in my mouth in case I moaned with malnutrition. He perceived her as monumental, over-powering: a jutting headland, a baby elephant, a sturdy battleship, an old battle-axe. To call her a hag would be to dignify her to a degree beyond which her dimensions did not dictate. She was, quite simply, gross.

He noticed that her hair was black and greasy, frizzled and frazzled, sticking out everywhere at odd angles, imparting to her the air gener-ally thought of as redolent of the more quiescent and malleable cata-tonic schizophrenic. It did not escape him that her eyebrows ran hap-hazardly like an untrimmed hedge across the fumaroles of her forehead, over the apertures of her eyes which beadily regarded the world as one set of importunate and vexatious obstacles after another, sent to try and test her, and to be outwitted and overcome. He observed that her face was a mess of puss-filled, malignant pustules, with an especially vile and viscid one at the tip of her proboscis, and that a goatee sprouted sparse-ly from her protruding chin. His olfactory channels told him that char-nel-houses have smelt as sweet as Chanel No. 5 in comparison with her malodorous pong, just as jakes have partaken of the aroma of per-fumeries when set against her stinking stench. In short, and not to put too fine a point on it, he saw that she was horrendously hideous to such a degree that it dwarfs my poor powers with a pen to render what he saw. Still, she is, or rather, I hope will become, for better or worse, my study in the grotesque. She has to; otherwise I will be hers. Maybe I already have.

I am more than aware that I am merely imposing my own reactions as regards my mother on to him and making them seem his, when they may not necessarily have been his reactions at all. But if I judged my mother in relation to what I knew of his, then it is probably safe to sup-pose that he did too, just as it is only reasonable to surmise that he evaluated his mother set against what he knew of mine, just as I also did. Why I should assume that he shared the same aesthetic sense as me, that he professed the same principles of good taste, is a mystery best not considered too closely or gone into too deeply here. Suffice it to say that subsequent experience and observation on my part have confirmed me in my original opinion, namely that his mother was to my mother as a divine creature is to a devil incarnate. I can only assume that his has done the same for him. I know it has, if what I see as the beauty of some of the women he has associated with over the years is anything to go by. Aside from being brothers, we are both also, *a fortiori*, men, products of a particular place and time, and as such have been conditioned to find broadly the same set of female attributes attractive. At least enough for there to be some consensus between us as to what constitutes an incontrovertible peach set against an out and out wagon. A clue to the difference between us lies in the fact that he acts on his impressions and impulses. I refuse to.

What is more notable and even remarkable, and worthy of examination and exegesis, is that I equate physical beauty, or at least being presentable, with moral goodness and rectitude, or a kind of beauty of the soul; and physical ugliness, or at most being plain, with moral bankruptcy and cowardice, an ugliness of the pineal part. Why should this be so? Is beauty truth, truth beauty, and is that all ye know on earth, and all ye need to know? Is a thing of beauty a joy forever? Is it only shallow people who don't judge by appearances? Is the mystery of life the visible, not the invisible? And can there really be any widespread agreement on a working definition of beauty? If beauty is in the eye of the beholder, then to whom is the beholder beholden? Despite what I wrote above, there is still room for argument on this matter.

Take, for example, the case of fat people. (Notice I didn't write 'fat women'.) By making my mother fat, and also unsympathetic, I am contributing to the tyranny of thinness. But some men like big women, just as some women like blubbery men. The obese have their place in the canon of allurement. Even regardless of personality, generally seen as the compensation or even triumph of the not so svelte, or the so very meaty, this can still often be the case. But my brother and I are in this regard tediously conventional, if one can venture to introduce a concept like conventionality into a discussion such as this one. You won't find any copies of *Plumpers* or *Porkers* girlie magazines in his bottom drawer, nor mine. I am not about to start contributing, consciously or otherwise, to a tyranny of tubbiness. Most people in this age find slimness beautiful, and they have always found beauty virtuous. That's the beauty myth, and this is, after all, a book of myths. When was the last time a knight in shining armour rescued an ugly, as opposed to a beautiful, princess? And when was that princess' beauty was bodied forth by her being a little teapot short and stout, rather than as sylph-like as a gazelle? When was the last time a frog kissed by a princess turned into an ugly, and not a handsome, prince? And when was that prince's handsomeness indicated by him being rotund, as opposed to reed-like? And when was the last time the beautiful princess was evil, the handsome prince corrupt? The ugly sisters are a permanently bad lot, while Cinderella just needs a make-over to let her true worth shine through. If the glass slipper fits, wear it. That's where the shoe pinches all those who can't get into it. Now the boot's on the other foot.

I do not intend to here go against the accumulated wisdom of the ages, husbanded and handed down from time immemorial. By having loving mothers, men learn to love women. By having beautiful mothers, men learn to love beauty. By having beautiful, loving mothers, men learn to love beautiful, loving women: read on. As for those with ugly, loving mothers, they do not concern us here. As for those with beautiful, unloving mothers, neither do they interest us. As for those with ugly, unloving mothers: read on.

I am not intimating that having the mother I did automatically predisposed me to hating all women. The roots of my misogyny are much more tangled than that. (The following instalment deals with, among other things, my father: how I saw him and what I learned from him. Subsequent sections broach, *inter alia*, the relationship between my mother and father, and what I made of it. None of them a pretty picture, nor a pleasant read, be warned.) But having her around certainly helped to plant the seed and nurture the tree with its twisted branches and fallen leaves that are my unflinchingly jaundiced view of the unfair sex.

Edward's experience was, of course, entirely different. Our syzygy continues in all things, despite my wish that it were not so. How could he not become a man who loved women, with a mother who doted on him and drooled over him from the first? She brought him up, and then set him free. Mine wore me down, and then tied me to her. So while I see them as duplicitous jades, he sees them as people, as friends, as companions, as fun, as well as rides. None of which is to say that they aren't all different. Maybe we should concentrate on one instance of the phenomenon.

Am I jealous of his childhood experience, over mine? I suppose I am. I have already admitted as much, so it would be futile to start denying it now, by backtracking and retracting. I feel it has accounted for so much that has happened, or failed to happen, since. But coveting one's brother's mother is akin to coveting one's neighbour's wife. There is a commandment handed down against it. It is forbidden; it is taboo. But the fact that doing so is a sin makes it all the more attractive a proposition. The unobtainable, or at least the hard-to-get, is always more desirable. I wanted to have had his mother. Just as I wanted to be rid of my own. Just as she wanted to get shut of me. I am that outsider. She is that Madame.

Another image, before we move on, again from our toilet-training days. We were both bed-wetters, although he grew out of it sooner than me. He had every encouragement to do so. He was brought to every urologist and psychologist going, bought model cars and colouring books to keep him amused. A rubber undersheet was placed on his bed, and his nappies were diligently put on clean every night and taken off and washed every morning. In the event of the urge coming on him for a nocturnal micturition, a fresh new plastic potty was proffered for his use. Meanwhile I was left to wallow in my own piss, a practice from which it was decided I would inevitably learn my lesson, and urinate only at the appropriate time, in the old evil-smelling cracked chamber-pot provided for that purpose.

When you wet the bed first it is warm and then it gets cold. One night, as he lay well wrapped up safe and warm in the smooth powdery balm, and I lay warm and wet and sticky in the prickly heat, and we were both privy to how the other one felt, as well as to how we ourselves were feeling, his mother came in and bestowed on him a little yellow teddy bear, which between them they christened Dub, after the town in which we lived. What an appropriate place to place us – Dublin, this Dubh Linn, city of doubles and doubling, literally the black pool. It's easy to see your reflection here. This gift remained with him all through his boyhood and adolescence and even into adulthood, and accompanied him on his many peregrinations, even when it started to disintegrate, and had an eye missing, an ear hanging off. I was never given such inducements towards continence.

I know this scene smacks of the contrived sentimentality of the on-the-spot reporter for a satellite TV news channel, who unearths from beneath the rubble left in the wake of the earthquake or the explosion a child's toy he has planted there earlier himself before the cameras had started to roll. It's not much of an image really, after all. But he's included in it, irreducibly, just as I'm excluded from it, irrevocably.

So what else is new?

Let us leave our mothers, Mrs Tough and Mrs Tender, there for the time being. We are neither of us such Mama's boys that we cannot do that for a little while. These women had consorts, as already mentioned, with whom they went through life. Let us turn our attention to these men, Mr Tough and Mr Tender, who many would have us believe were our earliest role models.

We will voyage around our fathers.

3

"THERE'S MANY'S A MAN rocks another man's child, when he thinks he's rocking his own." So said my father, many times. What I think he was trying to get at, put another way, could be rendered equally well by another old adage: 'It's a wise father who knows his own child.' As you know, he knew from the very beginning that I wasn't his child, but that didn't stop him trotting out this wicked little observation whenever he felt like it. Perhaps he doubted the authenticity of his part in making some of what were supposed to be his actual children. But then whom did he suspect my mother of playing false with to get them? Given the description I gave of her in the last instalment, who would want to go near her with carnal desire in mind or, more to the point, in body, without the proverbial bargepole in hand? And why, for that matter, did he? Maybe his possibilities were limited. Desperation can do dreadful things.

But if paternity is no more than a legal fiction, given what women may do and never say, where does that leave me as regards this man my mother was married to? And where does it leave Edward in relation to his mother's spouse? Motherhood is expansive; it grows with the months and years, until it flowers into an all-consuming passion. Fatherhood is contractual. After an initial coital contribution, it shrivels into near nothingness, until soon there is little hard evidence for its existence at all. And our fathers, Mr Tough and Mr Tender, didn't even have the comforting fact of being that first cause to fall back on, when it came to dealing with us. So what, if anything, did I learn from my paternal unit, if only negatively? And what did Edward learn from his? How can I say?

My father treated my mother with puzzled incomprehension, which shaded into dismissive disdain, as though she were a creature light years more alien to his mode of being than a Venusian would be to a Martian's. Theirs was a typical Irish marriage: they spoke to each other at least twice a year, whether they needed to or not. Otherwise he backed also-rans and drank pints of porter. His house, far from being his castle, wasn't even his home. It was a lodgings he inhabited solely to perform the immediate physical tasks necessary to continue subsisting. His more authentic life revolved around the twin poles of the book-maker's office and the public house.

Not that his existence was one made up exclusively of idleness and merriment. He'd had a job once. In fact, he'd had lots of jobs once. So he had made his pile, and there was no shortage of money. He had been what is usually referred to as a building contractor, but that was just a polite camouflage for having his finger in lots of different pies. He was the kind of person you went to if you wanted something, or if you wanted something done, if you were the kind of person who went to someone like him to get things, and get things done. But by the time I came along, he was already taking a more back seat role, living in semi-retirement, and singing the praises of his own past. He was a man who had made the wherewithal to live well, but who didn't know how to live well, if at all. Still, he lived well enough, according to his own lights, I suppose.

I had not formulated these judgements at the time, of course. I knew nothing then, or very little. My only knowledge of anything being any different from what I then knew had been gleaned from my vicarious witnessing of my brother Edward's experience. Even so, while as a young child you may be able to spot the differences 'twixt man and man, you don't know the reasons for their being there, or how you might go about interpreting them. Meaning, dancing wildly in the night with unmeaning, and then wandering home alone wearily at dawn to the increasingly *déjà vu* chirp of the tweety birds, may be pinned down only through noticing the differences, but how can you know what the differences mean, what they're meant to mean, how they mean, what 'to mean' means, at that tender age? Or in my case, at that tough one.

Mr Tender came straight home from work one evening, as he almost always did, took Edward in his arms and waltzed him around the sitting-room while humming the strains of 'Under the Bridges of Paris', which he did quite a lot too. This is a song, it transpires, that Mr Tender's own father used to sing to him. Then, at teatime, which they called dinner, he cut Edward's bread into long narrow strips, which he called 'soldiers', as he would usually do, so that the boy could dip them into the runny yellow yolk of his egg. Then, later again in the meal, he sprinkled sugar onto another slice of buttered bread, as he sometimes did, and gave it to Edward, saying, "All children have a sweet tooth."

I watched all this, in dumb amazement. You couldn't credit my incredulity. The only song I had ever heard my own father sing was a rather raucous, ribald rendition of 'The Ball of Inverness', and this wasn't even directed at me for my delectation and delight, but just happened to be bawled out in my general vicinity. Nor did he ever pay any attention whatsoever to my dietary intake, or whether or not I found it gastronomically pleasing. He, and indeed I, would have found the very idea that he might show the slightest interest in what I ate, or cared if I liked the taste of it, preposterous in the extreme, laughable to the point of absurdity. All that concerned him, in relation to me I mean, was whether or not I cried too long or too loud in the night and so interrupted his slumbers, or later, whether or not I had his boots polished and ready for him to step into in the morning. As I grew older, I realised that I was a complete mystery to him, as I suspect had been those of his offspring who had gone before me. Come to think of it, I don't even think he thought of me as a mystery. I think he never thought of me at all, or never thought of what he thought of me. I was just there to provide a service, to keep the place clean, to look after his wants. I was an errand boy, sent to pick up the tab, for his excesses and deficiencies.

So Edward's father, although a bourgeois gentleman who liked a quiet life, a business executive in middle management who wore slippers by the fireside and smoked a pipe, was no stranger to performing the little kindnesses that betoken genuine affection, and would even go out of his way to act in a way that would favourably impress an impressionable young mind. And why, indeed, shouldn't he? Maybe he wasn't even conscious of doing so. Or if he was, maybe he still wasn't aware of the effect he was having, or hoped to have.

For example, Mr Tender decided that Edward should have a dog, since he supposed that all little boys liked them, and he thought that it would be good training and preparation for the future responsibilities of adult life for his charge to have a charge, a four-legged friend of the canine variety to look after. So a small but lively black Scottish terrier was introduced into the household. They named it, with a typically imaginative flight of fancy, Scottie. Edward took it out for walks a couple of times, and then rapidly lost interest in it, until soon it just lay there, ignored by him. I am not trying to imply here that my brother was a spoiled brat. After all, he had never hankered after a dog in the first place, but had had one foisted upon him, unasked. However, I would have loved to have had one, but I knew there was no point in asking. I would never have been given one. After a few weeks, Mrs Tender summoned a man from the Cats and Dogs Home, and the mutt was despatched out of their lives forever forthwith.

Again, a bicycle was bought for the young fellow, and since he seemed nervous about keeping upright while riding it, his father would go out with him of an evening on an old bike of his own, and they would cycle around the neighbourhood together, the deputy Daddy extending a caring and helpful hand to his surrogate son's shoulder, to buoy him up and balance him when he showed signs of wavering and wobbling under the threat of an approaching or overtaking car. No need for artificial stabilisers there.

But what remains with me most clearly now is how Mr Tender would take that fortunate fellow, my fraternal unit, on little trips and excursions around the city and the country. On occasions he brought him on bus journeys, the first memorable time out to Howth on the northside, and subsequently out to locations as far afield as Dalkey on the southside, not because they didn't have a car or wouldn't use it, or because it wouldn't have been easier to get to these places by train, but because Edward, never having travelled by public service vehicle before, had an insatiable yen to do so. They sat on the front seat on the upstairs of a double-decker, so that the little lad could look out of the windows at all that passed him by, and pretend to be the driver. His father paid their fares, and the conductor gave him a ticket from his machine, and Mr Tender passed the piece of paper on to Edward and said, "Mind that in case an inspector gets on."

Edward wondered what an inspector was, and wanted to ask, but felt that he would seem childish and stupid if he did, and be shown up as such, so he kept his mouth shut about it, and his inquiry remained unspoken, his curiosity unsatisfied.

Other times they took the train for day trips to such exotic locations as Limerick, Galway, or Cork. All these places seemed the same to Edward: windy and rainy, occasionally hailstones too, with strange grey buildings that were not his home. But he liked the sound of their names. A man in the same compartment as them, trying to be friendly with him because he was a child, but without any apparent ulterior motive, told Edward that the wheels as they turned in the train tracks were really saying, 'We'll soon be there, we'll soon be there, we'll soon be there'. But the boy actually liked getting there much more than being there. Even then, for him, it was far better to travel hopefully than to arrive.

These jaunts by public transport were undertaken infrequently enough for the novelty not to wear off, and there was hardly any greater treat for Edward than a bus or train outing with his old man. But even when they went on private journeys by car, the lucky lad still savoured something, still added to his store of remembered impressions. Or maybe it is only me who is remembering them, for him. Perhaps he showed them to me, but has forgotten them himself. When his father pulled into a garage for petrol, he would give his son the football books, picture cards, coins or team coats of arms that were on offer, to build into a collection. Edward always accumulated the full set. He remembered, or only saw, Mr Tender take a wallet from the back pocket of his trousers with a casual flourish, a gesture that betokened that he did this often and with confidence, and the wad of notes that bulged forth from that billfold. He recalled, or just clocked, him opening a small book and writing in it with a fountain pen, tearing a piece of paper from it and presenting it to the man at the counter. He realised that these papers must play an important part in human intercourse. My father never took me anywhere, never taught me the seriousness of the abstract concept but concrete necessity called money. I was left to find out for myself. I never did.

While Edward was away with his father, his mother would usually be at home entertaining some close female friends, or preparing a repast against their return. But sometimes she would come too. For Mrs Tender was not excluded from playing happy families by a restrictive coalition of father and son. Nor was Mr Tender left outside the game by a similar strategic alignment of mother and her little boy. Nor did the elder Tenders gang up on their young pretender. They loved him tender. It was a three-way thing, this familial triangle.

One of the things that intrigued me most in my formative childhood years was not only that Edward's mother and father slept in the same room, but that they even slept in the same bed. I thought this arrangement most bizarre. Now I know it to be the norm. But Mr and Mrs Tough slept in separate beds, in separate rooms, so how could I have known any different, for better or worse? It seemed much more natural to me that men and women should keep as much distance as possible between them, than that they should encourage intimacy. As a boy, I wondered exactly what women were for. As a man, I have only one answer. See what I mean about my misogyny?

The most enduring memory I have of the atmosphere in the house where I grew up is how the sound alternated between an oppressive silence and an outright cacophony of banging, clattering, screaming, shouting, slamming and snarling. Sometimes the two parties in dispute (and they were always in dispute) would say nothing to each other for weeks on end, but they would use non-verbal modes of communicating their antagonism, of making their hostility for one another felt.

My mother was not a passive, put-upon woman, but my father still did his best to keep her in her place. She, in turn, made sure to make things as hellishly hot and sticky as possible for him. I remember the front door being shut with such ferocity as he went out one day to meet his mates that, looking back on it now, I am surprised it did not come off its hinges. I remember pots and pans crashing on to the cooker and cups and plates thumping on to the table as he rustled something up for himself when he came in drunk, before he went to bed. I remember the smell of the inedible burnt offering she would always leave in the oven for him as punishment for his unpunctuality those times. I remember him slurping his tea from his saucer at breakfast the next morning, just to get at her, as if she still cared, if she ever had cared, although he maintained it was the quickest way for it to cool. I remember it all, but I never interfered. I sang dumb, but I saw and heard all.

One morning, as he was putting on his hat and coat to go out and back a few horses followed by downing a few pints, their primitive interaction went so far as my mother saying to him: "Why don't you stay at home for once and do some things that need doing around this place, instead of leaving it all to me?"

To which he replied: "You're my wife, and you'll do what I say."

Which was met by the top volume rejoinder: "Well, I won't be your wife much longer."

Then he clasped his hands and thrust them out in front of himself, moving the palms together and apart, as though choking the living daylights out of someone, of a chicken, of her, and grimaced down at little me standing there, as much as to say, 'Strangling is too good for her', or 'What else can you do?' She flung the bedroom door shut in his face.

One evening, as he was sitting at the tea table (we didn't call it dinner), on one of the rare occasions when he deigned to dine with us, she began to weep. Only later did I realise that this was ostensibly out of character, but only later still did I come to know also that it was just another ploy on her part in the ongoing battle to which I was an unwitting witness, a last ditch attempt to get notice and get her way, and so not so out of character after all. I got up from my seat and went to comfort her, but he told me to sit down and leave my mother alone; she'd be all right in a minute. What was he feeling, insofar as he felt anything? Well-concealed compassion, or barely concealed contempt?

These are just more incidents which I am making into images. They may not mean much to you, but they are loaded with poignancy for me. It is not my job to make them more relevant for you. Maybe you like them for themselves, but if not, maybe you like them for what they tell you about me, about them, about yourself. If not, tough. Either they, or me, or them, or you, are not interesting enough.

I did not take my father's side against my mother, although I feel he would have liked me to. Such favouritism does not account for my dislike of the ladies. Nor did I take her side against him, although that's probably what she would have wanted me to do too. Such a bias does not explain this hatred of women, for making me hate men. Rather, my much-vaunted, by me, misogyny is just part of my overall misanthropy.

I should point out, in all fairness, that my parents' open hostility stopped short of actual violence. Perhaps they knew, somewhere inside themselves where they would not even have known if they knew or not, that psychological warfare was more effective than its physical counterpart. Plus, it had the added advantage of keeping that band of merry pranksters who dabble in other people's lives (I mean here, of course, the shrinks and the social workers) at bay for longer, and delaying them from entering the fray. That would happen later, with me. Do not reveal, if liberty is precious to you. Then why am I writing about my own life? Because we are all incarcerated, anyway. And, society being an open prison, it follows that the family is a closed cell.

I am in that same house now, as I think back over those times and write these reminiscences, but now all is silence, interminably. Save for that knocking on the front door.

I notice that I am painting a picture of the working-class Tough household as rough and uncouth, and the middle-class Tender one as nice and sedate. Is this mere envy on my part? A chip on the shoulder of a neglected boy pressing his cold face against the window and scratching his fingers down the pane of glass of the warm, cosy lifestyle of his more well-looked-after brother? Is it mere inverted social snobbery? The idea that the feelings and sensitivities of the better-off and more genteel must be more heart-felt and refined than those of the plain, simple, ordinary folk? Maybe. But who is not envious at seven? Who is not snobbish at seventeen? And who is not either at any age? I'm no saint. Neither were many of the saints. You have to sin to get saved.

What you learn later is that the plebeians feel the same as the patricians; they just don't know how to express it as well. Or, more correctly, that caste has very little to do with feelings and expressing them. Articulate people are prone to making the mistake of thinking that those who aren't as eloquent have nothing to say. But we all have to learn how to feel, and express our feelings, wherever we're from, if it can be learned at all, if we're one of those who needs to learn. Can you teach feeling if it isn't there? Should you?

I, for example, do have feelings, even if I pretend I don't, no matter what I may have said. I just keep them to myself, most of the time. It's not always good to talk, or even to share, even if sharing is what I've resorted to doing here. But we are anonymous to each other, and you can always take it or leave it. Besides, how do you know I'm telling the truth, the whole truth, and nothing but the truth? Sharing my true feelings with you might not do me, or you, any good. That's why this is a story.

There was, of course, rain. Did I forget to mention the rain? There are no camels in the Koran, so they say. They are so common in that neck of the woods, so taken-for-granted a part of everyday reality, that only a falsifying tourist would trouble himself to emphasise them as local colour. Although, now that I come to think of it, there are camels in that other big book from that part of the world, the Bible. For instance, the one that would have great difficulty getting through the eye of a needle, a simple metaphor for the impossibility of a rich man entering the kingdom of heaven. Although, I seem to remember coming across the fact somewhere else that the Eye of a Needle was literally a particularly narrow gateway into the city of Jerusalem, the bane of camel-drivers' lives, so although it may indeed be difficult for a rich man to enter the kingdom of heaven, it is not entirely impossible. I bet it was a rich man, or one of his spiritual advisors, who spotted this loophole, and got through it.

Is rain exclusively Irish? Apparently not. Is it so common in Ireland that no Irish person pays any attention to it? Again, not so. But maybe Irish people don't know this. They imagine that everything, including the rain, is intrinsic to being Irish. Can my childhood be Irish without some rain? Of course it can. But, into every life a little rain must fall, as they say. So, although maybe we shouldn't be bothered bothering with the rain, we will, just this once, just to get it over with and out of the way, once and for all.

Okay then: rain. Cue rainfall, bucketfuls of it, incessantly pouring down.

On him it rained too. But it didn't seem to get to him as much as it did to me. I wonder why? It must be because no one ever had it as bad as I did. I have suffered, and been more miserable, than anyone else, ever. Poor me, always caught in the rain.

It occurs to me that you may well ask: if Edward and I could see into each other's lives, why didn't we arrange to meet? By simply sketching out a time and place, when one of us was in the other one's mind, we could have got together and got things together.

Well, for a start, we were too young to think of such a thing at this early stage. But even when we were older, I suppose we tacitly agreed that if we were to encounter each other in the flesh, it might spoil everything, and we were afraid to do it. Identity is so fragile, and must be preserved at all costs. We could have done it a few years ago, before it was too late. We could still do it now, but maybe it is far too late. Or is it?

Sometimes we got in touch telepathically up to three times a day, but after we had become accustomed to the oddity of our new toy, sometimes a month would go by without an exchange between us. Even the extraordinary becomes ordinary after a while, and gets taken for granted. We didn't even think our ability was anything special anyway, since it had been with us from the beginning, and we had always had it. It was only later that we found out its uniqueness, or rather, its doubleness. We were holy innocents, wholly innocent of our power. So he could be inside me, so I could be inside him – so what? It was just as strange to us that there was a me inside me, a him inside him, a them inside them, a you inside you.

4

GROWING UP IN IRELAND then was very different to growing up in the same bog now, and it was different to growing up anywhere else, also. Growing up anywhere is different from growing up anywhere else, at any time. But sometimes, even quite often, there are odd similarities. Although growing up in the same place at the same time can produce radically different results. Take Edward and me, for example: so different, and yet...no, no. I do love these worn-out old words and phrases, and the ideas they embody. That's why this story I'm telling, or trying to tell, is partly an anatomy of cliché. That's why it, in turn, makes me melancholy. But even I have to draw the line somewhere.

True, you only really begin to compare and contrast when you get a little older, and have been around the block a few times, met all kinds of people, and learned a thing or two. But we terrible twins had a head start on everybody else in that department. We knew before we began, because of our gift of surreptitious signalling, that we weren't the centre of the universe, that our experience wasn't unique, since we knew at least one other person, our sibling, who had a lot going on inside himself as well, and had outside circumstances that didn't bear much resemblance to the other one's. But at the same time we realised, because of this very ability, that we were the centres – or, at least, the poles – of our own universe, that our own experience was unique – I mean duoique, since we didn't know anyone, besides ourselves, who had it. Mind you, it was only when we got as far as school that we discovered that not everybody, indeed nobody, was capable of this singular – sorry, dual – feat. But that's another story, for another time. Oh all right, I'll tell it now.

School: the very word conjures up macabre memories for most people, memories they would rather not remember, have probably repressed, and would prefer to forget. When they do remember them, they usually embellish and embroider retrospectively, to make the burden of living with them easier to bear. I hear that schools are all different now, that everything has changed, that they are more enlightened and humane. But I have my doubts, and will reserve the right to reserve judgement.

I'll allow that not all schools are exactly the same, and I seem to remember, from my perspective, that Edward had an easier time at his than yours truly did at mine. But they are similar enough in kind, in that they all have more or less the same objective. Schools are for teaching you how to live with other people, before they are for teaching you anything else. I didn't learn my lesson well. Edward did.

The first day at school came for the unwilling schoolboy. Such was my chagrin at being flung in among a throng of snotty-nosed kids, which inevitably increased my awareness of being one myself, that I immediately sought solace by dreaming myself into Edward's situation. His classroom was cleaner and quieter than mine, less cram-packed full of other boys too, but still an uneasy atmosphere was persistently present, an incomprehension at being lumped into a herd, at being thought of as being just like everyone else, at being part of a crowd whose only power lay in being such a crowd.

His mother had led him in by the hand, and the teacher introduced himself. Edward was asked to choose where he would like to sit, and opted for a place beside a boy whom he seemed to recognise as one who lived up the road from him. Mrs Tender had even bought him a little model car, a yellow and black MG, to help pacify any misgivings he might have had about this new departure. Still he bawled after her. My auld wan had dropped me, or dumped me, off at the school gate, told me to stop acting the baby, or the maggot, to make the best of it, to be a man, and then promptly scarpered. I could not, or would not, cry.

While I was lost in this reverie, the clamour and chaos continued around me, punctuated periodically by an uneasy silence beneath which a murmurous undertow began to build up yet again. Suddenly the teacher swooped down on me, wanting to know how much two plus two equalled, or something else I didn't know, something else he hadn't told us, and I was shook out of my pensive ponderings, which he

rightly surmised I was using as an escape route from so-called reality –
that is, the reality he was responsible for presenting to me – the reality
out there which is supposed to be so much more real than the one in
here. He berated me for my inattention, for letting my mind wander,
and wonder. He seemed to take it personally. All the other boys thought
his anger terribly funny, his agitation fully justified, as though I was
deserving of his wrath for being such a ninny. It was then that I began
to have some inkling that the others did not have this imaginative fac-
ulty, this telepathic tendency, that Edward and I shared. It had never
dawned on either of us up until then that this was a resource not open
to others, had never occurred to us to test whether or not they had it
too. Now we knew it wasn't, and they hadn't.

You will argue, no doubt, if you're interested at all, that everybody
cogitates, everybody daydreams, and lots of children have an 'imaginary friend' to whom they like to talk. How was what I was doing any
different from what lots of others do? Well, it seemed to provoke a
stronger reaction in those who accidentally witnessed it than the average obliviousness to one's surroundings does in those who come across
it. Moreover, from what I learned of Edward's world, it was so alien to
my own, or what I'd known, that I could hardly have made it up out
of thin air in my own mind all by myself, without some sort of external stimulus to spark my imagination. So I really was being transported into his mind, which showed me his life, just as he was into mine,
which did the same thing for him. Another reason I know this is that,
while we were both fascinated with each other's lives, I was delighted
with his, but he was disgusted with mine. We sensed this only subtly at
first, but it became more transparently obvious later on. Was it possible to have such strong feelings about a purely imaginary world? So
I wasn't just wool-gathering. It really was happening. I kid you not.

Such was the fury of my master's verbal onslaught, that I decided
there and then to keep my virtual ventures with my brother dark to all
and sundry from then on. Only he and I would know of them. The termination of our transmission that day was like a television picture suddenly being lost in lines of static interference across the screen, before
finally fading altogether to a matt black finish.

The teachers also gave us the Good News about God, and told us how
the whole shooting match would fall apart without Him. At last, I

thought I'd found out who to blame. They did this in both our schools, so there was no avoiding or evading it. Apparently they still go in for this sort of thing, although increasingly few people take it anyway seriously any more. But the forms must be maintained, the forms being all there are. They told us we were all God's children. They told us we were all brothers in Christ. Does this mean that I am, like Christ, the son of God, and saviour of the world? And is Edward? Are you? Is everyone? Every man his own saviour. Every man a son of God.

My narrative does not intend to descend here to the level of recounting our Atlantean struggles, our Herculean labours, to overcome the malign influence of the indoctrination of the Catholic Church. Other people have done that elsewhere, in stories even worse than this one. The Christian Brothers beat us physically, and tortured us mentally, like they did everyone else – it was all in a day's work, this method of preparing us for the harshness of the adult world that by their very actions they only added too – but we just got on with it as best we could, and tried not to let it affect us too much. Stiff upper lips, and all that. There was even one lay teacher – how appropriate the name – who had a fondness for sticking his hand down boys' trousers and fondling their privates, while they sat on his lap, as he had told them to do. To me he did it too. But I never complained. How could I have known it was wrong?

Because the Tenders paid fees for Edward's tuition, and the Toughs coughed up not a penny for mine, the authorities in his place of instruction spared the rod and spoiled the child a little more than in my kip, in an increased effort to appease the parents. The more you pay, the more you can say, and the more accountable the people you pay are to you. (Not that the Toughs cared one way or the other, mind.) But the attitude in both institutions amounted to the same thing. I wouldn't say it never did us any harm, after the manner of some people to whom it undoubtedly did do a lot of harm, to whom it continues to do harm, and who continue to do harm themselves. But I'm not going to go on about how much harm it did do us. What harm? The best way to deal with this particular brand of casual brutality, or any kind of smug viciousness, is just to ignore it, and hope it will go away. Or failing that, if they hurt you too much, to laugh at it. Nobody takes the slightest notice of it, or pays a blind bit of attention to it, any more anyway. Like Atlas, we shrugged. Like Hercules, we rested.

But the interesting thing about God was that you could supposedly talk to him, even though he wasn't actually there. This was called prayer. At first I thought that this attempt at getting in touch with an absent entity, and hoping to have it get back to you, would be somewhat similar to my relationship (for want of a better word) with Edward. But it wasn't. I could float into Edward's mind whenever I felt like it, as he could into mine. This was not the case with praying to God. Besides, I always knew when Edward was with me, as he did when I was with him. Ditto. Most of the time when I was praying to God, I felt as though I was talking to myself. Sometimes I felt I was about to be filled with a strong feeling of grace, peace and tranquillity, but then I would hear blasphemies, curses and imprecations in my mind, and the foul language made me lose my concentration. Some part of me would swear when I was at prayer. Edward fared a little better, but little better. For they had taught us to pray, using the words Our Saviour gave us: Our Father.... But even though we both had proxy fathers, one rather more congenial and less poxy than the other, neither of us knew our real father. So Our Father was not real, to us.

Religion, in this case Catholicism, entailed Confession, and then Communion. These were called sacraments. I'd had one sacrament already, Baptism, although I had no recollection of having had it. Later there would be Confirmation, and maybe even Marriage, Holy Orders or Extreme Unction. So they said. To go to Confession, you needed to have sins to tell. Sins were things you had done that were wrong. The Ten Commandments told you what was wrong. You told your sins to a priest, who was a man who represented God, and then he gave you your penance, and then God forgave you.

I feel as though I am an anthropologist, outlining the (for me) primitive but quaint customs and rituals of a remote and near forgotten tribe, washed aside by the relentless and unremitting tide of progress. Or an archaeologist, excavating the remains of a once great but now extinct ancient civilisation. Do people still believe these things? I suppose somewhere, somehow, in some fashion, they do. Here is the story of my First Confession.

We queued up in our pews outside the box, us seven-year-old boys in short pants, our knees brushing the red velvet of the kneelers, most of us suitably awed by the burning light of the candles and the lingering aroma of the incense, and cowed by the teacher's insidious presence. When my turn came, I went in, knelt down in the dark, and waited for what seemed like an eternity, while listening to the mumblings of the priest and the boy the other side of him, until suddenly he pulled back the sliding door behind the little perforated hatch, and I stammered out, "Bless me, father, for I have sinned," as I had been taught to do.

It was now up to me to confess my sins. Even at that young age, I had enough cop-on to realise that an open admission that I had harboured thoughts of killing my parents would cause too much of a stir if made directly to my confessor. He would be shocked, and there would be endless fuss and bother, even if he didn't betray me by breaking the seal of the confessional, about which we had been given the low down. So I settled instead for the less specific, more anodyne, "I had bad thoughts."

Bad thoughts, at seven! When probed as to the nature of these cogitations, I revealed that I heard bad words, while praying. Sometimes I even said them. This was evidently not as idiosyncratic an experience as I had supposed, for he merely cautioned me to overcome distractions, and to pray for the strength to do so. Pray for the strength to overcome distractions while praying! Then, for my penance, he told me to recite a good Act of Contrition, and to say one Our Father, one Hail Mary and one Glory Be. It was as simple as that to be absolved of your sins. So long as you didn't have bad thoughts or hear bad words while doing it. Or say them. But which was more sinful? Having bad thoughts, hearing bad words, or saying them?

Edward had a fairly similar time, I believe. He offered disobedience as his most objectionable failing. But we both knew well enough not to give away the most distinctively personal thing about us, which could conceivably be construed as an erring aberration: our ability to enter each other's minds at will. That was, and would always remain, our secret.

"Go and sin no more," they said to us, as they said to everyone else. We went and sinned for evermore, like everyone else. Otherwise, why would there be any need for Confession?

Then there was sport, being good and bad at games. At my school, which catered for the lower orders, we played Gaelic football. At

Edward's school, which serviced the orders which had aspirations towards social pretension, they played rugby.

My chief recollection of playing Gaelic is how constricting it was to be obliged to stay in the same allotted position, to keep the familiar regular formation. You would go off your head with boredom waiting for the ball to come to your neck of the woods on the playing pitch. In Gaelic, there were no full-backs doing forays forward on overlaps, no forwards helping out in defence, as there were in that foreign and forbidden game, soccer.

Edward's chief memory of playing rugby is of being selected for the middle of the scrum, or 'vice-grip' as he thought of it. It put him off the game for life. Being squashed to death did not appeal to him. He was put in this position because, in primary school, he was bigger than most of his classmates. By the time he reached secondary school, however, the situation had changed, since the other boys had caught up with him in size. By then it had become apparent that he was a good sprinter, so the sports master wanted him to play as a back. But memories of his early experiences with the game stayed with him, so he came to a tacit agreement with this personage: he would run for him during the athletics season if he was excused from playing for him during the rugby one. The arrangement seemed to work. He even got to win a few medals, gold yet, so fleet of foot did he prove himself over the one hundred yard dash. But, because of parental disapproval, he never got to play the game he liked most: soccer.

I played it, after school hours, with the lads from my class, in a park near our place of instruction. I was not the greatest player ever, or even among this small gathering, but I enjoyed the opportunities the game afforded for the display of skill, mostly to others, but occasionally to myself. I am here recording my participation in these matches solely because of one scene that remains forever etched with clarity in my memory.

I was hovering on the edge of the opposition's penalty area, as the ball came over towards me from a corner kick. Dodging behind the boy who was marking me, I stuck out my foot and hit the ball first time on the volley, and watched it sail sweetly over the heads of all those in the packed goalmouth, past the flailing hands of the leaping goalkeeper, right into the top right-hand corner of the billowing net. That tied the score at one-all, and we went on, as far as I can remember, to win three-one. I am sure I must have scored other goals, in other places, at other times, but none gave me as much satisfaction, or have stayed with me so long, as that one. I would hazard a shrewd guess that this is because, aside from that strike being spectacular in itself, and apart from the boost to the ego success in competitive sport is meant to provide, it was the first and only time in my life that I felt I was doing something Edward would have liked to have been doing, something he wasn't doing, something he never had done, something he never would do. He was watching me, from inside of me, and I was getting even with him, even going one up on him. He never got to score a goal like that, even if he would have liked to.

One evening around this time, as Edward was straggling home alone from school, he was pushed back into the ruined remains of an old castle in a park near where he lived by three young toughs from a less fashionable neighbourhood. They must have known that he was tender. Illegally, they asked him for legal tender. One of them pointed to a nearby tree with a rope dangling from it, and said that he would hang Edward from it if he did not give them money. He claimed to have hanged other boys from the same tree before this, just because they had failed to comply with his demand. Edward could not understand why this was happening to him. All he could think to say in his defence was, "I'm just a good little boy."

This offering did not mollify them. He gave them all he had, which amounted to threepence. They told him to stay where he was, and not attempt to follow them, or they would come back and beat him. Then they ran off out of the overgrown courtyard, leaving him in a most distressed condition of wretched helplessness.

Is it possible to hold back a torrent of tears until the time when they will have the most emotional impact? Does the force with which the floodgates are finally burst open depend on the amount of time the slew of sobs has been held back? Or if too much time elapses between the event which precipitated the lachrymal desire and its ultimate consummation in weeping, does the urgency of the need to shed those teardrops slowly but surely subside? This fine balance between too early and too late must be calculated and judged to perfection, and remain delicately poised and maintained with precision.

Edward ran home as fast as he could, and only when he had got safely through the door did he let his crying commence, as he told his mother what had happened, she holding him in her arms. She called the gardaí, who duly arrived, and took him on a tour of the district in their squad car. But they failed to find the culprits, and so drove him home again. He felt foolish, as though they had not taken him seriously.

He had summoned me inside his mind, to observe all this, and I had felt his fear. But what I had noticed, and what had frightened him the most, was that however much I might have wanted to, I could not help him, could not save him.

The day when we would make our first Holy Communion was fast approaching. We were made to learn by rote the questions and answers to be found in our catechism. Naturally, at that age, the great significances of these stentorian statements went entirely over our heads, but Edward found it comforting that there was seemingly an answer to every question, that everything could be explained. I found it vaguely disquieting.

"Who made the world?"

"God made the world."

"Who is God?"

"God is our father in heaven, the maker and creator of all things."

"What are angels?"

"Angels are beings of pure grace, made by God to adore him."

There were the wafers we were given to practice how to receive the host, the soggy taste of which I can remember still. These were unconsecrated, and so not yet the body of Christ (God's son, who died for our sins), but just pieces of unleavened bread, and so it was all right if you accidentally touched one before it was placed in your mouth. (Now, I believe, consecrated hosts are no longer untouchable, and it is permitted for everyone to grab hold of them.)

His big day arrived before mine. He wore neat, new clothes, and sported a spiffing white rosette on his lapel as I would, as everyone does (always excepting girls, of course, who get to wear white all over, and so do not need just one measly little appropriately coloured rosette to show how pure they are). Edward walked up the aisle, knelt down and took the host on his tongue, swallowed it and said "Amen".

As he left the altar rails, he was transported into an altered state, and heavenly raptures were his in the abode of bliss. On returning to his pew, he held up his face and gave his mother a kiss, and his father smiled with ill-concealed pride. This elevated feeling, like a light being turned on inside his mind, lasted for at least ten minutes. For the rest of the day, his parents went the rounds with him, visiting relations and friends, who handseled him generously with sums of money. His mother even got him another little model car for his collection, this time a white Aston Martin, as driven by action hero James Bond. Here was a boy who would definitely go places.

All this led me to half-expect something special for myself. It goes without saying, but say it I will, that I was disappointed. On my big day the blessed host tasted just like all the unblessed ones I had had before. Worse, because the pleasant effects my brother had been privileged to experience were denied to me, it tasted like ashes in my mouth. I am not sure what ashes taste like, but then, probably, neither are you. It's just a simile, and like all similes you are supposed to know what it is supposed to convey, even if you don't know the means of conveyance. Why I should associate in my mind a nice taste in my body with higher sensations in my spirit, I do not know. Perhaps there is some mysterious link between mind, body and spirit which I made back then, but which now escapes me.

After this let-down, it hardly came as any surprise that my parents' idea of a treat was to excuse me my usual chores, and leave me to my own devices for the remainder of the day, once they had got me home.

5

A FEW YEARS AFTER COMMUNION came Confirmation, and then we would proceed from primary to secondary school. At Confirmation we would become good and perfect Christians. At secondary school we would learn more difficult things.

With Confirmation came more questions and answers, and when confronted with the former, we trotted out the latter, like the reflex actions of laboratory rats to familiar stimuli. This time the rosettes were red, rather than white. This was because the Holy Spirit would descend on us in the form of tongues of fire, rather than God the Son entering us in the form of broken bread. As I sat in my pew towards the end of the ceremony, I found it difficult to be as devout as I might have been. An elderly man to my right kept trying to sneak a look into my special new prayer book, with illustrated biblical scenes in colour, but I kept opening it slightly towards him to tease and tempt him, and then closing it over away from him to thwart and torment him, hardly the action of a recently confirmed good and perfect Christian. Even then, my Pyrrhonic actions would confirm my sceptical thoughts. We set out only to meet ourselves when we return, to reinforce our own prejudices.

Edward wasn't quite as bad a boy as me, and managed to go through the motions more enthusiastically. But then, he had another round of visitations and presentations to look forward to. At this rate, I wouldn't put it past him to get married eventually, if only to get his hands on all those wedding gifts that would inevitably come his way.

Secondary school differed from primary school in that, instead of having just one teacher all day long, we had different teachers for every subject. These dispellers of ignorance struck me (!) as predominantly frustrated, faintly mad middle-aged men, although there were one or two who could either control the class or else knew what they were talking about, although the ability to do both rarely resided in the same individual.

Knowing what I now know, I realise that their main problem was that they had been given a little glimpse of culture in college, and were then condemned to serve out their days lion-taming the likes of us. But back then, we wouldn't have known or cared whether they knew what they were talking about or not, since it was just about now that puberty, as it is quaintly called, began to manifest itself, and our bodies became battlegrounds of hormones, with testosterone coursing through our systems, making our minds think of only one thing.

Ah, the absurd futility of endeavouring to educate rampant adolescents. Still, some of it must have rubbed off on some of us, somehow. But power and control, who had them and who didn't, were now the main issues, for staff and students alike, as they often are in later life. Is control controlled by its need to control? That's a powerful question.

One day a palpable stir passed through the classroom, with the mumbled message that so-and-so had a picture of a naked woman in his desk. With the teacher out of the room, leaving us to our own devices, this report provided a cue for most of my classmates, who went asinine over the ass, leered over the legs, tittered over the tits, were curious over the cunt. The lucky chap privileged enough to be in possession of this image was even able to go so far as to extract payment from those not fortunate enough to be his closest cronies, for the mere chance to peruse this *risqué* photographic portrait. I couldn't have afforded it, even if I'd been interested. For, while I admit it shows a woeful lack of imagination on my part, my first reaction to the situation was, 'Why would anyone want to look at a picture of a naked woman?'

It was not the case that this kind of material has never done anything for me, since I subsequently, albeit tragically briefly, became quite a devotee of this much maligned if admittedly reductive genre, which is loosely termed, with an insouciance that covers a multitude, pornography. For are not all genres, in their own way, reductive? And, in their own way, inclusive too, the macro lurking in every micro, just a small vowel shift away; and verse vicea, of course. Or is that arsy-versy? Pornography for the lonely man, romantic fiction for the lonely woman. Or is it the other way around? It was simply that I had not yet masturbated to orgasm, and so had not yet found out what all the fuss was about. I was still only at the uncertain erection stage. I didn't know what that thingamabob between my legs was for, or why it got hard and grew big. My time to cum was still a time to come.

Edward too was making progress in this direction, although he too had not yet enjoyed an ejaculation, pious or otherwise. However, unlike me, he had developed an exclusively aesthetic interest in women's bodies, divorced from the purely sexual pleasure that he was later to discover could be derived from them. Or maybe his aesthetic sense and sexual prowess were mingled in subtle ways of which he could not yet be fully cognisant. So it was that he started to keep a scrapbook with pictures of scantily clad, curvaceous young lovelies, cut out from newspapers and magazines that came his way. Some of them were culled from a foreign tabloid which he had to part with pocket money for, and sneak into his tiresomely correct household. His interest was not in what would now be termed hard-core material, but in more saucily suggestive pin-ups. He was astute and cute enough to keep his collection hidden, under some boxes on top of his wardrobe, but without fully understanding why he did. One afternoon when he was studying this treasure trove in his bedroom, he left it momentarily unattended while he went to the toilet, and returned to find his mother surveying it in his stead. This meant trouble.

"I'm ashamed of you," she told him in a low tone. "Those aren't nice girls." She confiscated his compilation, never to be seen again.

That night his mother and father and he prayed the Rosary together, for the first time since he had been four or five; why did you talk to God, and his Mother, after you looked at women? Thus, Edward was initiated as a carrier of the burdensome weight of guilt. Like me, he liked to watch, although he would not be content with just watching.

Despite parental censure, and the increasing prevalence of periodic mood swings in his mother, from warm and affectionate one minute to cold and distant the next, nature took its course for him, as it does for us all. It happened late one night as he lay alone in bed, his hand on the organ that was standing up against his stomach. I know this. I was there, as I was for all the most significant moments of his life, or the ones given significance here by me. Suddenly a wad of creamy white stuff appeared at its head, and his aspect was altered, shaken and stirred, as though he'd been struck out of the blue by a bolt of bright-flashing lightning. He pressed his face against the glass of his window, and stared up at the stars in the heavens.

After this incident he found himself becoming more and more interested in real live girls. I felt it too, if only through him, and it was exquisitely thrilling. I could not believe that something so nice could be openly allowed. Then I rapidly discovered it wasn't. Would I only ever feel it when he felt it too? As usual, I was insanely jealous of him.

But the ineluctable came to pass in due course for me also, just as I had almost stopped hoping, but still half-hoped, it would. I was sitting in my room with copy-book open and pen poised, reading an account of the Franco-Prussian War from my school history, fingering as I frequently had before the engorged flesh that stared up at me, when instead of subsiding dryly as it had always done, I felt fluid rising through it and popping out at the end, with all the force of electricity coursing through a cable. Strange, when the thing you piss through becomes the thing you cum through too. I was thoroughly satisfied afterwards, even if my clothes were rather messy and sticky, and delighted that I too had discovered this free and easy source of endless entertainment, and joined the jacking-off confraternity. Since then, I have always associated any mention of the Ems telegram with my burgeoning sexuality.

I hear that these days they actually teach courses in school on 'Relationships and Sexuality'. They didn't back then, but even if they had, would it have done me any good? For I have never been able, for the life of me, to fathom what sexuality has to do with relationships. That's what happens to you when your parents don't fuck each other, and when they, so to speak, fuck you over, or don't give a fuck about you. So it was that I took my pen and slowly wrote the word 'SEX' on my penis, in large ink blue letters, just so that I would remember what it was for. Should I have written 'LOVE'?

My life is not interesting. Why, then, am I writing about it? I should stick to placing more emphasis on writing about Edward and his life, even if it is refracted through me and mine.

Having learned of these coming attractions, we became an enthusiastic pair of wankers. We even compared notes, insofar as we could. Whereas he preferred to imagine an unadorned human being who was the object of his affections while he was playing with himself, I favoured focusing on more abstract, fetishistic fantasies. Masturbation has been called a poor pleasure. But what pleasure could be poor, especially when contrasted with pain? What pleasure could not but be poor, especially when contrasted with other possible pleasures? The fruition of the onanist is part of the function of the orgasm.

Thus it was that one evening, as I lay on my bed in my room with lad in hand, carefully contemplating a suitably sordid act of triolism (that's a threesome to those of you in the back row, who find this tome a tad heavy, both to read and to hold up with one hand) featuring, it goes without saying, myself as the sole male participant, my mother walked in and caught me *in flagrante delicto*. It had most definitely not been my intention, even subconsciously, I can assure you, to get caught. But I had never been so 'caught' in all my life. (My apologies, even in this relatively benign instance of the foul habit, for the quotation marks, which if you could see me would be accompanied by a flexing of my upraised fingers, but I have a bad dose of digitismus.) I had clean forgot to lock the door! Even if I had secured it against any invasion, she would have wanted to know why she could not enter, when it became apparent that this was indeed the case. Sometimes when she had asked me to account for my long absences, I would say that I was reading or writing, and my father would smirk knowingly behind her. Now I had been found out. Unlike Edward's mother on discovering his dirty little secret, mine uttered not a word. Her retribution took a more swift, savage and visceral turn. She went downstairs to the kitchen and got a bread knife. Back in my room, as I struggled to get my trousers up from around my thighs, without so much as a by your leave, she plunged it into the offending organ. If thy member offends thy mother, she will pluck it out. If you prick us, do we not bleed? Blood spurted everywhere and, not surprisingly, I screamed out in pain. She then left the room, turning the key in the door.

So there you have it. I am unmanned. The reason I hate women is tritely obvious after all: I've never had one; and the reason I've never had one is because of the genital mutilation I suffered at the hands of that woman. I can still get it up, as they say, but I feel pain simultaneously when I feel pleasure, and the more intense the pleasure, concomitantly the greater the increase in the pain. I became the subject of a particularly gruesome form of aversion therapy. This state of my affairs provided me with a neat introductory primer to the delicious and delinquent ambiguities of sado-masochism: to have the worst pain imaginable in the part designed for the most pleasure. The only sin is guilt, and the only crime is punishment. I could have been the Raskolnikov of jerking off, but Mother Nature ripped me off. Is it any wonder I feel cut off, so to speak, from the rest of humanity? Isolated, marginalised, outside the parameters of their perimeters. An outlaw, beyond their law.

So, now you know that, for me, the phrase 'the pains of puberty' contains and contorts, partakes of and provides, whole new layers and levels of mangled meaning. Is this occurrence also the reason why I have taken refuge in fantasy? Humankind can bear very little reality. How else could I have survived, or can I continue to, now? Face reality? Nonsense. Construct a better one, or, at least, a more comfortable one. The gap between myself and others, which had always been great, but was now so much greater, means that when I come to penning, as I surely will, one of my pet projects, more than likely entitled *A Brief History of the Male Orgasm* – an in depth dissection and discussion of the range of its intensity and quality, including diverting digressions on why they are just as multifarious, and therefore as interesting, as female ones – I will be able to do so from a purely disinterested, if not wildly warped, perspective. If I become the best chronicler of my sex's sexuality in the language, as I just might do, it will stem from the strength of non-participation. And it will undoubtedly stand me in good stead when I come to writing, as I fully intend to, a related study entitled *A Brief History of Male Obsession*.

However, notwithstanding the uniqueness of the angle of outlook imposed on me, as a result of what happened to me that evening, let me state from the outset that I still forgive no one: not her, nor him, nor the people who gave me to them. But one of the great advantages of this experience was that I never really believed anything, or trusted anyone, ever again. Or I believed in not believing things, trusted in not trusting people. If I display misogyny, it is only part of my thorough-going misanthropy. I, very occasionally, like some women better than some men. With similar infrequency, I like some men better than some women. Equally rarely, I like some women better than most men. With matching irregularity, I like some men better than most women. But mostly, I like no one. You behold before you a horrible example of the proof of the proposition that suffering does not ennoble. It is not good for the soul. A pain that serves no purpose, in that it is solely chronic in its lingering, and so does not alert you to the fact that there is something untoward going wrong with the body that needs curative attention, simply serves no purpose. It is good for nothing but the getting rid of it. Unless it is to make you disturbed, bitter and twisted. I know the argument that runs that, if you have knowledge of these emotions, you can have a better understanding of them, and so can try to transcend them. But it doesn't work. At least, not for me. I have never grieved for my grievance. I am not about to start now.

Mother came back into me the following morning, and bathed and dressed my wound. She said that it would heal, and that I should get ready to go to school. She assured me of my father's complicity in, and approval of, the drastic action she had taken against me, and told me that if I opened my mouth to anyone about what had happened, together they would make sure that things would go very badly for me.

Did I say my life was not interesting?

Shortly after this, I gave up school for good. If not for my own good, then for the good of those who were trying to teach me, and who were trying to me while they taught me, just as I was, I am sure, to them. I was troubled, I'm sure you will appreciate, by the affliction inflicted on me, and wanted to tell somebody about it, but couldn't find anyone to tell, and felt that they were all talking about me, which they probably were, because of my resulting increasingly erratic behaviour. Did someone say paranoia? If people suspect you're paranoid, they begin to play on you, which increases your paranoia, and it becomes a vicious circle. Just because you're paranoid, doesn't mean they're not out to get you. And just because you're not, doesn't mean they're not either. Although the fact that you were inclined to paranoia in the first place probably encouraged them to try to get you, to try to get to you.

I became the archetypal moody teenager, the troublesome adolescent whose schoolwork deteriorates, and who becomes estranged from their family. As if I wasn't estranged enough from my apology for a family already! The symptoms were so classic that the powers that be did not even bother to consider that there might be specific extenuating circumstances peculiar to my situation that would account for my anti-social hostility. My shenanigans went so far as to culminate in my playing truant from the institution where I underwent instruction, 'mitching' as it is otherwise known, or – my favourite phrase to describe this activity – 'going on the hop'. Inevitably I was found out, when the note I had spent hours carefully counterfeiting, in an attempt to pass it off as coming from the hands of my parents to explain my absence, was tendered to the teacher and exposed, much to my surprise, as a not very convincing forgery. Or maybe I wasn't really so surprised at all. Maybe, this time, in some secret part of myself, I had really wanted to get caught. The Toughs were sent for by the Principal and, predictably, they did nothing in the way of defending me. Edward never tried to get away with any of this kind of carry on. So, ergo, he never got caught. But if he had, and if he had, I feel certain that the Tenders would have made a better show of standing up for him.

Since my parents raised no vociferous objections to my subsequent demand that I be permitted to abandon my to date less than distinguished scholastic career, and indeed probably thought it better all round that I had as little as possible to do with the rest of humanity, particularly that part of it with any kind of authority, and that not being encumbered by studies would mean that I could be put to work doing more menial manual labour around the house, and with whatever legal requirements there were regarding the minimum age at which one could leave full-time formal education having been satisfied, I packed up my bag and baggage, and bade goodbye to my imparters of knowledge, who were, I strongly suspect, overwhelmingly relieved and glad to see the back of me.

So I became an autodidact, a self-taught student who was myself my own teacher. In lecture halls the world over, the bored lecturer's boredom increases in direct proportion to the boredom of his bored students. And vice versa. A professor is somebody who talks in other people's sleep. An undergraduate is somebody who sleeps while other people talk. But the likes of me, to whom was not given a sustained opportunity to learn about things in which I was not interested, in the vain hope that I would become interested in them, or a reasonable chance to learn about things in which I was interested, in the groundless expectation that I would remain interested in them, would have hung on their every word, and they would have loved to have got their hands on the likes of me.

I left school semi-literate. The more eagle-eyed among you may infer that this book is being written in an effort to redress the balance, and even accuse it of a species of over-compensation. But, since a little learning is a dangerous thing; drink deep, or taste not the Pierian spring, I took to my room and read omnivorously, with fine catholicity, tons of tomes. I robbed them from bookshops, borrowed them from libraries. One book led to another. I could have written a thief's journal. There's more to life than books, but not much more. Life's the thing, apparently, but I still prefer reading. Even reading my own paltry writing, when I write it, as I write it, as I am now. I'm sure reading books must have something to do with life as it is lived, but for the life of me I haven't quite worked out precisely what it is yet. Apart from a brief foray into not very gainful employment as a general operative at a local factory, detailed in a future chapter, after I had made it clear to the fearsome fosterers that I would no longer serve as their slave boy, and they consequently insisted that I should get out and support myself, I have stayed in my room ever since. Unless it is to partake of or to perform the quotidian necessities for the continuance of existence, such as alimentation, hydration, urination, defecation, and perhaps most important of all, the maintenance of a constant supply of bibliomanic and scribaceous materials, this is where I have remained to this very day.

Edward continued his academic training, spending a further two years in secondary school, and then proceeding to university, like a good little college boy. I was a middling genius only, while he shone. The advantage for me of his pursuit of further studies was that, as well as my own endeavours, I was able to learn from his, by being inside his mind at crucial junctures in enlightening lectures, so long as he stayed awake for at least part of their duration; or when he pored over notes, cramming for exams, so long as his scribbles were decipherable and made some kind of sense. But if I piggybacked knowledge from him, sneaking in on his coat-tails, I trust he must also have gleaned something from me and my more solitary pursuits. I would want some reciprocity. He is my brother, after all. I care about such things. I am still human. Human, all too human. I am only human. That is, I am an animal. What kind of animal? Why, a sedulous ape. For, if it was I who had acquired and assembled the nuts and bolts of an education for myself, it was he who showed me how to use to its maximum potential the machine I had made. You taught me language, and my profit on it is, I know how to curse. The red plague rid you for learning me your language.

It was around this time too that it was thought appropriate, propitious and even providential, to inform us of the uncertainty of our origins. It fell to our parents to fill us in. His duly obliged; mine didn't. His were preparing him for something, perhaps adulthood. Mine were preparing me for nothing, except victimhood.

His mother took him aside and told him about how men and women got to be Mammys and Daddys. She had got his father to broach this subject with him beforehand, and the preliminary sounding him out and ascertaining how much he already knew made this arduous and embarrassing task a little easier for her now. This knowledge is called The Facts of Life. Whereas most children's first question about these matters is 'Where did I come from?', mine had always been 'What's the difference between boys and girls?' Have I ever found out? Back then, I thought girls were exactly the same as boys; they just wore different kinds of clothes. I imagined they too had little cocks and balls, just like Edward's and mine, dangling droopily underneath their pretty skirts and dresses. Even now, I sometimes still think I was right.

She told him that some men and women who found that they were going to be Mammys and Daddys didn't always want to be Mammys and Daddys at that particular time in their lives, and so they gave their children to other men and women who did want to be Mammys and Daddys. He was such a child. She never did tell him that he was a twin. But then, how could she, if she didn't know?

As you know, we were both already well aware that we were foster-lings, from way back when in the orphanage, our memories stretching back to the day when he became the chosen one. But he knew that for present purposes he must pretend to be interested in this intelligence, to give the impression that this information was a revelation, to let it be believed that this news being given to him was indeed news to him. He duly obliged. Since mine, as aforesaid, hadn't, I didn't. Mind you, I'm sure I could have easily got away with not being able to simulate surprise credibly, even if it was incumbent on me to do so, since, given the bleakness and severity of the treatment I'd received in my time as pot-boy to that mad man and woman, it would have been perfectly understandable and need not have come as any shock at all that I was not their own flesh and blood. It could have been merely confirming what would have been my already existing strong suspicions. Mind you, they didn't seem to have treated their own offspring any better either.

The faint hope flickered that we might now find out who our irresponsible progenitors actually were. But we were left just as wise as we had been beforehand, in this regard at least, which was not very wise at all. We never did find out who our real – that word again – parents were. My origin has always remained as uncertain as my affections. As has his, as his. Just as my destination has always remained as certain as my enmities. As has his, as his also.

As for my termination....

And his....

6

THE PHYSICAL WOUND HEALED, but the psychic trauma remained. Persistent pudendal pain was a constant unwelcome companion, and I considered countless ways in which it could be killed. But, intractable as it was, this would have involved killing myself too, which, however bad things were, was not a viable option for me. At least, not then. That is, not yet. The pain was part of my very being now, having penetrated and integrated itself into the nerve fibres that were a mainline along which ran currents sending signals to the pleasure centres in my brain, scrambling the message, and capable of eliciting a response that was all too predictable as it increased or decreased in relative severity. Strange how the body can overpower the mind. Pain embraces the body, and although no suppurating wound can be seen, it picks and scratches as at a scab that wants to be a scar, until it festers in the mind and becomes a sepsis of the spirit. Its only goal is total control. It distorts character, alters personality. I am the plaything of pathos.

It would be disingenuous of me to pretend that I did not deeply regret what had happened to me, but, in the moments of my regret I was already regretting future moments in which I would regret my regretting; unless regret went on forever, and regretting regret went on forever too, and regretting regretting regret. Regret is not a particularly progressive emotion. You regret it, and regret regretting it, and regret regretting regretting it.

They say that what you've never had, you never miss. But I had before me always the example of Edward's experience, and I had to watch him go forward, getting on with his young life, from the vantage-point at which I stood still, having given up on that kind of life. He was expanding into the world, while I was contracting from it. Could I have modulated my behaviour otherwise, arranged it any differently? I don't know. I don't care.

What was his reaction to my grievously harmed body, my genuinely serious injury? How can I say? He averted his eyes, and put it from him. I think it made him distance himself more from me. Or maybe I just felt more distanced from him. Or both. He didn't want to have to feel my pain, but I desired desperately to feel his pleasure. My craving made me cling to him, but his carriage would not carry me. Nothing worse than a friend in need, especially one who insists on turning up to play the ghost who spoils the feast. Nothing worse than a poor relation, especially one who is an unacknowledged and unacknowledgable twin. In the midst of prosperity, we do not like to be reminded of adversity, especially when it could so easily have been ours. The delights and pitfalls of love's young dream were what beckoned to him now. All I could do was watch.

For, as mentioned previously, he began in earnest to, as my old man might well have put it, fancy the fillies. Apart from a few faltering, disappointing dalliances, over which I will not ask for the indulgence of the reader's patience, his affections came to rest fairly early on on as fair a specimen of winsome Irish girlhood as one could wish to see. Every epic tale has its dream woman, for whom the errant knight goes to the ends of the earth and back again, engaging in dangerous deeds of derring-do, while she waits for him in her ivory tower. It is time we introduced a new character into this narrative. It is time the heroine of this history was unveiled in all her glory. Let's give her a name. Let's call her Mary. Let's talk about Mary. Mary's not a bad old name. Although it has been popular to the point of saturation in this isle over the years, I'll grant you, even if it seems to have fallen into eclipse more recently, the bearer of this identifier was not of the average run of commonalty. She's Everywoman, but she's a special woman too. Because every woman is special, to some man, or some woman. Or so they tell us, so we're told. I will endeavour with my utmost skill to describe this paragon, though I am sensible that my highest abilities are very inadequate to the task. For never did your eyes behold, or your concupiscence covet anything in this world, more concupiscible than this Mary. Will I make this model of excellence and virtue blonde, brunette or red-haired? Blue, brown or green-eyed? Pale, sallow or dark-skinned? Small, medium or tall? And what of the thousand and one other attributes that account for attraction? It is difficult, if not impossible, to decide.

To conceive her right, sit down, sir, turn on your personal computer, position your fingers over the keys, and paint her to your own mind, as like your mistress as you can, as unlike your wife as your conscience will let you, it is all one to me, please your own fancy in it. And, ladies, make her look as near as you'd like to look yourself, if you could bear to be that beautiful.

INSERT HERE GENERAL ALL-PURPOSE DETAILED
DESCRIPTION OF MARY, AND ATTUNE TO INDIVIDUAL TASTE

So you see, and suffice it to say, her exaltedness lay in her exquisiteness, and there was no creature more exquisite than she was exalted. Let not this idealised idol be lost amid practical particularities. Who will now say that I cannot do believable female characters? Who will now aver that I can do believable male ones? Does the man define the woman he is trying to imagine into being? Or does the imagined woman define the limitations of the imagining man?

Was this how Edward felt about her, or I, or everybody? It was the consensus, felt with acute intensity by Edward, and merely recounted here by me. Look at me, trying to be nice about a woman. But the easiest way to knock someone down is first to build them up. If you begin by placing someone on a pedestal, there's no telling how far they might fall. Look out, Mary Constance Contrary.

Edward first put his eye on her at the local Saturday night discotheque in his sixteenth summer. He was permitted to attended these hops, since it was thought beneficial from the point of view of well-rounded character development that he mix socially with young people his own age. I, on the other hand, abjured them, oblivious as to whether my parents approved of them or not.

She was sitting with a group of friends, chatting away amicably, while he stood with some of his buddies, acting the lad nonchalantly. He worshipped her from afar, calculating how he could get near. He struggled to summon up sufficient courage to ask her up to dance, but, fortified with four pints of lager, the taste for which he was fast acquiring, and the smell of which on his breath he had disguised from the doormen at the entrance by eating oranges and chewing gum before trying to gain admission, he felt confident enough to risk a rebuff. To his relief, she accepted his suit. It was an up tempo number, since he did not feel he could handle her during a slow set just yet. Ah, the warmth of a girl's breath on your neck, and the weight of her head on your shoulder, and the tightness of your arms fast entwined around one another, as you slow-danced and smooched together. Such sensations were not vouchsafed to Edward until the following week. Instead, he talked to her for the rest of the evening, in spite of the jeering of his peers, and then offered to walk her home. Captivated as she was, she did not fob him off with a ready-made excuse, but consented to be accompanied.

As they strolled along together through the smell of honeysuckle in the air, she linked her arm in his. When they reached her garden gate, they stopped to say goodnight, and he bent and brushed his cheek against her cheek and then pressed his lips to hers. She opened her mouth, so he thought he'd better open his, and their tongues met and swirled around each other, darting here and there. They had a jolly good wear, as they used to say. They felt each other up and down, as they still say. Where did he get his know-how from? From his not wanting her to know how little he knew? Or from an instinct known to everyone? Except me. Search me. But witnessing your twin's first kiss is like experiencing your own first kiss, if only at one remove, if only at second hand. I have never kissed anyone, but I know what it must be like, because I know a man who has. He did my kissing for me. Lucky him. Luckier me. It started with a kiss. I never thought that it would come to this. Strange, how things start, and how they might finish.

How do I begin relating about a relationship that has lasted so long and endured so much, on and off, over the years? I suppose I just have begun, even if I don't know how. (I am referring here, of course, to the association between Edward and Mary, not to that between Edward and myself.) In its initial stages it achieved the improbable feat of being both whirlwind and dilatory, as they struggled to balance the conflicting considerations of being, on the one hand, mad for each other with, on the other, keeping a weather eye firmly fixed, however hazy the focus, on farther down the line. For neither of them wanted it to burn out after the original blaze up, to peter out after the first dam burst, as such formative infatuations, if such it was, have a habit of doing. How were they so wise, way beyond their years? I do not know, except to say that it was the wisdom of the ages, rather than the counsel of the age. Her female principle curbed his male one, just as his male principle coaxed her female one. In such sagacious but unconscious colloquy, something was worked out.

As almost always, a well-preserved image best serves to illustrate and elucidate Edward's part in this mercurial mixture of exuberance and reticence. One afternoon, when he was about four or five, he was found by his mother at the end of their back garden, explaining eternity and infinity to the elderly, portly, next-door neighbour, Mr Quincey. Even in the past, he could conceive of the future, and knew that you travelled through the uncharted passages of time to get from one to the other. Even in that place, he could conceive of others, and knew that you travelled through the farthest reaches of space to get to them.

"They go on forever," he told the intrigued septuagenarian.

Edward and Mary started going out together, and lasted nine months, until parental pressure over the need to study for impending final examinations forced them to cool off each other for a while. They were both of solid – or is that stolid? – middle-class stock, after all. But, during that pregnant period of no periods (and no pregnancies), they cemented themselves together so soundly that they were bound to take up where they had left off a little later.

A chief constituent of this adhesive was popular music. They would lend records and tapes to each other, and spend hours listening together. Around this time the bloated behemoths of Hippiedom were under threat from the graceless gazelles of Punk. But, since both subcultures had much more in common than they would have readily cared to admit, with each other rather than with the rest of what passes for society, there was some inevitable crossover in audience appreciation between them. Do you want me to list the contributors to the soundtrack that will press all the right buttons as an accompaniment to the first giddy rush of this great love? All right, I will: The Beatles, The Rolling Stones, The Who, The Kinks, The Yardbirds; Bob Dylan, The Byrds, The Stooges, The MC5, The Velvet Underground; The Sex Pistols, The Clash, The Buzzcocks, The Undertones, Elvis Costello; Patti Smith, Television, Talking Heads, The Ramones, Blondie. What, no Irish? Well, apart from The Boomtown Rats and The Radiators from Space, not much at this stage. The dubious pleasures of paying 50p to stand wrapped around each other in a draughty shed in a flea market called The Dandelion, to witness the fledgling U2 go through their paces, still awaited them.

Go and listen to some of the aforementioned artists now, to help you set the scene and try to get the flavour of what follows here. See you later.

Back again. Of course, having full sexual intercourse, as they used to call it, or fucking each other's brains out, as they still call it, came up. Given their backgrounds, and the mores of the place and time, it was not at all a foregone conclusion that they would go all the way. For he was, let us not forget, still a virgin, and so too, as far as he knew, was she. But Edward was blessed in that he was able to combine romantic idealisation with hot, adolescent lust. Indeed, for him they were almost indistinguishable. Besides, if you are possessed of a naggingly embarrassing virginity, what else is there to do but set about getting rid of it?

So, one evening in her house, when her parents were out, the not-so-inevitable inevitably happened. There had been many wandering fingers, and much fooling around, on countless occasions beforehand, so it seemed to be only the way of nature to now let nature have her way. She had stopped wearing a bra long before when she was going to meet him, to afford him ready access and make it easier for him to get at her. He had been charmed, and I perplexed, by some of the more curious questions she had posed in these intimate moments, like, "Why do men have nipples, if they don't have to feed babies milk?" or, "Why can't men come, without having to make such a mess?"

Despite the fact that they were, as it were, in love, when it finally came to pass, it proved fairly perfunctory.

"Come on, let's have it off," she said, in the midst of a clinging clinch.

There now, I'm glad that's out of me, he thought, when it was over.

Their technique improved in time. You can't expect everything to go exactly right from the word go. But you never forget the first time. Or do you? I don't know, never having had one. But I have never forgotten his.

I call to the eye of the mind this scene: them lying there spent, fast entwined in front of the fire, basking enjoyably in the warm afterglow, but conscious that they'd have to get dressed and make themselves presentable shortly, before her parents came home. I remember him feeling both elated and yet, unaccountably, vaguely disappointed. If, after love, all animals are sad, then, after first love, all animals are sadder than they've ever been before. But saddest of all are those who have never known the sadness after first love, or after any other love, or all the joys and sorrows love goes on to give rise to, and who now never will. Like me. For I am, unlike him, still a virgin, to the present day. Oh, I suppose that, purely physically, I could still be capable of trying it with another, but if the pleasure is more when shared than when solitary, so too, for me, would be the pain.

Edward didn't let his lover know of the ambivalence of his feelings. He always did know what side his bread was buttered on. I didn't let anyone know of the mixed-upness of mine. I never had any bread to be buttered. Feeling him feeling extinguished after being in another's body, I knew then that the only way that I, given my disability, would feel a similar feeling was through losing myself in words. The pleasure others find in sex, I would find only in text. I would forget the pain of sex in the pleasure of the text. The transformation of consciousness, the opening of yourself to another person, the being consumed and subsumed by them, the losing yourself in them, in other words, that which is called love, I would find only in language. I would forget the impossibility of love in the possibilities of language.

Does this definition of love describe the way he felt? In other words, was the love he felt really true and truly real? Was it totally transcending? Perhaps not quite yet. That would come later.

The I of the mind. I am sure someone else has made that joke somewhere else before. I wish there was no need for the word 'I'. I wish I could extinguish I. I will, with these words. There's an aporia for you. And him. And I. To say nothing of an *aperçu*.

The eye of the body. I spy with my little eye. I'm a spy, in the house of love. Peering in on his life, as he loves others. Pressing my fingers against his life, as his loves pass by, as though his life were a transparent screen I stand behind and can look through longingly, but cannot enter, penetrate, go through, get beyond. The walls of his reality are secured safely against me.

The I of the body. Did I say I was sad? But where did this idea that sex with others is superior to sex with yourself come from and gain credence? Maybe it is only the credulous who think that this is the case. Just because most people hold it to be true, does that make it so? If everybody else threw themselves in the Liffey, would you, as his mother used to say? This is the kind of thing mothers say. Except mine, who was not like other mothers. What was yours like, and what did she say? My only sadness is that I am not in a position to compare and contrast masturbation with copulation. For if the latter is really no better than the former then, presumably, it would be no worse for me. So I could test the truth of this universally held truth. But at what risk? What if it really is true? I am not prepared to take that chance. As it is, I'll never know for sure. So let's hear it for auto-eroticism. Don't knock onanism. Maybe sex is better with one, if only for me. Maybe I'm not so sad after all, alone with my own body.

Are these reflections culturally, or neurally, determined? Or should that be neuro-culturally?

There is, it must also be remembered, the procreative function of sexuality to be considered, so often forgotten during those heady teenage years, usually forgotten by me regardless of my years. So it was that, as a result of their first few physical encounters, Mary conceived of herself as gestating. She didn't want to be with child, no more than he didn't want her to be in such a condition, but she convinced herself she was, and her anxiety fuelled her conviction, and spilled over into him.

She was late with her monthlies; there was no trace of blood to be found. First one week went by, then two, then three. The longer she went overdue, the more she worried, and the more she worried, the longer she went overdue. With the benefit of hindsight, as they say, my brother's state of acute agitation at this juncture seems almost delightfully droll, to me at any rate, but I'm sure also to him. Everywhere he went, he saw babies, babies, babies: in buggies, in carry-cots, in carriages, in car-seats, in prams, in strollers, being wheeled hither and thither all over the place, or slung over shoulders with straps fore and aft. Who would have thought there were so many of the little fuckers in the world? It got so bad that he was sure he must be hallucinating them. But everyone old was young once. Every adult used to be a child. Every grown-up had once upon a time been a baby. The child is father to the man, or mother to the woman. But he didn't want to be the father to any child, boy or girl. At least, not then. And Mary didn't want to be a mother. That is, not yet.

Then one day out of a clear blue sky, a call came to say that the flecks of red had appeared. It had happened on a train, and she was calling from a public coin box at the station. Never before had she felt so blessed to be cursed. He too was relieved at the resumption of her menstrual cycle. But the scare of this phantom pregnancy had taught them their lesson. This pause had given them pause, and henceforth, both before they stopped seeing each other for a short while, and after they started seeing each other again, they made sure to avail themselves of more than merely adequate prophylactic contraception. They were ahead of their time.

The exams came and went, and Edward and Mary were reunited for the sunny summer of waiting for the verdicts to be handed down. When the results finally did come out, they both had done brilliantly well. This vindicated the actions of their parents in keeping them apart – to their parents, at any rate.

What would they do, now they'd left school? It was expected of both that they would proceed to further study. Edward was showing signs of becoming a reasonably useful guitarist, and his father, being pragmatic, thought he should follow his instincts and study music. But his mother, being romantic, knew that love costs, and encouraged him to do business. Mary bridled at the thought of continuing her formal education, but was finally brought to heel. However, she would study what she wanted. As would he. They were both going to university, but they were both going to register for Arts. Arts: where all the trouble begins, for it has no clear end.

I made myself comfortable in my room, and settled in for the long haul. I was eagerly looking forward to what I might learn through him. I had already started collecting words, and collating them. They were like numbers, in that you could play with them, even if you didn't fully understand them. I found these games a great comfort in times of distress. They alleviated my aches and pains, eased my worries and woes. Strange how the mind can overpower the body.

7

I T WAS NOT CUSTOMARY then for students from cities, embarking on higher education, to move outside their given metropolis to study. Nor was it usual for them to move away from the family home. These circumstances proved problematic for Edward and Mary, but for the meantime they had to be borne. He always did think it amusing when people asked him if he lived at home. Even then, he knew the answer: wherever you live is your home. Or as much of a home as you ever have.

> *Wherever I lay my hat, that's my home*
> *Wherever I lay my wife, that's my home*
> *Wherever I lay my hat, that's my head*
> *Wherever I hang my head, that's my home*

He is not *The Man Who Mistook His Wife for a Hat,* but perhaps I am *The Man Who Mistook His Head for a Home.*

But before they took up their respective places at the same seat of learning, they treated themselves to a two-week holiday in London, using money saved while doing summer jobs. Their parents acquiesced in their travelling together, since it was felt that they were deserving of some reward after their studious exertions. Mr and Mrs Tender even thought it beneficial for Edward's personal development, and the development of his personality, that he should pair bond with a nice girl like Mary from a good family like the Contrarys, since it would help to inculcate in him healthy attitudes towards boy/girl relationships and the precious gift of human sexuality, and so they encouraged the association, and approved of the trip. How liberal they were!

They were also, however, given to understand that the sleeping arrangements during the vacation would be communal, which, as it happened, was not the case. Had they known that the young couple intended sharing a double room, they would not have been so compliant about giving their consent. How conservative they were!

It was, surprisingly, Edward's first time outside Ireland, the land of his birth. Mary, on the other hand, had already visited London, with her family. They went by boat train, since they were in no hurry, and it meant that they could conserve cash. His previous vacations had been family affairs too, to provincial seaside towns with names like Carrigart, Curracloe, or Courtown. Now he was going forth to find out for the first time what it felt like to be a foreigner in a foreign country, a stranger in a strange land, if only for a fortnight. I observed his reactions by being inside him, though remaining in my homeland, where I lived, and still live, to this day.

As they sailed out through the mouth of Dun Laoghaire harbour, the place where the two enfolding arms of the East Pier and the West Pier almost meet, his excitement knew no bounds. He felt he was flying the confining nets, as someone else once almost put it, cast over him by the Three Fs – I mean here not fair rent, free sale and fixity of tenure, although later in his life these would assume much greater importance, but faith, family and fatherland – even if only temporarily, with his best girl in tow beside him. He thought he was beginning to fulfil his destiny. So did I (that is, I thought it about him).

Now I think: what a prat he was. But then again, so was I.

The crossing was calm, and the train sped them through neatly ordered, pleasantly patterned fields, which they watched racing by rapidly outside the windows. After arriving at Euston Station, they took the tube to Lancaster Gate, where they had booked to stay in a hostel.

The whole idea of yo-yoing underground through a big city was a novelty for him. He imagined all the different stations of the network as the extreme peripheries of a giant central nervous system, and the train tracks as the internal wiring between them, and himself as an electrochemical signal sent travelling along it, with millions of others, by the elaborate dance of sodium and potassium ions changing the charge from positive to negative. (He had worked on his chemistry and physics in school.) Or as the holes for entry and exit to an extensive warren, with each lagomorphic commuter knowing only the key to the secrets of their own journeys through the tunnels of the abstrusely intricate maze. (He had worked on his biology and mathematics in school.) He wondered if such images filled Mary's head too, but guessed they didn't. After all, she had been there before, and knew what to expect.

Such was the difference in size and scale, in those dark, distant days back then, between the cultural backwater that was Dublin and the continual buzz that London provided, that simply walking up and down those streets, savouring the spectacle of so many different people of such diverse races, and feeling dwarfed by all the tall, menacing buildings, sent an enormous rush of adrenaline shooting through Edward's bloodstream and circulating all over his body. They went to loads of galleries and shops by day, and concerts and films by night, and had a jolly fine old time all told, thanks very much. It never occurred to them that if they were living there all the time, they might sooner or later get tired of all the ceaseless, incessant activity, and become preoccupied with the humdrum exigencies of day-to-day existence. But how could it? Their situation was such that they hadn't become aware of these quotidian considerations, even in the place where they were permanently resident. Mine was, and I had. Or was about to.

I may as well remark, in passing, that this time away afforded them their first real opportunity, of which they took full advantage, to indulge in more than merely furtive, rushed love-making. They revelled in the chance to explore each other's bodies in the minutest, most gloriously lingering detail, and marvelled at the new-found freedom they discovered in doing so. He had by now, such was his regard for her, stumbled on and starting using a handy technique to avoid climaxing too quickly and having the whole show over before it had barely begun. He would focus his mind, and so I had to follow him in focusing too, on something entirely non-sensual for a while, thus staving off a little longer the inevitability of the desired resolution. In his case, it was usually the solving of a particularly convoluted *Irish Times* chess problem, with several possible permutations of equally plausible, at the first glance he had given it, competing claims, which sufficed to cause him indefinite delay. Check this out sometime yourself, you fool, since it can prevent, or at least postpone, things from going stale with your mate.

He would slowly circle one of her nipples with a finger, while letting the fingers of his other hand slip just as slowly down her spine to begin stroking her behind, and then slither himself down to lick with his wet tongue the pert little bud in the damp furry den between her legs, while those hands glided over her parted thighs, until she screamed with pleasure, and then screamed for more of the same.

She would let her fingertips float up and down all over him, brushing the great rooted blossomer that grew out of his bush, and then take it between her succulent lips and swirl it around in her swivelling mouth, until he howled in ecstasy, and then howled for the same again.

It is hardly necessary for me to state that I found all this carry on most peculiar, preposterous, and even perverse.

As a postscript to my account of the joys of the sojourn, I might just add that it was during this excursion that Edward first conceived of the inclination to write stories. Songs had long sprung from the mind and heart of this young man, but stories were like longer songs. He took to carrying a small black notebook and a ballpoint pen on his person at all times, as all true wordsmiths of whatever hue do, for jotting down the words, phrases, sentences and ideas, as they snapped through his synapses or, if you prefer, fluttered through his fancy. Mary made sure he did this as unobtrusively as possible, for fear he'd be pegged as pretentious. Maybe one day he would write a really long story. That would be novel.

Was it the increase in both frequency and quality of his sexual relations that gave rise to this burgeoning interest in practising imaginative writing? Or was it the liberating breath of fresh air that being outside Ireland provided him with? Or a bit of both? I cannot say. All I know is that from then until now he has usually associated being at his most productive creatively with having lots of good sex, as well as with being away from this country. He has also made a connection between the last two circumstances, regardless of their relevance or not to the former one. Interestingly enough, this *modus operandi* is once again in direct opposition to my own way of doing things, to what propelled me towards penmanship. I, as you know, have never had sex, except with myself, nor have I ever been in exile, except internally. The more Edward loves, the more he writes, or so he believes. The less I love, the more I write – that's what I believe. The more he travels, the more he writes – that's his creed. The less I travel, the more I write – I give this some credit. For him, life is elsewhere, anywhere but here. For me, life is here, and nowhere else. We have each found our own motivations, in those very conditions which act as disincentives to the other one. It was always so.

So as they sailed back across the water, even before landing, he knew what it was he wanted to do. Even as they were returning from this, his first time abroad, he knew it would not be the last time he would leave.

Back in Dublin, they began college. As I recall, he seemed to settle in well, the funereal atmosphere and dull impersonality of the great grey campus, with its ever-present equally grey overhanging clouds, giving him the anonymity he required to adjust to his new surroundings, and make friends at his own pace, or alternatively, to keep his distance and keep himself to himself, as he felt like or saw fit. He had Mary, of course, as a bulwark against any unpleasantness that might arise, owing to the competitiveness or unfriendliness of his fellows, and she supported him solidly while he found his feet. He hoped he was doing the same for her.

I, on the other hand, while present solely in mind and not at all in body and soul, and judging his assessment of his experience against my own view of it, couldn't make head or tail of the place, or of any dog or devil in it, and was very disappointed with what I saw of what went on there. Following a course of instruction in it seemed to me to be merely serving time at a glorified apprenticeship in a degree factory where, as in all such places of labour, it is bad form to be seen by the other operatives as being too keen in your job. What is the difference between 'I haven't opened a book, haven't done a tap', and 'I'm skiving off; watch out for the gaffer'? I do not use this industrial metaphor lightly, believe me. I know whereof I speak.

For it was about this time that I, as alluded to earlier, started a stint punching the clock in a neighbourhood sweatshop, and became another brick in the wall in these modern times, a cog in a wheel within a wheel turning like a ghost in a machine, running to stand still in strict time and perpetual motion, beside a cruel conveyor belt that spewed forth portable television sets, into the innards of which I was charged with the task of turning a couple of screws, before they passed by rapidly to the next worker bee up from me. It was the monotony that was new to me, and the monotony that got to me. I didn't last long. The factory would have taken my hearing, in exchange for a paltry living, if I hadn't had the gumption to get out pretty quickly.

This interlude came about when I downed tools at home, refusing to take any more orders from my ghastly custodians, and so they reacted by stipulating that I should take up tools elsewhere, very smartly. Since they would not help me to look for something to which I was more suited (and to what, if anything at all, was I more suited?), I took the first thing that came along, partly just to spite them (and was it possible, in any way, to spite them?). But, to use some locutions popular in this period, the factory was 'the pits'; it 'did my head in'.

Some people die as though they are living, which of course they are, but the factory was full of people who lived as though they were dying, which of course they also were. These boys had bad teeth, and strange skin conditions with protruding pimples, and at tea-break wanked away their frustration in the toilet cubicles. I do not know about the girls. These men had missing teeth, and dire dermatological diseases with pushed out pustules, and at tea-break drooled leeringly over tabloid stunners in the staff canteen. I do not know about the women. The brighter or more beautiful younger ones knew they were just being used as cannon fodder, and so gave free rein to their rebellious spirits, as much as they could. The more discontented or disillusioned older ones knew that nothing fundamental was ever going to change for them, and so kept their noses clean until retirement, as well as they could. Granted, I didn't fit in anywhere, but I certainly didn't fit in there.

So I issued an ultimatum to my finnish foster folks, made them an offer they couldn't refuse: either they let me quit my job, keep to my room, and leave me alone, in exchange for half my dole money, or else I would reveal my mother's malicious misdeed. This simple threat had the desired effect, and they were left with no option but to agree, and my contribution from my stipend from the Department of Social Warfare was enough to keep them off my back, for the time being, if only financially. All they really cared about was money.

Meanwhile, just up the road but a whole world away, Edward's studies were getting into full swing, and I was now ideally placed to make the most of his good fortune, if that is what it can be called. He had chosen courses in modern languages and philosophy, while his inamorata had opted for music and modern languages. How many tongues would they be able to speak to each other in now?

While I realise that I have just pointed up an essential similarity between the university and the factory, there were still many superficial differences as well, to which it is well worth my drawing your attention.

What greater contrast could there be, I remember remarking to myself when I floated inside him, while I stood there with screwdriver in hand among my comrades the proletariat, as we suffered fluently together under the heavy yoke of the capitalist oppressor, than that between the situation I then found myself surrounded with, and that in which I found my brother finding himself surrounded with, among his peers? From my perspective, how could I not but envy him yet again, and his ostensibly privileged life as a college student?

While we were required to stick to a rigid punctuality, they could cut classes whenever they liked. I remember how, one otherwise uneventful afternoon, a group of them just upped and decided on the spur of the moment to drive up to the top of the Three Rock Mountain, and dropping everything else, set off just like that. Such unappreciated, taken-for-granted freedom; such casual, indifferent selfishness. I wanted to be selfishly free, like them. So I rendered myself unemployed and unemployable, like them. So where is all the freedom I craved? Am I too selfish even to see it? Or have I not attained freedom at all? Am I not yet selfish enough? And what is the connection, if any, between these two terms? Has it got something to do with self-sacrifice and responsibility?

It was with just such conundrums as these that they were obliged sometimes to concern themselves, if only because of the pragmatic expediency of passing exams. The unexamined life is, after all, not worth living. Or so said one of life's great examiners, when he still had a stake in promulgating such a view of life, shortly before he took his own. As you can see, I have picked up a good deal of the jargon, and the various techniques, used for taking up ideas, throwing them around, and turning them this way and that. This happened while I was inside Edward's mind, while he was attending lectures and tutorials. So what if occasionally he had to sit in chilly halls and stuffy classrooms, his bullshit detector not as finely tuned as mine, the steel trap not as quick to come crashing down, his boredom threshold lower and interest level higher? So what if he noticed, albeit with less scorn than me, that his professors raised problems only in order to solve them, and brought their talks to a forced conclusion with maddening finality? So what if he had to listen to their third-rate rhetorical devices, flourishes designed expressly for impressing the freshmen, like him, such as, 'A table is a table only in so far as it is a table'? So what if the university flagstones were only a slightly more sophisticated version of the hell that was the factory floor? Being there gave him the chance to 'do his own thing', to do a lot of his own reading and writing, while doing a little of theirs. His presence there gave me the chance to find out what happened in these places, to see what, if anything, I was missing out on, or would have been missing out on, if not for him. His stint as a student gave him time to have a good time, and filled my time with something to do. We could both get what we wanted out of it, take what we needed.

Unlike the factory, the university probably didn't do anyone any harm, and it possibly just may have done someone some good. Or, at least, it probably didn't do anyone as much harm, and it possibly just may have done someone more good. Or, maybe, it did everyone more harm, and everyone less good. Ask Edward, not me. I was only in the university, through him, intermittently, and so can't really compare. Or ask me, not Edward. He was only in the factory, through me, occasionally, and so can't really contrast. Together, we might have made one fully integrated person, with a wide enough range of experience, and a balanced enough view of it, to be worth consulting on these matters. Apart, we might have made two fully integrated people, with narrow enough sets of experience, and balanced enough views of them, to be worth paying attention to regarding these concerns. But here we are, stuck with and without each other, in the half-light of this no man's land, neither together nor apart, both together and apart. He lives my life, and I lead his. But the fact remains that, for whatever reasons, and for all its faults, both of us thought that the university did less harm and more good than the factory, and so preferred it. But maybe someone else would have thought the exact opposite. Ask Edward, not me. Ask me, not Edward. Ask both of us. Ask neither. Ask no one.

Once again, my memory of one of his childhood memories can tell us so much. He would often ask his father, in all seriousness, his young brow furrowing thoughtfully, "Am I good?"

To which his father would reply, teasingly, a smile rising to his lips, "When you're asleep."

This would frustrate Edward, but he always came back for more.

I never asked my father such a question. He would not have known how to answer, or would have answered only with an uninterested grunt.

But do we really need to ask such questions at all?

Since it was at this time that I became more or less ensconced in my room in perpetuity, I feel justified in taking the liberty of describing it here.

In shape it is almost a perfect cube, in size it is nearly tiny, in colour it is off-white. There is a single bed in the corner farthest from the door, with a bedside locker beside it. Upon the bedside locker rest a book and a reading lamp. There is an old wardrobe with some clothes in it in the corner opposite the door (and also, of necessity, opposite the corner which holds the bed). In the remaining corner, that is, the one farthest from the one in which the wardrobe stands (and also, of necessity, opposite the one which holds the bed, and also, of necessity, the one which has the door) there is a table and a chair. Upon the table rest some papers and another reading lamp. There is a window in the wall which runs between the corner that holds the bed and that which holds the table. The longer sides of the table face the wall, and the chair faces the longer sides of the table, away from the window. We don't want the outside world intruding, when I'm sitting inside at the table working, searching for the word. For, as you may already have surmised, it is in this setting that what you are reading was first conceived of, and is now being written. This is really the only reason for giving you this description of my room, its only relevance to the rest of this story.

So now you know the awful truth, which of course you knew all along: I am a writer too, just like my brother. Well, not just like my brother, but a writer nonetheless. For, although I was reading more at this time than I had done before, because of the influence of experiencing Edward's recent experiences, there was still something vital lacking. During the few times I would venture out, and ride around on the buses, I became fascinated by the people on them who were reading books. They seemed to me to form a secret society, of which I was now also a member. Books had not been prevalent where I had grown up, so now I saw them as badges of high and noble honour to be striven for, signs of intellectual and spiritual superiority to be attained.

But even so, a sense of dissatisfaction lingered. How great it was to read books. But how much greater still it must be to write them. The more Edward read, the more it made him want to write, but the more he read, the less capable he felt of writing. So he read more, and wrote less. The more I read, the more it made me want to write too, but the more I read, the more I felt I couldn't do much worse than some of what I was reading. So I read less, and wrote more.

Edward and his chums were learning how to dissect, to take apart. But me, I found I could give them only the raw material to go to work on. Will they remember to stitch it up, to put it together again? Can they? Do they know how? Or do they murder to dissect, tear open to take apart?

This is my dead body, take it, so that you may live. These are my scattered remains, old bones, for you to pick over.

8

EDWARD AND MARY finished their first year of instruction and sat their exams, and as soon as this painful duty was discharged they went abroad together again, intending this time to stay away for the whole summer, on a working holiday. Any money they earned, or rather, saved, would be contributed towards their fees for the second year. This paying, or part-paying, for their own education was thought of by their parents as character-building, fostering as it did a respectful and responsible attitude towards money, although it wasn't, strictly speaking, necessary from the financial point of view of their families.

They had been looking forward to getting away again as soon as possible, because of the freedom they knew, from the time before, it would afford them. As mentioned, they still sheltered under their parental roofs, which severely curtailed any spontaneity in their modes of sexual expression. Like many young people back then, and even more so now, Edward could be said to have been born in a room with the television on. He too had experienced that almost obligatory initiatory rite of passage, which takes place in countless sitting-rooms across the globe every night, of having to sit through a televised sex scene with his parents, those who'd had to have sex to have him, and watch them behave as though they had at last been caught out in the carnal deed of begetting him. He was adopted, so this wasn't exactly the case here, but he aspired to the archetype enough to know what was going on, what was expected of those who'd brought him up, and what was expected of him.

I can remember being present with him, in him, through him, one such time. The curvaceous young vamp portrayed by the fast-rising starlet with the flirtatious, supercilious, even vertiginous eyebrows, was auditioning for a job in a luxurious bordello, and proved her potential worth as a high-class hooker to the Madame who was her prospective employer by tying a knot in a cherry stem with her talented tongue.

The significance of this small screen revelation was lost on the Tender *mère* and *père*.

"What does it mean?" shrieked his mother, uncomprehendingly.

He wasn't about to enlighten her, for the obvious reason of the embarrassment that would ensue. Neither did his father cast any light on the subject, if only because he didn't know the answer.

On another occasion, the hero and heroine of the piece being transmitted had just begun to remove each other's clothes, when Mr Tender fell to consulting the clock on the mantelpiece and checking his wristwatch against it, as a means of diverting his attention, pretending he was wholly innocent of what was going on, or at least entirely indifferent to it. Mrs Tender got even more stuck into her knitting. But if what was coming down the tube was of such little relevance to them, then why was the air so fraught with their uptightness about it? Edward felt the familiar onset of blushing face and dry throat, and his eyes started smarting from staring straight ahead and not blinking, in an effort to ignore his parents and to give the impression that, for him, nothing out of the ordinary was taking place in front of them. Before they went to bed that night, he heard his father mumble something to his mother about there being far too many foreign films on the goggle box these days.

Edward had begun to notice that his father's chief objections to fictions he did not like was that they were too 'far-fetched' or 'fictitious'. This struck Edward as strange, since he thought the whole idea was that that was what fictions should be. As do I. Accordingly, he started treating life with his parents as a surreal soap opera. I had always treated life with mine as a scary horror story.

So it would be a huge relief for this young man, and his young lady, to be relieved of such retrograde tension. A relief, incidentally, which I personally never needed, since I am one of the few whose parents did not permit the watching of television. Maybe that is why I have installed one in my room now, a small portable black and white job, scavenged from a nearby charity shop, that rests on the creaky bookshelf I've constructed from bricks and planks of wood, across from my bed. It is imperative that I retain some vestige of contact with the modern world. Besides, it is also incumbent on me to make up for lost time.

Edward and Mary headed for Holland, where they'd arranged jobs in food-processing factories. Yes, Edward in a factory, more of which anon! They hoped to go to France later on, to castrate maize or pick grapes. Travelling via London, they stopped off for a couple of days, briefly revisiting some of their old haunts. Old, that is, from the last time they were there together, which was the first time they had been there together, which doesn't make them very old at all, I suppose. But the haunts were old in themselves, regardless of who was doing the haunting.

The city was almost as exciting as ever, although a little less so than the previous time. Maybe it is the way of places, the way of the world, the way of places in the world, to be taken for granted upon increased acquaintance. Or maybe it is the way of ourselves, or some of ourselves, to take places in the world for granted the more we get to know them. Or maybe both perceiving perceiver and perceived perception play a part in this view. Whatever way you look at it, they pressed on.

Arriving in Amsterdam, tellingly enough, gave Edward the same rush that being in London had the year before, despite the fact that trams were running above ground, instead of trains below the earth. We agreed, insofar as we could ever agree, that this was a town with a split personality. Was that why we both felt so at home there? All great cities have many faces, but few divided quite so dichotomously as this one did.

One of these sides was composed of canals, tulips and windmills; the other of drink, drugs and whores; 'dikes' was the only term common to both. The tourist image trappings didn't interest him much, except for how they contrasted with what he saw was on offer as he strolled around the red light district with Mary. Had she not been accompanying him, he might have taken the opportunity to indulge himself hedonistically in the sex shops, cinemas and brothels that abounded, but she provided some restraint. Not that she showed outright disapproval, as such. She just didn't give thorough approval, and read any interest he evinced in seeking sexual gratification with anyone else, by any means that excluded her, as a gross insult to her femininity. Strange creatures, these women, I remember remarking to myself at the time. I would have quite liked to see the inside of one of those places, purely from the perspective of disinterested curiosity, you understand. But for the moment, at any rate, this was not to be. He wasn't going to do it for me, and I was hardly going to up and take off there myself, now was I?

Lest it appear that it was solely the possibilities for polymorphous perversity which preoccupied him during their stay, let me add that they took in the galleries too, as they always did. He was particularly taken with what he saw in the Van Gogh museum. I can see him still, staring at 'The Sunflowers' for a full twenty minutes, amazed at how no poster or other reproduction he had ever seen had come near to capturing the three- dimensional way the embedded paint gathered and swirled before him on the canvas in waxy impasto. He would have remained there all day had she not dragged him away. Even I was impressed, I have to say.

They went down to the small country town where their labours were to begin. I will spare you the stories of the youthful high jinks which ensued, of getting falling down drunk, of getting as high as a kite, of getting thrown into canals. Instead, I will describe Edward's reactions to factory life.

It all slid off him, as they say, like shit off a shovel. The noisy jangling of jars as they made their mechanised way through the steel loops, the condensation created by the steam that poured out of the ovens used to cook the fruit and vegetables, the tedium of picking out the burnt carrots, green beans, gherkins and cherries from the conveyer, the damp atmosphere produced by the hoses used to swish away this damaged produce. It all washed off him, as they say, like mud off a Wellington boot. But then again, he knew it wasn't his life. It was just a way to make some money and have a good time during an adolescent summer, which would be fondly remembered in years to come as something wild he had done during his youth, a fund of anecdotes to be recounted by the accomplished raconteur he would surely become. Moreover, he was working with others for whom it wasn't their life either. Besides, Mary was there. He could not have known, or understood, what I had felt in my factory.

Then disaster struck. Or rather, a mild inconvenience. He heard the news from home that he had failed his exams, and would have to return to repeat them if he wanted to progress. This happens to geniuses all the time, apparently, because they get side-tracked into pursuing their own interests, and diverted away from the main drag that must be followed by the common herd of lesser mortals. This intelligence threw a spanner in the works as regards their going to France. He expected Mary to jettison the French leg of their journey too, and go back to

Dublin with him, even though, much to his secret annoyance, she had passed with flying colours, getting first-class honours. She flatly refused to go.

"Do you think I'm your possession?" she wanted to know. "Where do you get your ideas from? Where do you get off? I'm not in your custody."

A compromise was reached. They agreed to visit Paris together for a few days, and then she would continue on down south for the agricultural work, while he would go back to the homestead in the north for a period of sequestration, burying his head in the neglected books.

Exams were, once again, the reason for their rifts.

What can I say about Paris that has not been said before? How were his impressions any different from the many that many others had already had? He discovered that every cliché that has ever been coined about the city is essentially true.

'The waiters are rude.' This they learned when they ate out at modest restaurants, or stopped for a drink at the umbrella-covered tables outside cheap cafés, the most inexpensive ones they could find, but still exorbitantly overpriced. How is this kind of behaviour good for business? Why do people go back to places where they have been made a meal of? The French have a word for what gaffs like this must have: cachet. To be unaware of such layers of prestige is to make a gaffe.

'The inhabitants have no patience with anyone whose French is less than perfect.' They had thought their French was pretty good, even if it was only first year college standard, but now they found themselves frequently ignored or hastily corrected, as they searched for words or struggled for structures. The natives may have been talking in a language that Edward and Mary didn't fully understand, but it was a language I didn't understand at all. But then, the world is full of languages I don't understand. Including, I sometimes think, English. To know everything about a language, and be able to say nothing in it. Or rather, not be able to say anything in it. That's saying something. Had I been there, I would have just spoken English with a French accent, and seen how they liked that. But that wouldn't have got me very far either, now would it?

'Paris is the most romantic city in the world.' Well, who would deny it, except a chauvinist who was not French? Do you want me to rhapsodise about his emotional reactions as, with her at his side, he promenaded up those boulevards and strolled through those streets and tripped down those alleyways, many of whose names are familiar even to those who have never trodden them? One has only to utter the sounds Champs Élysées, or Latin Quarter or Left Bank, for example, to provoke a predetermined response. Similarly with The Marais, Montmartre or Montparnasse. These places are already part of romantic myth, and do not need me to contribute anything more, even if doing so would tell you something more about Edward. It goes without saying they did not visit the high-rise housing-schemes which surround the city, just as, I presume, they surround most cities. Even then, they were not overly burdened with what passes for social conscience. But they did take in the galleries, as always, which are in the centre of most cities. Even then, they were inordinately enamoured of supposed artistic perfection. The thing that had the biggest impact of all on him, even more so than it had in London or Amsterdam, was the atmosphere which prevailed of it being okay to be in love, or at least to be demonstrative in public if you were. In France they kiss on Main Street (as an American might say). I could not understand this fascination at all. Maybe it was all just the way he was feeling back then. This is what I felt.

But I can remember how, the night before they left, they stayed out well into the wee small hours of the morning, running around from bar to bar, and club to club. Bliss was it in that dawn to be alive, but to be young was very heaven. They could not remember at what hour they finally got to bed, but when they woke up in their tiny double room in their cheap backpackers' hostel, it was already late afternoon and they were only mildly hungover. They made love sweetly, before leaving to catch their trains, his northward bound, hers going south. 'I love Paris,' he thought to himself, as they kissed goodbye in a station of the metro.

Despite all the drawbacks, Paris was the place, and he knew that one day he would live there. He knew he would be giving Paris one more chance. He would also be giving Mary another chance too. Which amounted to giving himself a second chance. That's a lot of chances to be giving, and to be given; and to be taking, or to be taken.

Meanwhile, things were not going so swimmingly with me. The pain from my wound had got worse, so I naively took myself to a doctor to see if he could help me obtain some measure of relief. I know that I had my parents wrapped around my finger and under my thumb, by keeping alive and dangling over them the possibility of revealing to the appropriate authorities the brutality of my mother's disciplinary attack, and my father's collusion in it. But the pain was at times so intense that I was left with no alternative but to seek outside aid. I did not think I would have to name the first cause of my infirmity. Or if I did, I could lie. What follows here is a cautionary tale, illustrative of a pet theory of mine, and I'm sure another before me, that all the problems of the world are caused by people not being content to sit alone in their own rooms.

The medicine man examined me and could not find anything untoward wrong. He concluded it was all in my mind, implied I was malingering, and advised me to look for work. How could he have failed to detect the damage to my body? Had everything healed up so well that no scar tissue, that tell-tale sign which would have provided ample evidence of my injury, could be found? Or was it actually being suggested that nothing at all had happened to me in the first place? Was I just a habitual liar? Or was something far more sinister afoot? Did someone say paranoia, or schizophrenia, or their dreaded combination?

He sent me to see a psychiatrist, who operated in tandem with a social worker, both of whom had their foot soldiers doing their dirty work for them. Generalisation is a fool's game (oh, I've made a generalisation!), and while there are exceptions to every rule (although the exception doesn't prove the rule!), I am tempted to comment: 'You know what these people are like'; or, 'You know what you're going to get'. If you're not distressed, you're obsessed, or if you're neither, then you're repressed. Although it's possible you could have any two, or maybe even all three. They win, every which way, and you lose, every time.

They divided fairly evenly into the 'pull yourself together' no-nonsense mob, and the 'let's talk it out' New Age psychobabble gang: Scylla and Charybdis; a rock and a hard place; the devil and the deep blue sea; damned if you do, damned if you don't. Either way, whether by a short sharp shock, stiff upper lip stance, or a softly softly, touchy-feely approach, these were can-do guys and girls, who liked to get results.

The head headshrinker interviewed me. I will not particularise him, just as he did not really particularise me. There and then I shrank in the presence of the shrink, so here and now let the shrink be shrunken by me. All I will say is that he was a specialist, and like most specialists in any one field, seemed to have glaringly obvious deficiencies in many others, owing no doubt to over-concentration on one aspect only. The specialist is the new barbarian. So we had a lot in common. But we found it difficult to understand each other.

It seemed to me that he spoke a completely different language to mine, another one I did not understand. To acquire this language you had to have massive self-belief, coupled with breathtaking stupidity. Given the lopsided distribution of power between us, I had a huge crisis of self-confidence, coupled with a still awe-striking intelligence. (He cautioned me towards humility. As you can see, I ignored him. From the first, he did not seem very humble to me.) So I could not communicate in his tongue, and he was too busy, or too uninterested, to learn mine. He was the conquering colonialist after all, and was seeking to impose his language and customs on me. Doubtless he treated all his subject peoples just the same, no matter how different they turned out to be. His attitude was that I was only pretending not to understand, and if he shouted the same words and phrases loudly enough for long enough, then they would be bound to get through my thick skull. It was a method which proved singularly and spectacularly unsuccessful. That is, it did with me. But as he will tell you, excusing his failure dismissively, I defaulted on appointments, and so he did not have enough of an opportunity to work his clinical hocus-pocus to do me any good. He had himself covered, either way. I always fancied myself as something of a rebel.

He asked the usual questions.

"Do you see visions?"

"Yes, magnificent reds and blues and greens, a beatific vision."

"Do you hear voices?"

"Yes, when I turn the radio on."

"How much do you drink?"

"As much as I can."

"Do you smoke cannabis?"

"Every chance I get."

"How many honours did you get in the Leaving Cert.?"

"Nine A1s."

"What was your childhood like?"

"Idyllic."

"Do you avoid cracks in the pavement when you're walking along?"

"Are you trying to find out if I've got obsessive-compulsive disorder?"

"Do you think people are trying to put ideas into your head?"

"Isn't that what the advertising and public relations industries are for?"

"Do you sometimes feel like swearing?"

"Fucking right I do, especially when confronted with fuck-witted questions like this."

"Are you troublesome in your home?"

"What business is that of yours?"

"What do you do all day?"

"I read and I write. I wash and wipe and eat and drink and piss and shit. Believe me, the time passes. There's no problem filling in time. Besides, as I'm sure you know, it would have passed anyway."

"Are you feeling suicidal?"

"Whatever could have given you that idea?"

It was enough to drive you mad. I would not be mad. I did not really give these answers. But he really did ask those questions. I'm sufficiently realistic to know that replying as I have done above would have been going too far into fantasy. But this account is fantastical, so in reality I could have gone as far as I liked. Sometimes things just don't seem real to me. Did he really expect me to tell him what my childhood was like in a couple of sentences? If he reads this book, it'll give him some idea. But he won't have time. What does he do all day? No two human beings are alike, yet he and his ilk ask everyone the same questions. They say this is to find out what each individual is like, but what happens if they run across a type of individual who is not of any known type, but extremely individual? Like me. Or maybe my brother. Or even everyone. His Parthian shot was a probe as to what I thought had caused the pain I thought I had. But I kept my secret.

He made the usual diagnoses.

I had an 'inadequacy of personality', and 'poor interpersonal relationships'. He was obviously an adherent of the shoddy thinking then prevailing, which held that how well one got on with others, one's integration into 'society' as it is called, was an indication of the well-being of one's mind. As though society were any great shakes to begin with. Back then, the big wish was to have everyone like you, and like you;

which somehow involved liking them, and being like them. It still is, to a uncertain extent, although as a trend it seems to be dying out. I thoroughly approve of this death. Personally, I think that there should be a fifty-year moratorium on the word 'relationship', even if I sometimes find myself stuck for a word to employ in its stead.

I was 'eccentric', and 'psychologically vulnerable'. As if there was a centre that could hold, a circle to be inside or outside. It is the eccentrics I find more interesting, insofar as anyone is. If only because we are all eccentrics, now. And aren't we all, to a greater or lesser degree, psychologically vulnerable, depending on the fineness of our minds, or how grievously we've been wounded? Put any organism under enough pressure, and it's bound to bend, even to the point of breaking.

I also 'intellectualised my difficulties', and was 'verbose'. This was, it seems, deemed wrong. And I might well have had 'mono-obsessional disorder' as well, and 'paranoid personality type' into the same bargain. But nothing great is ever achieved without a narrowing of focus, especially if you want to be a specialist. One man's obsession is another's determination. And it's easy to become slightly suspicious when someone you don't know well keeps asking you personal questions. Not all paranoia is delusional.

His prognosis was that it was 'difficult to be optimistic about his outcome', since I was 'refractive to treatment'. A win-either-way situation for him, since if I behaved in the way he wanted me to, and got better, he would enjoy the success and get the laurels, and if I didn't and didn't, it was not his fault, but my own. And if I obeyed and didn't obey and did, well that way just bad luck or good fortune. Any and every way of behaving can be codified and labelled, constructed and construed, in whatever way anyone likes. Nothing is good or bad, but thinking makes it so. Not so. This was bad, and thinking only made it worse. But he didn't think so. There are no facts, only interpretations. My own interpretation was that I was depressed simply because I was depressed, that my mental condition was as a direct result of my physical one. What a great mind is here oer'thrown. My little body is aweary of this great world. A healthy mind in a healthy body.

He offered the usual remedies.

Pharmacology had made great strides, he said, and proceeded to prescribe some lawful poison, to match his legalised character assassination. It didn't alter my perception, or change my conviction.

He recommended I should partake in group therapy sessions. Sitting around with a bunch of strangers talking about the pain in our souls was going to alleviate the pain in my body?

He advised me to move away from home. Giving some slum land-lord the best part of my meagre income for a hole-in-the-wall crummy bedsit was going to improve my circumstances?

He told me I should turn away from the fantasy I had flown to and face everyday reality. So he had clearly swallowed the received wisdom then popular, which stated that your appreciation of a world outside yourself, the so-called 'real' world again, was an index of your mental health. But I am making my own world, and Edward's, and yours. Am I artistic, or autistic? Every artist worthy of the name creates his own world. But does he live in it? Every autist who does not sully his calling lives in his own world. But does he create it? Sometimes I think that no one makes their own world. But I still think that everyone lives in a world of their own. Neurotics build castles in the air. Psychotics live in them. So everyone is psychotic, and no one is neurotic? Hardly. Vice versa? Not so. But we all do live in a world in which everyone is, at best, a potential, if not a reformed, lunatic.

He proposed electroconvulsive therapy, the old electrodes to the brain with the current charging through them, but I declined the dubious pleasures of this shock to the system, since it messes up your memory, and I had a good one (if not good memories in it) and didn't want it tampered with. Then you wouldn't have this book, bad and all as it is for memory blanks. Sometimes, to listen to me, you'd swear I was writing to be read. I can't remember what became of my good memory.

All that was left after that was lobotomy, since 'Lobotomy gets them home', as they used to say. But I forewent the tender mercies of this form of psychosurgery, since it cut off the energy which fuels ideas, of which I had quite a lot (if not much idea what to do with them), and didn't want the combustibles to stoke them with cut off. Then this tome wouldn't be yours, misguided and crackpot as many of its ideas are. Maybe I am suffering from delusions of grandeur, after all, if I imagine this work is going to find favour with the general public.

All in all, I concluded that the Hippocratic oath should be renamed the hypocritical oath. Any group of people whose use of language is so cliché-ridden and jargon-laden should not be put in charge of other people. Canst thou not minister to a mind diseased? So much for these mind doctors. I shouldn't pay them any mind. Never mind any money. These soul fixers, delving into the troubled psyche, have no souls of their own. That's why tampering with other people's comes so easily to them.

Some time after I arose from his Procrustean bed (as I dub the bog standard couch), the sociable social worker came by for a confab with my parents. I will not particularise her either, for the same reasons I did not do the good doctor. To socialise her would invite accusations of sociopathy against me. All I will say is that she had been through the self-help books and had attained high self-esteem. To quote that popular adage of affirmation, she had learned to love herself. So she found effective dialogue difficult to develop when attempting to interface honestly with the recalcitrant Toughs, but she adopted an other-considering and non-judgmental mind-set, in the hope of establishing a mutually inclusive, non-threatening space, where open sharing and full and frank discussion and exchange of views on core values could take place.

She asked more of the usual questions.

For the most part these overlapped to the point of replication with those of the shrink, although she did throw in a few of her own. Had I been a bed-wetter? Had I many friends? Was I prone to random acts of violence? How had they disciplined and punished me as a child? The Toughs did not welcome this unwarranted attention and intrusion, but since they were conscious of their precarious position as surrogate parents, and of the dire consequences for them if the truth got out about what they had done to me, they did their best to keep their best side out, and appear as caring, concerned, and responsible as possible. But they kept their secret.

She made more of the usual diagnoses.

Again, these mostly mimicked those of the Grand Inquisitor, with a couple of new ones added, for good measure. There was, she felt, a lack of conversation, communication and understanding between them and me, to say nothing of what went on, or failed to, between them. My upbringing, she hinted, had been too stern and repressive. This had caused me, she suggested, to become an under-achiever, although I also had over-idealised and unrealistic notions of my own ability. The Toughs sat there and nodded and pretended that they could follow her. They did not see the implied criticism of themselves, or care about the one of me.

She offered more of the usual remedies.

Once more, these were essentially carbon copies of those of the Chief Interrogator, with one or two further ones appended for good measure. I should move into sheltered accommodation in a settlement house, where I could undergo a programme of resocialisation, which would include courses in confidence-building and personal development, and outings to bowling alleys and McDonald's. Or, failing that, I could attend a drop-in centre, where I would be able to talk about my problems, and do light work making Christmas cards, packing greaseproof paper, or sewing mailbags. It occurred to me that this is what convicts do in gaol. But then, I was a prisoner too, of sorts. Incarcerated by them, by him, by you, and by myself. I still am. This is my prison notebook. This is my jail journal. This is hard labour. If you run away, they call it absconding. The Toughs promised to encourage me to co-operate, although they couldn't give any guarantee that I would. So much for these agents of conformity. I shouldn't conform to their agency.

If only I'd stayed at home, dealt with my pain on my own, and suffered in silence, look at the trouble I would have saved. A gentleman does not discuss his ailments. Nor should I. At least, not with them. I should do so only with him, with you, and with myself. But enough, for the time being, of this logorrhoea. Or is it echolalia? (It's great to have a dictionary in my small library, it's one of my favourite books.) Thus ends my coruscating critique of the self-styled, but self-serving, 'caring' professions. So much for these professional conditioners. I shouldn't dwell on their conditioning.

What did my brother make of this entire episode? I do not know. I seem to remember that he was too busy swotting for his repeat exams to pay much attention to what was happening with me. I'm sure the self-same social controllers whom I had fallen among would have much preferred to have got their hands on him rather than me. At least he had the odd tangible symptom or two that they could have got their teeth into and claim they'd eased. For he used to, and still does, get elated and depressed, not so that he requires medication or hospitalisation, but enough so you'd notice. I, on the contrary, do not. Try getting me excited about anything. But he was a scion of the coping classes, who tend not to have any truck with the social services, if they can help it, and so he avoided their clutches and the stigma entailed, never mind the trauma involved. This stratum is never marked out as the mentally ill. It is merely referred to as the worried well.

Edward passed his exams and proceeded on to his second year of studies. He was joyously reunited with Mary on her return. The birds were flying south, the trees were shedding their leaves, the sky was getting darker, the weather was turning colder. Another September came to an end, and more learning was about to begin.

9

WHEN JUNE ROLLED AROUND again, with the birds chirping in the abundant foliage, and the sun shining down from the bright, blue sky between showers, this pair did more exams, and departed yet again, this time to the Land of the Free and Home of the Brave, the good ol' US of A.

They flew over the depths of the Atlantic Ocean and descended into Kennedy Airport. After a couple of days there they were supposed to continue on up to Cape Cod, summer workplace of so many Irish students, where he had lined up a job tending to horses in a stable, and she had organised one looking after children in a mansion. But one night on the town in the tempting Big Apple was enough to make both of them reconsider their plans, and scotch any desire to go through with them.

So they remained by the banks of the Hudson for the season, where he found work selling ice cream in Central Park, and she got a gig waitressing in a nearby diner. They had temporary work visas, so everything was above board and legal-like. A place to live was also located, sharing an old house in Brooklyn with five others in similar circumstances to themselves, and they became part of the much reviled brigade of bridge and tunnel people, who commute to Manhattan to earn their crust of daily bread.

Discharging the duties associated with these occupations, and dealing with the necessities to maintain their accommodation, led to the acquisition of new interpersonal and social skills, or called forth the use of ones already present but lying latent, such as the ability to be both more persuasively friendly and more aggressively hostile, and to judge which mode of behaviour was appropriate to each given situation, in order to cajole people into tipping well at work or coax them into cleaning up at home, and to complain and shame them if they neglected so to do. I was amused and slightly perplexed to witness the emergence of this new confidence and poise in my brother, and in his significant other. In this way, they were growing together. If they could make it there, they could make it anywhere. And they did, and do.

That first night which so changed the course of their sojourn consisted of one manic pop thrill after another. After a trip to Lexington 125, just so that he could say he had officially waited for the man, they zoomed all the way back downtown to The White Horse Tavern in Greenwich Village, a place he'd wanted to visit for years, and now found as much to his liking as he had always imagined he would. Then they carried on to catch Johnny Thunders and the Heartbreakers at CBGB's.

"Get the needle in and get out here," yelled a peroxide blonde, spiky-haired, black leather and lace-clad girl in the front row, when the gap between the support band and the main attraction began to yawn. Sure enough, that's exactly what the gentleman in question seems to have done, since he came out and without further ado launched into a rambling, shambling rendition of 'Chinese Rocks', staggering and swaying precariously around the stage, so wasted and withered was he in his writhings. Edward was convinced it wasn't all just an act.

While Mary and he had familiarised themselves with light drugs the previous summer, neither of them had ever gone near anything stronger. Nor were either of them now about to begin mainlining heroin. But Edward was initiated into the insomniac joys of amphetamine sulphate that night, having a line offered to him in the toilet after the show by an unusually generous-minded, big-hearted fan, at what he was assured was a knock-down rate. When he told Mary, she disapproved vehemently, balling him out.

"That shit could be anything," she shouted, incredulous of his stupidity.

In this way, they were growing apart. But having warned him, she forgave him, and they still went on to have a very good time, drinking and dancing the night away. It was well into the early hours before their heads hit the pillows.

They had started as they meant to go on, and so stayed on. If London was a hit that was improved upon by the bigger hit of Amsterdam, and Amsterdam was a hit that was eclipsed by the increased dose of Paris, then New York was the most potent mix Edward had come across so far. New York isn't America, as they say, but Europe with more energy. It would seem that, for him, only cities mattered, at least at the expense of the countryside, and his need to experience new cities was growing exponentially.

While we're using this cheap metaphor of addiction taking hold through rising tolerance, it is worth asking: where is all this going to end? What will happen when, his ceaseless craving for new places having brought him all over the place, there are no new places left to go to any more, and he, and I, and the world, have run out of places? Will we have exhausted all our possibilities? Will all the possibilities there are have been exhausted by us? Wait and see.

What appealed to him most about this nominally American city was that its beauty was for the most part accidental and chaotic. The beauty of European cities, or what he had seen of the ones he had seen, was mostly intentional and ordered. It had taken centuries to build a cathedral, or construct a square. But the beauty of New York arose independently of human design. Forms which were often quite ugly in themselves turned up together fortuitously, and suddenly in this juxtaposing there was beauty, like in a surrealist or abstract expressionist canvas. The elements of beauty of the cities of Europe were as well-planned and painstakingly executed, down to the minutest details, as a late Renaissance, or Baroque, painting. I know that cathedrals and squares are organic, living things, always being added to and subtracted from, constantly changing and repeatedly rearranging themselves, often without human interference; and presumably there are town planners working in New York City Hall. But this difference between New York and Europe's finest is marked enough to stand up to close scrutiny.

Edward accepted, and even revelled in, this chaos. He fell madly in love with that crazy town. I, on the other hand, still maintained my rage for order, and would seek to impose it on, and so try to control, the formlessness I saw there through him, as well as the formlessness I see here around me. Why is such formalism always empty? It is no emptier than formlessness. Why is that realism always dirty? It is no dirtier than fantasy. How's the form? Are you content? I was horrified by New York, because my methods didn't work there. No more than they do here in Ireland. He was blessed in having no method, there or here. Except the method of no method. How methodical.

He was, it should be added, crushingly aware of the gap between the rich and the poor, the haves and have-nots, the have yachts and not have yachts, the well-heeled and the down-at-heel, that was such an oppressive daily feature of his latest and, for the moment, greatest foreign love. He had never seen this division so starkly before, the fur-coated, chihuahua-toting old dames tottering out of limousines on their way into Tiffany's, while the uniformed doormen kept the bums at bay, and the working girls served them behind the counters, dreaming of being taken away from all this to some better way of life. But the cash nexus was, he told himself, a fact of life anywhere and everywhere you go; it was just more pronounced and obvious to the eye there than in most other places. The poor will always be with us. Poor them. As will the rich. That's rich, coming from them. Besides, he was on the right, or the more comfortable, side of the divide. Life is what you make it, as the self-made always say. But not always what you make of it, as I would doubtless add. If not what it makes of you, as the unmade would like to be able to say.

At summer's end, he would have liked to head farther west, to see more of these cities of glass and steel, but they couldn't afford it. He had earned, and spent, an awful lot of money, and had very little left, little more than the little he had started with. But the habit had firmly taken hold, and he knew he would be coming back to New York, just as he had known he would be going back to Paris, just as he knew he would be going farther west. The cities were getting less important in themselves now, so long as there was always one more to go to.

He knew he would be going to the ends of the earth.

While Edward and Mary were settling back into their final year of college, I was dealing with my parents' reaction to the consequences of my engagement with the psychosocial programmers. They disapproved of my having sought help outside the family home, for fear that I might have divulged details of what they had done to me, but they were afraid to punish me any further, in case I did indeed betray them.

They pretended to the relevant authorities that they were counselling me to play ball, and placed the blame for my recalcitrance squarely on my own shoulders, but domestically they discouraged any such course of action, with its perilous risk of exposing their atrocity. They couldn't really do anything with me, and this pleased me, and vexed them no end, and led to strained relations. So I removed myself from their sphere of influence over me yet again, and retreated even more into my room. Everything back to as abnormal as normal, thankfully. Business as unusual as usual, reassuringly.

But what is that knocking at the front door? And what is that smell?

My other but not necessarily better half, and his other, much better half, sat their final exams, and then hung around Dublin for the summer, doing odd jobs and waiting for their results. It would be interesting to see if he could view the city of his birth as though he were not from there, as if he were seeing it with a fresh pair of eyes, for the very first time. But it seems such powers of emotional distancing were not yet his. He was not ready or willing or able to become an internal exile, like I was, even if he already felt like a stranger in his own home town, as I did.

They talked about what they would do come September, but so much depended on the grades they got that it was all just idle speculation. Their fate was out of their hands now, and in the lap of the Gods, or in the hands and the lap of the examiners. She favoured more musical study at home, he preferred finding work abroad, but it was too early to settle on anything. It was a trying time, for all concerned, like being caught in limbo. Their love-making, in the snatched moments in which it could take place, reached new peaks of intensity, perhaps in some shallow show of over-compensation, as the emotions between them began to ravel, and then disentangle.

When the results finally came out, they found they had gained many honours and distinctions between them. She had done slightly better than him, but both of them had done very well. Maybe now they could put an end to all the tension in the air.

Graduation had to be gone through, to give their parents at least one big day out, and after the conferring of degrees, they went on to a party with their class in a Leeson Street night-club called, I'm not making this up, The Drunken Boat. I will refrain from making cheap cracks about how it should have been named The Ship of Fools, or how they were being sold down the river into bondage and slavery. In saying 'I will refrain' I have not refrained from refraining. It was on this night that Edward finally determined that he would go away, either way, whether or not Mary deigned to come with him. Babylon, here we come.

I saw him, from within him, looking around at the crowd which surrounded him in that den of iniquity, and from the way I saw him looking at what he saw, I saw that it looked as if he thought they were a sorry crew. He despised these social circles, even the one he was part of, that periodically decided they were the centre of the universe, but then produced nothing but talk, and not very good talk. As do I. (Despise, that is, not produce.) You'd think that with all the honours degrees they had among them, they would have been able to string together some sort of decent conversation, one that was more than just talk, but no. He and Mary, along with the rest of their coterie, were now officially sanctioned as scintillating people, with sublime sensibilities and exquisite taste, capable of rare feats of ratiocination. But you didn't need to be the bearer of a badge of intelligence in order to converse with other bearers of the same badges, or indeed, with anyone at all. You just needed to be nice. That's a nice distinction. I've got it to a nicety. But they weren't nice, no more than you or me. But if they weren't really the clever young things, then where were such creatures to be found who were all those things? Maybe no one group was any of these things, or only was insofar as it thought it was. Like this group.

They had both had far too much to drink, even by their own astonishingly capacious standards, but stocious though he was, he still had no intention of formally announcing to the assembled multitude, in true self-dramatising fashion, that he intended to swell the ranks of the Irish Diaspora by going into exile. Such an ostentatious gesture would only have invited ridicule, giving some other young wiseacre the cue to quip, with scathing sarcasm in a long, slow drawn-out drawl, the kind of speech that if written would be in italics, *"Sure can't you do that here?"*, thus deflating his high heroic display of dignity. Always the hard word, always the phrase that meant its opposite. He knew that if he told them that he was leaving this place, he would be put in his place, even if he didn't know his place.

He confined himself to confiding in her, although he doubted that her reaction would be in any way different, or any more favourable. He told her he was going. No, he couldn't do it here. She told him she was staying. No, she couldn't do it there. Both were implacable on this point, impervious to pleas. Could the time they'd spent together not rescue them from this rupture? Was a shared history not more important than an individual impulse? If the world is made up of the leavers and the left, the roles are always interchangeable. He was the one who was leaving the country, but it did not follow that he was the one who was leaving her. She could just as easily be the one who was leaving him, by staying behind. Because she was staying in the country, she was leaving him. Because she was leaving him, he was leaving the country.

They agreed to keep in touch, and meet up again. But knowing how way leads on to way, he did not doubt that she doubted that he would ever come back. But knowing how what goes around comes around, he did not doubt that she doubted that he would always stay away. In this way, they had grown together. In this way, they had grown apart.

Closing time was looming, so he went to empty his bladder, so as to be ready to hit the road. Then there it was, facing him at eye level, just as he'd taken up his stand at the urinal and started cascading, a graffito that hit him like a punch in the solar plexus, stopping his streaming:

HOW'S THE NOVEL GOING THEN, EH?

Now what friend or other stranger could have etched this legend? Did they secretly hate him, or was it just a bit of fun? Did they, or he, even care? Misanthropist, philanthropist, what does it matter when you're pissed? But the writing on the wall had cut him to the quick because his writing, or the lack of it, had been on his mind all evening, and for some considerable time now. Although he hadn't admitted it to himself, much less to anyone else, the main reason he wanted to emigrate was because he thought that if he was away he would write more, because he thought that by being away he would meet many different kinds of women, and have a greater variety of sexual experiences. The old associations die hard. The old obsessions take hold. The dreams of youth are strange. He ended what he'd begun, and went back to join her and the gang.

Later that night, in somebody's flat, when they had finished a final fuck for old times' sake, that had struggled to be born somewhere between desire and desperation, I seem to remember, or did I imagine it: him imagining her vagina as a wet, heaving, humid, slimy, swampy piece of quagmire, inside a deep, dark, dank, damp, oozing cunt of a cave, in whose fetid moistness he would be smothered and stifled, if he did not slide out and slither away, like a snake in the grass, a viper at her bosom.

Where did this boy get his images from? From me? Where do I get my image of his images from? From him? Maybe it is just something he knew himself, and had always known. Just as it is something I know too.

In less than a week he was flying to London. It was his first destination because, like so many who had left Ireland before him, and were leaving back then, this spalpeen lacked the shekels to venture any further afield, though he intended after a little while there to have accumulated the wherewithal to advance wherever he liked. He told the Tenders he would be away only for a month, possibly two, and would definitely be back by Christmas. So they let him go. What else could they do?

He had done a good deal of cogitating in the few days before his flight, about what lay behind him, and before him, and even beyond him. Things had fallen apart with her. That centre could not hold, no more than any other, and now he is loosed upon the world. But maybe, in his own anarchic way, he had wanted all this to happen. How do I know? I don't. I mean I don't know, not I don't know how I know. I may be able to see inside his head, but I don't know for sure, or can't say for certain, why he does what he does, any more than you do, or can. Or, for that matter, than he can do. What I am telling you of him is coloured by its coming from me, and by its going to you.

It seems to me that he thinks he is setting out on a search for love, which he will find through exploring sex. One may as well search for sex by exploring love. And why does he make this silly distinction? It is senseless to me, not because I hold sex and love to be more or less the same and so not worth contrasting, or so completely different that they are not worth comparing, but because, you see, it is my firm belief, insofar as I have any, that one day we will live in a world without love; not to mention bitterness and jealousy and hate, and all those other little words for all those big feelings that make us so unhappy. We will be the dead. But in dying we will be born to eternal life. This is simply an evolutionary necessity, an essential survival strategy. Maybe we will even live in a world without sex. Or where sex, and indeed love, will not be thought of as anything special.

Please don't laugh at me, or pooh-pooh my proposition as unsustainable arrant nonsense. The reason these passions and desires are now thought of as being of any consequence whatsoever is largely an accident of history, in my view, rather than arising from any deep-seat-ed, definingly human, physical or emotional need. You can call the current situation the product of the wisdom of the ages, if you like. I call it the result of the folly of generations. Most people would never fall in love if they hadn't heard about it somewhere first. As it is, they probably never really fall in love anyway. They just think they do, because they think they should.

Religion used to have the market sewn up on achieving ecstasy, or avoiding agony. It was most people's way of accessing transcendence, their means of finding release. Anyone who looked for any other ways or means to these ends was castigated. Nowadays, a good sex life is commonly acknowledged as being the answer to everything, the new universal panacea, a one-way ticket to salvation. Once again, if you don't subscribe to this credo, you're an oddball, or a downright weirdo. But if everybody's doing it, it's no fun any more. What self-respecting, self-regarding, self-reliant elitist wants to do what everybody else is doing? To be sure, doing it in a different way to everybody else works for a while, but it soon wears thin. It's a neat trick by humanity, I'll grant you, to tell itself it should feel guilty about doing something it thinks it should enjoy, so that it will enjoy doing it even more, and then when it stops feeling guilty about doing it and so starts enjoying it less, to think up new ways to feel guilty about doing it all over again, so that it will enjoy doing it even more all over again. Sex without sin? A fine idea indeed. By thinking of it as dirty, you can postpone its being bad. Bad to do, that is, not bad in itself. By thinking of it as bad, in itself, you can think of it as dirty. Dirty to do, that is, not dirty in itself. By thinking of it as dirty, in itself, you can think of it as good. Good to do, that is, not good in itself. For a little while, at least. What is it, in itself? Fucked if I know.

So, the religious schismatic is one and the same as the sexual deviant. Both get their jollies going against the grain. But what is a schismatic? And what is a deviant? What were once vices are now habits. (And vice versa, habitually, even if they weren't dirty.) Humanity can't go on in an endless cycle of guilty enjoyment forever. At least, I hope not. For, if the free person must eventually ask himself: 'What do I do with my freedom?', then the sexually liberated person must similarly inquire: 'What do I do with my sexual liberation?' And so, one day, people will have come around so much that sex will no longer be perceived as being a huge source of pleasure, or even if it still is, this will no longer be perceived as being of any great importance, and so little or none will be attached to it. Sex will be as important or as trivial as anyone wants to make it. Just like religion. Don't let anyone tell you any different. Solipsists of the world, unite and take over.

My word, what an outbreak of ranting, what an outburst of raving, and from such a mild-mannered, gentle soul as myself. I am conscious that my tirade against the sexual imperative reveals only, by negative implication, how important it still is to me, just as apostates showed how much religion continued to exercise them by proselytising against it. But religion still meant something to them, just as sex is still of significance to me, only because it was still the prevailing way of doing things in the times they lived in, in the world around them, just as sex is these times, in this world. We are none of us such recluses that we are not touched somehow by what other people think, by what they feel, by what they do. More's the pity. But this will change.

Maybe you will call my bluff, or think you are doing so, by attempting to attribute my opinions to the trifling circumstance that I just don't get laid enough. Indeed, as you are aware, I have never got laid at all. Does it show? Maybe my anatomy, as they used to say, is my destiny. Is that how it seems to you?

Whatever way you look at it, it seems to me that Edward would have done well to remember that if, as was his belief, sex is one more victory chalked up against death every time you do it, then that must mean that when you stop doing it, you have finally accepted and even embraced your own passing on. Instead of flying from it, you're drifting into it. Rage as you may against the dying of the light, and call as you might for more light, death remains a certainty that will come to everybody, inevitably. Would Edward become the wanton wielder of a conquistador cock, a roaming rover with a woman in every port? His blood was fired up, as if some powerful potion was running through his veins, an aphrodisiac philtre made up of equal measures of wander and lust. As he looked down from the window of the aeroplane at the coastline receding in the distance below, he imagined himself as a soon to be ejaculated spermatozoon being carried along inside a giant volant phallus, and he was already thinking how gratifying it would be to be disseminated freely over all below him, a process he presumed to inaugurate presently, by picking a blooming English rose soon after his arrival.

All as a way of distancing death, a means of keeping it at bay.

 And what were his thoughts of the maid Mary? Would she have a second coming? Would she come to him again? It remains to be seen. She had shown him that almost everyone, not just him, is given a family to escape from. And maybe even to return to. He was grateful to her for that much.

 As for me, I remember this past time, not as a pastime, but as a time as lost as surely as all time is, or will be, lost. It was my seed time, my green valley. And his. How green was my valley? As green as any valley of the shadow of death. And his? I don't know. It seemed to me to be a happy valley, but should I dare to presume to speak for him? I have lived too much through him. To live through another is to live in exile from yourself, in exile from the kingdom. For thine is the kingdom, the power and the glory. As is mine. At least, because of him, I am now eminently qualified to take up office as a fully paid up member of the chattering classes. Except that I don't chatter. Except to myself, and to you.

 I was glad he was going. Think of all I would see through him. I was glad I was staying. Think of all I wouldn't have to do to see through him. His world was opening up, in my words, which are being written down in my world, which was closing down, in my words. What awaited me? Nothing. No future, as they used to say, in the past. What attended him? Everything. Look to the future, as they still say, in the present. He had finished waiting for life to begin. I had just begun. I had begun waiting for life to finish. He had just finished.

FIN

EUROPA

Poetry is both a going out and a kind of homecoming.

PAUL CELAN, *Essays*

1

Y OU WILL NOW LISTEN to my voice, and hear it, as it tells you of what I have listened to and heard, of what I was told, of what it has told, of what it is telling, of what it is telling of what is telling, of what I have looked at and seen, of what I am looking at now and see.

My voice will help you, guiding you farther and deeper into the labyrinthine myth, into the myth of the labyrinth. Sometimes you will want to escape my voice, to shut me up, to stop your ears, but it is not possible.

You will place this book politely to one side, hoping to forget it quietly, or you will fling it violently from you, confident of never stumbling on it again. Just as I have done. All to no avail, for you will find it, just as it will find you, waiting to be found.

For you will want to take up the story, if there is one, where we left off, you will want to know even still if there is a story, even if you suspect there is not, and you are curious as to how it will come out, if it will be resolved, if it is able to end, if indeed it is there at all.

You will try to sell the book, or give it away, or dump it, and with it the possibility of a story, and you will go about searching out other stories. But no one will buy it at any price; you will not be able to give it away, and even the refuse collectors will always return it to you. You cannot get rid of a bad thing.

You will find that what other stories there are are simply variations on those presented here. You will say that this book does not contain my voice, that my voice resides elsewhere, or that there is no voice, and, having made this excuse, take it up once again, resignedly, as though submitting yourself to the ceaseless, meaningless babble of an empty, antediluvian formula.

But how do you know there is no voice? It is your voice which proclaims this, and my voice which concurs with you, or not. And what other voices, then, if any, do you suppose are present herein? To find out, you must continue. You must hearken to me, singing a song for Europe. I was given a voice, and sing with it I will.

With my voice I can do many voices, including the silent one, the one that says nothing. I have spoken to you before now. You have already heard some of my voices (our voices). You have already seen some of my visions (our visions). You are acquainted of yore with previous episodes of my story (our story). Here are some more.

They are offerings which might light you on your way, in your frustrated and frustrating quest for finality, your obscure and unachievable urge towards completion. I have felt the flutter of the wings of madness. So too will you. As long as you stand by me and stick with me. So pay attention now.

Here is my voice. It is talking. Are you listening? Can you hear? Speak, you also. Use your voice. What do you hear? Yours or mine? Yours and mine?

I'll tell you what: you tell me. I'll tell you what you tell me.

Lo and behold, we come upon my brother Edward, last observed flying effortlessly above the clouds, discovered now struggling to stay swimming with sharks in a turbulent sea. I do not mean to pour cold water scorn on his dreams just yet, or indeed ever, but he has just found himself up to his neck in hot water, cast adrift amid threatening, tempestuous tides, fighting to keep afloat among encroaching, treacherous waves, and not be engulfed in the surrounding, tumultuous ocean. Still, despite how this description may come over, he did not go under.

You are ready to accuse me of exaggeration, I can tell. All right, I concede that I am embellishing, if only a little. Exaggerating is a way of attracting attention and being taken seriously, even if one is then largely ignored for exaggerating initially. I have no wish to be the boy who cried wolf. But, by the same token, neither do I want to be the boy who minds sheep. If I am given occasionally to gilding the lilies, I hope this will not give rise to a war of the roses.

Be all this as it may, there is a widespread misapprehension in circulation that the streets of London are paved with gold, a deceit of which Edward was a some time unwary but willing dupe. Having landed beyond in the Big Smoke, and been in residence there for longer than the wet weekend of a happy holiday, he was rapidly disabused of this naive notion. For all was not beer and skittles in his newly adopted city, and he sometimes wondered if there would ever be any more cakes and ale. For now the hassles of being out on his own struck him with their full force, and he had to start becoming responsible for himself in a way he never had been before.

Although not wholly unacquainted prior to this with the broad concept of paying the rent, he was now rent in two by the necessity of having to come up with it every month. That money is power is a much heard mantra, particularly from those who value money. (What a pleasant job that must be, valuing money, as every currency dealer knows.) But the relentless pursuit of money, not even for its own sake, not even for the abstract or even concrete power it could perhaps confer, but only for the power to pay the rent, rendered him almost powerless to persevere with what he really wanted to do, which was write.

He felt that this situation was not right. Why should he let the toad work squat on his life, especially if it was not the kind of work he really wanted to do? He had thought of squatting, as a means of obviating the crushing imperative of parting with money in the form of rent. But something sufficiently toad-like squatted in him too, a conforming fastidiousness steering him towards striving to maintain more than a minimum level of basic creature comforts. So he needed the spondulicks to subsidise his preference for such lily-livered luxuries.

At first, after a time, he sold his labour, over time, as a waiter. He did lots of laborious overtime, and was an unexpected success. I have not got it in me to be submissively subservient, under any circumstances, but Edward learned to smile smarmily, even while seething inside. He grew charming and attentive enough to encourage customers into the restaurant, and to bring them back again. His employers loved him, but he hated them. For the gains they made on account of his gregariousness were not reflected in what they offered by way of recompense as his remuneration. He knew he would have to vacate that situation, and labour in a different vineyard. But can one recoup rich pickings, picking someone else's grapes? Such employment only makes one wrathful.

He got another job, clerking in an office. He made a little more money, but not much more. (What a marvellous job that must be, making money, as every counterfeiter knows.) He had more regular hours, but not much more free time, since he was required to spend a significant amount of time travelling through a considerable distance in space, going to and fro to get to and from clocking in and out of his new place of work. Being a less than expeditious time traveller and a not very speedy space invader, he spent more time not having a good time by being a good time-keeper that he lost so much time that it was just wasted time. He could have killed time, and he did. The money he earned for the time he spent earning it did not leave him with enough spending money to buy him the time he wanted to spend writing about it. If he'd had more money, he would have bought some time. But the time spent earning money did not give him enough money to buy time. Time lost was not commensurate with time regained. The equation was not in proportion.

So, this being away from Ireland was proving more difficult than he had supposed, because of the tyranny money was allowed to have over him, or the despotism he permitted it to have. So, this being somewhere or anywhere other than Ireland was not as conducive to the production of letters as it had been cracked up to be, as he had dreamed it would be. With usury the stone-cutter is kept from his stone. The weaver is kept from his loom by usury.

It will be remembered that, as well as the notion of not being in Ireland, the other great catalyst that this young man, my brother, imagined would aid and abet his attempts at creativity and self-expression (if these have any relation to each other) was sexual experimentation and fulfilment (if these are not mutually exclusive).

It was with this other *idée fixe* of his in mind that he set about the sedulous seduction of some indigenous comely maidens, preferably ones who did not mind getting down and dirty pretty quickly, which, this being perfidious Albion, a notably secular society, a godless country entirely, meant most of them. You know the English: they see everything in terms of their genitalia. It is the sole reason for their existence, after they have fed their mouths. You know the Irish: they cannot see their genitalia. It is their way of not being English, those they hold responsible for once upon a time not having been able to feed their mouths. That's how it was back then, at least, back in the bad old 1980s.

The first such wench he hit on we will dignify with the name of

Sharon. How they met is unimportant: a night-club; a wine bar; a welcome home or going away party. Who cares? What her occupation was is of no interest: a student; a model; a physio or psychotherapist. Who gives a damn? You may think that by my giving you these pieces of information about her you would then know enough to be able to make a preliminary character assessment of her. But I don't want you drawing such inferences, if only because you'd probably be wrong, and it would be a great shame to waste your precious time. I could not live with myself for remorse if I were to lead you astray.

Cop for this instead, guv: she liked a good time, and was game for a laugh. Wantonly indulgent and lascivious behaviour was much to the fore, but proved unexpectedly disappointing for him in that it never became the source of a flood of rapturously liberating energy, as it had been with his first love, once they had got on their own and got it on all alone, but remained at best perfunctorily functional, at worst merely mechanical. Perhaps he had had unreal expectations. You get disillusioned only if you ever had illusions. Blame his first love for engendering these illusory expectations. Blame him for believing those unreal illusions.

The nub of the matter was that his meagre funds did not stretch to keeping his new love, if I can be permitted here to debase that much elevated term, amused and entertained in the ways she was accustomed to and preferred. There's the rub. His happy disposition and witty repartee, enhanced by the exoticism of a touch of the blarney, were not magnetically attractive and enticing enough to her to keep her hanging around for very long. He had been the young man carbuncular, and he had humped her. She, if not exactly indifferent, was glad when it was over. As was he. I am bored with her already. Let us leave her, just as she left him.

Then he took up with Tracy. It would seem his ego had not been bruised too badly, or his heart broken irreparably, if at all. We will take more time than a little over doing this new one, since he took quite a lot of time over doing her. He spent time with her, and over her, and under her. They took their time, and did time together, before doing each other over.

He met her at an exhibition one of his friends, another Mick immigrant, had invited him to. He plied her with free alcohol, and learned that she plied her trade as a freelance photographer. Not family portraits and wedding albums, but fashion shots for style magazines. Plus a little arty stuff on the side, in her own time. You may surmise anything you like from these few facts. I will not presume to set limits to your imagination. See if I care if you get it wrong. For how would you know whether or not you are right or wrong, in the last analysis, except by consulting me? I am an omniscient narrator. I am the only narrator. But I am also an unreliable narrator. For I am the voice of memory. The most unreliable narrator. The only narrator. The not-so-omniscient narrator.

Picture this as well, mate: she was just as capaciously carnal as the preceding one, although a good deal more feisty and frolicsome with it. They would take shots of each other in diverse locations, in compromising positions, using her camera. Because she was a little more with it than her immediate predecessor, and had a somewhat greater interest in the world around her, they managed now and again to be able to communicate on more than one level. This was a stroke of luck for Edward, the proverbial manna from heaven, since he was starved of female company to shoot the bull with, something he had grown used to with Mary, and now missed sadly. For he hadn't yet found the time to write a letter or make a telephone call to his first love. Tough as old boots sometimes, this tender lad. Sometimes I am prompted to the infernal inference that he was deserving of a good kicking. Devil the miss.

On the downside, she too expected some pecuniary indulgence, if not a downright lavishing with gifts, as a sign of his esteem for her, in return for the favours she bestowed on him, if only that of granting him access to her time, never mind her body. She would by times return the compliment, it must be admitted, but he did not always have the wherewithal to extend it in the first place. She seldom appreciated this stumbling block. The eroticism which our Ed had hoped would fire and fuel his imagination, or at least give some welcome respite from the constant constraining fumble in a greasy till, was turning out to be just as problematic as most other features of his life during this period.

Furthermore, she had the habit, which he found very annoying, of liking to talk about sex even more than she liked to do it. Their couplings were appraised in depth and detail after they had taken place. Other people were evaluated in terms of their sensual appeal, or lack of same. You know the English: always worried about whether they are, or you are, straight or gay or lesbian or bi or a, or good or bad in bed. It was their way of thinking themselves more advanced than the likes of the Irish. You know the Irish: always worried about the same things as the English, if for different reasons. It was their way of trying to be as advanced as the likes of the English. As if orientation mattered any more, to the likes of him. As if it had ever mattered at all, to the likes of me. Good and bad still mattered to him, but they were relative terms to me.

So, this having loads of mind-blowing sex was proving more difficult than he had supposed, because of the thraldom in which money was allowed to keep him, or he permitted it to. So, this having lots of sex with anyone and everyone was not as conducive to written composition as it had been talked up to be, as he'd imagined it would be.

It's all about money, and that ain't so funny. No mun, no fun.

So, all in all, his intention to write, if it can be written that one can have the intention to write, if it can be written that one can write what one intends, was sorely thwarted, and shifted to that always useful appendage, that ever rigid digit, the long finger. There is no time like the present, but his present, now past, presented him with no time for writing, for his time was spent getting enough money to get by, never mind to lay by for the future.

You will argue that he could have improved his position by taking up less menial occupations with higher salaries, ones that offered him more money for the same, or even less, time. Then he would have been able to afford to make the most of being out of Ireland, by covering the expense of the cost of living, and to take full advantage of the readily available supply of slap and tickle, for which he had to barter with these foreign ladies. He might even have got some writing done, whether or not it was as a direct consequence of these two felicitous and fortunate conditions obtaining, as he'd held it to be, for him. Whether or not his hypothesis is universally true, and the spilling of ink is always dependent on these two sunny and swinging circumstances forever being in place, I leave up to you. However, I strongly doubt that his steadfast faith in this particular holds good for many, if any, other than himself. Look no further than me, for a start.

As to your suggestion about him getting a better job. You will recall that he is a Bachelor of Arts, with no additional qualifications to his name, and employers were not exactly crying out for such hairy reasoners. He had to take what he could get, and try not to get taken in, if he wanted to get anything out of these go-getting risk-takers. Maybe he would have to retrain.

Time is money, they say. But if money is power, it can be the power of buying time. So money can be time. But time must have a stop. If only at break-time. That's the way the money goes. Made round to go round. Like a clockface with its hands, telling the time.

Now was the winter of his discontent, made glorious by very little, which he faced into with mixed feelings of fortitude and fear. He knew right well that being away from home and being with girls were not, as he had envisaged, helping him to write as he wanted. But he still believed that if other details were attended to, these factors might well see him right. Do not hold this against him. He was still young then, young enough to be convinced of his own invincibility. I was old enough to know better, although plainly of the same age. He could still think of himself as immortal, never having been reminded of his own mortality. He was as young as I was then, as it happened, although even then I knew that one day, no matter what, I was surely going to die. For I'd had a brush with death.

However badly he was doing and things were going, there was no giving up and going back home again for good, for him. He wanted to prove something, to himself as much as to everyone else, and would not return shamefacedly with his tail between his legs whence he had come. He grit his teeth in the face of the dispiriting London winter, and dug himself in.

He would be going home again briefly though, for Christmas, as people usually do, or did, until they had homes of their own, or had no homes to go to. He would not be bringing Tracy, although he was still stringing her along, as she was him. He would be keeping schtum about her at home. Was this young man growing cynical? That would be a deplorable trait, for a smattering of idealism is a very meritorious thing in the young. Especially when you consider what their elders, but not necessarily betters, are apt to get up to. For me, or for anyone else, to allow otherwise would be the height of cynicism.

Let us say that, while he may not have been satisfied with the way things stood, with himself and with the world, he was not about to go starting a revolution. No more than I am. But perhaps he is a sort of cynical idealist, or an idealistic cynic. Such creatures exist, you know. Look no further than me. What a complex character I have created. What a complicated person I am. I am a great character, but there is a plot against me. Have I made up a plot against him?

I saw him wondering if, during his upcoming excursion home, he would run across Mary Contrary.

Let it be known: I too have a problem with time, if not with money. For it was at this time, when Edward left Ireland, and found that he had no time to write because he needed time to make money to live, that I, not being bothered unduly by the need to make money to live, or indeed, by living itself, first took the time to put pen to paper in earnest. My subject would be myself, and him. My book would be both biography and autobiography.

But I found, as you have too, that not only did I have to record what happened to us from the moment I started writing, but I was also obliged to recount our lives over the previous twenty years. Because this is a chronological, sequential narrative, you can see that I have already fulfilled the second part of this requirement. But I am still slaving over, and getting bogged down in, the first. For, during the time I spent writing about the past, things were continuing to happen in the present, so not only did I have to write about what was already in the past when I began, but also about what was receding into the past while I was writing about what was already in it. So I was, and indeed still am, trapped in the cycle of trying to catch up with myself, and with him, so that the moment of my writing about things happening, and the moment in which the things I am writing about happen, are both taking place at the same time, in real time.

There is no time like the present. Now I've said that already. But there is no time like the past either, or like the future, as far as that goes. I could tell you what he is doing now, but it would spoil the story for you, if only because I do not yet know how it will end, if it ever does. So I am stuck chasing my tail, and his; chasing our tales.

When I was looking in the mirror, at the very beginning, telling you what I looked like, how old was I then? And, although always necessarily the same age as me, how old was he? Do I, and he, look the same now as we did then? When did I execute that description? When we were twenty, twenty-five, thirty? How old are we now? Did I do it yesterday? No, I haven't got as far as writing about yesterday yet. Will I ever? Not today. But some day I may write about yesterday. Some day I may even write about today. Some day I may even write about a today, and the today on which I write will have no tomorrow, because the today I write about and the today on which I write will be one and the same day. Hence, no tomorrow. Or, at least, none that I will know anything about. Or maybe I will, but not inside the bounds of this book, because I will have stopped writing it, and it will be finished, even if my life, and that of my brother, are still going on. Unless I abandon it, but that is another way of finishing, another kind of end. But you will know what happens after the book finishes, what will have happened after it has been finished, because you will be reading it after I have finished writing it. Unless you are reading it while I am still writing it, and it has not yet been finished. Unless it never finishes, and you read while I write, looking over my shoulder, world without end, words without ends.

It is another of the difficulties of this narrative, aside from its time-frame, that it is narrated by me, whose powers as a narrator are so pathetic, omniscient and alone and unreliable as I am, and so it may appear meandering. Or maybe, as already mooted, the harsh reality is that there really is no story, and I am just wittering on, with nothing to tell. Except that we've left my brother facing grim reality. Need reality always be harsh, or grim? You don't want to see him trapped in a cliché. So let's help him out.

That smell is getting worse, and there's that knocking again, at the front door. When is it taking place? When I was writing, or even as I write? Yes, it was happening then, and is still going on now. Is there much more time left for me to write? You do want me to get to the end of the story, don't you? So please help me out.

2

THERE IS A CERTAIN QUALITY of cold, mixed with vaporous mist, that insinuates itself into the bones, lingeringly, and brings you down hard. It is this lowness of mood that Edward would remember, in the years that followed, as defining what he would always refer to in an undertone, with a faint shudder, as 'that London winter'.

What a difference between the effect this city had had on him during his first visit there, and the one it was giving rise to now. Still so much to do, but now so little time to do it in. Then such light, such hope, now a gloominess bordering on despair. Before, so high was he on his own euphoria, and the rush of being where he was with whom he was with, he hadn't noticed the glum expressions on the weary faces of people shuttling along from station to station, being buffeted back and forth, on the tube, a system so dirty and clammy it was like living in a coalmine. Now he could see nothing else.

The return of this exile, however brief, to his native land for the festive season held the promise of some temporary respite from this awful scenario of going nowhere fast. Because of his straight-up straitened circumstances, and his unwillingness to lose face by asking for pecuniary aid from the ones who loved him and cared about him the most, the Tenders, this would be a boat-train job rather than an air flight. He deflected any suspicions that this expedient might raise among those malicious enough to make it their business, of which it was none, to find out about and put a malign construction on, that of him not doing so well over beyond and coming back with a scalded arse, by saying that he had time on his hands, and could read a book as he trundled over the tracks and sailed over the sea, which was something he liked doing with what leisure time he had, anyway. This excuse would have to act as a sop to these miscreants, if their taste for *schadenfreude* consumed them so much as to be so hungry for any titbit of idle gossip. How nosy can you get?

I am still here. I have not gone away. Talk about Edward going nowhere fast. Edmund, that's me, is going nowhere slowly. Or maybe, on the contrary, I'm getting somewhere slowly. Will he soon start getting somewhere fast?

A man walked into a bar in his hometown, after being absent abroad for a short while, and met up with some friends and acquaintances. He made sure to get a round in, and be seen to be holding up his end. Some of those present were solicitous as to how he had been doing, others patently couldn't give a good goddamn, while others still went out of their way to treat him with lofty disdain.

The scene was one of uncontrolled madness and utter mayhem, it being Christmas Eve, and you know, or can imagine what Dublin pubs are like on that night of all nights. People tumbling in, struggling under the weight of polythene department store bags full of last-minute presents. Not enough room to swing a cat for the sudden influx of returned emigrants colliding with the stay-at-homes who venture forth only on occasions like this one. Then out of the throng there appeared at his side a woman who had meant a lot to him, and for whom he had been something special. Am I wrong in using the past tense to describe the dynamic between them?

"Good evening, Mr Tender."

He knew who she was by the timbre of her voice, even before he looked around to visualize her and try to take her in, and so had enough time to compose himself and greet her salutation with a convivial, "Well hello there, Mary, how are you?"

He had been half-expecting to bump into her at some point during this sojourn, but was still mildly surprised now that it had happened. They chatted idly for a minute or two, exchanging polite pleasantries, awkward irony covering the acute embarrassment lurking just below. It occurred to him to apologise for his lack of correspondence, but he could think of no passable explanation to proffer, and since she did not allude to this silence, he opted not to advert to it either. He had not even sent her his address. She did not ask for it now. But he elected to give it to her anyway, along with his telephone number, in some slender stab at a pacific gesture.

As she tripped back to her circle of friends gathered amicably around their table, was it a vast emptiness he felt inside, the kind that comes of being carved out hollow? No, it was much worse than that, for he found he felt nothing so much as nothing at all. Some say the best feeling is to feel this nothing at all, but not him. To feel, how pleasant that must feel, he felt. Where were all the deep, rich emotions he was supposed to be feeling? To be happy is to be foolish. To be sad is to be foolish. To feel nothing is to be wise. Could have fooled me.

My mind wanders into nothingness. Here I am, pretending to convey to you how my brother felt, or did not feel, or felt about not feeling, when in actuality I am staring straight at the ashen, peeling wall in front of me, its surface as blank as my mind, and as the page I have yet to complete, beginning at the end of this sentence, commencing after this word.

Now you know what it's like. Every day I face this virginally white emptiness. I am like the man the priests and teachers used to warn us about, who could not concentrate while at mass because of Mrs Williams' hat, a florid creation displayed at an impossible angle on the attentively inclined head of a co-religionist seated in a pew in his immediate line of sight. Except that this article of headgear probably served as a much better excuse for distraction than my wall does, if it is distractions you are looking for. But in that state of mind, any excuse will do.

I am seeking such a diversion because perhaps I can no longer feel what my brother felt, if feel he did at all, or maybe I could no longer even feel what he felt at the time he was feeling it, if he was feeling anything at all. For all I know, a palpable physical ache may have possessed him, with every psychosomatic symptom in the book manifesting itself, those thumping heart-rending palpitations and stomach-churning vomitory beats, so perturbed was he as he watched Mary take her leave. Then I would be wrong in employing the past tense, when referring to how he felt about her then, and wrong in telling you that he felt nothing, like I do now. To feel nothing is to feel something. I hold on tight, to nothing at all. For had his body betrayed him in this way, he would even then have already been living in the past, just as much as I am now. He would have been caring about the past, as much as I do. He would have been past-caring, like me. I will sing of what is past, or passing, or to come. Even if I am wrong, about everything. Even if I may as well be talking to the wall.

The buses giving up the ghost early on Christmas Eve, Edward and a couple of his accomplices were forced to pour themselves into a taxi for the journey home.

Christmas Day proved as dull, tedious and boring as always, exceeded as it is in these respects in these parts only by Good Friday itself. But our man fugged his way through it as best he could, in a foggy hangover of his own making. I had long since ceased to celebrate either feast, which, incidentally, commemorate the birth and death of Our Saviour, respectively. Rather, I observed them.

It emerged around the dinner table that Mr and Mrs Tender were labouring under the misapprehension that their boy was home to stay for good this time, having got the travel bug out of his system, and satisfied his curiosity about living in a foreign country. He felt, I feel sure, that it was only fair to disabuse them of this mistaken assumption, and nip it in the bud.

"I'm afraid I'm heading back as soon as we've rung in the New Year," he declared. "Sure there's nothing here for the likes of me," he added, by way of explanation.

His mother looked to his father. His father listened in silence.

The waves of the Irish Sea solemnly refusing to part for him, he went back, as he had come, in a boat, into more only occasionally relieved misery. He would come to regard the next few months as the single worst time of his life. He was not to know then that his lot would improve, no more than did I, and this not knowing was part of what made things worse. It was not a foregone conclusion that things could only get better. He did make sure that he had Dub the Teddy with him, as usual, and his guitar, which he had judged too cumbersome to bring the last time, but couldn't do without now. Maybe these props would help to assuage his dark days, his lonely nights, as he waited restlessly for the darling buds of spring to sprout forth.

No sooner was his nose to the grindstone in the office once again, than Tracy announced that she was packing him in. This news was not entirely unexpected or unwelcome, but he rued the inconvenience of losing someone who had kept the bed warm during whatever nights they had shared it, and kept him entertained during whatever days they had spent together. Nor did he relish the prospect of head-hunting other prospective candidates to fill this gap, for it was only a tempo-rary/part-time position, and you just couldn't get good help in those days, no more than you can in these. If I didn't know him better, I'd say my brother was ripe and ready to resume the search for love. True love leaves no Tracys, or Sharons. They leave it. It leaves no stone unturned, and leaves every stone standing. Your true love never leaves you, if you're also theirs.

Tracy said she was tired of his hang-ups about money, and had found someone else who knew how to treat her well, and provide her with treats. The funny thing was, he thought that it was everyone else who was hung up about money, not him. He couldn't work it out, for love or money.

It is time to introduce the villain of the piece, and let him make his entrance, if only to perk up your flagging interest, even if it is a little late in the day for him to be putting in his first appearance.

His name is Wylie Sighfer, so that is what we'll call him. Edward and he had been aware of each other's existence since their college days. He could have been seen, if truth were told, lurking in The Drunken Boat that night when we were there, ready to deride the newly qualified, intending emigrant's plans, if I'd bothered to draw your attention to him then. Now he was turning up in London, anxious to renew old acquaintance, should it be forgot.

As to description, he was tall, dark and fairly handsome, in a rough-hewn kind of way, with a tight haircut camouflaging his incipient balding at the temples and thinning on top. A sallow-skinned, shifty-looking character, who nodded and twitched and gesticulated a lot, he had the raffish but edgy demeanour of a resting actor, strutting around self-confidently but self-consciously, with an elaborate display of plumage, in a vain attempt at masking nervy insecurity. I could tell you that in appearance he approximated the Devil, but I have never met that particular gentleman, the embodiment of pure evil. To be brief, you know this Wylie well: a serviceable villain.

What? You thought that role was reserved for me?

We have broached drugs. Now let us approach drink. We will address ourselves to it with circumspection, lest it creep up on us, unlike these two rogues when they got together.

Arriving in London, and in sore need of a place to stay 'while he sorted himself out' as he euphemistically put it, Wylie dialled a phone number that had been hastily scribbled on a piece of torn cigarette packet, and at some ungodly hour Edward heard the tolling of the bell. He knew it was for him. At first he had no idea at all who was on the other end of the line, and it was only gradually that the garbled message was unscrambled by the receiver in his brain. Bleary-eyed, he reluctantly consented to having this personage, whom he had never been especially close to, sleep on his floor for a couple of nights. He is just that warm, welcoming, open-hearted kind of guy. He did inquire as to which of their mutual acquaintances had so generously provided his new house guest with the necessary contact number, but he thought it unlikely that the person mentioned by Wylie was privy to this knowledge, unless it had come from yet another intermediary. So, was Wylie getting off on the right foot, by lying? If not, which of Edward's friends had spilled the beans to the chap mentioned by the prospective visitor? If so, who could it have been who'd really informed him?

When Edward got home from his place of toil the next day, he found Wylie sprawled on the sofa in front of the television, having already worked his way through several cans of beer, and with even more fresh supplies lined up in the fridge for imminent consumption. The house guest from hell invited his heavenly host to get started on one. Nothing loath, Edward laced in.

Perhaps it was doing a dull, dead-end job, or maybe it was the residual vibrations of Tracy dumping him, or more likely a combination of both, plus not being able to do what he really wanted to do, but my brother took to the bottle with unbridled gusto and undisguised glee. I do not mean to imply that, like my bugbears about whom you will have by now gathered I have a considerable bee in my bonnet – in other words the many eminent practitioners of the feeble professions of counselling, psychotherapy and psychiatry – I hold drinking to excess to be always and ever just a way of drowning your sorrows. Not everyone gets fluthered because they are trying to forget their troubles. People often get hammered simply because it's great fun. But there were, admittedly, reasons why Edward was less than totally contented with his lot in life just then. But then again, of whom among us could this not be said to be true, for a considerable proportion of the time?

The boys wound up going round the corner to the pub that night to continue their spree, and then getting a carry-out to bring home again to keep the binge going, and it was well into the small hours before either of them fell asleep, absolutely blotto at the end of their bender.

Thus, a regular pattern began to develop. Wylie, whose tenure on the floor of the flat was becoming more fixed with each passing day, would propose high jinks every evening, and the incumbent tenant from whom he was by now sub-letting his space proved only too eager to be led astray. The duo would get shit-faced, rat-arsed and gee-eyed most nights, and especially at weekends.

Various reprobates from the gin palace would wind up back at Edward's, and informal group therapy sessions would ensue, with the guys sitting around, liberally lubricated, attempting to be open and honest with each other. Since they were all male, the fake camaraderie was generally of the locker room variety, with the talk turning inevitably to the women in their lives, or more usually, the women who had been in their lives, and the conversation was peppered with expressions like 'ball-breaker', 'prick-tease' and 'tight-pussy', or whatever terms of disparagement and backhanded compliments men used back then, and presumably still do, now. Edward did not deign to join in, however much he may have secretly sympathised. He is, after all, from a good family. Unlike me. Even if we are both, technically, from the same family. But had I been there, I would not have been able to contribute either, not having, or ever having had, a woman. Unless, of course, I'd lied.

Edward did pick up and play his guitar for these laggards and lowlifes, though, if he was not too much the worse for wear to see straight and get it together. His version of 'Just Like a Woman' was particularly popular with this crew, who were obliged to listen, like it or not, holed up as they were in his pad. Then he would slope off and fall into bed, groping for and clutching onto Dub the Teddy, before succumbing as soon as his head hit the pillow to a sound, profound sleep.

He slept to dream, and what dreams he had, of the face, so unbelievably beautiful, of a girl he would prefer to forget, and of the face, so uncannily like his, of a brother he had never met.

It goes without saying that these nearly nightly escapades caused his work to suffer. On several occasions, after mild to severe reprimands from Inhuman Recourses, he undertook to do better and be more attentive, and not to miss so many days. But it was plain to all and sundry that he was letting things slide terminally. For he found he did not much care if he did get fired. He felt it was time for a change, and he was beginning to surmise intuitively that even if you do not lift a finger to seek an escape from your unbearable situation, sooner or later one usually presents itself anyway.

Not that he did not mean to keep the promises he made when he made them, after the dire warnings from his office manager. But there is a big difference, as far as I can see, between hungover man and unhungover man, between man sober and man drunk. When you've got a raging hangover, you never want to look at another drink for as long as you live, unless you've got to the stage of taking the cure the following morning to see you right and get you through, something Edward hadn't quite started doing yet. In this state, you feel so pained and dim-witted, such a useless asshole scumbag, that you can really believe all the old guff you hear yourself coming out with about cutting down, or giving up.

But when clouds clear and your hangover abates, and you're clean and sober once again, you find yourself fancying a couple of drinks. You think how nice it is to be pleasantly pissed, and even allow of the salutary benefits of going on a good tear every now and again. And when you're jarred, well, when you're jarred you're always glad you're jarred, so glad that you can't stop and want to keep going, pushing past that moment of euphoric madness that resides at the epicentre of every bout of drunkenness, the moment you've been pursuing, the crystallising moment of clarity when everything, suddenly and briefly for just that one single second, makes some kind of crazy, garbled, absolute sense, on into eventual dumb, numb oblivion. There's no arguing with you then. All discretion is thrown to the wind, you realise that rules are made only to be broken, and your resolutions go flying off out the window.

Or so it seems to me. For, although I like a drink or two every so often, and have even been drunk once or twice on rare occasions, I myself have never sought solace or delight in mere alcohol. It does not thrill me at all, as they used to say. All things in moderation, as some still say.

Nor did Edward and this sulphurous chap, who was so successfully insinuating himself into his life, draw the line at cans of beer. There is such a diversity of beverages, so inventive is humankind at devising ways to get out of its collective head, and Wylie encouraged Eddie, as he had rather irritatingly taken to calling him, to sample as many of them as he could manage. Eddie – sorry, Edward – felt it incumbent upon himself to comply, insofar as his meagre income would allow. So the beers they downed to bring them cheer were frequently the products of some highly exotic breweries, and the wines they consumed were more often than not fine, as they searched out some really rare vintages. They kept up this pioneering spirit when it came to the wide range of shorts, and whiskeys, brandies, vodkas, gins, rums, and many other firewaters kept them warm. As for cocktails, once they got started on these concoctions, the parameters were infinite and the permutations endless. Indeed, when one considers the variety of drinks readily available, and the amount of words in the language for drinking and being drunk, it is a wonder that those licensed fools who provide me with my hobbyhorse (shhh! – shrinks) have such a big thing about alcohol and inebriation. Drinking is the norm, rather than an aberration. At least, it seems to me to be so in these isles. If psychiatrists are failed doctors, then those specialising in addiction are failed psychiatrists.

So these fine fellows progressed on their merry way, carousing and getting up to no good, night after night. Edward was not without enough perspicacity to perceive that Wylie was a bad influence on him, as his mother would undoubtedly have told him. But in lieu of anyone or anything more interesting in his life at that time, he accepted this guy's presence, and decided to go with the flow, at least for the time being. He was getting to the stage where he couldn't stand to be alone. Unlike his brother, who had long been at the stage where he couldn't stand being in company. Edward was still fairly naive in many respects, and had about him the air of an innocent abroad. Edmund, yours truly, knew everything, as I have already told you, and so I am a guilty stay-at-home. Or in my room in this house, which is the only home I've ever known.

Whatever about Edward tolerating Wylie's hanging around, it might be interesting for the nonce to speculate about why Wylie continued to stay on. I know the answer, but I'm not going to tell you. At least, not yet. But perhaps you should ponder whether he had a motive, or if he was just being bone idle lazy.

So twisted would Edward become that sometimes he could almost imagine that Wylie was his friend.

Signs of the spring of the year were suddenly everywhere in the air, and the rapturous, riotous ferment of the new season turned the young men's fancy to planning a summer holiday. They both felt that they needed one, although neither voiced the opinion that it was from each other.

They settled on Greece as their destination, since it was relatively inexpensive, but not too plebeian. They flew to Athens, and after a couple of days sight-seeing, took off for the islands, like millions of others before and since. My brother's trip to the cradle of western civilisation with his buddy furnishes me with an opportunity to dig deep into the well-stocked myth kitty and draw on the overflowing image bank. But I will not indulge it. Oh all right then, but only a little.

They strolled around the Plaka, and Wylie haggled with vendors for knick-knacks to take back as gifts, although who he would give them to was not altogether clear. Edward didn't bother bargaining, he just paid the asking price for a beautifully designed ethnic rug, for lolling on at the beach. They took in the Acropolis, before taking a ferryboat from the Piraeus out to Ios, which Edward soon came to suspect was an acronym for 'Irish Over Seas', such was the amount of his compatriots he bumped into there. They lay in the sun by day, sleeping off their hangovers and having the occasional swim to keep cool, and got paralytic by night, as you do. There were girls too, since holiday flings were only to be expected, indeed were almost part of the package, even if the boys were not booked on an all-in deal. Sun, sea, sand and sex, that was the magic formula promoted in all the travel agents' glossy brochures, even if they hadn't bought their break from one of them.

One night, awash with booze in the midst of yet another Dionysian revel, in a bar-cum-night-club rejoicing in the name of, I kid you not, The Narcissus, I found myself inside Edward as I so often did, trying to feel what he was feeling. This time I entertained few doubts that my perceptions were genuine for, accustomed though I was to these jaunts, this time it frightened me, such was the strength of his emotions as they broke over him and washed back on to me.

He looked up at his own reflection in a revolving mirror-ball, and I could see him seeing himself, and not liking what he saw. The music dipped and swelled, and the big dark thoughts assailed him, as he wondered why minor keys are so melancholic, and then marvelled at the lacerating force of a 9th chord, as it chops and cuts through your being over a loud disco beat, and why it should make you want to race in and join the great human dance. He wanted to gather up the shattered shards of himself he saw spinning there, reifying and ramifying, and put them together again into some sort of beautiful unified mosaic. He was lonely, and the only way to alleviate this loneliness was to place his own heart on the line. It dawned on him in a flash in the half-light of dusk that he was going to have to learn how to love, if he was to know how to live in this world at all. In this endeavour, I remember thinking, he stood a far better chance of success than me.

He also had a dim inkling that there was some strange intertwining between falling in love, rather than just having sex, and telling a tale that touched people, rather than just cleverly putting words on paper. But I am giving you a moving story, yet I'm not in love. At least, I don't think so. I don't believe in it. Or so I believe. So how could I be? Or am I just typing, to put in time and fill in space? You are moved, aren't you? You're not sitting there chanting *We shall not, we shall not be moved*, are you?

All of which reminds me of another pet theory of mine, that the world would be a much better place if fewer people polluted pages by blackening them with words. But try telling that to my brother, in the state he was in then. Try telling it to me, the way I am now. Then why am I doing it? Well, the paper will be wasted anyway. He had been waiting to start writing until he was good and ready. I had already started writing, regardless of whether I was good or ready or not. Everything comes to him who waits, they say. But you can't wait forever. Or else nothing comes to you. And nothing will come of nothing. He didn't want to feel nothing. He wanted to feel something called love.

He looked over at Wylie through clouds of drunken befuddlement. Had he seen that man's eye stray over and catch Mary's, that faraway night in another dive like this one?

Lying on the beach on the last day of their all too short fortnight away, Edward realised, with the youthful clarity of the still just about young, that he was not getting any younger. He loved basking in the heat of the sun, shining down from up in the sky, feeling its rays fall across his shoulders, and breathing the fresh air and inhaling the intoxicatingly aromatic smells of the flowers and the fruits of the forest and the salt of the earth and the sea, and decided determinedly there and then that he must look for some way of prolonging this experience, of making it last as long as he would like it to, of turning it into as permanent a fixture as possible. The power of bucolic idyll is not to be underestimated. Although, speaking personally, I hated this scene. If I were ever, inadvertently, to find myself anywhere near a beach, I would opt to sit in the shade. I would also move around as little as possible, to keep the pesky sand from getting between my toes and into my crotch.

However, this simple desire to be warm was enough of a goad to make my brother want to do something about changing his life, rather than waiting for something to happen; and, when coupled with the dreadful prospect of returning to the dreariness of his life in London, it became an overriding imperative that something had better change, or he had better change something, soon and for the better. Having had to get out of Ireland, he would now have to get out of England.

The bulging boner he was nursing inside his swimming trunks, which had been easily brought on by the soaring temperature as he lay there prone, and was languidly pressing into that rug he had picked up back in Athens, may have contributed somewhat to his brief bout of decisiveness.

3

"IT IS RAINING. You have brought an umbrella."
"???"
"An um-brel-la."
"???"
(Pointing): "Um-brel-la."

***

"It is a fine day. It is not raining. You have not brought an umbrella."
"???"
"Um-brel-la."
"???"
"When it is pouring rain, you bring an umbrella."

***

"The cat sits on the mat."
"???"
"The cat catches a rat. On the mat. Fancy that."
"???"
"You're a prat. Drat. Look: there is tea in the pot. This is a pot. There is tea in it. I am pouring you some tea."
"Umbrella!"
"???"
"When it is pouring rain, I bring an umbrella."

***

"It is time to finish. See you tomorrow. Goodbye."
"Goodbye. Thank you."
"My pleasure. Don't forget your umbrella."
"???"
(Pointing): "Um-brel-la."

This is Edward, with a student, teaching the English language, in a classroom overlooking the Protestant Cemetery, where cats congregate around the grave of John Keats, as if they know the remains of a friend are buried there. 'Here lies one whose name was writ in water' reads the inscription below the poet's name on the tombstone, written in stone. We are indeed in the Eternal City of Rome. But how on earth did my brother get here?

Returning to London from his holiday in the sun, he adjudged the best way of leaving it behind again for warmer climes was to do a course in the Teaching of English as a Foreign Language, and then look for a job abroad. Implementing this plan shortly became imperative for several reasons.

Edward was drinking less now, since he had to go from his job during the day to his classes in the evening, although he managed to make some indent on making up the deficit at the weekends. But it was gradually becoming apparent to him that alcohol was not the sole intoxicant favoured by flatmate Wylie, who was still *in situ*, still with no visible means of support other than the modest subsistence doled out by the state. But the trainee teacher was nevertheless still a little surprised, and even mildly shocked, to arrive back to his abode unexpectedly one Friday afternoon to witness his partner in crimes of debauchery and decadence with a syringe in his right hand, filling up with blood through a needle stuck in a vein in his left arm, as he shot up some smack. Wylie looked up at him and, through a knowing, toothy grin, inquired, "Want a hit?"

It is, of course, a big deal to take heroin. That is, if you can get a big deal. It's bad for the fabric of society, you know, not to mention the health of the individual. But then, there *is* no such thing as society. The people who order society know this, which is presumably why they defend it and want to improve it. So you want to change the world? Best to start with yourself. The individual must be held responsible for his or her own choices. So why not take heroin? Horse, horse, my kingdom for some horse.

Edward shrugged his shoulders. Try anything once, that was a good motto, once. The bad thing about heroin is that it's good, once. Then it just gets to be a big bore, like everything else, a simple means of controlling people and being controlled by them, depending on where your link fits into the food chain, the chain of command, that great chain of being and nothingness. Or so I surmise, from Edward's brief dalliance with said chemical substance (dextropropoxyphene dihydrocodeine to you). I myself have never gone near the stuff. Why should I, when I had him to do it for me?

Sitting down opposite his tempter, Edward rolled up his sleeve. Not for him the preliminary sniffing, snorting and smoking of the tentative tyro. No apple-licker him, he got straight down to business and bit into the fruit of the tree of the knowledge of good and evil. An apple a day, as they say.

We are, you may recall, in the very early eighties, just before the AIDS virus became the big scare, as the scourge of happy hedonists everywhere. All the same, Edward, fastidious as ever, did not relish the prospect of sharing someone else's intravenous drug paraphernalia. But Wylie, tellingly, just happened to have a fresh set to hand. Be prepared, that was his motto. He liked to do good works. It helped him to do his dirty work. He produced the clean works, still sealed and shrink-wrapped inside its sachet. He cooked up the concoction, prepared the sumptuous feast. Edward felt as though Wylie was playing the role of high priest, or was it warlock, initiating the acolyte that was him into some ancient mysterious rite. Except that he was sure that this little ritual between alchemist and apprentice was not something he would be acting out again, with him taking either part. He who sups with the devil must use a long spoon. Needs must when the devil drives.

How does one set about describing the euphoria of the heroin rush to someone who has never experienced it? And how does one avoid redundancy when discussing it with someone who has? I should be in an ideal position to answer both these questions, having both experienced it, through my brother, and not, since I'm still myself and I didn't do it. But I find that I cannot either answer the questions or do the explaining. But wait a minute, Edward has both experienced it, since he's himself and he did it, and not, through me, too (if, indeed, it can be said that one has not experienced an experience through someone else's not experiencing it). Just as we have both experienced and not experienced all the other's experiences (and all our own?). So hang on now, and I'll hand you over to him:

> When Wylie banged me up, I lay back and saw God, not that I
> believe in that guy, of course, but you know what I mean. Actually,

I didn't really see God, I just felt great. And I felt great because I felt nothing. I mean I felt no pain. God and nothing must be the same thing. If arousal and orgasm are a few minutes of pure undiluted pleasure, a release before going back to the aches and pains and anxieties and tensions of everyday existence, imagine having the greatest pain-killer known to man coursing through your system, something that banishes all pain, and so renders the relentless pursuit of pleasure laughably superfluous. What heaven! Until, of course, you come back down and either have to take some more or else go back to being normal. And if you want more, you have to start pursuing it, and the money to buy it. Depressingly just like sex, in this regard, at the end of the day. But it's great while it lasts, again like sex. And though sex may be just as habit-forming, and perhaps just as costly and injurious to the health over the medium to long term, when you consider the lengths some people go to to get it and maintain a regular source of supply (sometimes they even go so far as to get married), sex probably has the advantage, even if only because it is more socially acceptable, in most circles, under certain circumstances, and less deleterious to the health in the immediate to short term. Although seeking out and then having to conceal something that's prohibited often adds to the thrill of doing it. But that kick wears off too, after a while. But, all in all, I'm glad I tried smack, just the once. It's so nice. Hey, it can even be addictive.

All right, you've guessed. That's not him, it's just me pretending to be him. So I could be him, or could have been him. Just like I could be you, or you could be me. But you never really know what it's like to be someone else, because it's always you imagining what it's like to be someone else. And your 'you' gets in the way. As I told you from the outset, we can enter each other's minds, Edward and I, but we cannot 'communicate' directly in any conventional sense of the word. (*Edward and I.* Good title that, for an anonymous, confessional, salacious little novel.) All my descriptions of what he was thinking and feeling about what was happening are just the speculative workings of my imagination. Is it all my imagination? Was it ever anything else?

I imagine it was that line about rendering 'the relentless pursuit of pleasure laughably superfluous' that gave the game away. It's a dead giveaway, along with my cynical notion about the motivation for conjugal union. Too much of my voice uttering my vision, my use of language expressing my way of looking at things, and not enough of his. But what were his, and how could you be sure they were his, except through me? Perhaps he shared my ideas about the ego junk of ambition, and would have approved of a junk that would banish ego, and set him free from the burden of ambition. Money, sex, power: these are what people pursue, in the belief that getting them makes you happy. Everyone wants to get rich, famous and laid, at least up until a certain age. But do these things deliver the goods? For a while, I suppose, they do. But then you want more of them, and that makes you unhappy all over again, until you get some more, and so on and so forth, *ad infinitum,* in a *reductio ad absurdum.* But what do I know? I've never had much of any of them. I've never even had love. Perhaps he would not have agreed with me after all.

So I copped out, and you caught me out, of giving a first-hand account of Edward taking heroin. (First hand by me, I mean, not him.) But then, there are some who would say that taking heroin is a cop-out in itself. If that is so, then out of what is it a cop? Would anyone like to know my views on this topic? Thought not, but here goes, for what it's worth.

Essentially, I think Edward's body is his own, to do with what he wants. As is mine. Would his description, having had the experience, have been any better than mine, having experienced it only through him? He felt serenely happy for a little while, is all I can find to say. But that is no small thing. Although something told him, clever boy that he is, that it might not be prudent to try replicating the intensity of that first time. What would his mother say, after all, if he became a junkie? Or, for that matter, his father? You may find his resolve uncharacteristically mature, for a young man who still bore many hallmarks of the ingenuous along with those of the ingenious, for someone whom you regard as foolhardy enough to mess around with those powerful powders in the first place.

But maybe there are hidden depths to the guy that you did not realise were lurking there. Perhaps he just does not fit into your neat little pre-ordained pigeonholes about what people are supposed to be like and not like, what they should and should not do, in your great scheme of things. Maybe he does not even fit into mine. Perhaps I don't even fit into mine. But then, I have hardly a prejudice to my name. That's my only prejudice. If you would like to see him getting the nonsense knocked out of him, then don't look at me. You've come to the wrong place. The nonsense is what's interesting, as far as I can see. And if you think these musings are composed entirely of *non sequiturs*, then that's tough. Since when should conclusions follow logically from premises? It's the *sequiturs* that bother me, when they fall into place too readily. You are stuck with me, as I am. As am I. My mind is my own, to do with what I want. As is his.

After this interlude, divers circumstances quickly compassed to push our Edward on into uncharted territory. Things started disappearing from the flat, and not being replaced. If Wylie was taking and even dealing in proscribed narcotics, and bringing unwholesome types to his lodgings for that purpose, Edward did not relish the prospect of being implicated in these nefarious activities when the constabulary came a-calling, as he knew they surely would, sooner or later. He could have kicked Wylie on to the street, after a more polite intimation at eviction didn't work, but that might have led to more trouble in the long run. He hadn't the stomach for a confrontation, especially when Wylie could so easily point the finger at him, if he took it upon himself to go to the powers that be. He also knew that having this guy around who had long since worn out his welcome was potentially detrimental to his own health and equilibrium, since it was so easy to succumb to taking advantage of what was on offer. Things were ready to fall apart at the seams, once again.

Then just as he was coming to the end of his night classes, he was 'let go' from his job. Personnel said he wasn't 'applying himself' during the day, whatever that meant. Possibly it referred to him falling asleep over preparing a report on sales figures for his boss. Or to drooling too long and absent-mindedly over a seated secretary's swinging legs. So what over-indulgence in high times hadn't done for him, trying to get out of the rut he was in did: got him sacked. (Although all that over-indulgence may have been just as much an attempt at getting out of the rut as taking night classes.) Luckily, he had just enough money to tide him over until he sat his exams and got his certificate, and then the school offered him a number of different jobs in several appealing locations, so well did he do.

Barcelona or Madrid? Munich or Milan? He wound up choosing

139

Rome as his next home away from home. True, it was not the rural idyll that had inspired him in Greece, but at least it would be warm. He could always take up residence in other places some other time, should he feel so inclined. So he bailed out, just as he could no longer keep bailing. He did not want to wind up out on bail or, worse still, find himself incarcerated at Her Majesty's pleasure in gaol, for crimes he had not committed, or had had very little to do with committing. It did not suit him to be an accessory after the fact.

"Thanks a bunch for putting me up, mate," declared Wylie as Edward took his leave, despite his ill-concealed pique at having to parasitically search out new digs. Putting up with you, more like, is what went through Edward's mind, although he did not give voice to it.

"I must pop over and visit you as soon as I can get it together," ventured the sponger. In a pig's arse, friend, thought Edward, tendering him a false address. He could be quite tough, when the occasion demanded. Sometimes, he could be just like me.

***

"Rearrange the following words to form a well-known English phrase or saying...."

***

"Complete the sentence...."

***

"Repeat after me...."

With what banalities was his working day not filled? But he had not been doing it long enough to become bored with it just yet. Besides, he was away from going nowhere in Ireland, because there was nowhere to go, and away from going nowhere in England, because of where there was to go. Maybe he was still only going nowhere, but it did not seem that way. Or it seemed a more pleasant journey. This would be his way of earning a living for the next few years, just as the peripatetic life would also be his lot. Frequent travel so often gives the illusion of not standing still.

Besides, imparting the basic building blocks of the language was not without some wonderful moments of spontaneous and uproarious humour too, for both of us.

"What is your favourite place in Italy?"

"I like nipples."

He liked Rome, for a time anyway. He was taking delight in what he took to be freedom, getting a kick out of what passed for fun. Who am I to put a damper on his enthusiasm? It is not for me to go spoiling his enjoyment.

He shared a small apartment with another teacher, a couple of streets away from his school. It was comfortable enough, and had all mod cons, although neither of them bothered to keep it very clean.

Must I bother doing the other chap? What's the point of my describing every new person, when he is constantly moving on, leaving them behind, never to meet again? They got on well enough, most of the time, is all you need to know, although they did come to blows once when, in drink, Edward kept chiding the guy about a pair of tatty sunglasses he was wearing, and was dealt a sharp puck on the chin for his trouble. Such is life. That's human nature.

He would go *fare passeggiata* on the Via Veneto, and stroll in the park of the Villa Borghese. He made sure to see all the sights, and sites, although he quickly learned to avoid them, the hordes of pilgrims he was forever falling over getting on his nerves after a while. The grandeur that was Rome is all fine and well, but he preferred to abandon the bands of tourists to the exploitation of their traps, and head down to the southern suburb of EUR, where the bombastic style of the buildings, so overblown to the modern eye, appealed to his taste for kitsch. Instigated by *Il Duce*, wouldn't you know, then interrupted by the war, the scheme was eventually completed in the 1950s. By the time my brother frequented the area it was already home to the administrative offices of many government departments, plus the odd museum. I cannot say as I liked it much myself. I prefer to save my needless rhetorical extravagance for language. I put the art into articulate, and into artifice; not to mention artificial.

Another reason he liked rambling around EUR was that not so very far beyond its clean wide streets, there were lots of hookers to be found loitering around, their short skirts fluttering in the breeze, ballooning over legs perched enticingly on high heels. He tried to take some comfort there, once or twice, but gave it up as a bad job, since alfresco couplings in alleyways, parks and up against walls were not really his *tazza di te*, not proving very comfortable, and so not very comforting at all.

Brothels are illegal in Italy, do you see, and the women would not go back to your place with you, or at least not with him. So he was deprived of the careless pleasure of walking into a *louche* lounge and being asked by the madam of the establishment to choose, for his amorous amusement, between a dark one, a fair one or a red one. Or being told he need not bother choosing, he could have one of each, or two or three of the same. For a consideration. Oh well. Most of the clients screwed the whores in their cars, but this option was not open to him, since he did not have his own transport. Sex in cars is big in Italy, he discovered, whether it is of the paid for variety, or between courting couples. Almost everyone lives with their parents until they get married, or until they're nearly thirty, whichever comes first, so you can hardly blame the young folks, now can you? There were also some Brazilian transsexuals on offer in the countryside the far side of EUR, but his taste did not run to such exotic lengths.

Nor did girlfriends feature during this extended Roman working holiday, surprising enough considering the ubiquity of beautiful women in the city. Maybe he was saving himself for Ms Right, or not putting himself out by dallying with Ms Wrongs, particularly if they did not put out, or as we used to say back here, do the trick. But how can you tell whether they're right or wrong unless you dally? You can't, but you can hazard a guess, educated or otherwise, as to how right or wrong someone might be for you, just by looking and listening. There's no harm in looking out, or in listening in. Most of the women in Rome didn't pay him much attention. In fact, they stared right through him.

More than once Edward could have been discovered dawdling home through the back streets in the small hours in a state of high insobriety. Lying scuttered in a gutter in Rome, staring up at the stars, he came closest to being the happiest he had as yet ever been.

Being as how his parents were of the Catholic persuasion, and had brought him up in that faith, he did make a point of popping along to St Peter's Basilica in the Vatican, if only just the once, just to see how they were still doing things there in those days.

Finding suspiciously few people knocking around this huge edifice of worship, he quickly ascertained that that day was the day for audiences with the Pope himself, which took place in a large chamber off to the side. The venue was thronged when he arrived there, so he stood at the back to watch the hordes of expeditions that had come there from every corner of the globe, just to see the man who is, for them, God's representative on earth.

Their leader sat hunched up in a big sedan chair on the altar, a mere dot from where Edward was standing, and read out the names of the places from where the pilgrimages had come. Each party took the enunciation of their own place-name as the cue to commence whooping and hollering at the top of their voices, ably encouraged by a rabble-rouser positioned in the pulpit. Then the Pope gave them a general blessing, making their whole journey worthwhile.

To my brother, and I must say, to me too, it seemed like the perfect incarnation of a cosmic, comic game-show. All the scene lacked to make it complete, and compete with television, was a giant wheel of fortune that the faithful could spin. But no one noticed the missing piece, and they all went home satisfied, having got their jollies. Even Edward found the entire spectacle quite amusing, if not wholly uplifting. Then it was time to go.

His institute offered him a job with a salary increase in another of their schools, in a nameless country town just outside Milan. Not that the town didn't have a name, but the name is unimportant, as is the place. What mattered to him was that it was near the city. Was the city any more important, as a name or a place, than the town? It was to him. He accepted the deal. He was ready for the country, so long as he could make frequent excursions to the city.

Should I give you my impressions of his impressions of the city and the town? Why go describing every new place, when he is changing them perpetually, not staying anywhere for long?

Here, I will give you some of what you really want. I will set forth in words a particular person and place, and supply lots of delicious detail. I will do this thing because they will prove to be significant, the place if only because it is where he met the person, the person not merely because he met her in that place. Although often I don't describe the people and places that prove to be the most significant of all.

Bar Magenta was where his eyes first fell on her. It was a big roomy bohemian art deco hang-out with high mirrored walls and a black-and-white tiled floor, situated at a V in the road with tables and chairs scattered all along outside in both directions, where the measures were generous and the company good. A couple of cocktails there and you were anybody's, among the students, media types and expatriates. She was sitting with some friends of a new-found Italian friend of his, so they joined the circle and were introduced.

Her name was Laura. Perhaps you have met her before, somewhere else, or was that someone else? Maybe you already know her intimately, or are you confusing her with another person entirely? This Laura's hair was the colour of blackest coal, a shiny, slightly wavy, crowning glory, cascading over her shoulders. She had those dark brown eyes, flashing and sparkling in the light as she rolled them this way and that, focusing successively on each person gathered around the table as they spoke. Her face was pale, like a porcelain china doll's, made of fresh, delicate skin, with a little *retroussé* nose resting above wide red-painted lips. Her figure, while quite full, stopped short of being over-ample, meaning she could best be imagined as a cuddly armful. Her legs, from what he could see of them, were not long but still well-proportioned, with pleasing calves swaying below a bunched-up black skirt. A white silk blouse and a black suede jacket and black leather boots comprised the remainder of her outfit, and she wore these clothes with casual ease, comfortable in them rather than constrained. An amber stone hung at the end of a narrow thong around her neck, dangling in her cleavage, and her fingers were adorned with rings, one of silver with green agate, one of gold with an emerald gem. Do you know her now?

Why was he subjecting her to such a thorough scrutiny? Ask rather how could he help himself from doing so. Even in the first five or ten minutes of being within her ambit, feeling the trilling cadences of her voice trickle over him, he was seriously smitten. She was already, for him, an obvious object of desire. She was the one for him. If she wasn't someone else's.

And what was her voice saying, in her native Italian? It emerged that she had just graduated from the university, having studied English and German. Now she was going to live in Paris for a while, to improve her French. The clincher came when, on learning where he was from, she announced, "I like very much the Irish writers I have read – Joyce and Heaney. Also the Irish rock groups, U2 and The Virgin Prunes. I would like to go there one day."

This was music to our man's ears. We were now moving into the mid-eighties, when you could hardly go anywhere on the planet without being aware of the unprecedented rise to near global prominence of certain home-grown, sort-of-homecoming showbiz stellar-types, who were intent on a bid for world domination. This was the cue for Edward to impress with his store of lore about having seen this fab four playing in the Dandelion Market, when they hadn't even cut a record and hadn't an arse in their trousers, and still walked the streets as mere mortals, and were still attending craw-thumping, no-fun, fundamentalist prayer meetings. He had been there at the beginning of that journey, too. He neglected to mention that he had been in the company of someone named Mary.

Then, next thing you know:

"I will be going to work in Paris soon too. Maybe we can meet."

That is Edward, again. He hadn't given much thought to going to Paris before that evening, let alone formed any definite intention of doing so soon. He had now.

Does his impulsiveness surprise you? It did me, then. But nothing would surprise me, now. At bottom, Edward did everything he did for love. He would do anything for love. He did it all for love. He even fell in love.

4

IN THE SPRING OF THAT YEAR Paris exuded its old world indifference and habitual decay, along with its modern bustle and annual rebirth. Faint sunshine filtered through the branches of trees, and shadows of leaves dappled the riverside pavements.

Edward took his bags off the bus that had brought him from the airport to the city centre, and then trudged off in search of a cheap hotel. He should really have put all this truck into a left luggage facility somewhere, for he was destroyed by the time he'd found a place to stay, and checked into it. Then, having had a rest and freshened up, washing his furrowed brow and bathing his weary feet, he set about attending to the business that was uppermost in his mind.

His heart was in his mouth as the tone purred in his ear, and then he heard a click, and the crackle of static kicked in over the hum of dead air on the live line between them.

"Hello, this is Edward. Is that Laura?"

"Edward? Oh, Edward from Ireland? Are you in Parigi? How are you?"

"Bene, grazie. And you?"

"Bene anche."

" ... "

" ... "

"Would you like to meet me sometime?"

"OK. I am busy tonight and tomorrow. Maybe Thursday?"

They fixed a time and a place. As you can see, although they had gone out together once or twice in Milan before she took off, and had a real good time, she was not exactly transfixed with expectation of his imminent arrival. But he was not about to let cautious embarrassment defeat him on his quest.

He spent the next couple of days scouring around schools, searching out work. He was lucky enough to isolate a source of income that would keep him going until something better turned up. Then he set about finding somewhere to live.

The night they met up he was in fairly capital mood, although more than a little nervous about how things might go with her, and still preoccupied with his hunt for affordable accommodation. What was going to happen? Would anything ever happen?

They greeted one another in English under the Colonne de Juillet, with its little golden statue of Liberty at the top, in the Place de la Bastille, near where she lived. He suggested going to a bar, and she brought him to Le Baron Rouge, a small, comfortable place with no pretensions, up the street from her apartment.

She was so beautiful in his eyes, even more so than the memory in his mind's eye told him she had been in Milan. He was enamoured yet again by her enamelled, perfectly straight, pearly-white teeth, that seemed to light up a room every time she parted her lips and smiled, her brown eyes dancing in animated accord with them. At such moments her face was like a freeze-frame from an advertisement, cunningly concocted by a crafty, almost too clever director, whose enthusiasm and ambition stretched to feature length proportions.

They drank, and spoke of their lives and their dreams, the way only people who are still almost young can do, with some hope that they might still find fulfilment somewhere, sometime in the future. They polished off a bottle of Merlot, and picked at canapés topped with sweet cheese. There was talk of going bar-hopping down the bright lights of nearby Rue de Lappe, but then a mutual realisation quietly flowed over them that they were having too good a time chatting away alone together to go swapping their surroundings for something more maniacally noisy. So another bottle was ordered, and they pulled a little closer.

She told him of her mad family, just as stifling but loving as his own, from which she was trying to distance herself. She was teaching too, but didn't want to do it for the rest of her life. She suspected she'd go back to Italy in a year or maybe two, and try to get into television or radio. He went so far as to confide that he would like to write books. Increased intake of alcohol, especially in convivial company, makes us trust to the truth of cliché.

And then they kissed, and canoodled, falling headlong into each other's arms, like excitable children let out early from kindergarten. So enwrapped did these grateful babies get in their rapture that even the broad bounds of Parisian propriety dictated that they take leave of her local, pronto. The bar-keep told them politely to give it up, or go, with a finality that would put you in mind of Dublin.

It would be oh-so-very-easy to say they shared a night of love like no other ever before, and that their lives were transformed forevermore. But it doesn't happen like that, now does it? This night, he didn't even get beyond her hall door.

"I have to work early in the morning," she explained to him at the bottom of her staircase, "and I don't want to be up all night."

The white light of a fluorescent strip on the next landing cast a garish shadow through the rusty metal rail of the banisters.

"But I'd like to see you at the weekend," she added, mock-coquettishly, and kissed him again, in the way for which the French have given their name to the world: deeply.

They made another date, and he wandered off in search of a taxi to splash out on. Was she only making an excuse, stringing him along, or was she just, by her own standards, playing her cards right? Was she teasing or was she serious, or was she teasing because she was serious?

The funny thing is, he found that he didn't care. It was not a case of not caring in the usual too-cool-to-give-a-damn kind of way. He was discovering the positive virtue of not caring, of accepting the way certain situations came about and turned out with a sovereign equanimity. What matter if he had to wait for a few more days for a much sought after consummation? What matter moreover if ultimately, unlikely though it seemed it would be, he had waited in vain. He had pursued her as far as Paris, and that indicated a kind of commitment (although, granted, she wasn't to know that he hadn't really been going to Paris until he'd met her). But perhaps it was the commitment that was important, not the outcome. He was beginning to understand that human relationships are not investment banking, even if sometimes you do have to cut your losses. This is an insight entirely lost on me, I needn't tell you.

Whatever happened, he was in the heart of the city that he had always known in his heart he would one day return to, and live in. And now maybe he might even love in it too. This Paris *au printemps* was proving to be not just another case of *déjà vu*. Was she the one that he'd been waiting for?

The fly on the wall sees it all. I'm a fly, crawling around inside his cranium. Can I tell you what I can see from this unique and unlikely vantage-point? Is it possible to make you feel what I feel he now feels? In other words, can I do love? I didn't do a very convincing job with him and Mary, did I? But then again, maybe that love wasn't true, wasn't mixed equally. Or maybe I just thought it wasn't true. Or maybe they just weren't ready. The ripeness is all. Will I ever be ready? I am a seedy old solipsist, a curmudgeonly young fogey. All this talk of Edward's new-found commitment trips uncomfortably over, rather than from, my forked tongue, if not my cloven hoof. I don't know which is worse: the general farce of men chasing women, or the greater farce of women playing hard to get. This is one of the main differences between him and me. This is how he thinks: 'Isn't it amazing that every woman you see in the street was naked this morning before putting on her clothes? Every man too, for that matter.' Whereas I think: 'So what?' This is more of how he thinks: 'Isn't it astounding that every person in the world is the result of an act of sexual intercourse between two other people?' Whereas I think: 'No'. The heart's a wonder, to be sure, as is having the heart to be able to wonder. He was capable of, had a capacity for, love, right from the very start. It is one of his many talents. I didn't, right from the off. It is one of my many defects. Will either of us ever change? Now he must learn how to use his gift, or it will atrophy and die. He needs lessons in love. But from whom will he get them? I am hardly the one to give them to him. But maybe I am too hard on myself. Maybe I too had the gift, but have not had the opportunity to exercise it, since my passages of joy became fountains of sorrow. Since I was mutilated, I've mutated. Now I'm going to mutate some more. If only I could help him. In that way, I might help myself. For, despite all the reverses I've suffered in life, I still remain not entirely unconvinced and incredulous of human goodness, in some humans, if not in most of them. If not in myself. Even in myself. I could be wrong, it wouldn't be the first time, but I think that this Laura is good. I could be wrong again, it would be the umpteenth time, but I think that by doing him and Laura well, I would be doing him a good turn. But would that, in turn, help me? Can anyone ever really help anyone else? The people who want to do most good usually wind up doing most harm. Can they even help themselves? Self-help is the watchword these days. But maybe reciprocal recompense is not the reason I should be doing it in the first place. How unreasonable when reason does not furnish the reasoner with reasons. But I do need help, from some source or other. I need lessons in love. But from whom will I get them? He is hardly the one to give them to me. For the thing which I greatly feared is come upon me, and that which I was afraid of is come unto me. In the middle of the journey of our life I found myself in a dark wood, for I had lost the right path. Actually, I lost the plot a long time ago. I think this is what is commonly called the dark night of the soul. I have what is usually diagnosed as the sickness unto death.

So my thoughts turn to self-destruction. Will I destroy myself? Would I hurt a fly? To be, or not to be, that is, famously, the only philosophical question worth taking seriously. That's a laugh, since there are many other problems concerning the nature of existence and the meaning of life which you could apply yourself to researching and dwelling over diligently, if you had a mind to go in for that sort of thing. It is also a laugh in another way, since you would probably not be very much the wiser when you had completed your investigations and had done with your pondering. But I am game for a laugh. Most people's lives are so shitty, they need a good laugh now and again, if not at others, then at themselves, just to be able to keep on going. In this regard, at least, I will prove no exception. So I will give you a laugh, like I should have been doing all along. But you can't have a laugh if you're always taking things too seriously. So let's forget the debate, and get stuck straight into the action. In a spirit of gentle fun, I will have a go at doing away with myself, or at any rate doing myself some not inconsiderable damage. Such a merry jape should give us both a bit of a giggle.

But now I am faced with deciding what means to employ to make an end of myself. How will I do this destroying? Has anyone seen the insecticide? Poisoning would be good, so long as it was quick and painless, or an overdose of sleeping pills, although that's pretty anaemic, and I might only go into a coma, or even wake up, like that chap in the Good Book who rises from the dead, what's this his name is?...Lazarus?...Jesus?...Edmund? I could cut my throat with a sharp knife, or get some rope and hang myself on the nearest tree. I could hurl myself off a high cliff, or throw myself off the top of a tall building, and let gravity prevail, or simply drown myself by walking into the sea. Or take a shower, the kind with gas instead of water, or the kind with water where you can keep turning up the temperature ever so slowly and imperceptibly, until it's so hot it starts melting the skin from your bones, but you don't notice because you've got used to it gradually.

But all these are all far too dramatic for me. Besides, I would have to leave my room in order to execute them, which is something I do only very reluctantly, and with increasing infrequency. I could stick my head out the window in the hope of being hit by a falling object, but I'd never be that lucky. Full-scale defenestration would be fruitless too, since it's only a two-storey house, so the most I could do is break a few bones and give myself severe concussion. Still and all, I could do worse, I suppose. I know: I'll take a running jump at myself, and dash my head against the bedroom wall. That way, all the impact will be at the same point and, you never know, I might do myself a proper mischief by splitting my skull open and hitting something really crucial, like a frontal lobe, or the hypothalamus, or some internal circuitry. Lots of irreparable brain damage.

Clear the decks, gangway, look out now, here goes: I run, head-first, bull-like, bullet-like, and heave the noddle into the plasterboard. WHACK! THWACK! THUD! Ah, the poor sconce aches. Stars orbit my crown, and I am like a dazed cartoon character sitting in a heap on the ground. Give me a minute to collect myself. Let me hold my head in my hands.

Well, a preliminary examination seems to reveal that my suicide bid has been less than successful, although there does appear to be quite a decent ooze of blood coming from somewhere, if the smears on my fingers are anything to go by. I must tear up an old shirt, and contrive a bandage for the cuts and lacerations. The run up was too short for me to gain sufficient momentum to really harm myself. Even in this I fail. I am a tough nut to crack. I have a tough nut to crack. I am a nutter, and I am cracked. But I am too nutant to be much craic.

But maybe it was only a case of parasuicide, an instance of the kind of attention-seeking behaviour that should be interpreted by all right-thinking people as a desperate cry for help. But who is there to pay me any attention, except you? And what can you do, except listen? There is also my brother, of course, but he is just as hamstrung as you, when it comes to me, as am I when it comes to him. The only cry for help it was was a cry for help to do it properly, or else for the proffering of one good reason not to do it again. Reason falls down on the job, yet again. Please don't tell me that what I need is a psychiatrist. When did they ever have reasons for doing what they do, or for how they treat you? But hark, what's that I hear?

The Reader speaks: "If you kill yourself, I won't know what happens at the end of the story."

So I reply: "Be assured, I do not intend, at this late stage, to give way and start presenting you with anything so prosaic as a storyline."

The Reader persists: "I've come this far, and I hate to let any book defeat me. Finish what you started, and put me out of my misery."

I point out: "If I kill myself, the book will finish, and all your troubles will be over right away."

The reader counters: "But then I won't know what happens to Edward."

I caution: "Maybe you won't know anyway."

The Reader probes: "Because you don't know, or you won't tell me?"

I confide: "Both, possibly. Haven't you ever heard of improvisation? You know, making it up as you go along, taking a line, or a line of inquiry, for a walk. And haven't you ever heard of sheer bloody-mindedness?"

The Reader confirms: "That's a chance I'm prepared to take."

So I acquiesce. In spite of everything, I'll go on. I won't be making any further attempts on my life in the foreseeable future, at least not until we get this business over and done with, and out of the way once and for all. Not only because I might yet succeed, but also because I might damn near kill myself. Thank you for helping me.

Are you surprised that someone suffering from my recently sustained acute head injuries, to say nothing of my chronic state of physical and mental decay, can have what is, at times, such an elegant and ornate, if not very original, prose style? What did you expect? Three or four hundred pages of 'All work and no play makes Edmund a dull boy', repeated over and over again with psychotic intensity? What do you want me to tell you: 'If you thought this was weird up until now, you ain't seen nothing yet. If you thought I've been hallucinating all along, that was just for starters.'? No. I have striven, as I still strive, as I will continue to do, to keep up appearances, despite any feeble-mindedness, real or apparent. And how would you, or indeed I, know whether I had been, or am, hallucinating or not, anyway? Let's face it, it has been some considerable time now since I was last in my right mind or knew what I was talking about, so a little dent to the pate isn't going to make much discernible difference from all that went before.

But there has nevertheless been a subtle change in my apprehension (such an apt word here) of the real. In essence, I can no longer tell the difference between myth and reality. I have put on antic disposition. But the trouble with this strategy is that you don't know when I have it on, and when I've taken it off. Hell, sometimes even I don't know. So you don't know when to take me seriously. Shit, sometimes even I don't know that either. Maybe the whole thing is a put on. How ironic can you be with irony? When does irony stop being ironic? But if you know you're insane, *ipso facto* you're not. But thinking everyone else is mad except yourself is the greatest form of insanity there is. So I'm not really crazy, but I'm not the full shilling either.

Where does this leave you and me, as regards the story? How can I help anyone else, when I cannot even help myself? How can I help myself, when I cannot even help anyone else? But I would not be doing him and Laura anyway, he would be doing them himself (along with her). I would merely be reporting on what he does, albeit in my own imitable style, admittedly putting my own impersonal slant on it. But I don't go in much for do-it-yourself. I am not, whatever you may suppose to the contrary, a fly-by-night freelance from the pack of paparazzi. So it's all up to him. That's where I'm leaving it. I'm buzzing off. I'm fucked. Is he?

Which reminds me, how was he getting on with Laura?

Saturday night rolled around, none too soon, for either of them. They decided to go to the cinema. The film was *Alphaville*, the futuristic science fiction one about the secret agent who travels across space to find out what happened to his predecessor, and arrives in a city where they have a loveless society. Except the city that is Alphaville looks suspiciously like Paris. Was this film more applicable to him or me? He was in Paris, but he was looking for love. I have never been there, but I don't believe in love. But Paris is not Alphaville. Alphaville does not exist. Or if it does, it is in the imagined future. In which case, it may well have already come into existence by the time Edward met up with Laura, since the film was made in the early '60s. It certainly had, for me. But apparently not, for him.

Then they did take off down the aforementioned Rue de Lappe, and got through more tequila slammers than was strictly good for them, in bar after bar. Italians have the name of being uptight about booze, but this night she did not seem too concerned about conforming to national stereotype. He did, if one credits the reputation the Irish have for liking to drink a lot. But more probably, neither of them were worrying too much about where they came from, and what it meant, or what it was supposed to mean. They relaxed into each other, and her natural vivacity shone through, igniting with the gaiety all around. She was careful not to get too far gone, though, for fear it would interfere with her plans for later, and she was anxious he did not go too far over the top either, since those plans included him.

And they kissed, and kissed again, and went on kissing, until they agreed to beat a retreat to her flat. As they were leaving, Edward overheard some artists in a dark corner of the bar, complaining about the complacency of the philistine bourgeoisie, as is their wont.

And they made love. How great it must be to make love. To be able to produce something which is always in short supply, and for which there is always a pressing demand, is an unalloyed blessing. I cannot make it. Nor can I do it. But I can tell you what they made and did. But I won't, because I'm shy. A discreet veil is here drawn. But here's an approximation: it was like...oh, it wasn't like anything, if truth be told, except itself. Best simply to say it was beautiful. That sounds so banal, I know, but so would anything else I dared to say about it. Suffice it to say that they made enough to want to make more, but however much more they made, they couldn't get enough. Enough said.

And so a courtship began, if that is not too showily old-fashioned a word to use nowadays. He found a room to rent near her, and they saw each other almost every day. He lavished her with little presents, and did not count the cost. Almost every time he met her, he had something for her. (Stop sniggering, you dirty-minded deviants at the back.) She was not to know that this marked a profound change in his outlook. But she gave him things too, chief among which was the gift of teaching him how to give.

With the benefit of hindsight it is easy to say that he moved into her place too quickly, barely a month after they started to consort, but they weren't taking the long view back then. Besides, even if they had waited any longer, would they have lasted any longer? Such speculation is not only idle but also futile, as you know it is impossible to ever know. To live with a woman is, it is commonly agreed, one of the most difficult things a man can do. Compared with it, writing a novel is considered a piece of piss. Yet so many men do it, he thought: why not? As did I, with jotting this stuff down. His way is a thorny way, beside which mine is a seeming doddle. But if this is a cake walk, I wouldn't want to walk his way. Let me eat cake. If this is a milk run, I would run a million miles from one of those who can lactate. Call me a milksop. I cannot say what any of this is like from a woman's perspective. And what, while we're at it, has become of Edward's novel?

The first six months are paradise, of course, and this pair thought that they had died and gone to heaven. Then all those little things begin to irritate and annoy: the dead hair in the shower, the faecal stains on the toilet bowl. Our Edward was not yet man enough to handle the fact that his woman might moult and shit. Let alone bleed. Or that she might talk back to him, and put him in his place. Nor could she, when it came to him. Perhaps if those first few months had been more infernally difficult, or downright hell, they would have learned how to live through them, with each other, and come out the other side, to mature and endure. But that was not to be.

Still, it was nice while it lasted. He enjoyed living in Paris and, for that first mad flush, he enjoyed living with her. No place was safe from their perpetual horniness, and the sighs and smells of their endless lovemaking filled the air. He disliked using public transport, and only did so when he had to, like for getting to work on time. Whenever he wasn't pressed by the base contingency of earning a living, and especially at weekends, he became a dedicated *flâneur*, who strolls and idles, observing and dreaming, captured and inspired by each new passing impression and sensation. Often, down by the river, the sound of his father singing 'Under the Bridges of Paris' would waft softly back to him. His unhurried surveying of the city would make a neat metaphor for his leisurely exploration of her body. He embraced both, wanting to know them intimately. He let love in, just as he let in the streets. He imagined that he was embarked upon a grand voyage of discovery, that might some day begin to mean something. As did I, once, nearly. I should have tried to tell him: it is always, more or less, almost certainly, not so. Why didn't he tell me? How could he, if he didn't know?

I have recovered, just about, from my abortive essay in self-annihilation. Do you think I was only suffering from sensory deprivation? It's easy to get cabin fever up here, and go stir crazy. There's nothing worse than being confined to barracks, I've heard it said. But if I was in prison, as I suppose I am, solitary is where I would like them to put me. It is a reward and not a punishment, as far as I can see. I like it here. It's where I chose to be. Or where certain events have made it more comfortable for me to choose to remain.

Still, maybe I should watch more of that television I was perspicacious enough to install. Things happen on TV. But I prefer it when nothing happens, even if it's only on TV. I have tried, inasmuch as it is humanly possible, to prevent things from happening to me. Unless I will them to. I have arranged things so, insofar as I can. I am one of those control freaks you have heard about. But even I realise I'm not in complete control. And that sends me right out of control. I do see the odd newspaper now and again which, when added to the transmissions I happen to catch sight of, keeps me in touch with contemporary patois, some of which may creep into this text, as I laboriously do my revisions.

But what need have I of modern methods of telecommunication, when I can watch my brother if I'm looking for a little bit of diversion? True, there is only one channel, which can drive even the sanest among us crazy, but so can chopping and changing between too many. And I do not require the excessive amounts of stimulation, available at the push of a few buttons, through such multi-channel hopping and surfing. My sexual needs have long since ceased to be over-clamorous, which is possibly why I am not terribly glamorous, and now my intellectual ones are no longer banging any gongs either, which could account for my thought processes appearing frankly bizarre. This lack might cause you to suppose that I would want more distractions, not less. Not so. I am content to wither away quietly. There'll be no raging against the dying of the light around here, even if it is only of the kind that comes down to you via a cathode ray tube in the corner, and is projected onto a screen. Henceforth I will practice ataxary. I will be the good man who does nothing. That's what makes me bad, and what lets evil thrive. But what good could I do anyway? If only such an obmutescence was observed by everybody, there'd be a lot less evil around all told, in my opinion. Those to whom evil is done do evil in return. So everybody should just do nothing, and then there'd be no evil done. Simple, but alas, far too utopian. Also, there wouldn't be any good, unless it is just the absence of evil.

What of my emotional needs? Sometimes I wonder if I ever had any to begin with. But I refuse to get trapped on the treadmill of a which-came-first-the-chicken-or-the-egg? argument about whether or not I was any different to what I am now before the evil that was done to me was done. The reality, if not the myth, of the situation is that I am not exactly awash with the Christian virtues of faith, hope and charity. Faith can move mountains. Hope springs eternal. Charity begins at home. And you can't have one without the others. And you can't have two without the other one. And the greatest of these is love. But there is no love in this house which serves as my home. And Edward is away from what was his loving home. Still, I get by, after a fashion, even though I'm stuck here. As, I'm sure, does he, where he is domiciled now. I am building a body of knowledge, as was he, except that I am using my own battered body, rather than another's beautiful one. The ballsache has cut me off from sex. The headache has messed up my thoughts. What do I feel about all this? Heartache, in the seat of my emotions. That's where the other wounds fester, making me bitter. But of itself, the old ticker hasn't been on the receiving end of any direct physical assault, yet. It's still pulsating away, sometimes pounding like the hammers, other times a mere murmur. When it stops beating, I will die, and as you have so rightly said, the book will end. Must I die for it to end? I am dying for it to end. It's breaking my heart.

What about yours?

And what about Edward's?

5

THERE THEN BEGAN for them what were, to my mind anyway, a series of fairly pointless peregrinations around the mainland of this great continent and, briefly, beyond. But I am duty-bound to tell you about them. Who is binding me to this duty? Him? You? Myself? Myself, mostly, I suppose. I have manacled myself here. But, sometimes, I let myself go. I am my own master, and my own slave. As everyone should be. Everyone needs discipline, whether they're a master or a slave. Everyone gets punished, sooner or later, one way or another. But it's better if you administer it yourself. I am a self-starter, highly self-disciplined, fully self-contained. Or I am, in so far as I can be. Which is, perhaps, not so very far at all. You cannot be the servant of two masters, as they say. But you can be the master of many slaves, is what I say.

This tiresome trail brought Edward and Laura to visit her family in Milan, when they had a month off work for summer holidays, and from where they went on to Florence and Venice, and did all that art and culture trail to the nth degree. Then there was going to see his people in Dublin the following Christmas, so that she could meet Mr and Mrs Tender, and they could have a look at her. Sometime after that, at Easter in fact, they spent a couple of weeks in High Germany. Then, that summer, they took a trip down to Spain, and there was a short cross-over into Morocco as an appendix.

What was the motivation for all this movement? As I implied, I do not know. But there is no premium on the amount of people who want to go here, there and yonder. Indeed, when I used to be out and about more, the speeds at which people hurtled themselves around from place to place was a constant source of mystery and amazement to me. As for me, there is no shortage of stillness. I mean there is, out there in the world, but not for me, when I can get enough of it. I do not miss being part of the hurrying throng. I like being far from the madding crowd.

But in this, it appears, I am considered somewhat unconventional. Edward and Laura, however, were not so different, so why should they have to explain themselves? That is, why should I have to explain them? They were young, and in good health, and in love, and wanted to travel together. What could be more natural? Maybe they thought they had a lot to learn. And maybe they did. Such as the fact that they had little to learn. Or that they were not going to learn whatever they had to learn by touring around. Travel narrows the mind. It is a great mass psychosis. It is something people do when they want to keep from thinking, or feeling, something else. It is supposed to be stimulating, but it is really numbing. It is a way of forgetting. What were Edward and Laura trying to forget? They've forgotten. Or maybe they remember only too well. I do not know about her, but maybe he was haunted by a shadow, named Mary, and this made him restless and contrary.

But I digress. That is, I am straying off the subject in hand. While we're on the subject, let's have a digression about digression, about going off the subject. Personally, I like it. I find digressions just as interesting as whatever they are digressing from, usually. Sure what discourse could be so interesting in and of itself as not to benefit from a little straying away from it, now and again? But maybe there is something in common between my fondness for excursus, and Edward and his then mot's propensity for travel. Like them, I like getting there as much as being there. There must be some kind of parallel between my circuitous, serpentine sentences, sprawling across these pages, and the couple's endless, winding journeys, unravelling across the globe. I like the byways off the highways, the back streets off the main streets, the culs-de-sac and blind alleys, as much as they do, in my own way. Maybe digression is my little individual psychosis, my way of travelling, supposedly enlivening but really deadening, my way of forgetting. What am I trying to forget? I've forgotten. Or maybe I remember only too well.

But what happens if everything becomes a digression, and there is nothing left to digress from, or return to, any more, except the current or previous digression? That's another story, called deracination. A nomad cannot leave his home. He is already in the desert. The desert is his home, but it is not exactly what could be called a fixed point of origin. That's not quite my scenario. Or Edward's. We knew where we had come from, if not where we were going. I should know where we were going, if I now intend to take you there. Or I should at least know how to get there, unless this is merely a case of the blind leading the blind, or even the blind leading those who can see. Do I know? Can I see? The ponderous, dangling interrogative has become an unpardonable mannerism, but an essential element, of my style. I wonder why? Because that's digression.

Laura's parents, Mama and Papa Pochini, seemed outwardly, to Edward, to be a nice friendly couple in late middle-age. Except that he was slowly dying of colonic cancer, and kept a paramour across town, whom he called on to cavort with at least twice a week; meanwhile, his wife polished off a good half bottle of whiskey a day, but more often than not more, in the not unjustifiable belief that it helped her to cope. Not that any of this should be taken to mean that they weren't really nice and friendly.

Similarly her younger brother Mario, who was ostensibly warm and welcoming, but went on frequent skiing weekends, taking the opportunity this afforded him to seduce as many different women as he possibly could, and record his trysts using a hidden video camera, for future exhibition among his hormone-addled chums, who delighted in watching him make each addled whore moan. Not that that made him any less warm or welcoming.

It was Laura, naturally, who had marked Edward's cards thus before they entered this minefield, as well as cautioning him as to how imperative it was that they maintain the pretence that they were not living together. Did her dire warnings prejudice him unduly, rudely pre-empting him from deciding for himself? He was conscious of a certain double-vision when meeting this clan, more pronounced than the protective layer of suspicion he was coming to feel, as a matter of course, whenever he was introduced to new people. Sitting around the dinner table with them, exchanging pleasantries and not-so-pleasantries, he found he could see not only what was going on in front of him, but also a blur around the edges telling him what it really meant, or might really mean. Would he have been able to discern this anyway, without her prompting? Very likely. All happy families resemble one another, but each unhappy family is unhappy in its own way. Who said that? Whoever it was, they were wrong. All families are unhappy in some way, and it is probably the same way. She was another person with a family to get away from. Like the rest of us. She was showing him why she had come away. As he would, in time, show her.

I have not shown anyone, except you. But then, I never went away. I chose to stay. It was my way of going away. As what I am writing is my way of showing. I did it my way. It does strike me that Edward was luckier than most, when it comes to from where he was sprung. Luckier, certainly, than me. Even if we were both sprung from the same place, technically. But I am always referring everything back to my stupid self. Can I not use my imagination to make you imagine what it is like to be someone else for a change, other than myself or yourself, for even a few minutes? I would find that very difficult to imagine, I imagine. Even if that is what I am repeatedly attempting to do. I rarely transcend myself. So much for my powers of invention.

It was so long since either of them had lived *en famille* that it was strangely annoying for them to return to the Pochinis' in the evening, after spending the day scooting around the city, and then have to talk about everything they had done. Of course, if no polite inquiries had been forthcoming, it would have signalled an insulting indifference that would have been even harder to take. One of the advantages, or should I say compensations, of living with a partner of your own choosing, rather than with people you never chose, is that there is slightly more chance, although it is still mightily slim, of having companionable conversation interspersed with understanding silences, rather than having constant conversation, understanding or otherwise, or constant silences, of the uncomprehending, even aggressive, kind.

But it is, in my view, I need hardly reiterate, preferable to live alone. Then there is no shortage of silence, if that is what you want. I mean there is, out in the aforementioned world, but not for you, if you can get enough of it. Why do people stay together, long after things have gone stale? For the children? Why do they have children? Because of what people will say? Why do they care? I suppose they stay together out of inertia, or so as to have someone come visit and tend them as they lie on their death beds. A new lover, or rather, sexual partner, doesn't owe you anything. Live alone, die alone. Live by the word, die by the word.

My brother and his sexual lover took to eating out, whenever possible, but there were a few times when they could not avoid taking their evening meal with her folks, just to pacify them. Like the night before they left for Florence.

All five, the Pochinis and their guest, were present and correct at the appointed time. After Mama had served up the *primo*, and they began tucking into it, Papa observed casually that the sauce could have done with more salt in the cooking. This seemingly innocuous barb, a standard salvo from his well-stocked armoury, was directed, however obliquely, at a woman who had, thirty years before, graduated with honours in organic chemistry from the University of Turin, no mean achievement for a female in Italy, or anywhere else, in those days. Edward wondered what accumulation of disappointments had made her settle for playing this role of long-suffering wife. Such behaviour in a hubby was enough to make you flirt with feminism.

Then, during the *secundo*, as Edward lifted a green bean that was proving intractable to his fork into his mouth between finger and thumb, Mama cried out in consternation, "Con le dita!"

To which our Ed could only regroup forces and sally bravely, "Si, perche no?"

Ah, table manners. What a great way to embarrass people, such an excellent form of social control. Anyone who is oppressed will usually try to find someone else to oppress, for whom they can become the oppressor, however limited their sphere of influence, however narrow their field of operations. Sometimes they even set about subtly oppressing their oppressor, and are in turn subtly oppressed by those for whom they have become the oppressor.

By the time the sweet came around, everyone was doing their level best to say nothing that could be construed as remotely contentious by anyone else, while still attempting to find something, anything, to say. A chance remark about the latest action movies led Edward and Mario to discussing their mutual admiration for the James Bond films, and Papa chipped in that he too was a big fan of *Zero Zero Sette*. My brother trotted out as obvious and conclusive proof of his great sympathy with the women's movement the fact that his favourite Bond movie was *On Her Majesty's Secret Service*, which had the worst Bond, but the best Bond girl, ever. But then Mama said curtly that she thought the 007 series ridiculously childish and just plain silly. Mario asked to be excused early.

Flailing and floundering in this sea of tension, Edward and Laura were relieved to light out the next morning on their tour of the antique towns. As they sat on the train, clanking out of Central Station, Laura was practically in tears. Edward knew, and tried to tell her, as she apologised and complained, that all parents are fallible, that it is essential for your development, if such is possible, that they fail you. But some, he allowed to himself, are more fallible than others, and fail you more spectacularly than is really warranted, or salutary.

But the monitory atmosphere, and the parental injunction to sleep apart, had not prevented our winsome twosome from managing a couple of clandestine, invigorating couplings, late at night when the apartment was quiet, and these people she'd brought him to meet were with any luck off in the land of Nod, if sleep had not been murdered, and they were still capable of nodding off. At these times, they felt as if they were chalking up little victories over repression. The little death triumphed, temporarily, over the big one.

Florence. How I wish I didn't have to do all the material you could get in any tourist guidebook: the Duomo, the Piazza della Signoria, the Palazzo Vecchio, the Uffizi, Santa Croce, the Arno, the Ponte Vecchio, the Palazzo Pitti, the Boboli Gardens. Plus all the great inheritance of priceless treasures by renowned masters: Dante, Giotto, Petrarch, Boccaccio, Machiavelli, Masaccio, Fra Angelico, da Vinci, Botticelli, Michelangelo, Donatello, Raphael, Titian, Caravaggio. To say nothing of all the local colour: American and Japanese holiday-makers armed with cameras and handy-cams, flashing credit cards in the upmarket jewellery shops on that old bridge, or haggling for the fun of it with the African immigrant street hucksters, who try to turn an honest few lire by flogging cigarette-lighters and other cheap trinkets, their incessant inquiry of '*Vuoi compra?*' usually the only Italian they know; the sights, sounds and smells of people bustling by about their daily business, or sitting chatting in restaurants and cafés. So I won't.

Why did I bring them there then, if I'm not going to take the opportunity to go on about how beautiful it is? The answer is that I didn't bring them there, they went of their own volition. I just tagged along, inside my brother's mind. I can tell you that they were not intimidated, as many visitors are, by the sensory overload of so much art in such a compact space, by the output of all those names and the spectacle of all those places, listed laboriously above, found in such close proximity to each other. I was, for once.

It's not that I was overwhelmed by the glory of it all, but rather that the supposed self-improving influence of these poems, paintings and statues was entirely lost on me. They failed to elicit the appropriate emotional response, and that made me uneasy. For it was not merely a case of my perennial uncouthness accounting for this deficiency, but of a dawning sense of the awful disparity all around, such as had borne in on my brother when he had been in America. These guys had done good work, in their time, and now it was put up on display for all the world to see, in the service of a sprawling heritage and tourism industry. But what did any of these sublime achievements of Western civilisation mean to those black dudes, hustling the sightseers for a meagre buck? I suppose it meant that there were sightseers to hustle. But why did the multitudes not clamour to see the artistic triumphs of the dark lads' tribes? Because they are the wretched of the earth. But they have not yet inherited it, however meek they may be. Such inequality can give rise to the venting of spleen, and even incendiary incidents, rather than the habitual passive resignation and acceptance expected of the exploited. It was enough to make you succumb to socialism.

I'm not trying to imply that I enjoy a unique empathy with the downtrodden of this world, which prevented me from having a full aesthetic appreciation of what was on show. I am not so peculiar as all that. It would probably have all been pearls cast before swine anyway, to the pig that I am. But I do say that if you haven't got the social conscience, it is far easier to abandon yourself to this version of beauty. Even pigs have their uses – to wit, nosing out truffles. But ultimately I don't relate to anybody, rich or poor, black or white, good, bad or indifferent. Edward sees something of himself in everyone. That's how he gets by. I see nothing of myself in anyone. That's why I can't.

Look, they really liked being there, even if I didn't particularly like watching them. You have probably already been. If not, you should go. Millions upon millions of Americans and Japanese, year in year out, can't all be wrong.

Or can they?

Venice. More information from the guidebook: I can't do this. More cultural heritage: I mean I can, but I don't want to. More local colour: please don't make me. I know I should make more of an effort, for you. If there is any pleasure to be had from my tale, after all, it is in the telling, not in finding out whether or not we all live happily ever after.

You already know that hardly anyone ever does. The novels of Jane Austen I dipped into, because my brother was obliged to study them in school, always seemed to me to end just when they should be beginning.

But it is not laziness that keeps me from giving you dazzling descriptions. I can do that with my eyes closed. It is fear of endless repetition of what I have written before, or of what others have written before me. Or of obeisant, if sincerely flattering, imitation of what they have written better than me. But how could it be better, if I mimic it perfectly? Because they did it first, presumably, and achieved a certain degree of mastery. But if I set about improving upon it, then it is not mere mimicry. No, it is just an unmitigated disaster, because I am sure to make it worse. Despite what they may tell you, upgrades aren't always necessary. If it's not broke, don't fix it, as they say. If it's not fixed, don't break it, as I say.

But complacency is a terrible thing, I hear you retort. It is possible to learn something about dabbling in words by finding out how others went about doing so. Not so, since what works well for one scribe may be directly contra-indicated for another. Don't talk to me about the anxiety of influence, and the struggle to find your own voice. The original terminus, and most outstanding accomplishment, of any voice, is to find a way of saying something about something about which you have nothing to say, about which there is nothing left to say. Like life and love, for example, or sex and death. But you would most likely be better off just keeping your mouth shut. Whatever you say, say nothing, as they say. Whatever you say, say something about nothing, as I say. As if there was anything else you could say. But you are already apprised of my pet theory, about the less writing the better.

To this end, I would even go so far as to propose the inauguration of a scheme, whereby most people would be paid a lump sum to stop writing, and thereafter receive an annuity to refrain from ever starting up again. In the case of beginners, they could be offered a pension to desist from even contemplating starting off in the first place. It could be called the 'Promise Not To Write' allowance. This system, coupled with the low financial returns that can be expected to accrue to an author, from most writing that is in any way worthwhile or has anything to recommend it, should be enough to see off all but the most dedicated and determined, or the most pig-headed and foolhardy, of practitioners.

Given my espousal of the twin virtues of stillness and silence, per-haps provision could also be made to extend this plan to encompass the spoken word as well as the written. Everyone would be encouraged to apply, through an aggressive advertising and marketing campaign, for the 'Promise Not To Speak' allowance. For it is another of my pet theories, that life will be greatly improved when people stop talking to each other, and give up believing the cosy all-embracing myth that argument and debate and the exchange of ideas will somehow enable us to arrive at absolute truth, or at least resolve differences and diffi-culties. That's not true, because so much gets lost, or comes out, in rhetoric. Aside from it being highly debatable whether or not there is such a thing as absolute truth at all. Beauty is truth, truth beauty. Who said that? Whoever it was, they were wrong. But maybe they knew they were wrong, since they put it in inverted commas. All right, if you want to be pedantic, you can say that they "wrote" it. Yes, and then everyone goes about quoting it. See how insidiously this virus spreads, from page to person, from person to person, from place to place, and back again. Get rid of words, I say, written and spoken.

But man is a social animal, you remonstrate, quoting somebody else. Language is the glue that gives us social cohesion. It's all about com-munication. It's good to talk. Well then, riddle me this: if reading and writing are solitary activities, but man is a social animal, then why are bookshops full of books, and people producing and buying and selling them? Huh? I'll tell you why: it's so they can be alone. Or at least fill up their aloneness. We read so as to know that we are not alone. Who said that? Wrong again. We read because we are alone. Which is also why we write.

But then you do get the dodos who will insist on talking about books they've read or written. Public houses and radio and television studios are full of them. Give them half a chance, and they'll talk about any-thing. Which is why it would be better if people found something else to do when they are alone, besides reading and writing. For example, they could watch television, with the volume turned down. But then they would probably want to talk about the picture. Damned if you do, damned if you don't, as they say. Don't do a damn thing, as I say, if you're going to be damned, either way.

Obviously I haven't obeyed my own advice. I work, alone here at home, at reading and writing. I am a homeworker. I am a homewrecker. I am an anti-social worker. I am a society-wrecker. But I have to spread the word, about not spreading words. Or, at least, not wasting them. I am only working to make myself redundant. I am talking myself out of a job. And I am already streets ahead of the rest of you, having dispensed with speech. But I wouldn't put it past some antagonistic bastard to take issue with me, thus drawing me into an argument to defend my position. But I am exempt from my own strictures, since I am an individual of very great spiritual and intellectual advancement. The page black with scribbles and the blank unsullied page, the silence behind the sounds of words and the wordless sound of silence, they are all so much nonsense to me.

Still, words might come in useful if I am to tell you something nice about Venice. And that is my job, just now. Is it any wonder that I am unemployed, and unemployable? I told you Edward would go there one day, and now he had. I cannot put it more simply than to say he fell in love with it. The reason for this passion, apart from being there with the woman he had fallen in love with, was that it was the only city he had ever been in where, every time he went out, he got lost. He was a traveller without maps, but he had a fine sense of direction, and after a couple of days anywhere could usually find his way around, gauging where he was by just referring to some prominent landmarks. But not in Venice. Its labyrinth of narrow, shady streets that would unexpectedly give on to the expanse of the great, wide square full of sunshine, and one bridge after another over quiet, lapping water, water everywhere, left him quite baffled. He couldn't get his bearings, and was in a constant state of amazement.

They did manage to find their way to the Rialto, and to climb the Campanile in St Mark's Square. After that they lingered together on the Bridge of Sighs, whispering sweet nothings. Then she told him that it had been built as a passageway between the Palazzo and the prison, and reputedly took its name from the sighs of prisoners being led into trial. The revelation that it was not called after the sighs of lovers, enraptured with the view, softened his cough. Terrible how digging into things means you cannot enjoy them any more. Maybe the trick is to learn how to enjoy them in a different way.

But there is so much in that place which is not what it at first seems, so many ways to turn that you don't know where they'll lead you. Venice is the digresser's digression.

They squabbled on the train back to Milan, which they were hitting for a weekend before returning to Paris. A bunch of *ragazzi* doing the compulsory military service boarded at Verona, and came into the same carriage as Edward and Laura. They sat down opposite a thin, buxom, blonde woman in a light, summer, cum-fuck-me dress, who was sitting across the aisle from our pair, and started chatting her up. What drew Laura's ire was that Edward had been stealing glances at this other specimen of Italian pulchritude all through their journey.

"You don't love me," she complained.

"Of course I do," he reassured her.

"You are not serious about me. I think of marriage, and a family."

These were things Edward had not thought of at all. He wondered if they precluded eyeing up other women. If so, this could lead to a life of tittle-tattle and tiff after tiff, until all the little petty quarrels amounted to one big mountain of strife, and you got past the stage of kiss-and-make-up, to the point of no return, and arrived at good old irretrievable breakdown.

Miss Italia in her chemise just about succeeded in fending off the boys' attentions.

They patched up their dispute before arriving back at her parents' apartment, since she didn't want Mama and Papa knowing any more than was necessary. She knew what kind of implications they would draw, and so always operated on a strict need-to-know basis when it came to dispensing information to them.

It being the end of their holiday, they were flat broke, so apart from long walks, they were forced to hang around her family home. As she went through old family photograph albums on the final afternoon, and came across pictures of Mario and herself as kids, her mother inquired (and here I translate from the original Italian), "Have you ever thought of having children?"

It was her notion of a subtle hint.

"It is good to be married," added her father.

That was his idea of same.

Was this the pressure that Laura was labouring under? Did she want family life for her own sake, or just to please them? He doubted if she would even have been able to say where one motive ended and the other began.

After struggling through two more days of this sly solicitude, they headed for the plane back home. At the airport her father, the philandering old cove, hugged his daughter close to him, and murmured (again, in Italian), "I hope it's not the last time I see you."

"Don't be silly, Papa," she told him.

Her mother just looked at her disconsolately, then resignedly.

There is always so much that cannot be expressed, in the bosom of your family. If there is something you want to say at home, but can't, then you suffer from claustrophobia. If there is something you want to say when you're out, but can't, then it's a dose of agoraphobia. But where do you go if you've contracted both?

Dysfunctional is the word they use these days, I believe, for people and families and relationships like these. But show me an example of any to which it does not somehow apply.

Mr Tender was there to collect Edward and Laura at Dublin airport a few months later, on Christmas Eve. Mrs Tender was waiting for them at home. Ever since his exile had begun in earnest, my brother had dreamed of making the journey back to Ireland, so often undertaken alone, with a girlfriend in tow. But the flight had been marred by piddling bickering. Why hadn't he bought Mr and Mrs Tender better presents? Why didn't he wear nicer clothes? Why didn't she shut the fuck up? These proddings were, as you have no doubt tumbled, merely the outward manifestations of a deeper underlying malaise, the one about the M word. But why did she want to marry him, he wondered, if she found so many faults with him? She found so many faults with him, he figured, because he didn't want to marry her. So the thin thread tied between them was tightening, strained close to breaking point, ready to bounce back at them. Fraught would be the word to describe the atmosphere they created on the plane. Funny how nothing turns out exactly as you imagine it will. But everything turns out more or less as you always knew it would.

His mother had grown frail, he thought, studying her from across the table at Christmas dinner. They had accompanied his parents to midnight mass the night before, and Mrs Tender had complained of being petrified with the cold. It now transpired that, because Edward had brought Laura home, all the way from Paris, and had been keeping company with her for nearly a year, Mr and Mrs T assumed that he must be serious about her. Which, of course, he was. But for them, 'being serious' meant getting married. Which is also what it now appeared to mean for her. Was he to be assailed from all sides, in this manoeuvre towards matrimony? And why was he so against it, when you get right down to it? It wasn't that he thought he didn't love her, because he felt that he did. Besides, you don't have to love someone to marry them. Nor do you have to marry someone you love. It was more that he was unsure if he could maintain fidelity, despite loving her, even if lots of people who entertain such doubts still go ahead and jump the broom anyway. Many women, and indeed men, put a high price on monogamy, in case you hadn't noticed, particularly in the times we had started living in then. Honesty is my brother's besetting vice. He likes to do right by others, and think well of himself. He was slow to discover that we all need secrets. Or maybe his views on family life were still too uncomfortably close to mine, even if he was more than aware that a simple twist of fate, in which he'd had some connivance, had dealt him a better hand than many. He was no longer too young to think about growing old, but he still didn't want a wife and kids for at least another five, and more probably ten, years, if ever. He was afraid of what it would be like, when pillow talk turned to nappy talk. Selfishness is my brother's besieging virtue. He likes to do well for himself, and have others do right by him. He was fast learning that he might have to share. Perhaps this is what kept him from taking the plunge.

They rang in the new year, 1989, with the bells at Christ Church, and he held Laura close to him, and kissed her passionately. Minutes later, just for a moment, he was almost certain he saw Mary disappearing around the corner into Winetavern Street. Who was that guy with her, in the long black coat? He didn't mention this sighting, real or imagined, to his prospective missus.

Rain was falling softly the night they wished his mother goodbye, as she stood shivering at the door, and his father waited in the car to drive them to the plane.

"Home is always here for you to come to," she told him, with a meaning look, when Laura was just out of earshot. But he no longer felt that this was his haven in a heartless world, even if he and Laura had also taken advantage of some of the nooks and crannies of the house, and used them as they had used the periods of privacy in her

170

parents' place. He would have to build his own nest, find a bolthole of his own.

They fell to discussing his Ma and Pa as the jet climbed into the sky.

"I think she is a very good woman," Laura opined, "only she spoiled you. And your father is a very nice old man. He was very nice to me. You are very lucky."

How long more, how much longer, could they drag on like this?

6

PAY ATTENTION, or *achtung*, as we used to say, when playing soldiers as kids, copying the old war comics and movies, and as they still say, in Germany. For that was where they were off to now. Why? Because neither of them had been there before, and she could practice the language. The language obscene, as one of her favourite poets has it, an engine, an engine, chuffing them off like Jews. She came across these lines only after she'd begun learning how to speak in this tongue.

Berlin would have been the place to go, since there was still, although its time was nearly up, the well-known wall they could have languished in the shadow of, like a heroic king and queen, and crossed over to see the other side. Lots of doom-laden cold war atmospherics could then be thrown in, and Weimar night-club associations. But they wound up in Munich for a week, since she had a friend there, with whom they could stay.

They found the Glockenspiel in Marienplatz as charming as everyone else had before them. The Chinese Tower Beer Garden in the greater Englischer Garten was as good a place as any other to linger for a while, although there were less crowded drinking dens nearby. People were tentatively starting to sunbathe on the sandy banks and islands of the dilatorily flowing Isar, in the nude yet. The streets looked grand and imposing, redolent of empire.

The fairy castle built by mad King Leopold II at Neuschwanstein gave them a fun-filled day trip, but it was the more disturbing folly of Dachau that really stopped them in their tracks. They took the S-Bahn the few short kilometres from the big, sprawling city down to the neat and tidy town, whose name has been made infamous around the world on account of the death camp that once flourished there.

The blocks where people were corralled for sleep had all been pulled down, ordered rectangles filled with gravel marking where they had stood. But everything else, including the crematorium, had been preserved, with the ruthless efficiency we have come to think of as typically Teutonic. However, it was all so spotlessly spick and span, airbrushed beyond belief, sanitised out of existence, as though no horrors had ever happened there, that the all-pervading, glossed-over eerie futility made Edward want to scream and shout out loud, or have a picnic or throw a party, as if in rebuke of the clean-up he regarded as a cover-up. There were no ashes left in the ovens.

You have heard of bird-song at Belsen. You have heard of poetry after Auschwitz. But have you ever heard of dancing at Dachau? You cannot be camp about the camps. That would be in bad taste, something I am ever anxious to avoid. Belsen was not great gas. Auschwitz was no barrel of laughs. Dachau just gives you the blues. There is no springtime for Hitler.

His parents' accounts of being young in Ireland when the war was on came back to him.

"Times were very hard. It was called the Emergency. You couldn't get sugar." So much then for neutrality.

Laura flicked her long, dark hair back behind her ear with her finger, and he thought of what she had told him about how the phrase 'still life' is rendered in Italian: *natura morte*, literally 'dead nature'. That was a good way to sum up the feeling evoked by being in Dachau. Still, life goes on. He wondered if they sneaked off and made love where they couldn't be seen, would it assuage the anger he felt inside? He couldn't be sure if such an act would be liberating or inappropriate, or liberating because it was inappropriate, or totally appropriate because it was liberating. He didn't bother asking her what she thought.

But who do you blame? Blame God. But there is no God. Or if there is, he is a right bastard. God is dead, and gone to hell. The Devil is in his heaven, all is wrong with the world. God never closes one door, but he shuts another. The Devil take him. God is love, God is good, God is patient, God is kind. Good God. No one moulds us again out of earth and clay, no one conjures our dust. No one. Praised be your name, no one. Blame no one.

Walking back to the bus station, he looked at the faces of the sturdy burghers they passed by on the way. These were the sons and daughters of the people who said that they didn't know what was going on down the road. The ones who had turned a blind eye, cocked a deaf ear, and kept their mouths shut. The ones who had willingly obeyed the ancient injunction to See No Evil, Hear No Evil and Speak No Evil. They were the Master Race, but they had a slave mentality. Now work had made them free. They may have lost the war, but they had certainly won the peace. So piss off.

But those Jews were just as bad, thinking they were the Chosen People, long before the Germans ever began regarding themselves as such. And the Jerrys got the concept of concentration camps from the English, who had used them in the Boer War. See how it all connects? All the same, there is some kind of Moral Absolute involved here. This is what we call the Categorical Imperative. What about the Sovereignty of Good? The Germans were wrong in doing all that torture and murder, in committing all those crimes against humanity. As were all the others: the English, the French, the Americans, the Russians. See how easy it is to categorise and classify by race? Millions subsumed under one banner, and presumed to be more or less the same. But no one stood up, stood out, and shouted "Stop!" You have heard that it has been said: an eye for an eye, and a tooth for a tooth. But I say to you, resist not evil. If anyone hits you on the right cheek, turn the other one to him as well. Love your enemy. Otherwise, we will all be eyeless and toothless, long before our time. Read the great lie called history, and learn how we learn nothing from it. The fields of Europe, festooned with flowers, are drenched in the blood of its young men, the innocent blood of lambs and the blood of the guilty beyond redemption, alike. As are those of many more far-flung shores, it goes without saying. Let's not forget the Chinese and Japanese, for example, and the big mushroom-cloud explosions made by those splitting-the-atom bombs.

But the suffering and death of these untold millions means next to nothing to us today. Some even go so far as to say that the Holocaust never happened, or has been grossly exaggerated for propaganda purposes. It is also argued with equal conviction, and maybe even some justification, that Hiroshima and Nagasaki brought a swift end to World War II, saving millions of other lives. It all comes out in the wash, this view seems to suggest. What you lose on the roundabouts, you make up for on the swings. Which is all very fine and well for the rest of us, but not much consolation to those who did not come out, or make anything up, or more especially, those close to them who did. 'Never Again' reads the inscription on the monument in that place visited by Edward and Laura. But it always happens again, somewhere or other. It is happening now, this very minute. My *Weltanschauung*, as you can see, is one of *Weltschmerz*. You would have to be an *Ubermensch* to see things any other way.

Nevertheless, I am not unaware of the Nazi that lurks in me. For I too have my mission. This book is *Mein Kampf*, or *My Struggle*. But it is not a self-help book, or only accidentally so. Rather, it is the meaning of my mien. My assignment is to make people feel things they have never felt before, or to help them make sense of things they have felt before, but didn't understand. And to render the same service to myself, in the process. I would have people thinking up names for emotions not yet felt, or imperfectly assimilated. Perhaps I should have gone into politics. I would have been a great dictator. What atrocities would I not have committed? What horrors would I not have perpetrated? All in the name of what is right and proper. All for a cogent argument that proceeds towards a given goal. There is never any shortage of people to pick on. Who will we demonise today? Just cast your eyes around the playground, and look for someone a little bit different. Are there any disabled people handy, any immigrants to be found, any boys who like boys or girls who like girls lurking around?

There is a Nazi in everyone.

Back in Paris, Edward took to fiddling around with computers, which were becoming all the rage. His French was improving too, so that he could do more than just get by. He had a facility for languages, the kind that use numbers no less than the ones made up of words. Maybe he could effect a transition in his career path, from teaching one to programming another.

Both Laura and he were still giving classes every day, and beginning to burn out. Domesticity was also playing its part in dragging them down, and so they were getting tired of it as well. Changes were afoot. Would they go to Ireland or to Italy, to try to improve their lot, and get on in the world? Or would they simply go their separate ways for the rest of their days, if they could not come to a meeting of minds and hearts, and get on with each other again? No point in taking all that trouble to be together, if they were only going to make each other miserable. Where had the sparkle gone? Could they get it back?

Term was ending, so with summer shining in her face again, they decided that another trip was in order. Maybe the heat and light of Spain would help them to see if they could sort out whether or not their condition was terminal.

I too have a talent for languages. Well, for one, at least. Despite, or is it because of, certain misgivings I entertain about my ability to comprehend it. But my facility is making me facile. My conceits are becoming conceited.

In the relatively short space of time since what I am writing about took place, and my writing about it now, anyone who writes any way seriously, and the very many who don't, tap away at an electronic keyboard, and look at a screen, just like Edward was starting to do back then. Computers have taken over the world. If the facilities exist, why not use them? If the conceits are out there, why not let them in?

But I don't need such technological aids to help me make things easier, or to help make things easier for me. I can manage quite well by myself on that score, thank you. So here I am, a lone Luddite, still scribbling away with a pen on paper, like some cobweb-covered, quill-scratching anachronistic anchorite. You can see the shapes of words on a page, like everyone else, like myself. But, most likely, the only time you hear their sounds is when they are spoken. Do you see their shape, when they are not written down? Am I the last person left alive who still hears the sounds of words, which is the music of time, even when there is no one speaking, and they dance on the page?

I can still hear that knocking, and smell that smell. I'm getting a taste for this, senseless though it may be.

And I remember Spain. He enjoyed it, more than I imagine I would have, being blessed, or is it afflicted, with a rather more gregarious nature than me. She was more reticent about the brand of pleasure the place afforded. It is not for nothing that the word *macho* entered English from Spanish, and she found this attribute even more pronounced in the men there than in those from her homeland. For her, this was not appealing. Maybe that's why she liked Edward.

They arrived by train in Barcelona, a city which it cannot be denied, chiefly thanks to the flamboyant architecture, is breathtakingly beautiful. So taking deep breaths, they took off down The Ramblas, a street he wished would never end, and watched the old men playing dominoes in the cafés, and the young folks flirting and strutting around, acting as smartly and sophisticatedly as they thought the *jeunesse dorée*, or is that the *juvens dorados*, of the best city in the country should. They lingered for a few days, walking the feet off themselves, doing the galleries and the cathedral, and whatever else there was to be seen.

Except a bullfight. These happened on Sundays, and he wanted to take one in, but she wouldn't go with him. All that false bravado, at the expense of a dumb animal, was much too boorish and brutal, according to her, and emblematic of the country as a whole, she added, with no attempt to disguise her disdain. He could have gone by himself, but figured it wouldn't be as much fun alone. The sun also rises, but for whom does it shine? He was about to launch into a spiel about how the ritual public slaughter of symbolic beasts was a rite almost as old as civilisation itself, satisfying a deep-seated psychic need in man. But he pulled himself up, thinking better of trotting out what she would tell him was barbaric balderdash.

This was the first of a steadily escalating series of disagreements they had, or failed to have, as they edged down the coast, like a river slowly meandering, stopping for a day or two here and there along the way, but giving the package holiday blocks a very wide berth. They journeyed by bus, because the trains were a mess, and didn't get you there any quicker. Neither of them felt like hiring a car, after reading in their guide-book that the roads were treacherous once you ventured off the boring highway. Tarragona, Valencia, Alicante all played host to them, and had good little beaches not very far away.

They took a detour inland to Granada, since anyone they met along the way who had been there told them that if they visited only one city in Spain, this was the one it should be. You don't see an edifice like the Alhambra every day, after all, anywhere in Europe. But then it was built by invaders, those Moorish infidels.

The abstract ornamental stucco decorations that covered the Palace buildings had a rhythmic repetition that was quietly hypnotic. It was an art that did not seem to seek to capture the eye, in the hope of leading it into an imagined world, but one that, on the contrary, liberated the onlooker from any preoccupations of the mind. No specific ideas were being transmitted, but a state of being itself. This recurring regularity appeared to be designed to promote and then mirror a repose and inner rhythm in all those who entered and dwelt there. The perfectly planned and patterned riot of colour on every wall whetted his appetite for continuing southwards, where there would be more of this tracery to savour, but also brought to the surface what had been irking her all along, what they had come away to work out, what was disturbing her own calm.

In the gardens of the Generalife, amid the tranquil gurgling of water running down stone balustrades and bubbling up in ornate fountains, she stood foursquare in front of him, finally confronting him.

"What is it that you have against marriage anyway, or is it just against marrying me?"

"Why do you want to marry me," he spat out, "looking at your parents?"

"To do better than them," she replied directly, and then, almost as an afterthought, "and so as not to be alone." He still loved the way her Italian intonation lent her sentences a strangeness, an almost-but-not-quite-the-way-we'd-form-them formality, which was so exotic.

Then she added, pensively, as though it was far too obvious to need stating yet again: "And because I love you."

They had reached that stage, in my considered opinion, that comes to all couples who allow their lives and relationships – ah, that word again! – to be governed by the time-honoured, tried and trusted conventions, which enjoin that either you tie the knot, or the string will snap. Shit, or get off the pan, as our American brethren would put it. And indeed, what are the options? The rules must have been laid down for some good reason, if only to be broken, because they are ways of controlling and being controlled. Much as I love the old clichés, for the eternal truths they unwittingly tell, and collect these gems of what often was thought but never so badly expressed, to add to my ever-swelling compendium, I have no wish to snow you under with them here. But what else can I say?

'He didn't feel ready to commit himself.'

'He wasn't sure he loved her enough to settle down.'

'He didn't want to inflict all his emotional baggage on her.'

All a load of bollocks! He was as committed and as settled down and as sorted out as he could ever envisage. Best to say that he was no longer in the first flush of youth, that phase when you still think that finding the right person is going to make you happy, and he didn't know if he was cut out for spending the rest of his life running around catering to her happiness. He was pushing thirty, an age after which one becomes increasingly suspect if one does not marry. (Suspected of what, precisely? Being gay, or worse still, a womaniser, or horror of horrors, not interested in sex at all, or worst of all, just plain weird. You can call him, not to mention me, a weirdo, but none of these things are against the law, round our way, any longer.) But he wanted to light out in a completely new direction, which did not involve changing his situation with her, unless it was to end it, completely. Besides, living together satisfied any untoward curiosity, didn't it? But maybe it was no longer enough for her.

So they were falling apart. But at least they were still engaged in dialogue. Or was it simply two intersecting monologues?

The water trickled on around them, wistfully carrying them away, out of that garden, flowing on always, as they flew farther south.

America, now that was an idea. He'd always intended to return there. Go west, not-so-young man.

By the time they reached Algeciras, to take a ferry to Tangier, she was tired, emotional and irritable. Not just from travelling all day, but for the past two and a half weeks. Or the past few years. They may have lain in the sun, but they had also moved around too much, more than was good for her. But lying around wasn't always good either. He was gung-ho for going on, not showing much sympathy with her exhaustion. She grew more distant, moody and morose. How easy it is for me to advance lists of adjectives for what she was doing and how she was feeling, which are utterly inadequate, less than useless in their more than meaninglessness, when it comes to capturing in any way accurately what she really did and how she really felt. But what else can I do, or feel?

The town was thronged with Moroccans in transit, lugging

unbelievable amounts of possessions. Our voyagers checked into a hotel close to the harbour, and promptly conked out, even though it was only three in the afternoon.

When he came to, it was still light outside, but he didn't know exactly what time it was. The heavy smell of spicy meat cooking wafted up to their window, mixing with the stifling heat to make the atmosphere in their room pungently oppressive. That's what happens when you're still in the budget accommodation category: you get stuck above kitchens. His watch lay on a rickety table at the far end of the bed, but she was still in a deep sleep beside him, his arm trapped under her neck. He would feel bad if he woke her while trying to look at it.

A memory came back to him from their first days together. Cosseted in her apartment one weekend, they'd begun making love some time in the afternoon, and long after darkness had crept through the shutters, they'd decided to dress and go get something to eat. As they pulled back the covers, she suggested they bet on what time it was. He'd guessed eight, she'd wagered half-past. They were floored with surprise when they'd found it was twenty-past nine. Time would not stand so still for them for very much longer.

As he detached himself from her now, she shuddered awake, with a startled look on her face.

"Why could you not leave me as I was?"

"I'm sorry, I didn't mean to—"

"You never mean to do anything."

He leaned his hand across to caress her hair, but she pulled away from him, curling up into a foetal position, cuddling herself. They could not go on without having a showdown. Would it be a fight to the death? He summoned all his energy, indifferent to how hers was depleted.

"I suppose the reason I'm not keen on getting married," he began haltingly, aware that hesitancy can, and often does, signify honesty, "is because I don't think of you as my possession. Why should I bring you to an altar or a registry office, and make you promise your life away to me?"

While charming at twenty, Edward's attitude might seem just a tad immature at thirty. He would be making promises too, after all, ones that he might not always feel like keeping. That's how she saw it, anyway, as far as I can see.

"People belong to each other," she told him. "We do. Or did."

"Then why bother getting married?"

"Because I want to have a baby. You don't, that's why you won't marry me."

He didn't point out that they didn't need to get married to have a baby. Or that they could even get married without having to have one. But she always had been a good little lapsed Catholic girl at heart, with the residue of a predilection for doing things the proper way that that inherited burden brings. Besides, what she said was true. The prospect of paternity, let alone parenthood, gave him the willies. Him as a father? He knew he was too selfish to look after a child, the kind of responsibility, if he ever took it on, he'd want to take seriously, and not embark upon lightly. For now, he regarded kids, or ones he'd be burdened with bringing up, i.e. his own, as a needless vexation.

"You're right," he acknowledged.

"Then I wish you'd leave me alone. You don't care about me."

"Oh yes I do."

"Then leave me," she shouted emphatically, knowing that intensity can, and often does, betoken conviction.

She started weeping to herself as he closed the door. The sounds of her sobs reverberated while he disappeared down the stairs, haunting him for days afterwards. He was crying inside.

He went out and got maudlin drunk on red wine and brandy in a small bar down the road. A young Moroccan approached him for a light, and introduced himself as Mustafa. Though wary initially, Edward was too drunkenly lachrymose to keep his defences up for long. They fell into conversation, talking in a mixture of broken English and broken French.

Mustafa was in his early twenties, and dressed in a cheap leather jacket, blue jeans faded to white, and worn loafers. He sported a moustache that looked too old for his smooth, olive face, and lent him a slightly shifty air. Well-bevied himself, he began telling Edward that he was a migrant worker, going home to visit his family for the summer holidays. Apparently he was only one of about half a million Moroccans who drive across Spain every July and August, from the factories, farms and mines of France, Germany and the Low Countries. But he warned Edward off taking too romantic a view of all the colourful hustle and bustle that was going on in the port. His countrymen were often victims of discrimination during their journeys, ranging from the standard verbal abuse to outright violent attack and robbery.

Was there no getting away from blasted people and their bloody bigotry, anywhere you go in the world? But I shouldn't prejudice you against people. I must be tolerant at all times, unlike them. Have I done people a great disservice, by constantly dissing and dismissing them? I think not. Hell is other people. Or rather, hell is the need for other people. Is this Edward talking here, or me?

Mustafa felt like getting all this off his chest. He was encouraged when he heard that Edward was Irish, believing he'd chanced on a fellow-sufferer. And why indeed was my brother (to say nothing of myself) not at all galled by injustice in his own native land? Well, he was younger then, and the other man's oppression always looks greener. Not that that is any excuse. And maybe it did move him, and I have not noticed. Could it be that it may even have contributed to his leaving?

Long before they fell out of the bar at four in the morning, Eddie and Musty had become bosom buddies, and shared their troubles and woes, political and personal. They arranged to meet up again, later that day.

"You come stay with my family in Tangier. You bring your girl. I show you city."

When he got back to the hotel she was gone. Vanished into the night, no note or nothing. He was too far gone to go looking for her at the bus or train stations. He flopped into bed, and slumped over into sleep.

He checked with the desk clerk next morning, but she had left no message, and no one had seen her leave. There was no point in phoning Paris, because she couldn't have got back there yet. Rather than pursue her, he decided to keep his appointment with Mustafa. It might be a long time before he again had the chance to set foot on African soil.

Tangier looked magical as they approached it from the sea, with all those minarets shimmering in the distance through the heat haze. Having driven Edward on and off the ferry, and extended him his hospitality, Mustafa did not then take him down to the teeming souk, and arrange for him to be kidnapped for sale into the white slave trade. Edward, for his part, although he may have met an Arab, did not then set about killing him.

Instead, he was introduced to his host's father and mother and innumerable brothers and sisters, in their small, ramshackle apartment, and plied with vast quantities of shish kebab and couscous, and the illicit hooch streamed for the entire weekend. He also managed to get very stoned, on the best hashish he had ever smoked. High times, indeed. If only he had been into young boys, his every need would have been catered for. Mustafa commiserated with him about Laura, but said he could do nothing to help. He did advise him not to take her back. There are plenty more fish in the sea, and bitches in the pound, and all that. The problem here was that Edward, however cold, was not a fish, so scaly creatures would not make very good mating material for him. Nor was he a fisherman, even of soles. He had no wish to step into shoes of stone. Nor did he want to have anything to do with dogs, in any fashion.

Standing on the deck of the ferry, sailing back over the straits on the Sunday night, Edward reflected that he'd liked Morocco better than Spain. He revelled in its being so radically different from anywhere he had visited before. The rest had been just the West, which is not necessarily the best. So what if he had stayed only for a couple of days, and hadn't made it into the desert as he'd have liked? Still it had made a lasting impression.

But he was tired of playing the tourist, who hits and runs, and misses so much. He preferred being resident in his alien environments. For me, there has always been an insuperable barrier between myself and the rest of the world. For him, there was just something vital missing at certain moments. Paris had been good, but it was probably time to move on. He doubted that he and Laura would be reconciled now. He was tergiversating from her, feeling their parting was a *fait accompli*. I must be careful with my terms, for she is not a termagant. He wanted to go somewhere he could remain for five or ten years. America might suit, and they spoke English there too. He could get a better job. A new career in the New World would be right up his street.

That was his first and last time in Morocco, up to my time of writing. That's him all over, isn't it? Everything's great once, and then he doesn't keep it up. Just look at all his relationships – agh! that word again. They are usually supposed to grow and develop, but his just peter out. That may be fine by me, since I am by no means their biggest fan, but what will everyone else think? Does he have no force of will, they'll ask, no inner resources or strength of character? He is the man without qualities. This fearful lack of purpose thankfully does not afflict me. Just look at this quantity of writing. I am the man without quality. I have been to the desert, unlike him. The one inside myself, is what I mean. I could have told him: there is no wisdom there. I am a one-dimensional character, even with my unshakeable will. I do not grow or develop, I just remain more or less the same. I have no insights to offer, nothing new to say. If that's what you're after, you'd better look elsewhere. How about looking to him?

There will be no section in this selection entitled 'Africa'. Or an 'Asia' or an 'Australia' either. And the 'America' we are going to is North, not South. I will not even bother to mention an 'Arctica' or an 'Antarctica'. What matter if my exclusions invite accusations of being mired in the First World fortress? This tome is already reader-unfriendly enough without my adding even more to its proposed length. You thought the amount of time available to me would determine the amount of space my book would take up? That the length of my life would fix the length of my book? Not so. For I cannot keep writing about him, or myself, for the rest of my life. Forty seems like a good age to call a halt, since it is generally about half-time in the game of life, and the time between now and forty will find him in America. He didn't go to all those other wonderful places, so how could I possibly put them in? He is sticking to something and getting stuck in somewhere, at long last. The best of luck to him.

Are you disappointed, or relieved, that I intend to give up halfway through? That you won't get the second half, that there'll be no volume two? I don't know if I'm up to a sequel, to doing the whole thing again. Can nothing happen twice? Let's just finish this part for a start. Is this book half-empty or half-full? (It doesn't matter, if there's another book on the back burner.) I have only one life. Should I spend it all in writing about our lives? I don't know. But let me know what you think at the end, and I may get back to you. I may return to the myth, if I find I'm still in exile. Or if I return to my mythic exile, once again.

Paris again then, one more time, after a hot and heavy train journey that seemed to last for weeks rather than days, cooped up in a compartment crammed with reeking peasants, and stops at every station along the way until the French border, and then a few more besides just for good measure. After this, he felt he could get to dislike Spain almost as much as she had. The whole dreadful experience seemed to crystallise and be encapsulated in a flash, when he went out to the toilet to take a shit, and there, in the foul-smelling cubicle, above the over-flowing commode, was a graffito in black marker which, roughly translated, read:

THEY'RE ALL ONLY BITCHES – SO FUCK THEM ALL HARD

Just how much did some men really hate women? He convinced himself that he was not one of their number. Not even now. Just how many women hated hate-filled men? Was Laura one of them? Even now? There are loving men too. They just have to be given time to fall in love. Perhaps I am not one of them. But maybe my twin is. How do we find out who we are? By having relationships. Or, of course, by refusing to have them.

His passage had not been helped either by thoughts of what would await him on his return. He may have been able to put his misgivings on hold during his Islamic weekend, but with every chug of the engine and every squeak of the wheels on the tracks, his dread at what he would be facing into increased. The pain in Spain stayed not merely in his brain, but strayed into his heart as well. Or is the seat of the emotions lower down? Either way, I wouldn't know. For if true moral worth is gauged by the capacity to evince feeling, or at least to demonstrate its outward signs, notably laughter and tears, then I am an ethical bankrupt, a coelacanth among the backboned. But he has a heart, and now it is ready to be broken, even if he is also a heart-breaker. But I must have some redeeming feature too, surely. What could it be?

When he arrived, the apartment was empty. A few lines scrawled carelessly on a piece of paper, torn from a jotter and left under a lamp stand, asked him not to try contacting her or following her, said sorry, and wished him well. Had he driven her to such uncharacteristic brevity?

He phoned Milan, and the third time got to talk to her. Their conversation was faltering, punctuated with pregnant pauses, and she told him she still liked him, but didn't want to live with him. He could not find it in himself to plead with her to come back, or to take him back.

He knew she would want too much, more than he could give. From her tone, he judged it useless to go down there and see her. A moment later the line went dead, and there was only the empty, infinite promise of the dialling tone buzzing in his ear.

He went back to Dublin, and sorted out his documents for America. 'Are you now or have you ever been a member of the Communist Party?' So much red tape made him see red. But bureaucracy keeps people in jobs, and the business of America is business. So mind your own.

His letters to Laura went unanswered. Four or five years later he got a card from her, forwarded from Dublin to New York, saying she was married now, and had a baby boy, and wondering how he was doing. He never replied.

But he kept her image in his mind all the days of his going. That's the good thing about having a good memory, like him and me. You don't necessarily have to be with people, if you can remember them. Memories of the past feed future desires. If memory serves, who does it wait on? It waits on everyone, unlike time. But with memories like mine, what desires could I possibly have? Me remembering to fuel my desiring is a waste of my time. But with no desires, I can be autonomous. I don't need other people, as he does. The only desire that comes to me from memory is one to be left alone.

But he still needs to relate to people, as you will see. Memories of old loves make him want to meet new ones. He had been not giving a shit so as not to get hurt. Now he was giving a shit, and getting hurt. This split-up caused him great pain. It pained him that he had hurt her. But what pained him even more was that he could not help it. Was there something terribly lacking in him? If so, it was nothing to the void that lay at the heart of me, where my heart should be. He could not face the country of marriage, so now he was off to another continent, called America. I'll be going along too, of course, just for the ride. Who will he meet there? I'll watch, and tell you. But I won't be meeting anyone, for I'll be staying here.

So with an extended work visa in his pocket, Dub the Teddy in his suitcase, and his guitar under his arm, he wished his ageing and ailing parents goodbye, yet again. He knew they had been disappointed about what had happened between him and Laura, but they hadn't said anything. That was the best thing about them since they had got older, he mused: they never said anything. What can parents say or do anyway, when it comes to their children? No matter what they do, you'll do what you want to do. No matter what they did, he always did what he wanted. Even if it was his undoing. Now, what was he doing?

DONE

AMERICA

It occurs to me that I am America.
I am talking to myself again.

ALLEN GINSBERG, 'America'

1

L ISTEN, BUDDY, one more time, for old times' sake, to the words. They will tell you everything, and nothing. I am not fond of the sound of my own voice, despite any appearances, or rather sonorousnesses, to the contrary. It is only the sure and certain knowledge of the untoward increase to an intolerable level of my already habitual self-disgust, that I would feel should I not finish after coming thus far, that persuades me that I must keep on going farther until I can make an end. It's too late to stop now. This gentleman's not for turning. Otherwise, all I will be able to present you with are *Notes from an Abandoned Novel*, or *The Unfinished* – indeed *The Neverending – Story*. You think I like this, take pleasure in it? No, I don't, no more than you do.[1] Unlike my brother. He is having all the fun. But then, he doesn't have to read this. No one does. Except me. That is why it occasionally, or even often, depending on the extent of your imaginative sympathy, lapses into self-indulgence. But you are reading it too. Are you indulging yourself, at my expense? Thank you for indulging me.

Will it be so perpetually?

The New York skyline is familiar to everyone, I feel sure, if only from postcards and photographs, unless they have been up a mountain in Tibet since birth, or in some similarly hermetically sealed condition of

---

[1]   Unless it gives you a very peculiar, even perverse, pleasure. Then it might please me too.[2]

[2]   I'm sorry, but I just couldn't let this book go out into the world (especially with a section entitled 'America' in it) without at least one footnote.[3]

[3]   Or two.

isolation. Edward looked down on it now, his second time to see its lofty indifference to his little existence, but still to believe it was welcoming him because he was a big man. It was my second time too, at second-hand, despite my reclusive situation. I watch all his removes, at one remove. 'Give me your tired, your poor, your huddled masses yearning to breathe free' – and I'll piss and shit on them. Give me, rather, your brightest if not your best, your mightiest if not your most righteous, desiring only to do as well for themselves as possible. They, at least, will have some chance of survival, being the fittest if not the finest. And who, indeed, can blame them?

In no time at all, he had settled in. He found a job as a computer programmer in a Wall Street banking house, where he could learn how to become a systems analyst. That's where the real money is to be made, where to be real is to make money. He moved into an apartment in TriBeCa, which he shared with two other guys, whom we will call Chuck and Chester. A swinging bachelor lifestyle ensued.

They hung out after work at The Odeon, a trendyish bar fashionable among the set he fell in with; at weekends, trips out of town to the mountains or the beach, The Catskills or The Hamptons, became routine. Having a job with social standing and excellent prospects, if only limited satisfaction in the short term, added a few more planks to shore up further his already nearly fully coagulated sense of identity, and gave him the one thing needful, a good self-image. The self-confidence he acquired from being more than just a mere salaried slave acted as a veritable aphrodisiacal beacon, a spoor to lure potential mates, or at least dates. Yes, Edward became what is commonly referred to over there as A Babe Magnet.

He was part of a circle, both Irish and American, and Irish-American, and girls would ask of each other, and their male friends, frolicsomely, "Does he have a girlfriend?" He became well-known for having girlfriends, or for not having them for very long. As a consequence, the more adventurous ones all wanted to try their hand at taming him. Everybody wants what everybody else wants, evidently. That's how your stock, not to mention your cock, rises and falls, in the free market amatory economy.

Even in retrospect, it is remarkable to me how many eligible young women of apparently sound mind and invariably sounder body, fell almost effortlessly into his arms, and his bed, especially considering the risk of HIV infection if a condom just happened to split, awareness of which potential danger was by then pretty much universal. You'd think these dames would have had something better to do, if they'd any sense in their heads, but no. Maybe it was the gift of the gab, a touch of the Blarney, or the poet, or the poetical Blarney, which he'd honed so well in London, or just being in the right place at the right time, but a succession of Cathy Anns and Debbies, Sarah Janes and Chloes did not so much succumb to his charms as practically force themselves on him, or in some slightly more subtle incidences, indicate discreetly that any advance would be very welcome, and meet with assent. There may even have been a Colleen or two, a name much more popular in Irish-America than it is in the old country, Ireland. But as soon as any of these damsels wanted to make things anyway more permanent, they were let down, or when he made it clear he wasn't interested in getting serious, they dropped him, as they had done their panties, in order to get something more malleable that they could more easily mould. This they usually dignified as 'teaching him how to fall in love'. He didn't care. For there was always another one just around the corner, who thought that she was somehow different. Maybe there actually was. One who was different, I mean, not one who just thought it.

But perhaps their enthusiasm for him was not so unusual after all. You know the average American: always innocently and bravely seeking out new territory to go gallivanting in, all the while maintaining that pragmatic sense of values which insists on recompense, dictating that they get something out for anything they put in. Like the typical native of any nation you care to name, in fact. Unlike me.

But this was worse. They struck me as possessed of an egotism so unselfconscious it bordered on psychosis. That was the nice ones. This has led to the enshrining of a principle called The Pursuit of Happiness. They are insane in their determination to be happy, since they've been told they should be, because they've also been told that they're worth it. They think they're entitled to it as their birthright, and expect to attain it, or better still, just send out and have it delivered. They hold this truth to be self-evident. It is how they are constituted, whatever state they're in, and they frown on anyone who lets the side down by not achieving it, or at least not striving, however modestly, but preferably with relentless positivity, in that general direction. But I speak here very much as a European, albeit one from the very edge of the old world, who, unlike my brother, stands in trepidation at taking any leap, great or small, into the new. How I wish I could modify these over-direct, inane generalisations, but I am a victim of increasing, unbridled globalisation. I am catholic in my tastes, as well as my guilt, which is why I might seem to be always protesting too much.

But we're not put here to be happy. We have not here a lasting resting place. It's not meant to be a bed of roses, all sweetness and light. It's a vale of tears, a veil of tears, only occasionally alleviated by the odd sunbeam of a smile. As far as I can see through them, anyway, when I avail of tears. Which isn't often, and never anytime and anywhere that anyone could catch me. But then, the much-vaunted pleasure principle does not apply to me, or if it does, then only negatively. These people were seeking pleasure, while trying to avoid pain. Pleasure is the source of all life. Pain is the origin of all death. I cannot, as you know, possess the secret of joy. So it is hardly surprising that I am in danger of succumbing to despair. But they are only too eager to have someone get them interested in their childhoods, their relationships, their souls, their sexuality, and get them to talk about them, preferably from a semi-recumbent position, and help them explore the extremities and limitations of them to the full. Like people the rest of the world over. Unlike me.

They've got a name for everything nowadays, too.

Exemplum Gratis #1:

"I'm just putting my books and CDs in alphabetical order."

"Oh, you've got obsessive-compulsive disorder."

Exemplum Gratis #2:

"Look, I'll do whatever you want me to do."

"Oh, you're being passive-aggressive."

Exemplum Gratis #3:

"I don't feel like going out tonight."

"Oh, you've got agoraphobia."

Exemplum Gratis #4:

"I can't stand staying in tonight."

"Oh, you've got claustrophobia."

Exemplum Gratis #5:

"I can't concentrate on this book."

"Oh, you've got attention deficit disorder."

Exemplum Gratis #6:

"Would you ever listen to me when I'm talking to you?"

"Oh, you're indulging in attention-seeking behaviour."

Exemplum Gratis #7:

"I've just bought some shares in a new company."

"Oh, that's risk-taking behaviour."

Exemplum Gratis #8:

"I like to remain faithful to the same partner, for the rest of my life if possible."

"Oh, monogamy just shows you're straight-laced and repressed, castrated or frigid. Your hankering for security means you probably lack self-confidence."

Exemplum Gratis #9:

"I like to have many partners, and change them frequently."

"Oh, promiscuity just shows you're a manipulative user, and totally irresponsible too. Your fear of commitment means you probably lack self-confidence."

Exemplum Gratis #10:

"I can do whatever I want to do."

"Oh, you're over-confident, arrogant and selfish, a true megalomaniac."

Exemplum Gratis #11:

"I really trust that person and get on very well with them."

"Oh, you're co-dependent."

Exemplum Gratis #12:

"There's a lot wrong with the world."

"Oh, you're a sociopath."

Exemplum Gratis #13:

"I'm very worried about this terrible pain I've got."

"Oh, you're a hypochondriac."

Exemplum Gratis #14:

"I finally feel good about being who I am."

"Oh, you've got narcissistic personality disorder."

Exemplum Gratis #15:

"She's the only one for me, I'd go to the ends of the earth for her."

"Oh, you've got mono-obsessional disorder."

Exemplum Gratis #16:

"I'm determined to be the very best in my field, and I'm going to put everything I've got into perusing my ambition."

"Oh, you're an obsessive."
Exemplum Gratis #17:
"I don't accept that about myself."
"Oh, you're in denial."

Talk about fixing you with a formulated, or is it formulaic, phrase. They do tend to rush to a diagnosis, which can wreak havoc with the prognosis. Everyone in America is in denial. That's why everyone in America is in therapy. But I deny denial. But I'm not in America. Maybe I'm in denial about that. For we are all, or pretty soon will be, in America. Or an America of sorts. Like my brother. Unlike me. For America is the Big Brother we look up to and want to live up to, but maybe this Big Brother is not the best role-model around. We are watching Big Brother, but is he looking out for us? You have heard it said: one half of the world doesn't know how the other half lives. But I would go much further: no one knows how anyone else lives. But now everyone thinks they know how everyone else should live. But they don't know each other. They don't know diddly-squat. So live and let live.

Not that I'm casting aspersions on such ways of behaving. As a matter of fact, I've often wondered what would happen if I got interested in the things that they're interested in too. For myself personally, I mean.

I'd probably be a lot more serious, for a start. Everyone is serious, except me. A man leads a sad life if he can take nothing seriously (and, oftentimes, if he can, and does, as well). Even his own emotions, or lack of same. Most people have something they take seriously, be it religion, politics, sex, their careers, or their husbands, wives or children. I have nothing, only these things: words. Words are all I ever took seriously, and even that faith is fading fast, the more I use them, and am used by them. Words are worn out, or they are wearing me out. This is accidie, or do I mean ennui? That's probably caused by my anomie. Funny how the French always have a word for it, or more often than not, more than one. *Les mots juste.*

Still, this scribbling is all I've got left. Rather, it's all I ever had. I may not be able to recall how or why, where or when, I embarked, but I'm not about to jump ship now. At least, not just yet. I still need the emotional protection the voyage affords me, against what I really feel. I'm hardly going to betray my emotions, if I have any, by portraying them, if they're there. For the writing is my last line of defence, just as it is my first means of attack. And I am very defensive: that's the reason I am so offensive. When you rub out the words, or punch holes in them, or I wear them down, or cease writing them altogether, will you be able to see the real me behind them, beyond them, underneath them? Or are they the only real thing about me, and if they disappear, so too then do I? Keep reading, and find out. If you're interested, that is. I can only show my bad faith is bad by putting your good faith in me, and my text, if indeed it is mine at all, to the test.

I'd probably be a lot funnier too, if I took more of an interest in what everybody else takes an interest in. Funny ha ha, the kind that makes people laugh, as opposed to funny peculiar, the stuff that makes them blanch. In short, I would conform to the norm. But I can't, and I doubt that I ever could, or indeed ever will. But you go right ahead and be my guest, by all means. For I am not saying that I know any better than you. I know better than that. But I do know different from you. I know no different from that. So get interested in whatever aspect of yourself and your life you want to get interested in. It will keep you occupied and out of my hair, even if it does make work for all manner of rogues and quacks. But, then, that in turn keeps them off the streets and out of my way, too. Except when they try to tell me that I'd be happier and healthier if I was interested in whatever they're interested in, or you're interested in, or interested in something, anything at all.

But I am not interested in having interests. Every bond is a bond to sorrow. Including the bond to having no bonds. That's not the kind of attitude they like to hear. So maybe I should set about acquiring some commitments. If only in a further bid to stave them off, and keep them off my back.

Very well, my words are my bonds. Which is where we came in. Back to square one. They've got you covered, no matter which way you turn. If only I could be literally unbound. But then I might catch verbal diarrhoea. Though there's some who'd say I've done as much, if not much more, already. My dentistry has been engulfed by dysentery. I am not so very foolish, or so much more cowardly than the next man, but maybe what I need is a custard pie in the face. Every old wife knows the delicious yellow filling to be an excellent binding agent, and the old jest of the ancient gesture will surely hand you the last and perforce the longest laugh, however hollow it may ring in the dark. But there is no one here to lend a hand, and perform this kind office for me. Except myself. Now that's what I call funny.

Can it be that I have been happy all along, or could have been happy sometime, and not known it? Can it be that I am, or could be, happy still? If you're happy and you know it, clap your hands. If you're happy, and you don't know it, how can you find out?

Then there is the question of why he, whatever about the ladies, was doing it, with them. Do I really need to ask it, on your behalf? Don't you know the answer, as much as I do? The great question: why? Always answered more than adequately by the other great question: why not?

If you want a long, boring, rigmarole explanation, I suppose you could say that promiscuity, like travelling the world has been for him, like writing words has been for me, is a search for something. A little something, to fill the big nothing. Something to be interested in, as it were, to compensate for our genuine want of interest in things. For maybe he is no more interested in things than I am. He just pretends better than I do. Although that wouldn't be too difficult now, would it, since up until now I haven't been bothering to pretend at all? But you probably find his wantonness very understandable. He was fucking away his pain. I couldn't understand it. I can't fuck away my pain. I can't fuck, period, because of my pain. If I were to try, I would only feel more pain.

Granted, he could have fucked the same person over and over again, instead of lots of different ones a few times, but he had found that this only causes more pain than pleasure in the long run, and amounted to merely a slower form of the serial monogamy he was practising now. One way or another, you always wind up getting fucked over. Or they do. Damned if you do, damned if you don't, as they used to say. You're caught every which way, no matter what way you go, as they still say. First you get the pleasure, then comes the pain. As for me, there is no time interval between them. I get the pain immediately, and precious little pleasure. Perhaps that is why I am trying to make my pain my pleasure. Its pursuit, after all, is only the way of nature, as they used to say. And nature will out, as they still say. All animals gravitate towards it, just as they are repelled by its opposite. The good life is demonstrably better than, and therefore more preferable to, a bad one.

But what happens to you, when doing what gives everyone else pleasure only increases your pain? Or doing what gives you pleasure gives everyone else a pain? Is it any wonder that I stand somewhat aloof, indifferent to everyday concerns, the common weal as it were, present in this, my own made-up world, only to the extent that I am absent from the so-called real one? But this one is real enough, to me.

So thank heavens for the anaesthesia of not caring, whether of the physical or emotional variety. For pain partakes of both, and sometimes both at once, although extreme emotional pain does tend to be the luxury of those not in extreme physical pain, although one of the chief consequences of prolonged extreme physical pain will be its emotional counterpart. Just as I am sure that extreme emotional pain will invariably manifest itself in physical symptoms, sooner or later. The metabolism is always disturbed in any emotional upset. The emotions are always disturbed by any metabolic upset. That's why I have buried my emotions. My metabolism can't handle them. Nor can my emotions handle my metabolism.

Which is worse: the pain of having no emotions, or the pain of having too many? We are always being adjured to control our emotions; that is, when we are not being encouraged to let them all hang out. I suspect that where and when and with whom you do it, or alternatively don't, is the key. But maybe those who do not show them really don't have any. However, while this anaesthetic may cut off pleasure as it blocks pain, surely this is a small price to pay for feeling no pain, if you're in pain. You wind up feeling numb, which means feeling nothing at all, bar your own numbness. Like I do, or rather, don't. Or rather, do. For this feeling nothing, this affectless lack of sensation, is in itself an extreme way of feeling. My mind tells me this. Whether it is pleasurable or painful, I will leave up to your mind to tell you. But don't knock it till you've tried it, as they say in these parts. Especially if you're always on the lookout for something new. There is some measure of the aesthetic, and the anaesthetic, in all of us. To say nothing of the ascetic. The solution is all about getting our own balancing act right. Am I being lucid or ludic, or a Libran in need of Librium? Whatever we are, we should all learn our scales, before scaling the heights or plumbing the depths, hitting the high notes or droning the low, or simply slip-sliding silently and surreptitiously away, when the scales have fallen from our eyes, and we see finally what fools we've been.

Maybe you incline to the view that justifying his promiscuity as a palliative is just an excuse for lots of shagging, just as making a case for my articulacy under the same rubric is simply advocating the kind of verbiage I've just put you through. But what is so reprehensible about sex for its own sake? It is, after all, one of the few saving graces of being alive, or so I'm told. And words are there to be used, by those who know how to use them. But such an attitude on his part, I hear you object, exploits those with whom he consorts, and is as abusive of them as my prattling patter is of this marvellously capacious language.

Well, they seem to like it, and he never led them to believe that they wouldn't be brushed aside if they became too demanding. Meanwhile, my going on and on in general about nothing very much in particular is surely no different to what happens in boardrooms and courthouses and lecture halls and schoolrooms and parliaments all over the world every day of the week, in the name of increasing wealth, dispensing justice, furthering knowledge, dispelling ignorance and improving life. Again, I ask you which is worse: our little games which make no secret of the fact that they are just games, or their big games which keep up the façade of being so much more important than just being games? It is all only a game. The deadly ones are the ones who think of themselves, and are thought of, as being engaged in anything more important than playing a game. We live in puritanical times, which may well be a mere veneer for a free for all, but I still see no reason to deride the ride, or to rein in the wild horses of words.

Nor, being me, do I see any reason to overpraise them either, or let them ride roughshod over me. I aim for the middle way, however tepid that might make me. Does that make you want to spit me out of your mouth? If the golden mean does not agree with you, it is probably best not to swallow it, although I find such individualistic taste extreme in the extreme. In this, I am extremely median. For it does seem to me that sex, so important to people when they are young that their interest in it can sometimes verge on the paranoid, becomes when they are older just another fact of life, so much so that their taking it for granted, or out and out lack of interest in it, can make it seem trivial. Just as over-interest in it can make it seem trivial too. Just as lack of interest in it can verge on the paranoid. Two opposite directions, which bring you to the same destination. You take the high road, and I'll take the low road, and whether I attain equilibrium afore ye or after ye, we will still meet up there. For all I see, they are as sick that surfeit with too much as they that starve with nothing. It is no mean happiness, therefore, to be seated in the mean. So long as you're not mean. That's The Facts of Life, according to me.

Still and all, despite my disability, which lessens my desirability, perhaps it is only incipient middle age that has given rise to, as it were, and can be held responsible for, as I say, my reflections and ruminations on the relative unimportance of sexuality. Better to have too much than not enough, is the counsel of the majority. Ask any hale and hearty seventeen-year-old, and he or she will contradict me. Except the seventeen-year-old I was. But then, I was hardly hale or hearty. The sexual impulse, which can be employed in the service of reproduction, as well as purely for pleasure – indeed the unalloyed ecstasy of which is the main ruse, frequently frustrated, of Madam Nature, keeper of this great terrestrial brothel, to seduce us to reproduce, and thus furnish new staff and clients for her dilapidated knocking shop known as The World at Large – is generally the first of our major faculties to go. Then it's usually the brain that seizes up, and you lose your mind. And eventually even the heart gives out, and you're a goner. Of course, the sequence is different for everyone. But dissolution, to say nothing of disillusion, one way or another, is inescapable, not to mention inevitable.

Similarly with words, but the other way around. They are tossed off so carelessly in our formative years, with little or no scrutiny, and it is only later we learn to weigh them, and judge their worth. Except me, who began so stiffly and stuffily, as tight-lipped as he was tight-assed, only to have my tongue loosened so that the phrases run riot from my lips and dribble down my chin, prodigally and profligately, as if bidden by someone. Or rather, as if unbidden. You can't have too much of a good thing.

You may say that such indiscriminate use of women, on his part, and words, on mine, is doing dirt on life. But life itself is dirty, before it gets clean. Otherwise, what need would we have of rubbing and scrubbing, polishing and shining? We need our fine style, to go foraging in the filth. We can all do with a little purgation and purification. Besides, I am not my brother's keeper, no more than he is mine. I hope you do not detect traces of sibling rivalry. We do not go in for fraternal strife.

So, maybe it is true that all this sex play and word play can't last. But it's all right while it does. He was having it all, or having them all. I was having none of it. I am old beyond my years. He is younger than his years. He wasn't girl crazy, he was cunt crazy. But girls were the only ones in possession of these wondrous organs. So it follows that he would have more than a passing interest in the purveyors of such remarkable items. Until, that is, the right girl came along. Or he came on her. Then he would see her whole, as well as her hole, and stop seeing the others. Or for me, until I found the right word. Or it found me. Then I would see the words around that word, and maybe even the world beyond them, and start making sense. That, anyway, is how the scenario is suppose to go.

But what is that word known to all men? Fucked if I know. Maybe it's the word 'girl'.

The computer screen in front of him flickered to life, as another day at the office began. The box emitted its squeaks and squawks and rat-tat-tatted, as it warmed up and slipped into gear. The more he learned about these newfangled machines, the more I was drawn into the vortex of taking them on board. The motherboard became my mother-lode. Oh, I didn't give a fiddler's about how they worked, the way he did. Leave that to the techies. I was more intrigued by their everyday applications. It seems I'm not such a lost cause, completely refractive to rehabilitation, after all. My interest can still be caught, just about.

Ah, technology: the knack of so arranging the world that we need never experience it at first hand, if we choose not to. What a boon for nerds like me. How quickly time catches up with you. We are in the '90s already. Have you noticed how much of life now takes place on screens? Ones you can interact with, that talk back to you. Soon we will barely have to live at all. As for living, our computers will do that for us. Unless those with the wherewithal to do so use computers to make us their servants, yet again, by gluing us to the ones they own. Soon I will cease competing with these gadgets altogether, and surrender sweetly to using one of them for putting an end to this miserable memoir, this chronic chronicle, and then for disseminating it throughout the world of real time and cyberspace. I am doing time. I am filling space. The subliminal is sublime. I will be the ultimate voyeur. I will be a virtual recluse. If only I could afford one of these miracles of modern science. For what can a poor boy do, if he doesn't stir outside the door, and hasn't got the readies to get his hands on one? Just go on watching his brother watching the screens, I suppose. If he is lucky enough to have one of *them*.

Look at him now, typing in a few commands, finding out what's wrong with some set-up thousands of miles away. He could easily be made to imagine himself The Master of the Universe, such is his opportunity for accessing so much information just by pushing some buttons. Infinite power in a little room. The trouble is, as always, everyone else in the same position could easily fall into the same trap too. All lost in little worlds of their own. Where would we be then? Too many Chiefs, and not enough Indians. A Democracy of Dictators, with each striving to be First Among Equals.

In the beginning, there was the cinema screen, as there always will be, world without end. People like things big. Then came television, a smaller, dirtier, more instant and intense hit, handier to score, harder to regulate, and so the drug of the nation. How addictive the fix of soap operas, their plot lines like brown or white lines to be hoovered up with needy glee, their characters' characteristics made to grow into a habit you just don't want to kick. Plot is character in action, as they say, and everyone wants a piece of it. To say nothing of the chat shows, where the famous, the fatuous, the infamous, and the as yet unfamed, share all, and we get high on the vibes of *craic*, like so many vials of crack. Then along came video, and you could have a little cinema in the discomfort of your own home. Now there is this internet, and these seedy ROMS. You can find anything on a screen. So put your hand against the screen, as these American televangelists tend to say.

Look at him again, back in his own room, stroking the keys, and stroking something else as well. Don't you think it odd that, when there's no shortage of hot snatch around, such an accomplished eroticist should have recourse to supplementing it by solo self-pleasuring, to the extent that it threatens to usurp the real thing? (Did I really just write the word 'real', expecting it to mean something? So much for reality testing!)

But there's the rub, as it were, for it is not so low at all, nor is it really unreal. He finds it queerly comforting to feel a keyboard caress from thousands of miles away, to fantasise and jerk off with people he has never met, and probably never will meet, on the other side of the globe. What's surprisingly soothing is that there's no involvement involved, or commitment made, and so he is free to hook up with, or even be, 'Tie

Me Up And Beat Me' from Pittsburgh, or 'Mistress Beatrice' in Aberdeen, or 'Master George', or 'Uncle Ted', or 'Sabrina the Teenage Witch', or 'Buffy the Vampire Slayer', or – dare it be said – 'Daddy', or even worse 'Daughter', or – whisper it low – 'Mommy', or even worser than worst, 'Son', and no harm done, because **no one gets hurt**. Except maybe himself, by himself, because he's by himself. So also may the others, by themselves, as they are also by themselves. They do it to themselves.

There is, on the one hand, something to be said for solitary sex: it's relatively inexpensive, and you don't have to dress up for it (if you don't want to), and you don't have to talk face to face to a partner, before, during or after (if that's what your usual partner(s) like). On the other hand, it is important, from the point of view of normal healthy socialisation, that people prefer sex with others to masturbation. I'm not in a position to take sides myself, at a loss as I am as to what constitutes normal and healthy, and caring not a whit for integration with society, but it does seem to me that lots of folks have had better wanks than they've had fucks. But there again, by the same token, maybe the redundancy of engagement in this supposedly synthetic world will spill over, as it were, to the allegedly authentic one, and my brother will find it impossible to forge meaningful attachments there. Then he will be like me, and I am not even working with the benefit of his adjuncts to distraction. You behold before you, at least in me, a horrible example of unaided and unrelenting solipsism. But how altruistic, rather than selfish, of him, if not of me, to take this risk for his fellow man and woman. Far from being dehumanising, how much more humane could you get? This is not a sign of underlying inadequacy, but lends whole new strata to the personality. Fluid identity flows, roles switch, positions shift, in a way they can't possibly under the tedious restrictions of the polite conventions imposed by the everyday social round. So much for a coherent plot, with well-rounded characters. We will have to make up names for sensations yet to be experienced, emotions as yet unfelt, thoughts not yet formed.

So what if half the women to be found out there have the bodies of men? That just proves the point about us being amorphous, androgynous beings. Besides, there are lots of creatures with the bodies of women who take full advantage of what's on offer there too. You can still put a 1 into a 0, with these ones and zeros. Why do you think

Soho, St Denis and Times Square are all cleaned up now? Because everyone's surfing and cybering away at home, that's why! These terminals are where it all originates. Far out in space, with the slaves of the waves, is where travel and words and sex, the things us boys have been doing to fill in time, are finally mingled and mastered, without us having to go anywhere, or do anything. To understand a society, you must understand its pornography, and what a veritable pornucopia of psychosexual corn erupts from this goat's horn. It is a state of the art recording of the basso profoundo known colloquially as the collective unconscious, and played straight back into every single one, like turning a loop the loop, through our auricles. It is a computer-generated film in those deep lurid tones shot in the depths of the shared psyche, and projected right back into each individual one, like running a lap of honour, via our retinas. Sex will always be more interesting and revealing in stereo, and on a screen, than it is in the humble flesh. Who said that? Whoever it was, they were right. I think everyone should be a machine. Who said that? Whoever it was, they were right again.

If we have indeed been dehumanised, let us embrace and play with our dehumanisation, if only for a while. Besides, it's always possible to combine man or woman with machine, and have sex with someone while you both watch a screen. We must look into that.

Strange, that Edward should be coming across these advances, which make being alone so much easier, in America, where to live alone is seen as a sign of failure. People shouldn't live together. But they do. Maybe they won't. In future, everyone will live alone. It's the only way to go. Life is about learning how to live alone, not how to live with other people. Mine has been, anyway. Have I ever learned how to live? I never did get the hang of this life thing. But there is little to learn about living alone. In fact, there's nothing to it. For it is barely living. Living and partly living. But that's how I like it. Alone again naturally, I used to think, when I worried about being alone. But being alone is not necessarily being lonely.

So do not dismiss the net he is captured in as simply for the saddoes. We are all sad sometimes. If they're the butterflies, who's the collector? Nor should you condemn the web he is caught in as nothing more than a playground for perverts. Maybe all those who log on are just feeling lonely, like him, or are thoroughgoing loners, like me. That doesn't make us losers. For who does not feel lonely from time to time, and what loner does not like to be reinforced in their aloneness, by being reassured that many others are alone too? If they're the flies, where's the spider?

But maybe they're alone precisely because that's their idea of kicks, and maybe not all the lonely are sliding inexorably towards being alone. Maybe it is merely a self-deluding rather than a self-fulfilling prophesy to say that everyone, Edward included, will live, and die, like me.

The knocking continues, and the smell abides. I wonder if it's not the front door at all, but my heart pounding to get out of my ribcage, and my putrid flesh rotting with intense self-loathing?

Looking up from the screen in his office one day, he descried a tallish young woman of slender proportions standing across from his work-station, chatting cheerily with a mutual colleague at the watercooler. Her hair was long, thick, strawberry rather than platinum blonde, cut in a fringe, or should I say bangs, that flopped down and stopped just short above a pair of champagne eyes, while her skin, so soft yet perfectly porcelain, traversed over altitudinous cheekbones, and her smile was a row of straight pearly whites. This striking appearance was enhanced by a well-cut, two-piece, hound's-tooth business suit, the skirt of which was no longer than it should have been, that is, at least four inches above the knee, revealing a generous display of long perfect American legs that simply kept on going up and up, tapering down into shiny black patent pumps, and sheathed in sheer black tights…or was that a stocking top that showed through the neatly cut little slit down the front at the left-hand side, every time she adjusted her posture against the wall she was leaning against, and flashing just the merest millimetre of bare flesh above it? Yes, those were surely the outlines of her suspender clips, or garter belt as he'd learned to call this nifty garment here, vaguely visible when the material tightened over her thighs.

It is easy for the non-fetishistically inclined to sneer here about silly little boys and dirty old men, and invoke the example of Dr Pavlov's famous dogs, foaming at the mouth and straining at the leash, but any aficionado of hose and heels worth his low grunt of approval, which can go on to register on the scale of delight as anything from a furtive giggle to a raucous guffaw, will not be slow to appreciate the effect this sight would have had on my brother.

To top all this off, her jacket was hanging open, and he did not fail to notice her breasts pushing tautly, and, some would say, even tartily, against the diaphanous black lacy chiffon of her blouse, stretching it slightly, and the two small but significant protuberances at the centres of these generous mounds suggesting the pert nipples beneath. She was, in other words, in the parlance *de nos jours*, A Babe.

The fellow-workmate she was shooting the breeze with was also female, indeed one with whom our Edward had on a couple of occasions found himself in a clinch, even if he considered it bad policy to become embroiled with women from work, and generally heeded the by now familiar maxim, 'Don't Screw the Crew'. So when he caught this new girl's eye and beamed hello at her, his sometime former squeeze introduced her coyly with the words, "This is Amanda, the new girl on the block."

"Welcome to The House of Fun," he ventured, with what he hoped would come off as a roguish air of good-humoured bonhomie. He liked doing the hail-fellow-well-met in the New World, which he liked to think he combined well with the sangfroid of the Olde one, to break the ice that lay between them.

"Thanks," she nodded.

"I'm Ed," he said, using the appellation he was now most frequently addressed by, and extended his hand.

"Pleased to meet you," she told him perkily as they shook hands, his a polite grip, hers a gentle grasp.

She gave a little hair flick, media-taught, and went back to the girly confab.

It is not as though Edward had not had his way with some certifiable stunners in his time, or that he popped his cork, peed his pants, or strutted like a peacock displaying its iridescent, variegated tail for every nice bit of tail that crossed his path. But there was something about this one. But sure wasn't there something about everyone? Yes, but not that certain something. But sure wasn't there a certain something about everyone he got involved with? Yes, but not as certain a something as this.

She seemed flighty yet demure, sassy yet shrewd, effervescent yet serene. She looked like a picture, and could be in pictures. But then, everyone could be in pictures. All right then, she looked like she could be a star, and not everyone can be a star, despite whatever you may have heard otherwise. Or, at least, they cannot sustain stardom for very long. The very beautiful, and the merely plain, though we'd like them to be so, are not the same. She was, in short, all that the male gaze would like to gaze at, all that the female gazed at would like to be. Would she prove to be a nice little man-pleaser, or would this graven image talk back? They all do, eventually, even the sphinx-like, and the sylph-like, even if it's only to pose a riddle, or wriggle out of a pose. Still, he felt like inquiring of someone, as soon as an opportunity arose, "Does she have a boyfriend?"

Maybe Edward was trying to show me, if only inadvertently, that not all Americans, and by extension, not all people, are the same. There are, after all, quite a lot of them. Americans, that is. And people too, come to think of it. There's good and bad everywhere, and in everyone, as they used to say. There's more to this than meets the eye, as they still say. So maybe there are nice Americans, as well as nasty ones, the same as there are nice people and nasty people the rest of the world over. Plus, the roles are constantly interchangeable, and some are one one minute, and the other the next. So maybe it's places that are more or less the same, or rather, no place is that much better or worse than any other place, when it comes to its people. It's just that America is so much bigger and, although it might be difficult to always remember this, it was pilgrim paranoia, followed closely by evolutionary eugenics, that drove its non-native peoples there in the first place, and helped them to survive and thrive, so everything is a bit more pronounced and magnified there than everywhere else. This world writ large can make the rest of the world seem small, and viewing the small world from this grand perspective, other countries may appear to be lagging behind.

But the saving grace, no matter where you are, is that you can't hide common, and this woman was class. American girls – well Californians at any rate, which is what Amanda turned out to be – are renowned, as Every Good Boy who Deserves their Favours knows, for being Good in Bed. It may not be politically correct to say as much, but they 'let you', as it were. Or, as Statesiders themselves put it, they 'come over', and 'put out'. Not only that, but they have an undeniable reputation as consummate sack artists, the nice girls as much, if not more so, as the nasty ones. Back in Edward's and, if you can stifle that grin for a second, my formative years, back in the Ireland where we were born and bred, it was only the cheap, dirty, little flibbertigibbets who slept around, the very fact that they did so confirming that they were what they always were, scrubbers and slappers, slags and sluts. Nowadays well-brought up young ladies do too, and so so too can you. Except, sometimes they're choosy. So, maybe you should be too.

So, would Edward be successful in this mission he had unwittingly embarked on – to whit, converting me to his less damning view of people, and Americans, who are, of course, people too? Even if it is I, after all, who is assigning him this motive, so why should he care? It should prove instructive to test how far floccinaucinihilipilification can get you, if only by demonstrating that it doesn't get you very far. (To say nothing of providing a similar service for the sesquipedalian.) And will Amanda deliver on the exceptional promise outlined above? Or would she just prove to be another male-made maid, a fantasy figure girl? Maybe that's what she really was, or wanted to be. She could even be both, at one and the same time.

Ho hum. Here we go again. Third time lucky? Well, she's once, twice, three times a lady. He was a daydream believer. He had not yet given up on attaining his ideal. She was a homecoming queen. She seemed dangerously, dreamily real.

2

T HERE WERE DRINKS AFTER WORK with the office crowd, as is *de rigueur*, but it was only when he'd made what she seemed to be taken with as some slightly *risqué* but irredeemably scintillating quips, of the order of, "Ah yes, Aran Sweaters and Thatched Cottages and Leprechauns: in Ireland we still progress from the breast to the potato...or the bottle of Guinness..." – here a slight pause for dramatic effect and emphasis – "...and then keep trying to find our way back again...", and so responded by fluttering her fair eyelashes at him, that he succeeded in enticing her for an intimate assignation at Elaine's on 2nd Avenue.

This bar still had some of its old literary associations, and since he still had some vague pretensions in that direction, he divined it would be a good haunt to get her alone in, since even though she was a graphic design graduate, it had come to his attention that she did read the odd novel now and again, and Irishmen, as is well known, and the women too, which is not such common knowledge, are dab hands at writing stories. It comes as second nature to them, like downing the above-mentioned mother's milk, or plates of spuds, or pints of porter. He would impress her with his impression of an impressionistic scribbler. In playing this role there is much he could have learned from me, had he troubled himself to look, for I am even more of a past master at imitating a writer, or at imitative writing, than he; viz.: the book you are holding.

During this tête-à-tête he plied her with Old Fashioneds like they were going out of style, along with a few more well-chosen droll witticisms, such as, "A Graphic Design Major? But you look too young to have been in the army...", or, "Of course, the next best thing to a lesbian relationship is to go out with an Irishman...", which kept her amused while he got her, or she got herself, drunk. For it was not as though she needed much persuading to open her mouth and loosen her lips with him or, as it transpired, to open her legs for him and have her other lips loosened by him, or by many others.

I do apologise here, before we venture any further together, to readers who are of a more sensitive disposition, whether it stems from prudishness or prudence, for this apparent increasing coarsening of the language. But it is hard for me to kick against the pricks, and perforce the cunts, by persisting in and acting on my belief that soon the majority of people are not going to be interested in sex any more. Especially with that boy my brother around. You see, although these lines may well be being penned with a more astute and select readership in mind, I am still going to have to put some good old ordinary out of the ordinary sexual perversity in all the same, otherwise the work won't shift units in sufficient quantities to ensure its safe arrival into the public domain. You are the market that doesn't like the market, or like to think of itself as a market, but the whole world, yourself included, is as yet still eagerly aroused by egregious rumpy-pumpy, or at the very least, by the very thought of it. In this sphere, as in others, your tastes may well be more recondite than those of the Average Joseph or Josephine Public, the Man or Woman in the Street, the Boy or Girl Next Door, and the World and his Wife, but since when was sex ever merely a simple pleasure, even for every Thomas, Richard or Harold? They have their peccadilloes too, just like you do. That's why sex sells. It is, since we got rid of The Man Above, or He gave up on Us, in other words in the wake of religion, the opium of the people. So, more opium, I say. You know you want to. And so, therefore, must I. And so, also, does she.

And when I told them, they didn't believe me. But when she told him, he believed her. Why shouldn't he? So, so should you. She was, after all, an attractive, good-humoured, untraumatically and unabusedly well-brought up, reasonably intelligent, liberally educated, unhung up twenty-four-year-old woman in the whole of her health, with a zest for living and loving, and a lust for life and love. Living life had not diminished her love for it, for life had not yet dealt forcibly with her, by forcing her to live without love, or at least it hadn't made much of an effort in that direction, in fact so little that you could be forgiven for being tempted to wonder if it ever would. In short, she was hot to trot, whether you like it or not.

Now, why is that such a problem for you? So, she enjoys sex. So, she does most everything. It's not her fault. It's not a crime. Why are you so adversely averse to the polymorphously perverse? Are you just jealous because she wasn't taught about God and the Devil, and made to lie awake at night sweating in the dark about Heaven and Hell, and saving or damning her Immortal Soul and all that ghastly old tommy-rot, or had to hide what she thought of the priest or the minister, or was told to co-operate with the psychotherapist or psychiatrist? Well tough titty for you. You should show some tender mercy. You should be happy for her, for as long as it lasts, not accusatory.

No, the shrinks and therapists would come later, if I'm any judge of horseflesh, or what becomes of fresh young flesh, when it goes the way of all flesh. This thought could give you gooseflesh. Who knows, maybe her parents did indeed send her to one of their kind, just as I myself had been through their mill, because they cared and didn't want to see her go astray and thought it was for the best, and she had lived to tell the tale, but did not tell it, or did not tell him, yet. Were I to tell you, one way or the other, if she had been or not, or whether or not she told him if she had been, that would be telling tales, way out of school. I am not yet a tell-tale. Although I do still have a heart.

Or maybe you are someone who is somewhat over-zealous in your quest for the total feminisation of society, who is more authoritarian than authoritative in holding that no man, even one as disinterested as me, is authorised to write about a woman in this way, who does those things that way, because what would he know anyway? Any woman who looked, much less dressed, like that would live in a non-stop gapping garrison of hair-trigger hard-on, you say, and those attentions would be most unwelcome, and would be wished away. You think men shouldn't do women, especially ones who look like her. But you only have to look around to see that lots of women look like that, and I want to do them. Can I? I don't mean I'm asking your permission, like can I do them at all? I mean don't you think I can do them well? Because I do do them, so I can do them, no matter how I do them, even if I no can do them.

But just suppose for a minute that there was a woman who actually liked doing all the things that you're about to learn she liked to do, and not just to please the ones with money and power and influence by abasing herself before them, but because she got off on these acts herself, in themselves, for themselves, for herself. For if there are ladies' men, surely there are men's women, even ones who aren't looking to get anything else out of what they do beyond the pleasure of the moment of doing it. Maybe it turned her on to turn guys (and girls) on, and she smiled to see their cocks stand, and revelled in the sybaritic abandon of any orgy. She took it for granted that most men would shag a lamp-post, given half a chance, and didn't look for her security there. If preferment came, then so be it, but that's not what she set out to get. She was just her own woman, just as they were their own men, insofar as anyone can be so indiscriminately independent, man or woman.

Or maybe she merely typifies the trend of people mimicking their emotional and sexual lives, how to feel or not feel, to behave or not behave, from the television screen, or the silver one, or that of the computer. You can't see her because of what's expected of her; and because of what's expected of her, she can't see herself. The made-up self has become herself. But so what, if she's happy like that? You're only young once. She won't have the ass she's got now forever. So, should he love her for her soul, or nail her while she's hot? Whatever which way it is, be assured: she is no mere male fantasy fodder, she is a real deal female sex-fiend. Or rather, she is both. Because she wants to be. Even if in reality she is the product of fantasy.

If you forgot I was writing this, would you believe it then? If I forgot I was writing this, would it be more believable?

Not that everything came out that first night. She'd have to see how shockable he was first. She wouldn't want to scare him away. Plus, they were with the same firm, which might throw a spanner in the works, or the work. She knew her way around, because she'd been around.

She didn't think much of the food at Elaine's, even if he found it passable enough, so after a couple more drinks, they took their leave. It was back to his place then, where a tie knotted around the outside door-knob of his room signalled to Chuck and Chester that manoeuvres were taking place within. And what action! What they didn't get up to, or down to, on this and many subsequent nights, is not worth even considering.

You never really know someone until you know them sexually, so they say. But maybe you never really know someone until you know them intellectually and emotionally as well. (Or until you've lived with them every day for twenty-five years, and even then....) And surely extravagant sexual indulgence can just as easily be a way of not getting to know someone too. We all have our ways of covering up, including showing off. And vice versa, of course. But Edward *knew* Amanda.

"That's a difficult skirt," he laughed knowingly, trying to run his hand up her stockinged thigh under her green A-line, as they sat on his bed, kissing deeply.

"I'll take it off," she smiled placidly. "I'll take all my clothes off."

Which is what she stood up and proceeded to do, with a little help from him. She lent a hand with his divesting too, a shirt button here, a fly zipper there, and the laces of his shoes. He noticed that she had had herself adorned with a diamond navel ring, and a tiny tattoo of a butterfly fluttering up and away was etched on her mons veneris. There's nothing like being with a new person, as she herself told him much later, explaining away one of her careless infidelities. It all seemed so right, as though it were a preordained event that couldn't help but happen, and it appeared to unfold in slow-motion, in moments suspended outside time.

You may have thought of her as a bit of a flake, but she was no fool. In fact, she was his best ever. Maybe it's no fluke that this should be so, what with her hailing from that New Eden which many see as not only preparatory to, but fully embodying, the forefront of The Fall of Man. Can silly girls be good lovers too? Possibly, if they put what passes for their minds to it. But that was not a problem with which she had to contend, being the proud possessor of a fairly useful mind, to complement her compact and delicious body. She was fully conversant with modern cosmetic sexual techniques, and diligently aware of the endorphin rush which is such a vital concomitant of orgasm, and is deemed essential for continued good health and all-round well-being, for painkilling and pleasure-giving. There are numerous bright girls who go in fear of their sexuality, of course, or are not even very cognisant of its existence at all, or who for various reasons of their own choose to be reserved about it. But that's another story, for another time.

Their tongues twirled around each other, as they lay back on his divan bed by the window, and went at it hammer and tongs. His tumescent, non-servile member slipped into her willing, non-virile sheath like a knife cutting straight through butter, such was her ready wetness. She licensed his roving hands, and let them go before, behind, between, above and below. She was his America, his new-found-land. His wandering fingers had found a home. Their respective mouths transmogrified into veritable suction pumps vacuumed together, and he sucked maniacally on her tongue until he nearly swallowed it down his throat, while his middle finger sought and found and slipped inside the tiny puckered orifice secreted between the folds of her bum-cheeks, and she began rotating vigorously, like one possessed, on the half-buried digit that protruded from the comfy saddle supplied by both his hands. As their separate crises approached, which would happily arrive simultaneously, she obligingly prised her lips away from his and whispered delicately into his ear, "I'm going to cum soon", and so he rapidly ascended from his then current plateau of pleasure to an apex from which vantage he could easily bring all the foregoing to a satisfying conclusion, letting go a shot into her darkness that caused explosions of light to go off in his head and power to surge through his limbs, her grinding against his thrusts at their point of conjunction resulting in the self-same effect being created in hers, or so she assured him a little later, as they lay together in the warm afterglow, she stretched out on top of him, positively purring like the cat that had got the cream.

After a suitable, restful interval, she slinked her way slowly down his body with all the grace and danger of a practised feline, stopping to kiss his nipples and stomach on the way, and as he opened his legs to give her more elbow room she dragged her tongue tantalisingly across his testicles. Then she smiled up at him conspiratorially as he raised himself slightly off the mattress on the soles of his feet, granting her easier access to his perineum, to which she duly attended with lavish licks. She had a tongue that knew all about how to get on in the world, as her skilfully rhythmic butterfly caresses along his proudly upstanding shaft, before plunging it into her succulent, industrious mouth, amply evidenced. Such was the extremity of the pleasant sensations supplied by this dual action, that he was forced to fall back on his old reliable ruse of getting to grips with an as yet unsolved chess problem in the back of his mind, although now they were stockpiled from the *New Yorker* rather than the *Irish Times*, or he might have erupted again almost immediately, which would have been a tad too soon for both of them. This was, in its own way, a welcome reappearance for this recourse, since with the majority of Amanda's fellow female citizens whom he had bedded, it had become necessary to resort to the equal and opposite expedient of fantasising outrageously during coitus itself in order to reach the point of getting off, if not getting up. They said he came too late, but it was they who came too early. Thus can being retarded be as bothersome as being premature. No such problems prevailed here, for after she had crawled back up him once more, and he deftly parted her buttocks and glided the same middle-finger in a maddeningly ticklish manner along the super-sensitive hollow that bisected her behind, she closed her eyes and visibly quivered, her face radiating undiluted contentment, and then opened them and murmured, "There are some things I like that I don't like". Unfortunately, the last vestiges of my brother's buttoned-down, lower middle-class, suburban Dublin upbringing, which I am shamefaced enough to admit envying him for, craven soul that I am, sprang to the fore here. In short, he was a little slow on the uptake when it came to apprehending her true meaning.

Such misunderstandings between the sheets are not as uncommon as might be supposed, however, and his incomprehension can be mitigated somewhat by the fact that not only was this their first time together, but it was also the first time he had been invited to attempt congress by thus reversing the charges, so to speak, and in such a casual and open-hearted manner yet. (Hence, it was also, *a fortiori* – or is that *a posteriori*? – the first time he had been encouraged to proceed so during the first time he had been encouraged so to proceed.) So it is understandable that he was a little nervous.

As she slid off him, and lay beside him prone and primed, he turned and lay his chest flat against her back, smelling her hair, nuzzling her neck, kissing her mouth when she twisted her head so that her cheek brushed his. His hand found its way around into her lap, and he fingered her damp bud as he strove to breach the front portal from the rear. "No," she burbled softly and, reaching back her hand, redirected her new beau's batterings so that he might with some justification in future refer to himself as her Back Door Man. Not to put too fine a point on it, love hath made its nest in the place of excrement. Well, ass-fucking is the most pleasurable, as some have said, and who am I to argue with what some might say?

I was not about to pass up the chance to feel what he was feeling during these unprecedented moments of his erotic career, but as soon as I began dreaming myself into sensing his sensations, the practical consequences of that ancient injury to my nether regions, received courtesy of my maddened maternal unit, made themselves all too apparent. The ailment in my equipment caused the derailment of my desires, however modest they may have been. His pleasure pained me. Once again, I would have to be content with watching. I can guarantee that he felt something decidedly different from anything he had hitherto experienced, but in its own distinctive way, every bit as appealing as the more conventional approaches with which you are doubtlessly familiar. She too revelled in the deed, if appearances are anything to judge by, and afterwards she told him that it had been, "Beautiful, completely equal, not a bit like Norman Mailer." Well, she was An American Dream, after all. So that's the story of his First Tango in New York, or rather, the first one worth reporting in detail.

When he turned on the television a while later, after they'd slept a little, on the first channel he happened to flick to, three hideously ugly middle-aged hippie women were talking to the host of some sub-Oprah late-night cable chat show, who sat all agog, about the ineffable bliss of tantric sex. Edward's and Amanda's eyes met, and they began to laugh out loud in unison.

Then he fell to wondering how many others she'd had before him, and how many of them she'd done this other thing with before.

In the weeks that followed, this fledgling twosome got to know each other even better. Amanda replaced Dub the Teddy as Edward's most regular bed-sharing companion, in his place and hers, and they spent time getting out and about and getting out of it as well. There was so much high jinks, and lolling around, that work was bound to suffer.

A case in point was the night they first did that aptly named concoction, ecstasy, together, curiously enough abbreviated to x on that side of the pond and to e on this one, a first for my brother, though not for his lover, who turned him on to it. It did make a happy alternative, and sometimes occasional accompaniment, to the powder that things go better with, bags of which were not that hard for him to find, given the circles he moved in, and how far he was prepared to march.

They were ensconced in a dimly lit Lower East Side dive called The Scratcher, and the booming drum'n'bass beats ascended through the soles of his feet as they cavorted on the dance floor, so that it seemed to him he was made of music, it was no longer outside him, but was the motor that powered him, regulating the finely tuned mechanism that was his body and brain. The lovey-dovey stuff that night was superfine, two became one as close as they can, until one was the other, and the other was no longer just one. But oh, when they came back down. It is foolhardy to run the risk of trying to land without wings, whether you're a hawk or a dove.

Never had he been with someone so coolly uninhibited, yet who displayed an affectless incredulity, which stopped just short of guilt, about some of her past actions. She wanted to be good, but not yet. Wryly she referred to her "periods of rather extreme promiscuity", but it wasn't regretful, just the indifferent shrug of a woman who'd chosen the wrong dress to wear for dinner, or ordered a dish that turned out to be not quite as appetising as she'd imagined beforehand. There's no use crying over spilt milk, as they say. Tomorrow is another day, as they also say.

But she had a need to confess, as though he was perhaps the first true friend she could talk to honestly about these things, because with most women they think you're a traitor to the cause, and with most men they are only too eager to take advantage of any perceived or self-confessed vulnerability, so there's all that brinkpersonship, one-uppersonship, and general jockeying for position involved. So, such phrases as "So much sexual satisfaction is based on dominance and so forth" were heard by him to issue from her lips, and were music to his ears. He liked the idea that she knew the ropes, and the value of a good spanking. For he could comfortably contemplate his current lover's string of former liaisons without any implied reproach to himself, so long as she also assured him that he was the best, and the one who would last. Or – somewhat easier for her to aver – that there was nobody else quite like him. The more she'd had, the more he loved her, so long as she loved him the most. Besides, he could creditably think ill of his partners – past, present and prospective – without it occurring to him to hold any undue prejudice against himself on account of his dealings with them. This is an invaluable asset to possess, it seems to me, when venturing into the cut and thrust of today's lethally competitive mating game.

It transpired that she had been in some sticky scrapes in her time, like screwing a French exchange student while baby-sitting for her college supervisor who was separated from his wife, and then catering for said Professor's not altogether legitimate cravings when he arrived home after the younger man had departed. Then there was the Hollywood B-actor she'd had an ongoing thing with for years, who was over twice her age, after initially getting rid of her troublesome virginity with his son at the ripe old age of fourteen. She'd had the obligatory tentative, exploratory lesbian affairs in high school and college, and recounted how she'd had long afternoon baths with her friend Susan, during which they'd soaped each other's breasts with suds, "hers so different from mine". She'd even tried a threesome sometime in her mid-teens, with a nice married couple who owned and ran a local delicatessen in her home town, where she helped out all day Saturday.

Unfortunately, the downside of all this unbridled expenditure of libidinous energy was that she'd succeeded in picking up the herpes simplex virus somewhere along the way. Alarm is insufficient to describe the state of shock Edward was plunged into on learning this fact, despite her reassurances that it could be contracted only when it was active, usually about once a month.

It happened like this:

"My roommates have been pulling my chain, saying since you're Californian, I should make sure you don't have herpes."

"Well, actually Edward, I do have herpes."

"*WHAT?*"

He dashed to a doctor post-haste, and gladly forked out $80 for the privilege of having the medic confirm what she'd already told him about it not being all that easy to catch, and then giving him the all clear. Nothing but the truth had issued from her mouth, as far as her disease went anyway.

She'd also had an abortion, I need hardly tell you, her first long-term college boyfriend being the other party responsible for the conception. A senior when she was a sophomore, he'd gone to the big city when he'd graduated, and despite giving it her best shot, she'd found it impossible to remain faithful to him in his absence, when she'd been left behind. She'd been so young, and her whole life would have been wrecked, she hadn't thought twice about whether or not termination was the best option.

She recounted how her brother Anthony had brought her to the clinic when she'd been home for Christmas. Everyone at a big pre-Nativity feast, called a Christmas Goose, thrown by her aunt and uncle, which she had stopped by *en route*, wondered why she couldn't be persuaded to eat anything. She'd been told to come in fasting for the operation. All she remembered was waking up in a lovely warm Demerol daze, and the cover of the Raymond Chandler novel Anthony was reading as he sat by her bed coming slowly into focus. No, it wasn't *The Simple Art of Murder*, nor yet *Killer in the Rain*, or even *The Little Sister*, and certainly not *The Long Goodbye*. It was *The Big Sleep*. The whole procedure didn't seem to have taken a feather out of her. Meanwhile, back in Edward's and my native land, debate on this issue still raged, unabated. The isle, as ever, was full of noises. But, far from giving delight, they hurt. Well, it is the land of the little people.

He swallowed all she said, as he had no reason not to. She wasn't boasting of exploits, just unburdening baggage. The absence of any crippling pangs of the aforesaid demon guilt impressed him, and me more so, brought up as we had been to feel ashamed about almost everything, to a greater or lesser degree. He listened and lapped it all up, bemused, but it was water under the bridge, and so also off a duck's back. It made such a welcome contrast to what he remembered of his time in the part of the world from where we hailed. Or it did, at that time.

For me, her manners and mores were no less striking. But I, on the other hand, was aghast at, and appalled by, them. That a creature could be so vacuously, vacantly happy after leaving such a trail of emotional destruction in her wake just didn't seem fair. It offended against the moral order. The one I knew wasn't there. It was an insult to the commonly held, conventionally decorous standards of civic life. The one I took no part in.

He was growing softer, mellowing. I was hardening into a bitter, bellowing rage.

After a few months, all was still going well, so it was time to meet her folks. When summer vacation rolled around, offering two whole weeks of untrammelled freedom from toil, they flew out of JFK, bound San Francisco way. Stranger things have happened, but there was a highly unusual occurrence shortly after take-off.

Enjoying the view from out the window, by looking through his eyes, suddenly my heart started palpitating at a panicking rate. Please don't chortle, but have a heart, because despite all appearances to the contrary, so do I. To hide the heart, you must first have one. Now it seems I am suffering from heart failure. But that doesn't mean I am one.

The constriction tightened around my chest, and I keeled over. And I dreamt I was dying, and my spirit left my body, and turned to look back down on me, and smiled reassuringly. Or maybe it was just Edward, come to see what was up this time with his neglected other half. My dreams are very surreal, if dream it was. My random access memory gives me rapid eye movement. I can no longer tell the difference between the most grotesque of fantasies and what passes for reality; or hallucinations from hearsay.

As far as I can remember, from my period of unconsciousness, my brother set to with a will to revive me, and then helped me to recondition my clogged up arteries and capillaries, and rejuvenate those blocked valves and veins. By exercising his steely will over my more than suggestible mind, he made me press my hands against my own torso, and pound away methodically at my seized-up pump. Soon, after a little rough handling, a tell-tale pit-a-patter was puttering through my body, and slowly I came to, and was back in the land of the living once again.

But I could not go on as I had been going. I could not bypass the need for radical surgery. However, I was not prepared to leave my room to have it. The stress induced by renewed contact with family immediately beyond the bedroom door and society at large beyond the hall one could have easily lead to a relapse in my life-threatening condition. I would not want to threaten anyone, least of all myself, with life. I was already suffering from post-traumatic stress disorder. Indeed, could not life be said to be an agglomeration of traumatic experiences and the stress which Research Has Shown (perhaps the most fearsome phrase in the English language, superseded only by Research Will Prove) follows on from them? Nor, incidentally, did I entirely trust total strangers in white coats or green scrubs and surreptitious 'This-is-a-hold-up' face masks to go poking around in my vitals. So, how to proceed? There was nothing for it but a spot of D.I.Y.

Thankfully, my brother stepped in smartly, as he had done before. The nice, buxom, tits'n'teeth, All-American, trolley-dollies, so like nurses in their ministrations, wouldn't let him use his laptop while still in transit, and adjourning to the smallest but most necessary room (or 'the bathroom' as he would now have called it if dealing with women, or 'the john' as he would have said if talking to men) was not really an option, since what he had to do would have taken longer than such provisional privacy would have permitted, so he waited until he and Amanda had deplaned and, whipping out this lightweight, portable information retriever and communication tool in the arrivals terminal, logged on pronto.

He ran a quick search that threw up a few websites which furnished us with the rudiments of performing open heart surgery. Downloading these, he printed them out and read through them carefully, giving me a chance to peruse the salient features and bone up on as much of it as I felt I needed. I have a very improvisatory attitude to such invasive procedures: they should be performed with the requisite dash of *sprezzatura*. No point in approaching these interventionist practices too earnestly: you'd only worry yourself into an early grave without adopting a certain cavalier poise. There is always room in my best laid plans for the aleatory music of chance. Don't take life too seriously, you'll never get out alive. I have an open heart, but it is not quite full. Fill up my emptiness, please, if you have something to fill it with.

First it was imperative to administer a little local anaesthetic. Some whiskey I had lying around more than sufficed to numb me, when I injected it into my chestal area using an empty pen cartridge I found on my desk. Not the most hygienic implement, I suppose, but I have it on the highest medical authority, albeit off the record, that the germ theory is 'largely a nonsense'. Next, the knife and fork I keep handy to eat the morsels that are mysteriously left for me outside my door were pressed into and did sterling service for tearing open my cordial cavity, and cutting and splicing the malfunctioning parts. The sight of my own heart beating away before me filled me with fascination rather than dread, but I knew that I had to snap out of any incipient idle speculation, and concentrate conscientiously on the job in hand. I was painstaking. I was taking pains away.

In no time at all I had fitted myself up with a brand new pacemaker. The internal mechanism of the old clock beside my bed, after a little fiddling about and fine-tuning, was admirably adapted for this purpose. No longer would I feel so oppressed by time, since I had made the space to bring it inside me, its tick becoming my ticker. Given the trouble that Edward was taking over me, with his sourcing of up-to-the-minute expert advice, this device could also be termed a peacemaker.

After that, it was just a question of sewing myself up neatly and tidily, so the seam didn't show, with the needle and thread I used to use to keep my few duds in passable nick. He couldn't talk me through it all, but he did all he could possibly do. I wouldn't want him to go having a sympathetic heart attack along with me. What good could be served by him leaving his heart in San Francisco? But it was wonderful to feel that we were co-operating so well, teamwork flourishing in our fraternal collaborations. It's enough to break your heart, but hearts are made to be broken. Only then can they be fixed. Together, we can cure them. Everyman his own card-carrying cardiologist (to say nothing of psychiatrist). Metaphysician, heal thyself. With a little help from his brother, if he is a man after his own heart, and has his best interests there. I may have lost my heart. I may even have lost heart. They may have taken the part that was my heart, or part of that part. But they did not take all of me. The heart doesn't die when we think it does.

Soon I was as right as rain, almost. Except for a great grey scar that grew across the site of my self-inflicted wound. I will admit to bouts of post-operative depression but, what with everything else that had happened to me, I was very much an old soldier by now, a grey dog who'd been around the block more than a couple of times. I knew that, when all is said and done, I was little better than the stuff that hangs on hooks in butchers' shop windows, that I was, like that table mentioned by that lecturer Edward (and therefore I) had listened to so long ago, just a bunch of random atoms held together by an invisible force that could disintegrate at any second. But I also knew, strangely, that I was also something else as well. Because I had survived. I felt, more so than ever, that I was leading a posthumous existence. But all the best existences are posthumous. I am a stoic hedonist. I have a whale of a time, until the house falls down around me. Then I just shrug my shoulders, say, "Oh dear, what a pity, never mind", grit my teeth, and get on with things as best I can. Even if that makes me, sadly, just another hermetic nihilist. Regardless of your interpretation, I too can be hermeneutic. Do not say that my heart is not in it.

As I lay healing, Edward and Amanda explored the city. I remember that first night, while I ached with inadequate access to pain relief, they were moved through the Tenderloin in the taxi they took from the airport to her parents' place, and she spoke of the fun times she'd had in this district during what she jokingly called "my wild youth". It looked like a tough place to me, an underbelly full of flashing neon-lights, but she told him that it wasn't nearly as bad now as it had been back then, when barkers stood outside peep-shows and strip clubs promoting the wares that would entice customers in, and bars crawled with wall-to-wall minge. Amanda was no stranger to such decadence, although she claimed she had calmed down a lot since getting into her twenties, just as the place itself had done.

Such sexual misadventuring, common enough in adolescence, had evidently been lent an extra thrilling frisson by forming part of *Her Secret Life*, given the prim and proper sedateness of Mom and Dad, which was the impression Edward got of them when they were introduced. His accent had acquired an American twang by this stage, but there was still enough of a brogue in it to lend him a cutesy, folksy charm. This was not lost on Mr and Mrs O'Hara.

The thing that struck me most about my brother's girlfriend's family, even more so than it had been borne in on me by his own kindred, was not just that they talked to each other, but how they talked to each other; not just that they were polite to each other, but how polite they were to each other. In short, they were normal, or what normal is supposed to be, but so rarely is, normally. I had the impression that if one of them had inadvertently knocked over a chair, and no one else was there, they would have still apologised to the chair. Which would be a bit abnormal, I guess. They would lead you to believe that everybody's happy nowadays. At least, that's how it appeared to me, at the time. But they could well have divorced a few years later, amid much acrimony and recrimination, and the services of a private, professional conflict resolution specialist, for all I know, though somehow I doubt it. Even if they ever parted, I suspect that the whole business would have been conducted in a terribly civilised fashion indeed, without recourse to the courts, and maybe even no need of a family mediator to arbitrate between them. He was the curator of a Museum of Ancient Oriental Art. She was a homemaker.

Then there was Amanda's brother Anthony, whom we've already met, who taught social anthropology in some small college town in the middle of that great land mass. It was nothing new, but it was clear, that this was a nuclear family, but with none of the explosive capacities inherent in such volatile structures. Or maybe it was just an example of the effectiveness of the nuclear deterrent. They had passed their own version of the Official Secrets Act.

If Eddie had brought Amanda to visit Ireland, and they'd stayed over with his folks, he would have had to pretend to his parents that he wasn't sleeping with his intended. Although they hadn't announced their engagement, and he hadn't even popped the question yet, there was a presumption on the O'Haras' part that their daughter wouldn't have turned up with this guy in tow unless he was more to her than just another passing fancy or flying fling, and so my brother and his lover were not only allowed to share the same room, but the same bed. Mom and Dad may have been a bit staid, but they must have decided that Amanda was old enough now to do whatever she wanted, even in their house. Or perhaps they despaired of ever seeing her tie the proverbial knot, and were prepared to assist her in any way they could in that direction. Thus their unprecedented solicitousness on her behalf, and relaxed moral latitude.

As before, Edward had no intention of being shamed or cajoled into marriage, but he knew he was gradually sliding towards being reconciled to the idea. He would soon enough be forty, which is not a young age, even if it is the age at which they say life begins, and his bachelorhood was by no means confirmed. It is better to marry than to burn, as they used to say, not realising that you can still burn after you marry, and also that it may be no bad thing to burn before you do. It is not good for a man to be alone, as they still say, although personally I have my doubts about the wisdom of that adage.

As far as I'm concerned, in future anyone with any sense, and the wherewithal to facilitate it, will live alone. In future families will be thought of as as quaint and outmoded a mode of social organisation as the steam engine is of transport. Or does my earnestness give me away, again? No, I don't think so, although I do freely acknowledge that my denunciations of the connubial state and the basic decencies of family life may be influenced by my less than blissful personal experience of same at the hands of my foster parents. Marriages, it seems to me, even the best of them, are kept together by an unlikely but sustaining admixture of concupiscence and inertia. It's an institution that allows for women's increased controlling of men's raw, rampant sexuality, into bricks and brats and brickbats, so the poor suckers are forced into becoming good little worker bees in an overpopulated hive, rats running on a treadmill in a race they can never win, because they oftentimes don't know they're in it, and because it never ends. It's all about possession, and possession is nine-tenths of the law. But the law is an ass, as is possession. Why should men marry women, when women are going to dry up anyway? Why should women marry men, when men are only interested in one thing?

The cock-eyed optimists among you will dismiss what I say as merely the sour grape juice drainings of depressed decrepitude. But isn't the latter an inevitable acquisition in life, after a certain age, and the former a natural reaction to it, when it becomes part of life, at any age? Apart from the setbacks, disappointments and failures that are attendant on life as it is lived, the ability to manufacture vital serotonin is diminishing, since brain cells are disappearing and not regenerating themselves, and nerve centres are getting ravaged, irreparably.

But where will the next generation spring forth and sprout from, you ask? Well, I don't suppose the human race is in any imminent danger of dying out, just yet. But this reminds me of yet another of my pet theories, namely that man (embracing woman, that is) will have reached its apogee of evolutionary development when it exercises whatever discretion it still has at its disposal, and stops reproducing altogether, plain and simple. But I don't expect my brother agreed with this less than life-affirming, or enhancing, prediction.

What finally tipped the balance in favour of marriage for him was, one day, when Amanda was out shopping with Mom, and Dad was at work, and the sun shone lazily through the bedroom window, Edward took down one of his girlfriend's old diaries from the shelf, and started browsing through it. He didn't view this as an invasion of her privacy, because they were on intimate enough terms already. He didn't even so much decide to do it, premeditatively, as just find the tome in his hand, almost accidentally. He wouldn't hold what he found in it against her, but was operating in a spirit of disinterested inquiry. Or so he told himself, with his characteristic lack of honest self-appraisal, or his ability to not let his right hand know what his left one was doing.

Amid her schoolgirl and college years' reflections gathered together there in what the Americans revealingly term a 'Self Book', his eyes devoured the riveting observation 'I should have been a man.' This entry went on to explore how she felt more like she imagined most men must feel, rather than like what women are usually supposed to feel, especially when it came to sex. 'Making out doesn't mean that much to me,' he read avidly, which she then contrasted with irrational women, who frequently attach so much importance to such actions.

226

An account of a date when she was fifteen ended with, 'I gave him a blow job. I felt he deserved something.' All this was interesting to Edward because he had sometimes had an equal and opposite emotion, to whit: he felt like a woman. (Sorry, let me clarify, I mean that he felt he should have been a woman, not that he felt like having a woman, although as you will have gathered, this desire was not unknown to him.) He liked to think of himself as a cunning manipulator, who could control members of the opposite sex by giving them what they wanted or, if more efficacious, by withholding it. He seemed to associate this way of functioning with women, rather than men. But nothing of what she had written in her youth put him off her in the slightest. Rather, it turned him on.

This diary had been kept long before they met. It never occurred to him to wonder if there was another book somewhere else now, full of less than flattering scribbled *pensées* about himself.

Whatever about him falling for the man in her, and even she going for the woman in him (and my own gen on this gender thing is that the sexual differences between bodies matters much less than the minds they carry around with them), he decided to splash out and ask for her hand. Well, he'd already had the rest of her. It was a mark of maturity to be wed, and women do like to see that you are capable of sustaining a committed relationship for a significant stretch of time, so that it mounted up like credit at the bank. Not that he was thinking like that. I'm just putting my own unfavourable construction on things, once again.

Under a star-sprinkled, darkening sky, with wisps of fog gently rolling in below them while they were walking the boards on Fisherman's Wharf, he tried the notion on her for size: "Would you like to be mine forever?"

Not that he put it quite like that, what with its dated overtones of proprietorship. Nor did he launch the more traditional Irish inquiry, "Would you like to be buried with my people?"

What he actually said, because he knew it was the kind of way that she talked and so would, he hoped, appeal to her, unless it was his very differences from her that proved so appealing, was, "It could be the real thing between us. How about it?"

Linking him, leaning into him, looking up at him, loving him, she did not say, as she might have, "I'll have to think it over."

Or even, "Are you out of your fucking mind?"

But, "Sounds good to me. I thought you'd never ask."

I don't mean to imply that they hadn't skirted around this topic before (and not necessarily only when he'd been watching her take off or put on her skirt), as there had been hints here and there along the way about the pearls, pleasures, perils and pitfalls of the matrimonial state, but he was still taking a risk. He wondered how and why it all seemed so easy now, and, as if reading his thoughts, she told him, "I've never met anyone like you."

This tickled me, because I have never met anyone like him either. Just as I have never met anyone like me. Indeed, I have never met anyone who was exactly like anyone else. If only because I have rarely ever met anyone else.

He had received the promise of marriage. They kissed and held each other tight, the way lovers do. Thus can once nubile co-eds slowly metamorphosise into punctiliously correct matrons.

They broke the big news to her parents, and were congratulated effusively. A joyous mood prevailed because of these glad tidings. I know I should write a scene here, but just take it from me, on trust. Would I lie to you? I could be lying to you, even in a devilishly detailed scene. I would be lying to you anyway, if you believe this recounting is a polished work of fiction, in other words, a complete fabrication. The devil is in the detail. But I am not.

"My Daddy was so pleased," she told him afterwards. "And my Mom too. They like you."

They decided to celebrate by hiring a car and driving to Las Vegas for the second week of their holiday. Then it would be back to San Francisco for the return flight to New York. He just had to see this garish temple to the Mammon of Unrighteousness, built in the middle of the desert. Just as we visit Europe to get a flavour of the past, so we go to the western regions of America to see the future. California is the anti-Auschwitz. But I'm not so sure about Nevada.

All hail the American highway, even if it represents flight as much as freedom. Was Edward on the road to rescue, or the road to ruin?

3

"SO, YOU HERE FOR THE CONFERENCE?"

This is the opening gambit, the most common pick-up line, used by almost every hooker, sitting around nearly every bar, sipping an artificially coloured pink cocktail concoction through a straw, ass hugged by a micro-mini, as she sways sweating into the leatherette stool, to proposition potential clients, in your average Las Vegas hotel. Which particular conference is never actually specified. That would be otiose, even if it was known.

Edward would take a table, waiting for Amanda while she worked out, toned up and wound down in the gym, or made merry trawling through the multitudinous merchandise in a sprawling mall, but sometimes he wasn't safe from the harlots' advances even there. Nor did telling these working girls politely but firmly that he was otherwise engaged to be married always succeed in doing the trick of repulsing their advances, since they then assumed he was there on his bachelor party, a tribal ritual where a chap soon to take the plunge gets together with his immediate male peer group and gets up to very bad things during his last few days of freedom, a custom the covert message of which is: 'No more nights on the town for you, my lad. Best knuckle down now and tow the line.' See, the prostitutes thought they probably did things, and allowed things to be done to them, that his wife-to-be would never countenance, much less consent to. Indeed, even if he had been married, and sporting a band of gold, it's a fair bet they'd have taken it for granted that he was still looking for a bit of strange, rather than wanting to keep them at bay. This is Vegas, after all. Folks don't come here out of motives of self-mortification. The self denies self-denial, preferring self-indulgence. Between having to negotiate, in the blue corner on my right, the rock of Family Values, and, in the red corner on my left, the hard place of Political Correctness, everyone in that great nation is entitled to let their hair down and have a holiday once in a while, where they can gross out on their favourite hobby, before going back to being blamelessly wholesome and puritanically straight laced. But the hustlers had not bargained for Amanda, who didn't think she was giving anything away. Edward wasn't there to gamble, not even on losing her.

For my part, it seems to me that prostitution is the only sure-fire way of vouchsafing that sex between men and women is 100 percent honest. But then, aren't we all, in our own ways, prostitutes? And don't some of us fall in love with our tricks? Then we become the proverbial golden-hearted hookers.

"They're like flies on shit," a grizzled old-timer, who had lurched into the same booth as Edward, roared across at him one afternoon. "If it's not the whores, it's the airline stewardesses, or flight attendants as they like to be called. Heh heh, the way some of them carry on is legal only in Nevada."

Edward, not normally given at this stage of his development to idle banter with garrulous interlopers, found himself, I'd like to imagine at my prompting even if it wasn't so, returning the ball, in typical jock fashion, with, "Which cost more, in the long run?"

"Heh heh, that's a good question, pardner," his new companion conceded. His pronunciation of 'partner' sounded like 'pardoner'. Was Edward hearing his confession?

They introduced themselves. This was Alvin, a janitor who'd been living in the town for close on thirty years. He was as surprised as the ladies of the night (and the afternoon and the morning) were when Ed let slip that he was visiting with his fiancée.

"Heh heh, ya don't bring yer apple to the orchard, buddy."

My brother, warming to his role as one of the boys in the laddish locker room bonhomie and male camaraderie of this spontaneous bull(shit) session, which he enjoyed playing because he didn't do it often, much to his shame, or rather mine, shot back,

"Just because you own a masterpiece doesn't mean you don't go to the gallery."

Alvin was in quick with, "But ya don't *take* yer masterpiece with you to the gallery, buddy, heh heh. They might want it back."

There was more talk about how Edward wasn't American, Alvin inquiring was he British, and brightening perceptibly on learning that he was Irish.

"Hey, my grandmother was Irish, heh heh. Great people." Etcetera, etcetera.

The veteran then fell into tearful reminiscence, but not about the Old Country.

"This town is dead now. The people used to come here had a little class – the gangsters, the stars. There was glamour, excitement, risk, ya know what I'm talkin' about? Yeah, class. Those guys used to pay cash for everything, off a big roll of fifties, fat tips all round. Now it's just uptight little Johnny Salespitches kept in line by their dumb, uptight wives, who they can't wait to leave behind. Herds of them. Assholes. They've got the airfares down to next to nothing, so the herds of ass-hole nobodies can keep the asshole new hotels full, and run up credit-card debt. Gamblin' is legal now in half the states, so they've built these horrible humungous hotels for the bozos all along the Strip, all the way to the airport. The Eiffel Tower, Venice, The Pyramid, it's all there, you've seen it, all for the bozos. It's disgustin'. It's depressin' as hell."

"Well," Ed put in, "that's the American way. Freedom of choice."

"Maybe so, pardner, maybe so. But how much choice d'ya need? It's a sad day when the nobodies can choose just like those with class. What's the point of havin' class, then? That's why nobody's got any class any more."

Ed was rescued at this juncture by the appearance of his betrothed. He could see how impressed Alvin was by the bob and weave of her fresh femininity, the hop, skip and jump of her uninhibited yet care-fully constructed and modulated sexual appeal, that would put a pep in the hep step and quicken the pace and pulse of any red-blooded male. He was not a Johnny Salespitch, henpecked by a nagging, down-home shrew. She was a doll-face, with an hour-glass figure to match, so he was a very lucky man. It did not seem to occur to Alvin that you could pos-sibly be kept in your place even more effectively by a raving beauty. I would venture that they're the ones best at doing it. Maybe he thought it was worth it. I do not know if he had ever been married. But then again, nor have I.

That night the happy couple went to an Elvis Presley impersonation contest in The Meridian Hotel, entitled, if you please, Elvis Ate America. The deal was that, not only did the aspirants to the throne have to give a rendition of a song from the early, middle and late peri-od canon of The King, but they also had to munch through as many cheeseburgers and knock back as many uppers and downers, washed down with as many milkshakes and bottles of Wild Turkey, as was humanly, or rather inhumanly, possible between their turns on stage. The judges gave due heed to how well both the on and off stage antics of the contestants approximated the trajectory of the iconic singer's paradigmatic career through fresh-faced, dangerous but guileless charm, a post-military service move to the mainstream, total excess, sad deterioration, careless self-destructiveness, grotesque behaviour, physical bloating and insults to the brain.

The Elvises included a Chinese Elvis (Ervis Plesrey), a Mexican Elvis whose show-stopper was a tear-jerking 'In the Barrio' (El Voz), a black Elvis (Elvus 'The Stud' White and His Honkieploitation Experience), a contortionist Elvis (The Fantastic Elastic Elvis), a wheelchair-bound Elvis (Elvis Pelvis Suffers Reverses), a bald, Puerto Rican Elvis (Elvos 'Hair Loss' Preslei), a chimpanzee dressed as Elvis (Evolving Elvis and His Darwinian Revolution), a schizophrenic Elvis who didn't sing the words, but mumbled 'Umh Ahh Umh Ahh' along to every song (Paranoid Presley and His Suspicious Minds), Elvis's stillborn twin (Jesse Garron and The Doppelgängers) and a female Elvis (L. Vice Pessary and The 'Sing-From-Your-Diaphragm' Girls). There was even an Irish Elvis (Seán 'Elvis' O'Presley and his Little Green Men). They take their Elvis seriously there. Or not, as the case may be. And there's some who say Elvis is dead. *Au contraire*: Elvis is everywhere.

It was during the bauld Seán's rendition of 'When Irish Eyes Are Smiling', the climax of his set, with him looking distinctly tubby and wobbly, and laying on the 'Pray for me, baby' asides to the ladies in the front row, that Edward was told by a waiter that there was a very urgent call waiting for him at the reception desk in the lobby, redirected from where Amanda and he were staying. He hadn't brought his newly acquired cell phone.

On his way out to take the call, he caught sight of a poster advertising the following week's floor show, a Marilyn Monroe lookalike contest, with a special spot prize for the Marilyn who could best mimic the agonising symptoms of endometriosis, which the starlet herself suffered from, along with displaying visible evidence of alcohol and barbiturate 'dependence'. Was this unprecedented thrust towards honest authenticity influenced at all by Reality TV? Strange the things you notice, and how they set you thinking, at times like these.

As soon as he picked up the receiver and heard the steady, level tone of his father's voice begin to crack and choke, he knew that this was the telephone message he had been dreading, while trying not to dwell on it, for some years now.

"Your Mammy's dying, son. We'd like you to come home, if you can."

They didn't stick around to find out which Elvis won. Back in their hotel room, Amanda put her arms around him, and held him close. She was giving him consolation, as lovers should do. Then her leg came up, twisting itself insinuatingly around him, and he found for the first time that he was not responding to this little one-note prelude which was supposed to open out into a full-blown symphony. He was not in the mood, at this precise moment. She stroked his hair, telling him it didn't matter. But he was afraid she was disappointed, and he feared this disappointment. She had power over him.

Edward was on the next plane out of there to New York, and then on to Dublin. Work commitments prevented Amanda from going with him, but she stayed behind to tidy up the loose ends, before going back to the isle of joy herself. Could she not have made more of an effort to accompany him to the isle of sorrow?

Is this a ghost in the machine, or a god coming out of it?

He arrived in off the redeye, dishevelled and exhausted, in time for the deathbed scene. Mrs Tender had several ailments, all of which were now conspiring against her. Mostly it was heart, a murmur therein. No operation to save her though, it being deemed too hazardous, what with everything else that was wrong with her. The priest had already been to anoint her, in what was now known as, with less extreme unction, the Sacrament of the Sick.

She could not speak very well, but smiled with her eyes when she saw him. He held her hand, and she asked him with her eyes to lean forward, and he put his ear close to her mouth. Her fragile voice whispered faintly, "Kneel down and say a prayer for my soul."

Edward was not about to stand on principle, and object, decrying the Catholic Church in which she had such fervent faith as a pervasive force of social and sexual control, only lately superseded by psychosocial and psychosexual medicine, and the theories of social and political science, legally enshrined. At least, not at a moment like this.

He bent the knee, and began the rosary, with the old man joining him at the other side of the bed, just like all those years ago, at the terrifying onslaught of puberty. When we're confronted with sex and death, that's when religion comes in handy. Or do I mean, dare I say it, spirituality, which has damn all to do with organised, mediated manifestations of religiosity? The institutions have their ceremonies for hatch, match and dispatch, but the spirit, over which they need have only as much temporal power as you let them, knows its own know when it comes to the elemental rites of getting born, getting laid, and getting out of here (regardless of whether or not you get it together to reproduce your genes before you go).

Funny how easily he could shed his eye-rolling, stifled-yawning, suppressed-giggling, New York-acquired, pseudo-sophisticated poise. If his friends could see him now. But to be free of all past conditioning is akin to permanently defying the laws of gravity, something it is difficult to do this side of the grave. You can take the man out of the bog, but you can't take the bog out of the man, as they used to say. That's if you're from the bog. You can't make a silk purse out of a sow's ear, as they still say. Are you a sow's ear? It's not far from this he was reared. Besides, if it meant nothing to him, but helped her have a happy death, then why shouldn't he do it? He was making something out of nothing. Correction: he was making something mean something different from its usual meaning.

As he intoned the incantatory Our Father, Hail Mary and Glory Be, his mother gripped his hand more tightly, her other one holding on to his father, for dear life, and their praying helped ferry her across the river from this life into the next one, or into whatever, if anything, happens next. She pushed out her last breath, and closed her own eyes. Her last words were to the adopted son she loved: "Make sure you marry that girl." She didn't say which one. He hadn't got the chance to tell her that he was engaged to Amanda.

His father went into a silence, which was to last more or less for the rest of his days, broken only intermittently, out of bare, and rare, necessity. The woman Mr Tender had loved and lived with all his life was gone from him. How could he either control or express his grief? I am moved beyond belief; more than I ever believed I could have been. Maybe my customary cynical tone merely masks a childlike naiveté and wonder, that heart of pure gold I hinted at above. Which is a difficult feat to sustain, given that I have, quite literally, a heart of steel.

Still, do I still take religion seriously enough that I will not kneel for my own mother's death? And which would make me happier, or less unhappy, or more unhappy still: kneeling or refusing to kneel? And which would be the right or wrong thing to do? The chief consideration in the ethics of this situation is that I am not, unlike my brother, overfond of my mother.

It rained at the graveside, as it always does, regardless of whether it is the rainy season or not, and the wind blew some of the many mourners' umbrellas inside out, and set their scarves afluttering. They had brought their umbrellas. Odd the trivial things you recall, at these momentous moments. The undertaker and his three assistants lowered the coffin down into the hole in the ground, each gripping either side of two long leather straps, gradually feeding them out.

"Ashes to ashes", the officiating *padre* proclaimed, "dust to dust", as he threw a handful of clay down onto the lid of the box. Edward stood shoulder to shoulder with his father, but they did not touch. He had not slept well, and felt disorientated, almost as though he were dreaming. This was a waking nightmare. The worst part had been the previous night, when the remains had been brought to the church, and after the few words from the altar, friends of the family, relations and neighbours lined up and trooped by the front row, shaking hands with Tender *père et fils*, saying, "I'm sorry for your trouble." It was a worthy custom, meant to express sympathy and communal solidarity. But Edward drew little solace from the condolences of people he barely knew. Now he watched the gravediggers set to, shovelling the mound of dirt back where it had come from, and it was almost as bad as the comfort of relative strangers, but not quite. It was not as bad because, even though he was watching the last of his mother disappearing forever, he understood that she was now beyond time, out in space, even if what was left of her on this earth was buried six foot under it, covered in soil. So he didn't cry, because he didn't quite feel that she was gone, and because big boys don't cry. Except me. Had I been in his position, I would have bawled. I always cry at funerals. In fact, they are the only occasions on which I cry. With relief, more than anything else. Is that inappropriate behaviour? Not that I've actually ever been to one.

The relatives and strangers stood around chatting desultorily, the men generally about politics, business, sport, cars, anything to hide their emotions; the women mostly about births, marriages and deaths, the intimacies of how everyone's children were doing, in order to display theirs. As they began slowly to disperse, a face from the past thrust itself at him from out of the crowd, the face of someone he really had known. She said, "I'm sorry," but did not complete the formal expression. Cliché was not the style of one Mary Constance Contrary. She did add, "I'm sorry I couldn't be there last night." Would she have said, "I'm sorry for your trouble," if she had been? No, she would probably still have used the abbreviation, a jettisoning of the official version that signified greater personal connection. She skirted dangerously close to a hackneyed phrase with, "If there's anything...," but fortunately trailed off with room to spare, when they regarded each other closely.

"So, how've you been?" he asked, failing to meet her high standards. She looked older, as was only to be expected, since, as is inevitably the way with these things, that is what she was. Skin was hardening, wrinkling; hair was losing lustre, the odd grey root showing despite the dye. But then, had he bothered to examine himself, he would have seen that he was no spring chicken any longer, either. Nor, indeed, am I, not that there had ever been anything remotely springy about the chicken I once had been. But she had worn well, and was still everything any man could desire. Or any mature man, of which there are, apparently, not too many. I will not treat of my own brother's incipient state of disrepair, or my own advanced decrepitude.

"Oh, you know...." she shrugged. "Give us a call, if you've time," and she proffered a card.

ASPECT Advertising and Marketing
Mary C. Contrary

Ph: 00 353 1 6610207   e mail: mcontrary@aspect.ie
Fax: 00 353 1 6610965

So that's what line she was in: selling products to people they didn't know they needed, until she told them that they did. Well, if people had disposable income, they needed to be helped decide how to dispose of it. Prostitutes, indeed. But was there really a market for marketing in Ireland? This must be fresh evidence of the much-vaunted Economic Miracle he had heard distant reports of during his extended American residency. Like most boasts emanating from the Old Sod, he had filed them under Greatly Exaggerated. Now it seemed there was some substance to it. It also transpired, from the cursory glances he'd already given some newspapers during this flying visit, that rumours to the effect that the various tribal factions in the North Country Fair were no longer beating, bombing and shooting seven shades of shite out of each other, in the hope of uniting once again, or preventing such a reunification, the fabled four green fields of popular song, were proving fairly true too. This was known as the Peace Process, a slow, lumbering beast, but could only be described as a sure sign of progress. He shoved the piece of cardboard into his pocket, solely out of politeness, it never occurring to him that he might use it, as she sloped off.

Late that night, as he sat on the sofa in the front room in the gathering autumnal gloom, nursing a long measure of Jameson whiskey, with his father tucked up in bed, the ghosts of his past gathered too, assailing him. His mother, knitting by the fireside there. Mother, father and junior sitting around here watching an innocently funny film like *Around the World in Eighty Days* or *Bringing Up Baby* or *Seven Brides for Seven Brothers* of a Sunday afternoon. Him and Mary, madly making out where he was lolling now, one eye on the clock against his father's imminent return from his Sodality and his mother's from the Residents' Association Meeting, his tongue down his new girlfriend's throat and hand up her skirt, as she felt his prick, first outside and then, undoing his belt and slipping down his fly, inside his jeans, but still not going too far, because they'd only started going out together. Never such purity again.

Memory fuelled desire, as it always does for him, and he fell to thinking: "Well, what harm can come of giving her a call?" Just for old times' sake, you understand, just to see how it's going, find out what she's doing. He did not seem to have any difficulty reconciling the prospect of this proposed meeting, after such horny reverie, with the reality of a top drawer, stunning bride-to-be back in the Big Apple. Did he know he was lying to himself? You'd be amazed at the extent to which some people can tell themselves one thing and act in another. I know him better than he knows himself. At least, I imagine I do. I know he was lying to himself about how seeing her was just to catch up. Why was he doing this? Don't you know? For who among us does not sometimes act out of mixed motives? And who among us does not put on an act, when acting so? The possibilities for self-deception know no bounds.

So it was that he found himself waiting for her at the entrance to Bewley's Oriental Café, Grafton Street branch, on a wet Friday lunchtime, after finding himself dialling her work number the day before. She breezed up to him, busy busy, and they went inside, queued for food, and took a table for two.

There was awkwardness, not the high-pitched jumpiness of youth, but hesitation about what to say and leave unsaid, an increased self-consciousness about being tactful. I heard him wondering to himself why men, or the man he was, met former girlfriends. You pretend it's just out of amity, but there's usually something else going on too, at least on one of the parties' parts, if not both. Was she here to see if he was attached, just as he was not entirely disinterested as to what she was up to, and with whom? A torch may be just embers, but it can be rekindled into an eternal flame.

What was she doing working in marketing?

"Well, it's really more just keeping people happy than hard sell. It's a job. Have you not seen or heard any signs of the roaring Celtic Tiger? It's a time of radical social and economic change in Ireland, as the pundits in the papers say, when they dig down deep into their capacious bag of clichés. [Attentive readers will be aware that this last clause is, in itself, a cliché. But she enunciated it, as she had the initial well-worn-out phrase itself, as though she knew that's exactly what it was. Not even she was now immune from the creeping disease of cheap and easy irony.] Everyone has jobs now. We have to import cheap labour from China for all the knee-jerk jobs Irish people won't do any more. Remember the Algerian bin men when we were in Paris? It's just like that here now. Except they were working legally. We encourage the black economy, by just giving the Chinks, and everyone else, tourist visas. Yeah, my job's bullshit, but it pays the mortgage and the bills. Maybe I'll pack it in in a year or two, and do a round the world trip. So, haven't you sold your soul yet?"

He told her he was a systems man in a big investment bank. It wasn't selling out, it was buying in. He hadn't had a chance to look around that much since arriving, what with one thing and another, but he would. It was his first time back in Ireland in yonks.

Whatever had happened to her music?

"Couldn't make a decent living at it. Got tired of damp flats and brown rice. Didn't want to marry for money. What about you? Do you still play guitar?"

Not much. He was surprised by the sudden and increasingly unguarded directness of their exchanges, almost as though they were taking up where they'd left off, regardless of the accumulated silt of the intervening years. What was it about her that made him talk so loosely like this?

Why had she come to the interment?

"Curiosity. I wanted to see how you were. And to show my sympathy. I always liked your mother. I saw the death notice in the paper. It's my morbid habit to scan the obituaries these days. Just like my father always used to do. I couldn't understand why he did it so religiously then. I thought he was a stuffy old crank. Now I know what he was at."

He inquired if there was some reason for this necrological activity.

"When people you know start dying, you do it. Or that's what got me started. First my father. Then one friend, then another. Leukaemia, car crashes. And I was engaged to someone. He died too. You might remember him from the old days: Wylie Sighfer?"

You live and learn. Now how did that come about?

"He started hanging around after we split up and you went off to London. But I wasn't having any. I suppose I was still pining for you, even if I told myself I wasn't. Then he disappeared to London for a while too, and when he turned up again, I'd kind of got over you, and I'd heard through the grapevine that you'd gone to Italy, or wherever. So I succumbed."

What carried him off?

"A drug overdose. I didn't know what he was into. He managed to keep it a secret from me. That's a couple of years ago now."

So even such an experienced user can fuck up. Was there some arsenic in the opium? But why was she with Wylie? Edward didn't think the swarthy one would have been his erstwhile inamorata's type.

"He was a handsome man. I prefer handsome men. I made an exception for you. I didn't know any better. And he had a rakish charm."

Is my brother really so ugly? Am I? He ignored her jibe. It was probably just her little joke. He disclosed that Wylie had in fact stayed with him in London.

"Really? He never said. It was me gave him your number. I didn't think he'd look you up, much less stay with you. You hardly knew him, did you?"

Indeed not. So all becomes clear, in Edward's chaotic brain. Mary had sent Wylie to him, unwittingly. Wylie must have been trying to get Eddie hooked, my brother's decline or – better still – death a quick route into Mary's affections, so long as she didn't find out that Wylie had anything to do with Eddie's downfall. Or, in any event, a nice piece of revenge against the man he had so unceremoniously taken up residence with, having intuited that his reluctant, put-upon landlord still occupied a special place in the palace of the heart of the woman he himself wanted. That's how bad people can be.

Let's hope our narrative is not descending (or is that ascending?) into the realm (not exclusively woman's!) of romantic fiction. I couldn't bear to see a storyline, sentimental or otherwise, developing at this late stage. But it seems to be doing so by itself, of its own volition. This book's got a mind of its own. It's got a hold of me. Is it grabbing you?

Was she seeing anyone now?

No time. Him?

Yes, actually he was engaged, as it happened. To a real live girl.

Mary glanced at her watch, and decided she was due back at the office, without a moment to spare. He walked her out to the door of the restaurant, and she faced him, saying, "It was nice to see you again."

He held her arm in his hand, just above the elbow, as a parting touch. That was intimacy enough. Tears were turning from hot to cold in her eyes, as she walked away. Tears for her lost first love, lost once again. She allowed them to fall down her face only after she'd turned her back on him. But I saw them, I swear. Yes, people still cry.

What, you thought I could only see what he was seeing, when seeing through him? So did I. But it seems I can see through myself too. See for yourself. I see it feelingly.

Yes, I can see through him. But what if you can see through me?

He wandered aimlessly around the city as the afternoon gave way to evening. They had hardly alluded to his bereavement. Then again, what was there to say? For what do old people do? They die, usually after suffering a lot. Everyone old was young once. We will all die. Which is why it's important to get your kicks when you're young and able. It's not what you did that you regret when you're old; it's what you didn't do, as they say. Maybe you regret both, either way. Then such unavoidable regret is added to your suffering. Of course, this particular old person was his mother. The only mother he'd ever had. Or rather, the only mother he'd ever known. Still, as far as the world at large was concerned, she was just another old person. Mary had known her a little, but she wasn't Mary's mother. Would Amanda offer him any more comfort than Mary had done?

Walking down Grafton Street, he could almost conceive of himself as on Fifth Avenue. The store front mannequins, in Brown Thomas for example, were dressed just as elegantly and expensively as in Manhattan, no longer mere functional showroom dummies. The salesgirls too were glamorous stunners, marionette equivalents behind the counters of their inanimate counterparts in the shop windows, living dolls who had probably been asked only one question at their interview for these posts: "What was your last modelling assignment?" No *curriculum vitae* needed, just send a recent photograph. Although they probably did all have degrees of some shape or form too, just in case.

Time was, when Edward was coming to – please don't make me laugh, it hurts too much – emotional and sexual maturity, when one would be hard put to pick out one really attractive girl while strolling down this street, one who looked like she had taken some time and put some effort into dressing with a view to impressing, and was at ease with her own appeal. Now a fair proportion of them could easily have walked off the covers of glossy magazines. This could only be all to the good, it seemed to Edward. They all 'put out' too, or so he surmised. But out for whom did they put? More than likely those guys driving all those sports cars he saw parked all over the place, another addition to the scene. Although women could drive sports cars too, if they chose so to do.

Around Wicklow Street, up South William Street, back down Drury Street, into Exchequer Street, on down Lower George's Street and across Dame Street into Temple Bar he ambled, and everywhere he surveyed there were designer bars, juice bars, wine bars, and continental-style cafes. There was no need for him to essay employing the faculties of imagination required to view his own place objectively as though it were a place he had never been before, for so changed was it in his years away that it might as well have been a different place entirely anyway. He was as a much an alien as all the Africans and Asians who were everywhere to be seen. He felt as much a foreigner here as he would have anywhere else. Indeed, he felt he might feel he belonged more somewhere else than he ever would here. Or else, if he belonged nowhere, then he might as well be here as elsewhere. Or else, to remain judiciously arbitrary, elsewhere as here. Deracinated is, I believe, the word.

Rambling up Dame Street, he fancied himself back on the Ramblas, what with The Coffee Rio Company and The Queen of Tarts Café. He could even have had a coffee in a cafe called Phoenix Perk, a thin Irish spin metamorphosed from the American one that is Central, courtesy of the friendly cathode ray tube. Well, you can't live in the televisual era and not expect the medium to have some influence, and disseminate its messages far and wide. You can't live in the past, even your own. Fictions supplant facts, at every turn, and so become them. The whole town was just a gigantic stage set, an elaborate backdrop, and if you looked behind the shop fronts you'd probably see that they were props, held up by angled supports at the back. Just like the rest of the world.

He wound up in a rowdy pub, with three or four floors to its overtly mercantilistic name, and got stuck in a raucous ruck, there being no venues in the vicinity for a quiet drink, leastways not of a Friday night. Carousing was much in evidence, matched by behaviour indicative of impending casual sexual interface, and not just among tourists or students or bowsies, but your average gormless young office workers too – boys and girls. From Catholic Church Police State to scenes redolent of Imperial Rome, all in the space of a few short years. And to think they were once, not all that long ago, so reticent about matters sexual in these parts. Did you think I meant country matters? Of course the country matters. Are you ready for the contrary? But after being made to feel ashamed of certain primary urges for so long, could you entirely blame them for conspicuously indulging them now? They had a lot of catching up to do, these poor folks. Even if they were only chasing their tails. Too much laughing ends in crying, as they still say. There'll be tears after bedtime, as they might say. If there was hope, it didn't lie in the proles. But where was all this new money they were awash with flooding in from? Simple: IR£ = € + $. It's always easier to spend other people's cash. Especially on impulse-buy, luxury items.

The drunker he got, the lonelier and more out of it he felt. He was tempted to call up the one or two friends of old who'd shown up at the funeral, but he didn't really know them any more. Between one thing and another, he had lost track, not kept in touch. The convenience of Hotmail and Yahoo accounts was not prevalent when he had taken off on his travels. Text messages had not yet caught on [unless you consider all printed matter to be messages in text, like this book, for instance]. So he found his own solitary way to his father's house, at approximately four o'clock in the morning. But not before standing on the Ha'penny Bridge for half an hour to clear his muzzy head, watching the river flow slowly down to the sea. *If everyone else threw themselves in the Liffey, would you?*

All day Saturday was spent with this father, while palliating a hangover with industrial strength doses of wonder drug Solpadeine [this realistic reference may be used as a product endorsement in future advertisements, for a fee to be agreed with my agent, should I ever find one]. Soon his father would die too. How long would the old man hang on, with the old lady gone? Then Edward would be orphaned, twice over, and alone. Except for his choice of mate, so long and for as long as they stayed together. And except for me. But he has not visited me much over the years, not nearly as often as I've visited myself upon him. Still, can you blame him? A man may lead an interesting life without ever leaving his desk, but it's not much fun watching him sitting at it, surrounded by four grey walls.

And so he comes to me. Of course, nowadays there'd be no call for all this mysterious overlay of telepathy. We'd just need a laptop and a cell phone apiece, and the job would be Oxo, with far less fuss and much more efficiency. But, as yet, these accoutrements are beyond me. Although you couldn't exactly get inside the mind with these implements. They only serve to bolster the communication of one's exterior reality, what you want others to know about you, rather than what you know about yourself. Such a means of camouflage is a handy tool, but we are not solely concerned here with image, having already been too enthralled by, and in thrall to, the power of images.

I sense he is disgusted with what he perceives. I do not expect he'll be dropping around in person to see me any time soon. Well, it hasn't been a bowl of cherries slopping out all this time, especially since I boarded up the door and stopped even going onto the landing. I've had to fire the shit out the window in plastic bags, and pour the piss out in bottles. But it can, and does, pile up. Even if sustenance is in short supply, despite cultivating my own vegetable patch in the corner, with the aid of the water supply from the tap and sink unit I took the trouble to plumb in.

What would he say, if he could talk to me, and I could hear him? "How can you live like this?", he would surely ask. "Get out and live, while you still can." Life may be less than ideal, but it will not be gainsaid, even by saying words. You can't shirk it, you have to cut it, so up and at it. "Fuck life," I would tell him. "Choose life," he would retort. Yet I know that he is not resoundingly happy.

As darkness drew in, Mr Tender put on his hat and coat, and told Edward he was going to Mass. Would his son care to join him? What class of newfangled foolishness was this? Mass on a Saturday evening? Edward tumbled that it must be some last-ditch effort on the part of the clergy to plug the hole of dwindling attendances, by being more accommodating, flexible and user-friendly. The customer is always right, no more so than when business is bad, which it is just now, for them. For their monopoly on salvation has taken a severe dent around here and been badly shaken in recent times by repeated revelations of certain paedophiliac predilections among a goodly proportion of their godly number who do not have and hold as their sole goal the sovereign good of body and soul. Ah, 'paedophilia', the Greek love of children. But I myself love children, and old people, or at least I would, if I could deal in meaningless generalisation, and so loved the whole of humanity, abstractly and abstractedly. However, I'd sooner take my chances with them over the mature adult portion of the population, which the very young probably will be and the very old certainly once were, since it's predominantly just that bit in the middle that really gets to me, and gets my goat. Better to call the offence sound, blunt-sounding Anglo-Saxon: 'child abuse'. Suffer the little children. It takes only one bad priestly apple for there to be no laughs in the little blighters' barrel. They can all go rot. The rotten carrion corpses of the raptors in black, I mean, not the victims in their charge, and under their tutelage, who have some legitimate claim, however illegitimate they may have been, to take their place in the pantheon of victimisation. Given my own background, and experience, I can relate to them. Now there's a first. I wonder why I cannot also identify with the ungodly men of God?

But enough of this editorialising. I will leave that to my editor, along with the editing. S/he can edit Edmund, thereby editing Edward. (Just you wait – Ed.) For, what do my measly opinions count for? On with the, ahem, story.

Ever anxious to uphold tradition, my brother made known his preference for going to Mass on Sunday morning. He had a dispassionate interest in seeing how they still did things. His father acquiesced. So, instead of sidling out, they stayed in, and sat facing each other by the fire in the by now familiar front room. Time was running out, so it was also ripe for Edward to put his father in the picture about a woman named Amanda, and how he was going to be married to her.

"I've met a girl I like in New York, Dad. We've got engaged."

"Well, it's about time. This is good news. If only your mother had known. She would have been pleased, God rest her. We often wondered what was taking you so long."

Mr Tender also ventured that he trusted Amanda was a nice girl, and that he was looking forward to meeting her. Ever get the feeling you were talking at cross purposes with someone? This is a prime example of what a previous generation used to term the Generation Gap.

No more than thirty or forty rickety brethren sat around disparately in their pews in ones and twos at the 11.30 a.m. offering, while the elderly ~~celibate~~ (sorry, slip of the pen, you can't be too sure these days [a slip, incidentally, which inadvertently shows that I am still writing in longhand; I hope that, if and when my manuscript comes to be typed, there will not be many such mythprints]) celebrant sermonised to his sparse congregation, with a blithe disregard for the niceties of public relations with regard to the possibility of wooing the floating voter, about the obligation all believers were under to attend Mass on the Sabbath, and how it was a mortal sin if they were in any way lax or lackadaisical in their approach to the execution of this solemn duty. Edward couldn't help feeling that the P.P.'s impassioned message wasn't quite reaching its target audience. There again, maybe the hapless cleric was aiming low, merely trying to consolidate and keep the meagre following who still practised their belief. Even so, it was surely a clerical error to suppose that performing this particular party piece might not serve to alienate his remaining parishioners. You cannot trust the ones who are too careful, I'll grant you that. But you cannot trust the ones who are too careless either. So whom can you trust? Certainly not yourself. Which one are you?

A swaying derelict (not the spiritual father), who had probably just stumbled in so he could wank himself off in the warmth, began holding forth unintelligibly to all and sundry while the preacher droned on in his own onanistic way to those still listening, not snoozing. None of the faithful paid the poor tramp the slightest regard, least of all the personage up in the pulpit. But he wasn't getting his flock's undivided attention either, owing to the tenor of his homily. When Edward last attended, it used to be screaming infants who disrupted this sort of ceremony; now it was the garbled outpourings of doddery old men. All in all, a dispiriting, rather than spiritually uplifting, experience.

Afterwards, Mr Tender assured Edward that more skulls, or was it souls, showed up for the Saturday evening show. Scandal piled on scandal was not about to make the paterfamilias relinquish one of the cornerstones of his identity, especially since he was now closer than he'd ever been (exactly like the rest of us, when you think about it) to meeting the one he'd made into his maker. Still, that shrewd bastard, my insidious sib, knew the scene he had just witnessed was emblematic, if only by synecdoche, of the death of something he had grown up with, something the man he had gone to church with, the man who had grown him, had tried to pass on to him. But, as far as Edward was concerned, it was a well-deserved good riddance to bad rubbish. Even if all we are left with now, in its stead, is money. So, a resounding good old Cead Mile Failte to the bright new rubbish of the future. Can I have some money, please? It is the last remaining currency, even if its rates are base. I hardly ever move, but I am susceptible to shaking. I shake enough for two. So surely that qualifies me as a shaker, if not a mover.

I'm sorry for this rash of social commentary, rushed as it is, but I fear it is mandatory if you want to get your name on the score-sheet. I am everything I hate. He is everything he hates. She is everything we love. Which she? What she? Who she?

Yes, there was more choice to choose from than ever before in Dear Old Ireland, so long as your choice was not a return to the bad old ways of the not-so-good old days. But how much choice do you need, as the wizened drunk had speculated, in the not-at-all-plain City of the Plain? How much choice do you really need?

The choice is yours.

At the airport, Edward did what he hadn't done since he was a child: he hugged his father tight, as they said goodbye. He promised to bring Amanda for a visit soon.

Back in New York, he decided he'd give his intended a pleasant surprise by arriving unannounced at her door. Judge then of his own surprise, to say nothing of his chagrin, in this penultimate chapter of coincidences and surprises, in the turbulent turmoil of this second last section, when he stepped out of the elevator at her floor in the apartment building, to catch sight of a broad-shouldered, well-made, middle-aged man closing her door behind him. This fine specimen of affable masculinity started towards where Edward was standing, with a carefree air of satisfied self-possession, and they brushed passed each other in the corridor. Maybe there was some perfectly reasonable explanation. But at ten o'clock in the morning?

Let us now address the theme of jealousy, particularised this time as that of Edward about Amanda's other beaux, not that of me for him. Theme, madam? No, it is. I know not "themes". If that earth could teem with women's tears, each drop she falls would prove a crocodile. The term they have for obsessive jealousy is Othello Syndrome. They got this name from a stage production. Is it therefore not really real? Oh yes it is. Is jealousy a sign of love? Only for those looking for a sign. Hello jealousy.

Should he go in, or go away? If he identified himself, it would give the game away, since she could clear away any potentially incriminating evidence. Never one to be stuck, he quickly devised a cunning stratagem. Activating her intercom, he barked, in his best imitation blue collar Yank accent, "Special delivery, flowers for Miss Amanda O'Hara. Must be signed for."

She opened a crack in the door, wrapped in her favourite orange silk robe, wisely leaving the latch chain on, and he saw that worried, alert look dart into those cool champagne eyes, like the cat in the adage caught in the proverbial car headlights. He knew that she knew that he knew that she knew (to infinity, for eternity) that telling him to wait there for a minute, while she tidied up, would only arouse his suspicions. Furtively, she opened the door and let him in, composing her face into a sparkle of unexpected pleasure.

Although she began lallating light-heartedly, and pressed her body towards him for some louche lollygagging, it didn't take long for her defences to crumble. For a start, where were the flowers? The heavy, voluptuous smell of sex hung around the bedroom, which she could hardly tell him not to go into, and lingered on the air. He got the scent of another on her, the closer she came, her pussy loose and sticky with a moist essence not his.

Now, despite my relative inexperience in, and indeed indifference to, such contrary matters, it does seem to me that this might well not be an altogether welcome development for my brother, and could well open up an appalling, unappetising vista for any prospective husband. He'd assumed, and she'd tacitly agreed, that they would maintain a certain fidelity. They were, after all, to be married. Many marriages have doubtless survived the odd extra-marital episode, or pre-marital one, or even a long-standing affair – be it discovered, undiscovered, uncovered or covered up – but he had taken it for granted, perhaps presumptuously, that she would be easing off with others, indeed giving them up altogether. That this less than adult augury for a life of wifely adultery was taking place while Edward was away burying his recently departed mother only piled insult on the already grievous injury against his *amour propre*. The loss of a mother's love leaves even a grown man ill-prepared for losing a love he thought he'd found that turns out to be less than what he'd expected. She wasn't, as they are fond of saying, there for him.

"But, we're not married...yet," she whined punily, a self-justification that struck him as downright perverse, so short-sighted, spineless and self-serving did it sound. He may have chased her, but she would not be chaste. If she was shy, it was because she was sly.

He did not resort to violence, not even of the verbal kind, but she launched into a confession of sorts, perhaps under the impression that ventilating the ether would facilitate them starting over. The happy chappy last seen leaving her abode turned out to be that Fine Art lecturer she'd made herself available to as a student. They liked to touch base, and touch basely, every now and then. While she was at it, she might as well own up to a hot afternoon a few weeks earlier in the hotel room of a beautiful black man from Mozambique, in town on business, when she was supposedly off sick.

"It's great the way sex can break down the barriers between people from different backgrounds," quoth she. Soon she'd be chanting gangsta rap.

Then there was a chef who took her cruising in his Pontiac convertible, some nights when she was having a night off from the gent who was beginning to feel like a dope because he felt he'd been her dupe.

"He's very working class; so different to what I'm used to."

How did she manage to fit Edward in, or is that to fit in Edward? It was well she had boundless reserves of energy.

To top it all off, she let him have the benefit of the fruits of her considerable research:

"There's something so powerful about a man's orgasm."

A turn on from a groupie, or even a mistress, but not the most stirring string of words to issue from the mouth of a proposed lifetime companion, if you have reason to believe she will not be confining herself to receiving swelling tributes from you alone. That is to say, only from you. The more enlightened sectors of those among you who have stuck with my monologue this far may argue that Amanda was merely indulging in a final few flings before accepting the inevitable changes the weighty responsibilities of conjugal union were bound to bestow. She would not necessarily treat her sacred wedding vows as onerous sacred cows, and chaff against the chains these cruel restrictions imposed on such a free-spirited if flighty young female, but would with due solemnity rise to the gravity and import of such serious and supposedly lifelong commitments.

But it didn't look that way from where Edward was standing just then.

Why should she limit her choices? But then, why had he bothered being faithful to her? Should we have one rule for women, and another for men? What's sauce for the blander gander is sauce for the loose goose.

This apology for a life was, and would be, his apology for his life.

Knocking, knocking, knocking getting louder and louder still. It's not inside me, that's a different kind of beating, it's definitely the door, and the door of my bedroom, not the front one downstairs. Shouts, seriousness, courtesy of gruff, authoritative men. They are growing impatient. Soon they'll be in on top of me. The real world, putting an end to fantastic words. From now on, I'll have to tell it like it is. I'll have to pretend I know how it is, and why. If a man has a reason to live (the why), he'll soon find a way (the how). I've found a reason: to finish off the book, so that you can finish it too, and we'll know what happened. We are moving into real time, and solid space. A one and three nines, waiting for a two and three zeros. Quickly now, quickly now, there's no time to lose, it can't stand still, we have to do everything faster, faster, faster. I don't want to be late for the millennium. That would bug me. My chiliasm is being challenged. Let us work to end the story.

Could you stand a happy ending?

He decided to stay on, for a while. It wasn't so much a choice, as a fear of change. You fall into something, and it gets harder and harder to crawl out, unless things get so unbearably bad that major exertion is preferable to just sitting still. I know whereof I speak. He was making a virtue of necessity. Of chance I am making a vice. He would give her a second chance, a seventh chance, an eleventh chance, an eighteenth chance. As posited above, a few infidelities are not the worst things in the world. Everyone's at it. Everybody's doing it. The fly goes to it. She had only to raise her eyebrows and send one of her smoky smiles in his direction for his heart to melt, or his prick to stiffen, leaving his head to straggle home, after such *ad hominem* advances, a very poor third. Maybe one day she would turn to him in all sincerity and say, "What difference did one more man make, or ten, or twenty? I can't believe I actually slept with some of those losers. I'm much happier now, just being with you." To everything there is a season, a time for every purpose under heaven. She was ripe fruit, but was she to be harvested by him? It was his season in hell.

Eventually it was something as simple, yet of such far-reaching consequence, as her phraseology that put him off. Phrases echo, like voices off, long after they have been uttered, reverberating at the back of the mind. They are tin cans tied to the back bumper of a 'Just Married' going-away car, their clatter an undignified racket, mixing in with the blaring horns, when all you want is some peace.

So, during a discussion about his collegial pursuits as against hers, which veered into a comparison of the advantages, or lack of same, of creative writing workshops over the good old-fashioned study of literature, she came out with, "English is just what a bunch of old guys wrote."

Pity the poor Dead White Male. I am white, and I'm male (well I was, when last I looked), and some day I'll be dead, after getting old, if

I live long enough. Pity me. Pity all living white men. Mary would have phrased it better, in the unlikely event of giving utterance to a similar sentiment.

Of her juggling multiple, live, multiracial males, if not mates, she readily conceded, "I like the variety."

Girlpower, indeed. How much choice did she need? What if she should, or could, choose to stop choosing? What if she never did? Unable to make up her mind, she would seem to have relinquished it. Never mind how much choice you really need. How much do you really want?

Visions of Mary began rippling through Edward's dreams. Amanda may have been slender, but she wasn't very stout. Unlike Mary. Mary was, if memory serves, anything you wanted her to be. Well, not quite. Because this is what boys don't discern: the beauties talk back. They have personalities, and you may not always get on with them. Mary had a personality. He just hadn't seen it, bedazzled by her beauty. Amanda has one too. He hadn't seen it either, different though it was, blinded again as he was by her undeniable visual appeal. For most men, what is commonly called 'growing up' could really be described as moving from the second dimension into the third. So few ever grow up. But better to take a chance on a real person, than some flat projection of your own fantasies. The moral of this story is finally becoming clear: don't ever think you've got everything worked out. I never do. I don't even think I've got that much worked out. The meaning of this book is being glimpsed at last: my brother's life is a journey from the fantasy of youth to the reality of maturity, via the discovery of women's bodies, followed by their often not inconsiderable minds. That is, their total personalities. Perchance so too is mine.

Amanda, being bright and bouncy, was not wholly oblivious to the fact that this guy she was still with was increasingly absent in reverie. She knew the score, as well as how to score. Things deteriorated to such a degree that, one evening after a more than usually mundane exchange of bodily fluids between them, she turned away from him in bed, spitting: "Fucking you is like fucking a corpse."

He could not say, of her necrophiliac, or rather -phobic, simile, "This is the worst", because he could still say "This is the worst." Still and all, it did not make him feel great.

He got up and dressed, and left her apartment for the last time, leaving her life forever, and walked down the lonely street of chance after midnight, to the deserted subway station. On the side of a carriage that swept into the platform opposite from where he was standing, an aerosol can kid had spray-painted in large, lurid, day-glo letters, orange and silver surrounded by black, with lack of training and primitive technique:

ARE YOU HAPPY NOW?

This was the worst.

He should choose. Even if for him it's just a silly old binary, rather than, as it is for her, a multiple choice. How much choice do you need? He should call it a day with Amanda 'Scarlet Woman' O'Hara. He should be gone with the wind. She was hardly in a position to sue for breach of promise.

Yet why was all America, for him, just this one woman? Because women are all the world, to him. America is a void, a vacuum that sucks you in and makes things weird. Just like Amanda, one of its many personifications. She may be of use for infatuation, but is she any good for love? She was extremely orgiastic, but not big on sensuality. Mary, on the other hand, was someone to grow old with. She might even do all those things that Amanda did, and care about him too. It wouldn't be just the old in and out, however well-executed, but then the getting tired and the thrill wearing off, and having a pleasant memory. It would be for life. They'd be in it together, for the long haul. Always supposing she'd have him.

For it was not a foregone conclusion that she would even look at him twice. But he was no longer too young not to think about growing old. He was, just as he had been when he started with that American girl, nearly forty, only now only more so. Where do the decades disappear to? Who knows where the time goes? This moment of manifestation, insight and decision is what we in the trade like to refer to as an epiphany. Nowadays, it is more commonly called a paradigm shift. I apologise if, real life being what it is, they tend to work better on paper than they do in what passes for real life. Maybe that is why I am making this one not work so well on paper. It is a more realistic representation of life. For coming of age, and becoming a citizen of reality (even if it is only your own) tends to happen incrementally, rather than as a result of a blinding flash. For maybe this is only what he wants these women to represent for him now. The subsequent realisation that they aren't what he has just started seeing them as, no more than they were what he saw them as before, could function as a further epiphany. But let's stick to one instant of growth at a time. I will sacrifice much verisimilitude for the dramatic effect. There's some who might say that things appear more real the more dramatically they are rendered. But that is not my experience of reality.

Yes, America is rich in promise. It is the final frontier, for making new starts. So if, or rather, when, the dream starts going sour, there's farther to fall. All promises are breached. He is learning now what he should have learned years ago. Wherever you go, you're always yourself; and maybe wherever you are, you always think you should be somewhere else. Oh fuck, always me, wherever I be; and wherever I be, being me, I always don't want to stay. But, wherever you go, there's no place like home. There's no place like any other place either, I'll give you that too. But there's no time now to watch this space. It's too late for 'I'd like to live here', but just in time for 'I wouldn't mind dying here.' The eschatological can quickly become scatological. Enough of this endless preoccupation with last things. What about first things first?

He should stop pretending to be someone else. Edward is a sexy, passionate, intelligent man. What was he doing, marrying the office floozy? He was letting himself in for having to listen to strangers lecturing him for the rest of his life about the damage to his self-esteem and sense of personal worth. He would wind up taking part in men's discussion groups, where they sat around and talked about their feelings. It might even be suggested that he undergo a course of assertiveness training. (Maybe that's what I should have done.) But has his life become a chess match that he has given away too much material in, and got himself into too irretrievably bad a position, to have any hope of ever winning? Should he settle for a draw? No. Go down fighting, even if your faithless fiancée no longer goes down with you, or on you. Play to win, even if it's not just a game. Or simply knock the board over, accidentally-on-purpose, and start all over again. Did you think he'd make a life of jealousy, to follow still the changes of the moon with fresh suspicions? Jealousy, that most private and personal manifestation of paranoia? No, to be once in doubt is once to be resolved. It was passing strange.

For why should he slouch around the world with a gesture and a brogue and a faggotful of useless memories? It's all the one gaff, more or less, always allowing for its diversity. There is, as the sing-song see-saw saying goes, good and bad everywhere. Ireland might not be much better than anywhere else, but it might not be much worse either, and sure it's cool to be Irish, at this point in history, and sure, as luck would have it, he just happens to have been born there. I mean here. Like me. It's the luck of the Irish that it's lucky to be Irish. So he might as well belong. Even if I have never been able to. He would climb aboard the bandwagon. Even if it's careening out of control. It would be a shame to miss the boat. Even if it's a sinking ship. That is what it means to be Irish. Even if all the children of the state are not cherished equally. Tell me, where in the world, and how on earth, is that noble ideal ever realised? That is what it means to lay allegiance to any nationality. That is what it means to me. That is what it means to be me. And to be him, to him. To be sure, to be sure.

He would go, or is that come, home. Wherever that is, was, will be. To seek what he could seek, find what he could find.

And so his steps did tend around the bend and he did wend to where he could fend and they would not rend but would mend and be able to vend or also lend what we will send post pending.

THE END

IRLANDA ONCE AGAIN

Having set forth from that place, it was only natural I should return
to it, given the accuracy of my navigation.

SAMUEL BECKETT, *The Unnamable*

1

LITTLE REMAINS TO RELATE, to be related, or to be related to. Or to fail heroically, or miserably, in the attempt to do so. Memory is selective. Memory is defective. Memory is a love detective. This is the last time you will hear the voice over, for even I wish this voice, be it mine or another's, were over. I have not been suffering so much from aphasia, as much as aphonia. I have grown exhausted, exhausting this voice. I would like to hear a new voice. I will speak with one voice. The voice that does not use I. I have used up all possible possibilities of the I. I want to forget about me, myself and I. Ask not, "Where did 'I' come from?", but rather, "Where am 'I' going to?" I am in search of self-forgetfulness. I am not the first person to stumble onto the liberating resources inherent in using a second, or more usually a third, person. Neither are you. Nor is he. The I topples into ⌐, and is no longer a vertical support, piercingly upright, but a horizontal foundation, lying flat and laying low. Not rampant, but flaccid. Out of such authorial impotence does fictive omnipotence issue. Instead of a prop to hold me up and hold on to, it becomes a bridge for other characters to walk across, to liberty, or perdition; to freedom, or to their doom. [NOTE TO SELF: Lyric becomes Epic, Poetry becomes Prose.]

Here comes the denouement. Help me unravel this knot. Even if it is Gordian, and must be roughly cut. Let us tie up the loose ends.

Is there an opening for closure?

Disentangling from Amanda proved less fraught with difficulty than Edward thought it might be. She was a modern girl, in more ways than one. She hated fuss and bother, and looked at those who made scenes, and then looked away, as at a gross display of disorder and bad taste. So he didn't make one. Strangely, they'd never got it together to move in together, so there was none of that uncodified divvying up of the spoils to be gone through.

He threw himself into work, but it was work he could do with his eyes closed, and so not very distracting. Like me, he had odds and ends to take care of, before extracting himself, and moving on. Still, late at night, in the still of the night, that face from his past rose up in his dreams, as if briefly breaking the surface of stagnant water in a murky pool, before disappearing back down below again. He would watch, from overhead, balanced on the edge of the diving board, his heart thrumming, his balls tightening, blood rushing to his head, unwilling or unable to take the plunge. Would you like me to have a stab at interpreting this recurring dream? You're welcome to have a go yourself. Step right up. Jump right in. After you. Are you diving, or drowning?

Her card still lay scrunched up in his wallet, which he'd learned to call a pocket book, growing more dirty and dog-eared every time he took it out to consider it, like when he was sitting in some crowded downtown bar, getting well-oiled, or riding home alone in a taxi. What the hell:

To: mcontrary@aspect.ie
From: et@easyserve.com
Subject: Hi
Sent: Friday, 24 September 1999, 22:25:43

Hi Mary,
How are you keeping?
I'm still working away here, for my sins, making my fortune. But I plan to return home soon. I can make a fortune there now, too.
Things have been difficult since Mam died. I don't think the old man can look after himself, or anything else, on his own.
I broke up with the woman I was supposed to marry. She wasn't that interested in what I was going through.
How are things with you?
Love,
Edward

He could be as laconic as I can be bombastic. Note the signing off salutation. He'd thought long and hard about that closing 'Love', but decided in the end to go with it, over 'Take care' or 'Keep in touch'. That was the good thing about a final love: it could be as innocuous or as portentous as anyone wanted to read into it; and it could be wriggled out of as having been grossly misinterpreted, should the need arise. Men: you wouldn't know what to make of them.

So a sustained correspondence got under way, tentative at first, but the ball was set rolling, and kept being returned. A hot shudder of pleasure shot through his febrile nerves the day he opened a message from her that began 'Dear Darling'. Amazing what one little word can do, depending on who it is directed at, and by whom. But that was a greeting she could easily discount, too, saying she was just being playful, or didn't even know she was playing at all. Women: you wouldn't be up to them.

Then, late in the evenings, half-cut in one of those plush hotel bars he'd go to drink alone in, the nights he didn't want many people around, or other nights, lying sprawled on his unmade bed in his apartment, staring vacantly at the ceiling, he took to phoning her up, for a quiet chat. I happen to know that all he really wanted was to hear the timbre of her voice. Although I must admit that after a while their voices carried sweet nothings on the air. But I will not quote them to you. Use your imagination. Use it again, if you want their telephone exchanges to grow more heated, and stray into the stratosphere of transatlantic phone sex, where fluids fly without fusion, and are produced, if not exchanged. I am not a content provider. I am not a contented provider. I am a discontent provider. I am discontented because I cannot provide. But I am turning, as are they, into a contentment provider. How's the form? Are you content? That's the style. There'll be no substance abuse around here. This facility of mine will no longer make me facile, but will be used felicitously. These conceits that I have will no more be conceited, but well-considered. And to think there are some who say genuine romantic attachments cannot flourish electronically. But such tender endearments are not natural in an age like this. They tend to be mechanical. Or maniacal. It was loneliness that drove them together.

He handed in his notice at work, having made sure to secure something similar to do in Dublin. They were sad to see him go, but the show must go on.

There once was a systems man
Who thought he was indispensable.
When systems analysed him
His view was found reprehensible.

But hang on. Wait a minute. Not so fast. Who's to say if she would fit right along with his dreams and schemes? That would be a tad pat for this ex-pat. Why would either of them want to read the same book twice? The only books worth reading are the ones worth reading more than once. Or, in fact, many times. The thing is, she knew him, and he knew her, and not just in the narrowly biblical sense. They could read each other like a book. A book you could read twice. Or many times. Like the book about them. Like this book. Like it, or lump it.

They arranged to rendezvous in Paris, while he stopped off on his journey home, for a strange interlude of renewal. Separate rooms, but the same hotel. There was a time, not so long ago, he reflected as he flew over in the jumbo jet that put him in mind of nothing so much as a gigantic male member wantonly bisecting the sky, when the idea of travelling all that distance to converge with, or upon, a woman, and not commence ripping her clothes off at the first opportunity that presented itself as soon as he arrived, would have proved laughably anathema, a potential slur on his manhood. But love is sweeter, or slower, second time around. If love it is. For it might just be, or become, symbiotic. How do you know if it's true love, or simply symbiosis? Perhaps they are just one and the same. Or is unrequited love the only true one?

Maybe you consider this revised gentlemanly approach merely pathetic, the way the milksops or coxcombs of old would have behaved. The modern man is much aware that today's woman will castigate him thoroughly for being too combative and competitive, urging him to evolve, and then, by gross and fiendish feat, drag the old ways in again through the backdoor, complaining that he's a softie and a wimp. Maybe what a chap needs is inner strength and resources, which don't depend on what women think of you, but don't depend on what men think of you either, and so are also a far cry from good old buck naked aggression. Although if you're fairly quiet, doing the strong, silent type, you'll undoubtedly come in for accusations of being terribly uncommunicative.

I think he prefers to think of his new-found finesse as the enactment of a latter-day, if down-at-heel, chivalric code, even if it does at times tend towards the cavalier. This is a courtship ritual, like a slow dance; and we must now proceed from ritual to romance. Allow us that much. We have spent too long travelling in the opposite direction.

But if a man chases a woman, until she catches him, then who gets caught, and who gets caught out? Maybe there is no catch, after all, at this late stage. Can the passionless recollect, or re-enact, passion convincingly, in tranquillity? Maybe modifying intensity is a necessary survival strategy, the price of staying alive. To burn out, or to fade away? Or to rust? What difference does it make, if the end result is the same? But it isn't, because the means have to justify the end. What's interesting is not where or when you end up, but how you managed to get there, and what you did along the way. Without feeling the burn – the hope, frustration, anger, rage, despair, redemption and love – we wouldn't have the fruits of sustained intensity. That is, ecstasy. You can't have life itself without some risks, so it follows that you can't live without them either. Did I imply that you couldn't get me excited about anything? I know about obsession, believe you me. All passion is not yet spent.

They weren't just trying in desperation to warm up some stale leftovers, reheating the remnants of an already, or almost, faded passion. They were just getting used to a new way of eating a more delicate dish. They were both, and so am I, need I bother reiterating, pushing forty. That is too old to believe anything, or believe in anything, or at any rate anything new, even if you ever did, even in yourself. If other people have personalities, then you must have one too. Personality is a mysterious construct, all to do with volume and projection. You can programme yourself to the point of not having one. You can also amplify whatever it is you've got. When you're in a room, it's you in a room, whether it's crowded or empty, empty but for you. If you weren't there, would it matter that you weren't there, even in a crowded room, would you just be one of the crowd? You must impress people positively with the force of your personality.

Maybe that's the key to all this relationships shenanigans: to realise that passion is bound to get done in, one way or another, either because you stay together, or else because you don't. So you must grow adept at adapting, and promise to compromise, as passion is tempered with compassion, and you develop personally, expanding your personality.

That is, if you want to stay together. Do I envy those so controlled, who are usually the controllers, who do not have to learn this lesson the hard way? Certainly not. They have never risked passion, with all its attendant risks. One wonders why they should be supervising the passionate, or the victims of thwarted passion. The best may lack all conviction, but so too do the worst. They had no previous convictions to look back on. It's best to have known passionate intensity. Even if it doesn't last, and fades away all too soon.

This man and woman went to all those places they had last seen together when they were still young, so many years ago, before the passage of time and the forces of circumstances had altered them. Edward and Mary, I mean, although I suppose the places may have changed too. They drank champagne, and sauntered by the Seine. Flowers were bought. Candlelit dinners were consumed. He was even able to savour, and then lay, the long lost ghost of Laura.

For the lovers made love, on their final night there, after kisses and cuddles and walking arm in arm and holding hands all week. Only this time it takes place behind closed doors. This is all I will say, although I could say more. This is what men can learn from women, the women who do not strive to emulate men: it's not quantity but quality, not frequency but intensity, and these depend more on who you're with than on what you, or they, do. To be one with one you don't feel you have to pay because you'd like her to go away. To want to stay with her, and want her to stay.

His first is his last. His next will be his first. His first is not next to last, but was made to last. She is his alpha, and his omega. So he must be one of those alpha males, just as I am the omega man.

Ultimately, we are in our prime.

Herewith some hints, consisting of puffs, encomia and vicious dismissals, being for the benefit of sundry puzzled or lazy publishers' readers, literary editors and book reviewers, who, on perhaps finding that thinking of something to say about this progressive work is proving too difficult or demanding for them, may care to dip into and take advantage of at will. The fragments may be cut up and pasted in as caprice or discretion dictates, and can serve as stimulation to forming one's own opinion, be copied down comprehensively, or strung together willy-nilly to bolster any particular argument.

this little allegory of pain and pleasure/examines the extremities of
agony and ecstasy/an ambitious but deeply flawed magnum opus,
which through its repeated failed attempts and stops and starts winds
up oddly mirroring the human condition/a tiresome tapestry of allu-
sion and reference, parody and pastiche/any text as referential as this
one cannot have any organic life of its own/a bumbling, doubled
Bildungsroman that portrays a preposterously protracted coming of
age, an almost interminable rites of passage/it's the next step in fiction, Irish or otherwise/the elongated, uncontrolled ravings of
a madman/obviously the product of a diseased mind, and quite probably a diseased body as well/treats self-consciousness as a disabling
affliction, but by the very probing of its paralysing effects on action,
paradoxically finds it enabling/absurdist mandarin/streetwise aristo-
crat/patrician urchin/nouveau riche plebeian/discovering riches in
poverty and poverty in riches/hovering between high style and low
burlesque, deep philosophical excavation and vernacular knock
about/a sorry spectacle/an epic of nullity/the arid anguish of a soul in
torment/low on the much-needed 'feel-good' factor/I can't
see him selling the film rights/a powerful argument for more stringent
censorship/a threat to family life and the very fabric of civilisation/
disturbing that it has been published complete and unexpurgated/
sad triumph of style over content/a formal formlessness pervades/
predictably unpredictable/a formalist joke, in which some very
strange and macabre things happen on the way to no punch line/a
mere demonstration of muddled thinking and garbled reasoning,
which gets lost in its own ongoing groping for meaning/isn't that
all any of us are doing?/whilst in many places the effect on the
reader is undoubtedly somewhat emetic, nowhere does it tend
to be aphrodisiac/self-indulgent, testosterone-fuelled, ego-driven
drivel/challengingly idiosyncratic/wilfully obscure/that guy's up
his own arse/but then again, so is Ireland/to say nothing of the
world at large/if he was a bar of chocolate, he'd eat himself/Traynor
displays a blithe disregard for the conventional injunctions: 'Show,
Don't Tell', and 'Less Is More'/relentlessly punctures the fourth
wall, but from the wrong side/makes mince meat of the intentional
fallacy, and the pathetic one too/doesn't know whether it wants
to be comedy or tragedy, and so falls between the two stools,
winding up as farce/can't put two words together/there is no

reason why any one word should follow any other/graduate student bullshit/reads more like a treatise than a novel, because of the writer's incessant interrogation of the very basis of all discourse/ongoing irony is the song of a bird that has grown to love its cage/we are all caged birds/I know why the caged bird sings/there are no 'real' people here (quotation marks optional)/the very fact that people refer to people in books as 'characters' means they can have no real existence outside of the books they're in, for they are merely characters, not real people/this torturous, tortuous text/this loose, baggy monster/this summa contra omnes/this apologia pro sua vita/this distillation of alienation/this synthetic symphony/straining, striving and struggling for sophistication/portentous plodding/pretentious poppycock/without knowing to what it is pretending/ridiculously overwritten/the second-rater's peculiar but predictable penchant for an awful lot of alliteration/the characterisation is paper thin, reminding us that it is indeed written on thin paper/all the characters are totally believable, I was enthralled from start to finish and couldn't put it down/walks a tightrope between embarrassing ponderousness, and the excitement of discovery/if it seems a little precious, that's because it is/dense, compendious, learned, turgid/ a triumph of control, until it loses control/lets it all hang out, while keeping it all in/the author shows little awareness of, or adeptness for, constructing the basics of plot and character development, or even having a coherent theme/ exquisitely crafted exposition and exploration cannot be sustained, and dissipates in sloppy, ragged ranting and raving/an amoral sensualist transmogrifies into a fundamentalist preacher/one rapidly grows tired of the nasty Toughs and the nice Tenders/paranoids think everything is connected, but they're right, because everything *is* connected, except, of course, the paranoid/dangerous admixture of superstitious myth and perverted logic/deals in endless theoretical generalisations only to demonstrate their practical limitations/'words, like a sword'/ savage indignation designed solely to make us savagely indignant/ sly satire which pokes fun at how the confessional memoir has become the ideal vehicle for victim culture, and is its most authentic voice/if ever a man suffered/can there be misery loftier than this author's?/maybe not, but much of it is self-inflicted/he may have been hurt once, but he has been hurting himself, and others, ever since/the mechanistic gives way to the human, even as humanity

264

becomes more dependent on machines/engages valiantly and viscerally with the zeitgeist, and the polter one to boot/ludicrously immature, in fact frequently fatuously infantile/awakes from the nightmare of history and escapes the prison house of language/a closed text that just about manages to remain open, a chink of light coming through the crack in the door left ajar/the increase in the rhythm of the prose towards the end is a poor, imitative, syncopated trick to mimic the giddy rush of intellectual, emotional and sexual release/writing that is a mere preparation for writing/a meticulous but mendacious manifesto/so self-absorbed is the narrator, and so self-conscious the narrative, it is surprising that any story emerges whatsoever/"It would be nice if the incessant monologue were to give way to some dialogue." "Would it?"/like all great works of art, it contains its own criticism of itself/covers his ass by anticipating the more obvious criticisms/destined to become a *succès de scandale*/ only written to be controversial/a melange of words that has little to do with life as it is lived/writing in pursuit of itself/tendentiously verbose, a mess of wordage, a wordscape of pottage/goes to alarmingly elaborate lengths to prove something that every dog and devil in the street already knows/sometimes to state the obvious is to state what needs to be stated/ a manual of how not to go about writing a novel/a hotchpotch of cliché/ simultaneously denies yet reaffirms the primacy of the individual, but only when that individual is cognisant of responsibilities within the broader social context/blah blah blah/a celebration and condemnation of the book as entity, object and end in itself/blah blah blah blah blah/ you'll either love it or loathe it/unless you're completely indifferent (to it)

Hark to their contumely at my contumely, and to their praise. Life is hard enough, without criticism. As is art, without more of it. Now for some really hard but fair criticism, constructive as they like to call it, rather than deconstructive as others like to say, that which comes directly from the author himself, as he tries to make of criticism an art in itself. These disjointed, failed attempts at explication may also aid the unfortunate reader. Am I a chancer and a charlatan, or am I ahead of my time? Over to you now, for you to decide. Here is the *clef* to this *roman*. But don't expect to find answers to such standard queries as: 'What is the author's purpose?'; 'What is this guy trying to say?'; or, worst of all, 'What's his message?' These are the facts, as opposed to the myths.

Myth's organic source lies in fable and neuron. But myth is consolatory nonsense. It deals in false universals, to dull the pain of particular circumstances. Like this book. But that's what we need. But what do you want? What you think is good for you might not necessarily be so. But who's going to tell you? Logic is useful only for solving problems in your own mind. It is useless for tackling questions with other people. Because they are either more logical or less logical than you. Whoever shouts loudest gets heard most. To be bright enough to know that you aren't that bright, even if you're brighter than others. To be bright enough to know that others aren't that bright, even if they're brighter than you. To have heard all arguments before, and be thoroughly unimpressed with all of them. I love what is left of my ignorance, and wallow in its contours, appreciating its value. I owe to it anything I've achieved, everything I will ever achieve. Much more so than to my knowledge. But to be able to wield words, like a sword. This pen is a needle, this writing is probing, the intimate, cruel, excavation of the scalpel. His cock, head and heart are bringing him back to Ireland. Mine have always kept me here. My wound was the taut bow by means of which I shot the arrow of his journey across the terrain of these pages, and it propelled my pen too. But such suffering is not good for the soul, or for the work. To say nothing of the psychological scarring involved. Why am I using a mode of expression I despise? Because it's the currency. It's tough, but sometimes I have to trade in that legal tender. I have just been venting my spleen, raging at the outrage perpetrated against me. By this I mean life, which happens to everybody, although it does happen to everybody differently. I have little hope of attaining full genitality or, for that matter, gentility, after that fiddle-de-dee in my solar plexus, the complex of radiating nerves at the pit of the stomach, that turns us on like the light of the sun, that makes us feel good like the shudder of sex, that happened spontaneously before I ever knew I had an autonomic nervous system, much less that it could be subdivided into the sympathetic and parasympathetic nervous systems, and that they are in turn regulated by the limbic hypothalamic system, which is ultimately responsible for physical consciousness of all emotions, and their expression. The question should not be how, but where do you feel? I have been searching for the seat of my emotions. Does it turn out that it's all psychosomatic? Only if everything is. If only the whole shooting match hadn't got done in somewhere along the line, during one of my many mishaps, maybe I would feel more, and feel better, and not feel numb and hollow, affectless and ineffectual, literally and metaphorically. [NOTE TO SELF: Literal + Metaphoric = Symbolic.] I would not have been obliged to visit and dwell in regions of my psyche most people don't even know they have, much less have to consider going there. They don't call it 'deep inside' for nothing. That's the man'll get you right in the guts. Or maybe I was born damaged, as the priests used to say, and the therapists tell us now, and this life has just been more damage accumulation, while they work on its limitation. Is there any chance that all this was meant to happen? Did I will it, or was it forced on me? Or was I complicit, and does whatever happened subsequently serve me right? That sounds like a classic case of what they would call survivor guilt. No, I'm not about to start believing or implying that. I'm a survivor, after all. That would be succumbing to them, and their ways. Everyone is born free, and then they put them in their chains. But will we be born again?

All I know is, back before the attack, when the sun came inside my tummy and warmed me up, I poured forth warmth towards other people. Then I shrivelled up, ran dry, and grew cold. So I resorted to the counsel of that ancient maxim, 'Say it, don't spray it'. But still I stuttered. To be so deprived would be enough to give anyone a sore head, much less a heart condition. If only it hadn't happened, I might have had a sunny disposition, instead of a style that grates. If you have style, they say you have no ideas. If you have ideas, they say you have no style. What if I have ideas about style? What if my style is to have ideas? If I'd been busy having a good time, you wouldn't have this book. I should have had a good time. I would have liked to have had a good time. I could be out in the garden now, taking the sun, instead of stuck in here, writing this. Or alternatively, stuck in an office in a job I hate, or don't much like, enduring a vile commute twice a day to get there and back. I was trying to express the inexpressible, and F the ineffable. I have made an exhibition of my inhibition. Anything that can be said isn't worth saying. Anything worth saying cannot be said. I'm sure I'm trying to say something. What is it I'm trying to say? Whereof we cannot speak, thereof we must scream. If you think this is unreadable, it's also unwritable, probably unnameable, and definitely unsaleable. Did you think I was writing in the expectation of being read? Think again. But, with everybody at it, the paper will be wasted anyway. I have been alienated by considering language too carefully. To say nothing of the incessant examination of other people's motives, and my own. Maybe I should copyright the English language. Then no one else could use it, only me. Unless they asked me for permission. The Dictatorship of the Proseletariat. From each, according to his paeans. Then I'd have my very own personal language, which we may as well call Slanguage, complete with its own grammar, syntax and vocabulary, capable of describing all those sexual intensities yet to be experienced, emotional extremities as yet unfelt, and intellectual complexities not yet thought. Or thunk. Otherwise, I'm doomed never to hear an original idea or argument again. To have been around so long, you've heard it all before. But isn't a dictionary of slang a contradiction in terms? No, because even if you think genuine communication is rare, if not impossible, if you're trying to communicate something, you have to show some respect for whoever it is you're trying to communicate with. Otherwise you'll get lost in a terminal tape loop of idiosyncrasy. Or an interminable one. But if I have felt these things, doesn't that mean others have too? Or have to? Even if only one human being has felt them, they are therefore not inhuman. These are my feelings about thoughts. These are my thoughts about feelings. Even if no one else has had my experiences, does that invalidate them? Maybe it was the singularity of what happened to me that gave rise to the uncharted, unchartered feelings. As it does with everyone. All writing is but a preparation for writing, unless it's a finishing it off.

Gather round. Hear ye. See here, it's not hearsay, or heresy: you can go through most of your life, whoever you are, with that clever clever, smart-alecky, loftily indifferent, wryly ironic tone, putting on the style, but life will always catch up with you, and break your heart. There are ironies too great to contemplate. What tone will you adopt then? How will your fine style save you then? Will you show the requisite grace under pressure? Or will it all come tumbling down?

When your six-month-old baby daughter dies out of the blue one night in a cot death?

Or when the son you've tried so hard for is born autistic, or with cerebral palsy, or cystic fibrosis, and your husband or wife leaves you because the relationship couldn't take the strain, and you lose loads of money in the divorce settlement, and you wind up in a low status job in a remote corner of the globe, because it's all you can concentrate on or be interested in?

Or when the son who was born perfectly healthy and whom you brought up lovingly to appreciate the beautiful things of life, or say your best friend whom you had all your formative first experiences with, is found wall-eyed, mouth-agape, sitting slumped backwards on a toilet seat in a cubicle in Amsterdam or Tangiers or Bangkok or one of the wild cities of the world, with a needle sticking out of the crook of his arm and the dropper full of his blood, and he's treated as a waste disposal problem by the local sanitation authorities?

Or he wraps the family car around a street lamp while swerving to avoid a dog its owner had just let off its leash to have a crap in a field, and now he sits immobile in a corner making gurgling noises with a silly smile on his face that makes him look dumber than the average tree stump?

Or when the daughter who didn't die in infancy, and has just started studying medicine or law or architecture in the best college in the country, comes home one day and tells you she is hearing voices that are telling her to kill you, and then herself?

Or when your uncle, whom your parents trust implicitly, sticks his hand up your dress while dandling you on his knee when you're nine, and nearly penetrates you, and then slaps your bottom and says, "Easily courted, easily tickled, easily made a fool of", and no one believes you because everyone likes this rich uncle, and you're put off sexual relationships with men until you're in your mid-thirties?

Or another uncle you love is left in severe neuropathic pain after a routine appendectomy, and the surgeons and the hospital administration close ranks and admit nothing, and no one believes him because he's poor and has one previous conviction for a minor drugs offence and they make like they've never heard of iatrogenesis, and so he kills himself because he can't stand not being able to work and being a burden and not getting a proper diagnosis or appropriate treatment and not receiving any kind of settlement for damages because negligence can't be proven?

Or when that arse-licking, cock-sucking, sexual favours-trading bitch at work with the big tits and cute ass and long legs gets promotion over you, even though you did all the work on the project, and she just sailed right in and made it look as though she'd co-ordinated everything?

Or that flash bastard with the sports car gets it because his father is a Master Mason, or a Knight of Columbanus, or a Rotarian, or a Rosicrucian, or a member of the Golf Club, or the Tennis Club, and so is the boss?

Or when your mother has a massive stroke, followed by a series of small ones, and goes from being bedridden to wheelchair-bound to getting around on a Zimmer frame, and needs constant care and attention that you haven't the time to provide or the money to pay for, and even though she gets meals-on-wheels she can't even feed herself?

Or when you're picked up in a night club one night by a luscious femme fatale and later castrated, or dephallicised, or both, during the filming of a snuff movie?

Or when you contract alopecia, and all your long flaxen curls fall out, and you get into a flat panic about whether they'll ever grow back or not, and in your case they never do?

Or when you get grotesque facial, spinal or abdominal injuries after a skiing, hang-gliding or bungee-jumping accident, and you don't get a penny in compensation because the travel agent and leisure centre were well within their statutory rights, having provided the proper safety instructions?

Or your billionaire industrialist father won't pay the ransom when you're kidnapped by anti-corporate anarchists, even though they chop your toes off one by one and send them to him by registered post?

Or some freedom fighters, who believe fervently and so violently in their cause, park a car bomb in the wrong place and blow half the town you just happen to be a foreign exchange student in sky high, and unfortunately blow you or yours to smithereens as well in the process?

This isn't just happening on TV. It has happened. To you. Read the front page headlines.

Or a robber cuts your ear off because he thinks you know the combination to a safe you're guarding while working part-time at night security to pay your way through college, but you don't because the gaffer doesn't give that information to anyone?

This isn't a movie. This is really happening. To you. Read those brief little filler stories buried in the middle of the newspaper. Watch the human interest snippets on the television news.

See what happens to the little people? And to the VIPs too? What makes you think it won't happen to you? The unbearably awful happens to people every day. Always remember: your worst nightmares can come true. There's a lot of bastards out there. They have been legitimised. They can dream it for you, wholesale. Life will break your heart. Say what you like, do as you may, whatever you do, whatever you say.

Or something really ordinary and inevitable and predictable will happen, like your mother will die, or your father will die, or your husband will die, or your wife will die. *SOMEONE YOU LOVE WILL DIE.* (If there's someone you love.) Hell, you'll die yourself. What makes you think you're immune? What makes you so invincible, so invulnerable? Not so much fun now, eh? Now the smile's on the other side of your face. Too much laughing ends in crying.

Nothing is funnier than unhappiness. Who said that? Whoever it was, they were wrong. Just wait until unhappiness happens to you. War, Famine, Pestilence. Emotional or Financial Bankruptcy. Personal Betrayal or Bereavement. It's not hard to come up with a Litany of Disasters. I have enunciated my own, in an effort to rescue genuine emotion. The only problem lies in making it particular, while at the same time making it partake of the majesty of myth. But either way, your days are numbered. The end is nigh.

That's when you'll need love. Being cool and arch and deadpan won't help you at all then. You'll be sad and fucked up and depressed, but not gullible enough to be taken in by therapy, or the attendant pharmaceutical industry, shelling out a small fortune to lie on a couch in a plush office, or sit in a group meeting in a dingy hall, talking about and working through your childhood traumas and your problematic relationships. Their drugs don't work. Not nearly as well as the ones you buy privately from your dealer. But even they can't go on working forever. You don't trust the shrinks, but you don't trust in God either. The supposed consolations of religion or even philosophy will hold no comfort for you. Nor will the psychic healers and snake oil charmers. No, love will be all you need. It will be the only thing that can save you. If you're lucky enough to find it. If you believe you're lucky, you probably will be. Or maybe you won't. That's what I believe. I'm lucky to believe it. Millions don't. About themselves, I mean. And about me. You have to stand up for yourself, and what you believe in. You have to believe in yourself. Until your luck runs out. But, if you're lucky, you just might get it back again. Or maybe you won't.

So, no more Mr Nasty Guy. It's nice to be nice. But it's better to be good. Being good is great. Being good is the best. Sometimes the best just isn't good enough. Sometimes the good is better than the best. It's easy to be clever. We can all be clever. That is, those who can be, can, and will. I have been clever. I was dumb enough to be clever. Can I be clever enough to be dumb? Because cleverness isn't love. Now I would like to be good. It's hard to be good. It's good to be good. It's good to love. So more Mr Tough Guy. Tough enough to be tender. This is where having your own personal style comes in. For what are words worth? Words must begin to mean something again, and not remain forever detached from meaning. I was shoving words around. But they will not be trifled with. Neither will thought, or feeling, to say nothing of what goes on lower down. I grow weary of theory. It is making me bleary. The idea's everything. The very idea! Ideas matter only as much as the idea that ideas matter. The trouble with a lot of books is that they're usually written by people who read books, who know very little about understanding people who don't read books, which is the vast majority of people, who the vast majority of books are about. The trouble with a lot of other books is that they're written by people who don't read books, and so haven't the remotest idea how to go about writing them. You must love words, to overcome suffering, evil and death. You must have style, and that will give you meaning.

I concede that the following may well have been very good optional titles for this tome: *The Mystery of the Missing Penis*, *The Diary of a Madman*, *The Hurt and Hurting Heart*, *The Opposite of Odyssey*, or even *The Man Made of Words*, or, better still, *The Man Undone by the World*. Why not *City of Words*? For that is what this huge edifice is: a sprawling suburb that is struggling to connect with others to form some sort of mass conurbation and make some kind of ragged, higgledy-piggledy sense. Might it some day, if not now, begin to mean something? I sincerely hope so. Maybe my book is utopian, since it is set nowhere, although you could say it is set anywhere and everywhere, which makes it dystopian too. We need a town-planner, to have a place we can get around, without finding ourselves stuck in gridlock, and getting into jams.

I have shored these fragments against my ruin. And his. And yours. In remembrance of time nearly lost, of things almost ruined, but partially recovered, and now reclaimed. After our thorough investigations, all we have discovered can be encapsulated in this silly, circular syllogism:

Life will break your heart.
You'll need love, to heal.
Only love can break your heart.

Here endeth the lesson. Don't mess with the preacher man. If you eat at the mission, then you have to listen to the sermon. You cannot dine and dash. No doing a runner here. I have had my say. Have I said what I wanted to say? Maybe we'll never know, for sure. And so, we shall not cease from exploration.

"Knock knock."
  "Who's there?"
  "Police."
  "Police who?"
  "Please open up, or we're coming in after you."
  I must now make good my escape. I am an escape artist. I am a quick change artist. I look to the window. I look at the window. I look out the window. Outside it is sharp, cold but clear, as befits a winter sky. For today is New Year's Eve, Friday, 31 December 1999. It is also, I've heard through the bush wire, or the grapevine, Edward and Mary's wedding day. I wonder why they chose the last of the old, over the first of the new. Probably so as to be in time for the party, and to have their night of nights on that very special night.

I take the handle of the side window and force it open, just as the head of an axe comes crashing through a panel of the bedroom door. I scramble onto the sill, daring to look down. It is quite a drop, much too far to jump. But if I launch myself across, I can grab hold of the drainpipe, and shimmy down into the backyard. That is what I do, as the boys in blue burst into my room, shouting after me. If I hadn't already had a nervous breakdown, I'd say I was having one now. Though there's nothing to say you can't have a second one. They say the second is usually worse than the first.

Landing in the garden, thankfully without breaking any bones, I take a second to peer in through the parlour window, even though the Cops are in hot pursuit. Now I know the source of that vile smell. Two bod-

273

ies lie decomposing in chairs on either side of the fireplace. I can only presume that they are all that is left of Mr and Mrs Tough.

But how did they arrive at such an advanced state of decay? I hope you aren't hopping to the banal conclusion that I did for them. Or maybe I did, and have successfully repressed it. Or did they have at each other? Maybe they simply expired away, either together or one followed by the other, and didn't bother to tell me, or anyone else. But then, how could they, if so expired? The second to go could have announced the demise of the first, but would not have been in optimal position to broadcast news of his or her own, after he or she had gone. Or before going, come to think of it, not yet having gone. I really don't know. That is, I can't remember. That is, I don't want to. It would be some primal scene to witness your parents, or those who stand *in loco* or in lieu, murdering each other rather than making love. So let's not go there. And let's not have recourse to the annoying jargon either. Primal scene, indeed: it's enough to make you want to give a primal scream.

"What is truth?" said jesting Edmund, and would not stay for an answer. For I cannot linger, if I want to avoid the long arm, and full rigour, of the law. What will happen if they catch me? Would I be accused, found guilty, and imprisoned? Or could I enter a plea of insanity? Maybe I'd then fall eligible for a mental health disability payment, on condition that I commit at least one act of public lunacy per annum. For instance, the publication of these mindless musings, or others like them. But then they'd probably make me do therapy to keep it. They can't afford to have too many arty farty, airy fairy nutters, many of whom are of course just chronic malingerers, on the loose and at a loose end in a full employment economy. They must be put to work, however lowly.

Yet maybe I have been incarcerated in prison all this time, and not realised it. Or, indeed, in a mental institution. Or maybe I knew I was in some such place, and didn't tell you. In which case, you will think me one with Pinocchio, Munchhausen, or Judas. Are all tellers of tall tales always liars and betrayers? No, I am not, for this is my home. My surrogate parents lie dead before me. It was they who were creating that god-awful stink. Granted, the knocking on the front door has been going on for the best part of twenty years, before the authorities decided to break it down. But at the start it was intermittent, only lately growing more persistent. It was just a cheap device to keep you reading, and is now revealed for what it is, solved and resolved. But that's not to say it wasn't happening, and I wasn't reporting it faithfully to you.

What to do, what to do? The Feds are coming down the drainpipe after me, but fortunately, in typical Keystone fashion, one has landed on top of another, in a gloriously riotous collision, pinning him to the ground. I don't want to be lagged, and had up before the Beak. Justice may be miscarried. If you look guilty, you might be found so. I might not be as nimble-witted or silver-tongued as my prosecuting cross-examiners. That doesn't mean I did it. So while the Rozzers lie squabbling, I give them the slip, climbing swiftly over the garden fence.

Where to go, where to go? Is there any place that can offer me safety and sanctuary? I know, I'll make for the church where my brother is espousing his bride-to-be. It was most neglectful of him not to send me an invitation anyhow, even if we have never met.

I can kill two birds with the one stone, by getting confession before the nuptials get underway. For, if I really and truly did kill my parents, then confession takes the sin away, and makes everything okay. Hmm. A very likely story. Believe it or not. When shriven, its seal will not be broken, by the man of God, or by me.

How can I be writing this, and doing it at the same time?

Anything can happen, and it probably will, but maybe it won't, and maybe you want it to happen, or maybe you don't, or maybe you're not sure.

Arriving at the church grounds, I run up the front steps, and in through the doors. All the guests have assembled and are seated, and Edward is waiting at the top, by the altar, with his best man, some old school buddy I know nothing about. Surely it should have been me, his only brother? He knows I am here. He saw, or I let him see, what happened at the house. I think he is feeling a little disgruntled. He fears I will rain on his parade. He would rather put me from him. His father is there too. Mr Tender, I mean. The whoreson must be acknowledged. For unlike only one of our illustrious forebears, both of us are bastards, and neither legit.

But why this getting married in a church lark, for God's sake? Are two middle-aged atheists playing the hypocrite merely to please their two remaining parents? What's wrong with a registry office?

Well, maybe Edward, in love as he is, is coming around to the notion that it does seem a little hasty to throw out two thousand years of beautiful, if sometimes bloody, tradition. The baby with the bathwater, as they say. Even if there are older belief systems and faith expressions around. Maybe all this God business bears looking into, after all. A First Cause, a Higher Power, outside yourself, as they say. Or else, he doesn't much care one way or the other any more. Is that not where we came in?

What an outstanding instance of bad timing. I stopped believing in God when most everyone else still believed. Now that most everyone else no longer believes, I'm tempted to start believing all over again. God *is* good. Or rather, God is a good idea. It's his invention, Man, who in turn thought him up, that's the problem. What a piece of work is Man. Personally, I've never been entirely sure that I did exist, much less been tempted to start speculating on the existence or otherwise of some Supreme Being, with a view to trying to make sense of the predicament that is my own existence, or lack thereof. To say nothing of that of the rest of you.

> *There once was a metaphysician*
> *Who proved that he didn't exist.*
> *When the others had learned his position,*
> *They agreed that he wouldn't be missed.*

I have been in search of, and in flight from, myself, and the world. Which doesn't leave a lot of room for God. I am self-defeating. I am self-deluding. Aren't we all? But I am as comforted, if credulous, as any believer. It took me a long time to learn to believe in nothing. I am not about to renounce my faith now. It hardly matters what you believe in. What counts is the strength with which you believe. Life is so fleetingly short and brief, and so essentially absurd and meaningless, that it ill-behoves anyone of any intelligence or sensitivity whatsoever to take it anyway seriously at all, by embarking on the perilous course of trying to make some sense of it. [NOTE TO SELF: Philosophy + Fresh Findings = An Unlikely Headline, at this late stage.] Nevertheless, I will try. In the final analysis, dying concerns only the living. In the finish up, death worries only old bones. In the end, immortality preoccupies only the mortal. But apparently that's all part and parcel of being alive. So I hereby declare a curse on all the rebels, busy trying to prove that nothing can be proven. I am not trying to prove that nothing can be proven. It does not need to be proven. I am living proof of the truth of this proposition. I do not need to prove myself, not even to myself. However, I will anyway.

I am taking my place in a pew at the back. Good Lord! I see that the Confession Box is now called, more comfortingly, the Reconciliation Room. I cannot reconcile myself to such a change. Still, I was only pulling your leg about going to confession and getting absolved. I must confess, I've nothing to confess.

Suddenly the organ strikes up its high-flown drone. Here comes the bride. Is she all fat and wide? Does she wobble from side to side? Not so as you'd notice. Still, it wouldn't surprise me if she was up the proverbial pole. Mary takes her uncle's arm, so she can link him up the aisle, and he can give her away, in place of her father. Then, casting her eyes around, she catches sight of me, and does a quick double-take, presumably because of my battered resemblance to her soon-to-be husband. What is this bedraggled version of her childhood sweetheart doing at the bottom of the red carpet, while the genuine article stands waiting at the top? I admit, I cut a poor figure, on account of my accumulated injuries, but there is no mistaking the similitude beneath the dishevelled disarray. From her unconcealed bewilderment, it is obvious Edward has not told her anything about me. What is she marrying into? There again, maybe she's just nonplussed to find me here, having heard my full story.

Then, for no reason I can explain (so you shouldn't try to either), she creates a kerfuffle as a diversionary tactic, and while her father's brother is busy searching the middle distance for whatever it is she pointed at, she reaches out and touches me. There. How does she know? Is it psychic powers? Whatever it is, it has a physical effect on me. Maybe I have just been suffering from arrested development, mentally, and precipitate old age, physically. Now I can feel the power surge through my body, and I orgasm automatically. What a climax. She has cured me. Simple as that. She has the healing hand, and has given me the rub of the relic. After all this time, I hope you will not denigrate my offering, which releases me from solipsistic prison, by calling it a premature ejaculation. We do need to institute some kind of reward system, and where better to situate it than in the pleasure centres of the brain? Perhaps I was only an example of the character distortion brought about by chronic pain. Or a bad case of performance anxiety. Stage fright can lead to showing off, once you get it together to go on. It's hard to get started, or to start getting hard, but when it gets to the end, you want to do it all over again. What if everything I've written here has just been coloured by mood rather than determined by disposition? Is all this just the result of one very long bad humour? Is it my permanent temperament talking, or was I just being temporally temperamental? I will leave you to ponder.

But remember, there is such a thing as depressive lucidity, I'll grant them that much. They describe this as a withdrawal from ordinary human concerns, which usually manifests itself by a profound indifference to things which are, genuinely and objectively, of minor interest. So it is possible to imagine a depressed lover, for example, while the idea of a sexual adventurer feeling a bit down, or indeed of a national patriot having the blues, or a religious zealot in the glooms, seems laughably incongruous, frankly inconceivable. That is to say, it seems so to me. Nevertheless, you can get a good insight into a character's character by finding out what they consider important enough to get depressed about. One person's genuine objectivity is another's telling subjectivity. A lover of sex might get depressed if they couldn't get a bit, a lover of country if their land wasn't free, a lover of God if they mislaid their faith. Where is the moral centre, or determining principle, as to what's major and what's minor? Is that why we have music? [NOTE TO SELF: Music = Emotion > Words.]

Still, maybe this depthless despondency is my true condition, be it innate or acquired. Just as it could be yours too. How low can you go, before getting high again? Solo we can't hear you. Do you like the view from down there, or would you like to get back up? No matter what they say, I was all times a decent lad, no matter how decadent I may have been. Taste is a matter of taste. This is to my taste. Unless my writing has the force of orgasm, it is utterly useless. Because my actual orgasms had no force, they were worthless, and what I wrote became displacement activity, or what they used to call, I fear to say, sublimation. Although, depending on how you look at it, it is possible to view all human endeavour as such. But not me, or not any longer. Now I can come like a train, and so write like a dream. Now that I can fuck properly I am free to think clearly and feel deeply, perchance to fall in love. Or is that putting the platitudinous cart before the axiomatic horse? In other words, to be like everyone else. If, perchance, they can do these things. To be just like my brother is now. Sometimes I imagine I have always been him.

What would you say to that, if it turned out that it were so?

Her good deed for the day done, Mary proceeds up the centre parting, to her final destiny. All the relations are there. The world is a wedding, as they say. She looks like a looker to me; and to everyone else too, it seems. She has got her big day, and the white dress, as lots of women secretly crave, and is eye-poppingly stunning. Even if no spring chicken, she is not mutton dressed as lamb. The worrying abscesses on her earlobes, where she got them clumsily pierced, have all but cleared up, and the annoying blue vein showing in the hollow at the back of her left knee is not visible now. She is even getting over being sick in the morning.

As Mary takes her place beside Edward, he turns his head to the left for a full view. She is his radiant vision, even if veiled. He lets me see her as he sees her too. As well her as another, I can just hear him thinking, because she's not like any other. Mary was a woman who loved too much, or too little, I cannot make up my mind as to which. Edward is now in touch with this inner child, has discovered his feminine side, come to terms with his negative aspects, dealt with ongoing issues, and intends to grow old gracefully. Sometimes she cries: is it because she's a woman? Sometimes he drinks to excess: is it because he's Irish? Sometimes he has vague, but deep, spiritual yearnings: is it because he was raised a Catholic, but has long ago lapsed? Sometimes his longings are more palpably sensual: is that because he's Irish, or Catholic, or a man, or a human being? Sometimes he gets short-tempered and impatient: is that because he's a man? She's always wanted to have a baby: is it because she's a woman? He is masculine, she is feminine, while I am neuter. Or I was, until she made me better.

Do not suppose that this is a mere marriage of convenience. For are not all the best marriages marriages of convenience? That is, if they are convenient for both parties most closely concerned, if both those halves of the one whole couple find it convenient to feel true, mad, deep, passionate, heartfelt love for each other, and for the other only. For who would want to inconvenience themselves, in this day and age? Self-sac-rifice has been sacrificed, on the burning altar of the search for self. Don't give yourself away. But make a certain sacrifice. Maybe you have to sacrifice yourself in order to find yourself again. What you give is what you get. Which makes me wonder about the wisdom of instigat-ing such a search in the first place. It is just that these two have got over their pathetic delusions of boundless sexual freedom. They've realised, as is supremely difficult for their whole spoiled rotten generation, just as it has been for every over-indulgent lousy generation before it, that you can't base a marriage on mutual sexual attraction alone. Because what'll happen when pneumatic bliss turns to not being able to piss, and the voluptuary shades into a valetudinarian? Sex is messy, that's what you tell yourself when you get too old to get horny enough, or wet enough, to derive much pleasure from it any more. But fluid reten-tion is fairly unsanitary too, not to dwell overlong on urinary inconti-nence. I am not taking the piss here, or jerking you around.

So I do hereby recant my former negative reflections on the solemn institution of matrimony. It is a truth universally acknowledged, that a single man in possession of a good fortune, must be in want of a wife. Or it was, back when there were universal truths. If indeed there ever were. It does, however, seem to have served those who went before us, adequately if not admirably.

Oh, I know all about how when trusting someone can slide into tak-ing them for granted, and it can be a chore to keep fancying someone you sleep beside every blessed night of your mortal life. But, in a rough world, it's nice, not to say good, to have a friend to hold on to. And if that friend is your lover as well, why then, that's all the better. Even if the *Kama Sutra* gymnastics can get less than riveting, and become a bit routine. You never know, she might not mind him having the odd bit on the side, so to speak, so long as it isn't a serious threat, and he doesn't do it in her face. There again, isn't that how most of these extra-marital dalliances begin?

Instead, try envisioning her vagina as the petals of a rose, lush and sweet-smelling, exfoliating and enfolding him. Perhaps the site of the soul we've heard so much about is actually the nervous system itself, rather than the pineal gland. Maybe the CNS is where mind and body meet, and the elusive self resides. Imagine their two nervous systems meeting and tingling in consort, no longer straining against each other, but melting together. That is what will happen, later tonight. And many other nights, I'd venture to hope. For, the possibility still exists to be married to someone, and to go around worshipping the ground they walk on, and feeling grateful for breathing the same air they breathe, and sensing yourself expanding peacefully into the universe through every pore in your skin as you lie closely beside them after making wholehearted, uninhibited, rapturous love.

For, I ask you now to conjure up a world without love, or its possibility. It would grind to a halt. After spinning dangerously out of control, as it is now. As it always has been, world without end. Love makes the world go round. Edward does not want Dub the Teddy, who still keeps him nocturnal company, to be his only steady sleeping partner for the rest of his life. Like me, he needs some stability. It had been so long, before Paris, since his penis had found solace in this lovely woman's body. Or mine in any bodies – sorry – anybody's. He now knows that's what he wants, and on a regular basis.

So, no more sowing wild oats for him, even if he indulges in the occasional fun-filled fling, from time to time. It is time to reap. For, as I've hinted, her womb, that last resort of eternal wandering and eventual homecoming, so long as it has not been made to suffer the hysteria of hysterectomy, is full, and not just with child, but children. Yes, it's twins, and what's more, they're girls. That's what the scan says. It's another *fait accompli*, and they're going to keep them. The most banal, but still beautiful, ending, and beginning, of all. You could call one of these ripening mites The Golden Fleece we've spent so long searching for, while the other might as well be referred to as The Holy Grail, although I'm sure you've got other suggestions for far more suitable names.

Will these girls make a better fist of things than us boys ever did? I wish I knew. I can't wait to find out.

Vows made, undying devotion and loyalty pledged forever, the congregation rises, the organist strikes up again, and the now united couple turns and walks down the aisle as one. As they approach my pew, Edward acknowledges me with a nod, and they pass on, smiling for the clicking cameras and rolling video. Now is not a good time for our long-awaited first meeting.

Outside in the grounds, as they are gearing up for the official photographs, and his side and her side are mingling and chatting away convivially, I am feeling a bit out of it, and not suitably attired. So I decide to slope off somewhere else where I'll be less obtrusive, and won't stick out like the proverbial, or pre-verbal, sucked-sore thumb. Just as I'm making my exit through the church gates, the groom, my brother, intercepts me and says, "Hello there."

Well, it's a start. But it turns out that we don't have that much to say to each other. I suppose that's because we know each other too well. This is where that paradox you've been patiently waiting for makes a point of not happening. Remember when I thought there was no me inside me? Well, there is, and it isn't him. What, you thought that he didn't exist, that I made him up? Or that I didn't exist, that he made me up? Or that I made myself up? That my wound didn't happen, or my suicide attempt, or my heart surgery? That they were not the reason for, but part of, the fictional fantasy? Oh no. Think again. We have not been the same person all along. I do not intend to crown this story, such as it is, with the effect of so startlingly paradoxical a revelation. We are not one. But we are two-in-one. A bit like him and Mary. Or is it one-in-two? Two into one won't go. One into two goes twice. Come together, go forth and multiply, only to divide and conquer. You can multiply by dividing. Let's split the difference. For my ego has been altered by my alter ego.

Here, take a look. I am running up to the video man, and grabbing his camera. After a knuckle-wrenching scuffle, I rend it from his grip. Now I am turning it on my brother. What do you see?

I see me. He sees him. You see you. That's all we see. (Wait a second, is that someone else, looking over your shoulder?)

As it is, I eat my words, I swallow my shite, I take it all back. I am bringing it all back home. I became a stranger to myself. I am now myself again, and no stranger than when I began. I'm more like myself than I ever was. I'm more like who I used to be. More like who I might have been. So too is he. I was away from my true nature for a while, but now I have come home. Just like him. Absence makes the heart grow absent. Presence makes the heart grow, and glow. My nerves aren't what they used to be. His are what they always were. I am of a nervous disposition. You can't hate what you haven't loved. You can't love what you haven't hated. Hate and love are mirror images, as well as being direct opposites. Like him and me. Like him and you. Like you and me. They are each other turned inside out. Like he and I. Like you and him. Like thou and I. I am stepping through the mirror. It cracks, from side to side. My mask falls. I will walk naked. I will be myself. I will be like myself. Just like you are like you. Exactly like he is like him. Hate is the same as love. Like we are the same as each other. Only love is stronger than hate. Which one of us is stronger? I have had a love/hate relationship with myself, and with my brother. To say nothing of with you. Now I am meeting myself coming back. And him. And, how could I forget, you. We are running into each other. He is a rich man, I am a poor man. I had pain, while he had pleasure. I laboured with the word, while he laboured o'er the world. He is prodigal, I am prodigious. He was the scapegrace, I was the scapegoat. This is a goat's song, full of grace notes. He wanted to be famous, I wanted to be anonymous. I am the lost sheep who becomes the black sheep who becomes the sheep who is found. He is the stray dog who becomes the dog in the manger who becomes the dog who minds sheep. Some people are perfectly happy being by themselves. Now I know that I am not. Even I am human. Even I need someone. If only for a vigorous shag now and again, or even a slow, gentle, luxurious one, if loving me for the rest of my life is out of the question. Like him, I'd like to have my cake and eat it. So let me eat cake. I've been on bread and water rations for long enough. Because what you don't get with doing it on the net is spontaneous gesture and real feeling. Which is what people still want, even if it's becoming more difficult to find. At worst, cybering is a craven retreat, at best it's a temporary adjunct. But it is not a lasting alternative. People may not come over and say 'Yes' quite as easily in what passes for reality as they do in what goes on in your fantasies (unless you pay, but you always pay, one way or another, so why pay more, at least in the short term?), but maybe that's what makes them all the more interesting when they do give it up and get it on, in the long run (always supposing you were interested in them in the first place, that is). There were times when he could have done better but, for the most part, at least did no worse. Why have I been labouring under the misapprehension that he is more brilliant, gifted and talented than me? There's geniuses and geniuses in it, and genius and genius in it. Thinking I'm not good enough is what makes me great. Thinking he is great is what makes me not good enough. The race is not to the swift. The snail gets there too. Sometimes he finishes first, the roadside littered with causalities and dropouts, pull-ups and pile-ups, climb-downs and let-downs. I have finished a book, while he hasn't. Well, almost. A book about him and me. And her. Not to mention you.

But just because I'm not him, doesn't mean we cannot have a pointed piece of role reversal. For, just as he is arriving home, and even settling down, I am setting out, and going abroad. Is that paradoxical enough for you? Dissatisfaction with one's homeland is, after all, one of the signs of a healthy questing and questioning spirit in the young, just as indifference to it is an equally salubrious indication of a measured maturity in adults. There is no need for nostalgia now, since people do not leave, so much as come and go, for longer or shorter periods. Nostalgia ends in neuralgia. We don't emigrate so much as relocate. Location, location, location. Or, in my case, loquation, loquation, loquation. People used to think exile was a terrible thing. Now it is thought of as advantageous to spend some time beyond. Unless you're dealing with those who are so well established where they started off from, because they got dug in and never left it. It's a wide world, and a wild one, and yet a small one too, getting smaller every day. But it is still big enough, and not always bad. Remember that story about that ancient monk who vowed as penance that he'd never see Ireland again or set foot on Irish soil again, but then one day he had to come back to save the day, and so he blindfolded himself and tied clods of foreign earth to the soles of his shoes? That's what we call a symbolic gesture, but who did he think he was fooling? I think he was cheating, because he was still back where he started from. He had, in case you didn't know, been accused of 'book copying', which is what we would now call infringement of copyright. So shamed was he that he went away. A similar fate will not befall me. I have nothing to hide, so will wander where I list. A journey is the ideal metaphor for a search for truth, but that doesn't mean you'll ever find it, or that you can't go home again. Life is a journey, as they say, but you don't always have to stay away. This is the journey home, as well as the one away, which is rarely one way. How far into myself can I go? How far around the world can he go? How far into the world of myself can I go? How far out of himself can he go into the world? No matter how far into myself I go, I am still in the world. No matter how far around the world he goes, he is still himself, into himself. We all send a self out into the world. We don't always get it back in one piece. Hence this experiment in representation, these lines from the edge of meaning, from the precipice of nothing at all.

For look at all I thought I saw, and didn't see. There are many lands my feet have not set foot on, or travelled far in. Come to think of it, they have not trod on any land but this, and not that much of it. The world of this book did not even traverse all the anglophone world, much less a lot of the rest of it. Not, I'll readily admit, that it was me who was doing the roaming. I was the mental traveller, he was the physical one. But my brother never made it to Canada, Australia, or New Zealand. The canvas was too broad. That's what makes the picture narrow. I would like to visit these places, and many more besides. What about darkest Africa, and the wisdom of the East? Or the many unspoilt corners of the Caribbean? There's the Caymans and Cuba, Barbados and the Bahamas, Antigua and Jamaica, and let's not forget Bermuda. And what about Haiti or, if we ventured farther afield, to the South Seas, Tahiti? I want to go to all of them, while I still have time, before it's all too late. Is it already too late? It's never too late. It's too late to stop now. It's too little too late, but that's preferable to too much too soon. I will go to Portugal, and the Czech Republic, and Sweden, and Cyprus, and why not Egypt and Russia, China and Japan, Mexico and Peru, Bora-Bora and Bali, and Papua New Guinea? I'll be off shortly to book two sun-soaked, drug-drenched weeks in Ibiza. I might even use the internet to hunt down a bargain. Although it might not look too good being the oldest swinger in town. Not that I've ever swung. My brother did that for me. But now I can swing with the best of them. Or rather, I wish I could. For is it possible to dispense with the habits of a lifetime, or of my life up until now? Alright then, I'll swing for them. But a quiet little island in the Cyclades should do the trick nicely.

Well, now all that's out of the way, maybe we can relax. To my surprise, that Ed invites this one to the happy couple's big millennium wedding bash. I can but reply, "Just try stopping me."

Because it would be so great to have some fun. People want to be happy, you know. Why shouldn't they pursue happiness? Because they won't get it? That's beside the point. That's the pettiest of details. You won't find out if you never try. But maybe too much trying only makes you unhappy. You'll never get to heaven in a rocking chair. That's true, if only because there is no heaven. But that doesn't mean you should necessarily stay in your chair. Or not try to be happy, either in or out of it. Have the Tough and Tender brothers only been knocking on heaven's door, all this time, while, at the same time, raking hell?

I mean, take a look at biochemistry, genetics, all that science of the body and mind. I am a dying breed. I am surplus to requirements. Why create malcontents who will grow up to be unhappy people? All my suffering, and yours, will soon count for nothing. Our most tragic moments have been drained of all human significance. We are merely the result of some bad chemicals sloshing around in our brains. We should be nipped in bud. Let humanity start all over again. Am I part of the problem, or part of the solution?

So, here I am, at this swinging party. All the swells are here, looking swellegant. Except for my brother and his new wife, who have by now taken their leave to enjoy their wedding night, before taking off on honeymoon tomorrow. I suppose I better mingle. Ah yes, one must integrate with society. Even if it is, and always has been, a chaotic shambles, made all the more so by its pretensions to order. But becoming part of it is the only way meaning can be attached to you. Just like a word in a sentence, a paragraph, a chapter, or a book. It means nothing, or next to nothing, but itself by itself, and I must begin to mean something to others. I will do so by telling stories. Man *is* a social animal. So even if you think that's unfortunate, it's better if you try to train yourself to think it's quite the contrary. Let us work to end this story. Let us try to finish these sentences. That's the story of my life. It's my life sentence.

So I will chase my little share of happiness. I have been my own amanuensis of my own anamnesis, but I refuse to continue as a mere spectator of my own life, and life in general. Just watch me become an apolaustic apostle, seeking enjoyment. I will do so by going out into the world, and telling heartrending, moving tales. Get ready for some ripping yarns. I will now pull the wool over your eyes. With any luck I'll pull it off. If truth is stranger than fiction, let's make fictions stranger than truth. I must get the hang of dealing with other people, like they tried to teach me in school, if only I'd paid more attention. I pray it's not too late. I will be a rejuvenated revenant, done with my exile down among the dead, and returned up top to the land of the living. This is the return of this native. Henceforth I will be a 'people person'. People are neat, despite their manifold contradictions. Or rather, perhaps because of them. It was not for nothing that I observed my brother's adventures in America. Up with people. Also, people are all very different. Don't let some people tell you any different. What he got up to in Europe was not wasted on me either. It is right and fitting that their faces and names are, for the most part, dissimilar from each other, that no two of them are exactly the same. All hail the great diversity, which can prove so diverting. Oh brave new world that has such people in it. For the past while I have not been very interested in people, or what happens, or what happens to people, or what people make happen. But all that may be about to change. For there is a bigger picture. It involves other people. Other people than you. Or him. Or me. Other people than us. So I no longer wish to type about types. Words were more real to me than people, than things, than events, than the world. Obviously experience must have something to do with expression, but whatever the relationship is, it is so nebulously tenuous as to be resistant to explanation. But there's still a world out there, called the world. So I will drown my book. Stay hungry. Remain vigilant. Trust nobody. Question everything. I am sceptical of everything, including my own scepticism. But that's not scepticism, that's reverse credulity. What if everything you know, or thought you knew, is wrong (including the stuff about everything you know, or thought you knew, being wrong?)? What if you've always been living the wrong life? What if everything you've ever seen, you've seen assbackwards, or rather, backassways?

Confidence comes from doing stuff, and from not thinking about doing stuff while you're doing it. People who stay home have more difficulty acquiring confidence, except confidence about staying home. I must get out more. Maybe I'll take up golf, or gardening. Or perhaps getting hooked on fishing would be more my line. Even if I haven't made my fortune, I will still go in search of girls. Or a girl. What an adventure that'll be. You thought I shunned the world, and women, because of unresolved tensions with my foster-mother, or the bad example of my foster-father? That would be a little too predictably casebook, now wouldn't it? But if my horn was nicked, who was it by? Maybe I did it to myself. Finally, it'll be the mundanity of the filthy lucre cash value kicking in, the dreadful but inexorable financial necessity to earn my own living so that I can make my own life, that'll drive me out into the world and into accepting its inhabitants, even if nothing else does. I must put some time into developing a career. Maybe I'll become a psychotherapist, just to have something to fall back on, if the storytelling fails me. It's so much in demand, and there'd be loads of material I could glean from practicing, as they say, even if I don't quite get it right, however well-versed I am in the psychopathology of everyday life, however many scenes of everyday madness I have witnessed. Or maybe I could learn to do massage; that'd be a good one. Or reflexology; it's great too. Or good old creative writing. *Dear Human Resources, I am a team player, with good interpersonal skills.*

But no, no more of my dark imaginings, especially about having no imagination; or of my bleak visions, particularly about having no vision. I won't let myself get waylaid again. For I am now partial to a tolerable life. No more self-harming behaviour. You won't get far on welfare. I will be a gregarious recluse. Until death wraps me in its quietly forgiving arms. I have even thought of a fitting epitaph for my gravestone:

He may not have done much good
But he never did anyone any harm

Most people do not act consciously, much less conscientiously. If they did, they would not act. Or rather, they would. Or rather, they do. Everyone acts, the only difference being that some know it, and some don't. But, either way, it's all only acting. Forgive them, even if they know what they are doing. As it is, I am a cloistered nonentity, capable of only the meanest interaction with my fellow creatures. Aren't we all?

Or, at least, aren't all the best contemplatives? Like those monks, priests and nuns. They live in obscurity, as I have done. Do they wank, I wonder, before or after a long prayer session? They don't seem to make much money. They take a vow of poverty, plus chastity and obedience. Although they're usually well-fed, get the odd squeeze in now and again, and generally prefer telling other people what to do than being told what to do themselves. Maybe I should have joined up with them, and taken their Holy Orders, to legitimise my solitude. It's their vow of silence that would have appealed the most to me. But not any more. Now I'd like to start talking. Now I'd like to keep talking. Now I'd like to keep you talking. Look who's talking, and who they're talking to. Look who's talking too! But now I'd like to go towards the light. I will be more light-hearted, and less heavy-handed. I've seen life, if only at second-hand, and I haven't been too impressed. Now to try it first-hand. I would like to live now, if you please.

Because life is not a conspiracy. I got into paranoia, when irony failed me. These are the twin poles of the contemporary condition, the dual modes I have oscillated between. My experience is, dare I say it, representative. He too used irony to stave off paranoia, but here's the difference: when irony let him down, he let love in instead. Not being in a position to go about this, like most of my species, I made myself paranoid. But I did it to myself. I am a self-made man, who takes full responsibility for the mess he has made of himself. You try spending the best part of twenty years in a room with no wine, women, or song. For the benefit of my fellow creatures, albeit not entirely voluntarily, I conducted such dangerous experiments on myself, or rather allowed them to be carried out on me, and reported my findings in my writings. There was no plot against me. There was hardly any plot at all. If paranoia means you think they know more than you do, especially about you, then why not make them think you know more than they do, especially about them? The world may not be for you, but that doesn't mean that it's against you. The world is neither for you nor against you. It just is. They weren't out to get me. So I won't go after them. They won't get me now. I've got iron in the soul, titanium balls, plus a good head on my shoulders. No one makes his own world, but everyone lives his own life. You cannot live in your own world, but you can try to make your own life. Time exists, but cares nothing for how it is reckoned. It does not ask for or need these seconds, minutes, hours, days, weeks, months, years, decades and millennia. Space exists, but cares nothing for how it is measured. It does not demand or require, these inches, feet, yards, furlongs, miles etc., or even these millimetres, centimetres, metres, kilometres etc. This was not the story of a man of character. I was not such a great character after all. Neither was he. Nor were we bad ones.

I will say only that by inadequacy of personality I have overcome my disabilities. By force of personality I would have buckled under them. Out of my powerlessness I have fantasised, or is it fashioned, an absolute supremacy. Sometimes being passive is the only way to be active. If the bitter lie, the healed tell the truth. I have been healed by her, and by telling this story. You've heard this one before, but it's the way I tell them. How much of it is true? All of it? None of it? What does it matter? Who cares? It is all true. Even the lies.

Even so, I must declare, self-effacingly and shamefacedly, that I am proud of myself. It is, after all, no inconsiderable achievement to write a book with not very sympathetic characters, and no discernible plot to speak of, and bring it to a fitting conclusion. It is not easy to say so much about having nothing much to say. The mistake is to think you have to have something to say. The mistake is to think you have something to say. I am too much like the others: I have too much to say – even if it is about having nothing to say. I have not said anything new. I have said nothing anew. Because I have obeyed certain formulae.

Take a sympathetic hero and put him in adverse situations, chief among these that, to all intents and purposes, he either appears, or really is (and how can we ever know, will we ever find out?), broadly unsympathetic. Was that his nature, or his lack of nurture? Do I mean myself, or him? Is this a biography, or an autobiography? He has to battle against everything he does, and is done to him, being at the whim of an increasingly erratic author, be it himself or another. Then let him triumph over the forces arrayed against him, after many hair-raising adventures. That's what happens in stories, as far as I can see. People are going along, just the same as always, and then something happens to them, and they learn something about themselves, or the world, or their place in it, and they are forever changed. Or something happens, and they learn nothing, or very little, but we learn that they are incapable of learning, or that they are unwilling or unable to change, or only very little. Or they have to do something, before a certain time, and time is running out. That's the knack to making up stories. You're just playing a game, you say. But I have not played the game, in order to show you that it is all a game. As if you needed to be told. As if you could give a shit. I have only played another kind of game. Just so you know that I know what we all already know. Next thing you know, I'll be telling stories. As I get older, and stop making sense, I must get wiser, and start making cents. I will play the game.

What kind of stories do I like? The ones people won't tell me. Yes, in future I will tell stories, and tall tales, even if this was supposed to be the story to end all stories, the tail end of tales. The difference is, next time out, they'll be of my own devising. I'll make them up myself. I'll write something real, about real people, and real things happening. Even if I'm making up the people and things, I'll make them seem real. Otherwise, I will expire. I will expire anyway, but perhaps not quite as soon as I would have, had I not set about telling my stories. What would that matter? Well, it matters to me. One must drag on, even if it's a drag, and face up to things, and put a brave face on them. Or a brave voice. Stories are not passé. I will try to be nice. I am trying to be nice. It's trying to be nice. I will be good. I'll give it a good try. There's a million stories out there, and in here. There were stories at every turn, if only I'd bothered to stop and look, if only I'd taken the trouble to stand and listen, if only I'd had the courage to sit down and tell them. For what about Sharon and Tracy, or Laura's Mama and Papa, or Mustafa, or Chuck and Chester, or the pre-Amanda American girls, or Amanda's Mom and Dad, or good ol' Alvin? They all had stories to tell, or to be told about them. I bet Alvin's had a really interesting life, if you only get him talking. And how could I forget the dastardly Wylie Sighfer? What demons drove him? Wouldn't you like to know? I know I would.

So, from now on, suns will rise and shine, and dim and set, with tremulous falls of light; flowers will grow and bloom, and wither and die, the shrivelled petals lying scattered on the grass. Heads will roll, hearts will pound, tears will fall, sperm will ignite. There will be detailed descriptions thereof. There will be well-crafted scenes, with just the right amount of revealing and withholding. There will be characters with characteristics, tics and traits at every turn, plot lines interweaving to beat the band, and relationships all over the shop, right, left and centre. Just like in the soap operas. [NOTE TO SELF

$$\text{Relationships} = \frac{\text{(Social) Ethics} + \text{(Personal) Morality]}}{\text{Time} + \text{Action}^2}$$ Plus images.

Images, images, images. It is worth repeating: image are worth repeating. I might even stretch to a symbol or two. Although, come to think of it, maybe I already have, since when it comes to symbols, twins tower over all. The appropriate emotional responses will be elicited. Catharsis and purgation will take place. Far from highlighting artificiality, they will help me believe, and so believe in, my stories. They will provide the same service for you. For what if I cannot credit my own fictions? Then it's unlikely anyone else will either. My credibility will be at stake. It was my lack of interest in other people that made me a bad man, and this a bad book, if such it is, if such I be. Did a bad man ever write a good book? Why yes, it happens all the time. You are holding living proof of this proposition, in my humble opinion. But you have to relate, even if you alienate, and are alienated. People will kill for a good story. They'll even die for one. No matter how well or badly written, if it's a halfway decent – or indeed more usually indecent – story, than they'll be all ears. That's what'll put their bums on seats, and keep them turning the pages. But they have to believe in the story, and the characters, or be able to suspend their disbelief. Otherwise, they'll know it's all just pretence, and their hearts won't be in it. Even if mine is.

However, I respectfully suggest that the divided self of Eds -ward and -mund, is a very human image of now discredited dialectic. To reason in twos splits the reasoner in two. If everyone has a dual, or indeed a multiple personality, with which they duel constantly in an effort to control its multiplicity, then the schizophrenic represents the very epitome and perfection of humanity. They are completed. They are men in full. That's obviously why there's a high incidence of the condition in Ireland, notably the farther west you go. Nowadays, it has even been given the nicer name of integration disorder. Well, yes, I do sometimes find it difficult to fit in, and to make things fit. I've had problems with my adjustment. So I should disintegrate. Modern life is rubbish. You couldn't make it up. This daft non-story is a history, and a product, of our even dafter culture, from the daftest of centuries. That makes it a social document, and an historical necessity. So what if you think it's all a load of old crap? What did you expect? I was just doing a bit of ground-clearing, which is hardly ground-breaking. I promise to do better next time.

For now, I will sit here and sip my wine (or is it beer?; and what does whichever it is say about me?; and what does what kind of wine it is, or what kind of beer, say about me too?; or should I dare to mix grape and grain, and what would that say about me as well?; would that be courageous or foolhardy?; wouldn't it be getting off on the wrong foot, waking up to my dream of a new life with a viciously debilitating corkscrew hangover?), and smile and make small talk with all who come and go, many of whom I will get to know. Here they are, gathering in the garden, drifting in in ones and twos, for the final countdown. Pleased to meet you. Nice to know you. Here's my calling card. The story of life began in a garden. Where will it end? Or, more to the point, when? No man, or woman, is an island, entire of themselves, on this tiny island of ours, or on this spinning island planet. But Everyman, and Everywoman, is. We have journeyed, together and separately, from the beginning of time to the end of the universe. Are you lonely tonight? Well then, come on over and join us.

If this book can be interpreted, it has failed in its intention, conscious or otherwise. I do not intend interpreted with ease or difficulty, but at all. For if it has an intention, conscious or otherwise, it is not to be interpreted, with ease or with difficulty, but at all. This is a self-fulfilling prophecy, an instance of telediction. So my anality comes to an end, in inanity.

This is not the key to all mythologies. It is not even the key to any mythology. Those kinds of keys are not given. I was in danger of turning into an unimaginative pedant, who could not finish his book, and so dies instead. Now it is completed, and I am not dead yet. To tell you the truth, I'm just beginning to live. I've never felt more alive. I've never felt better in my life. I am as happy as the day is short. Welcome, Oh life! Or what is left of it. Or what passes for it. I come to encounter for the first time the reality of experience and to hide in the hollow of my heart the dead conscience of a race that was never mine to start with.

Young daughters, young makers, stand me now and always in good stead.

The stars are out tonight. They are not obscured by clouds. There's Gemini, the twins, shining brightly. For once, it is not raining. A bit chilly yes, but no sign of a downpour. Look, there goes a firework, flashing as it ignites, painting up the night sky with fine sparkling points of light. Another is exploding too, bursting through the

blackness, and yet another still. The wedding guests are chanting loudly, and loudly clapping their hands. Everyone is joining in, including
me.

All together now: ten, nine, eight, seven, six, five, four, three, two,
one.... Happy New Year, Decade, Century, Millennium....

BEGIN